OCCULTATION

Eric Lahti

I0609022

Nightmare Press
Shepherdsville, KY

Dedicated to everyone who recognizes reality for the farce it is.

Also by Eric Lahti
The Henchmen Series

- *Henchmen*
- *Arise*
- *Transmute*

Short Stories and Novellas

- *The Complete Saxton*
- *The Clock Man and Other Stories*
- *All the Bad Things*

Better Than Dead
Roadside Attractions
Greetings from Sunny Aluna

OCCULTATION

Eric Lahti

Occultation: n. The passage of one celestial body in front of another, thereby obscuring the view of the original celestial body.

CHAPTERS

1 - Dr. Funkenstein's

Last Request

Kind of sad that my last view of space was probably going to be nothing more than an enormous boulder with two distant glints orbiting it.

Outside, barely visible in the inky dark was one of the gold-standard mysteries of the galaxy. A planetoid about 1000km in diameter. A planetoid nowhere near a planetary system. Nowhere near a star. Just a hunk of rock in the literal ass end of the outer regions. Weirder: The three Predecessor space stations orbiting it, the one I was staring out of, and two smaller ones, completely automated. All quietly ticking away for 14,000 years as near as anyone could tell. Just hanging out and thumbing their noses at reason. Endpoint was the name of the primary station. Out here, we called the rock *Temnyy Muzhchina* – Dark Man.

"Should have been a supernova," I muttered to myself and tossed back my whiskey. Winced. It was like swallowing something random from a lab.

"They're not as glamorous as you think," a voice said. It had a singsong quality to it, like the speaker was used to seeing nothing but clear skies ahead.

I flicked my empty glass across the table and said, "I really hope you're not a Prudist, because I'm spending my last night alive and I don't want to hear a bunch of bullshit about salvation right now."

"I don't party with Prudists," the voice said. "They have chosen a different path to Heaven. I wish them speed and happiness, but they and I don't see eye-to-eye."

I turned my head and found a man with dreadlocks and a suit made of tiny square mirrors. Only one group of people in galaxy could pull off the look. "Didn't see the mothership dock," I said, motioning to the chair opposite me. "How's the party business?"

He sat and eyed me for a moment like I was something he'd never seen before. A tube wreck of a person maybe. There had to be dozens of us lurking on this alien platform. He shook his head. "The party business will always thrive because we sell the one thing everyone needs and desires."

"More whiskey," I said.

"Not everyone prefers whiskey," he replied.

"No, I meant I need more whiskey if I'm going to listen to Pfunk Gypsy propaganda."

He smiled and my anger withered away. Say what you will about the Pfunk Gypsies, they knew a thing or two about spreading good feelings. Interstellar monks who preached that partying was the best way to salvation. Turned out the best way to their financial salvation was to party with them. A ride on the Pfunk Mothership could cost a month's credits but it was a ride you'd never forget.

"I am Bick Parameter," he said, extending his hand. "It is a pleasure to meet you."

"Rex Kormer," I replied.

"Rex Kormer," he said with a sparkle in his eye. "Vagabond, thief-"

"Appropriator of-"

"Purloiner of," Bick said. "Own yourself, my friend. Be proud of what you are."

Bick held up his ring-encrusted hand. I swear, the guy had more jewelry than an old-school Terran love-broker. A moment later, a robo gently placed two drinks on the table. Bick lifted the glass and inhaled deeply. "Whiskey. United States. Pacific Northwest. Probably Oregon circa early 2000s."

"We're   drinking   five-hundred-plus-year-old Whiskey?"

Bick downed his in a gulp, sighed contentedly, and smiled. "Of course not. But this is an excellent synth."

"Good enough to be real?" I asked, sipping mine gently. It was smooth as silk and warm as bare flesh.

"If anything is real, then yes, this real."

Bick slid a holo puck across the table and tapped the center. A woman with bright pink hair sprang to life. She was smiling and waving at someone. Coveralls pulled down and tied around her waist. AniTats running up and down both arms. Then her face turned serious and stared hard at the HoloLens. The serious stare ebbed with a toothy grin, a middle finger extended straight up, and the animation repeated itself. At the bottom of the holo, a name a bunch of numbers scrolled by in chyron. Devore, Natasha, 03141592:1.0CPD, Presumed-Terran.

"Pretty gal," I said. "Legit Terran?"

"Legit. Just like you."

"Not a whole lot of us left," I mumbled.

"Did you know her?" he asked.

"There were 12 billion people on Terra when the Diaspora hit. Most died in the fires. A bunch of us escaped. Some even lived out productive lives filing paperwork and fixing computers."

"But not you, Mr. Kormer?"

"Not my bag. I'm still trying to be an adult. Bounce around a lot. Looking for work, sex, stuff to steal, myself."

"Well, then, that explains your youthful appearance," Bick said.

"B/S drives warp time, buddy," I told him. "Like I said, I bounce around a lot. If she's legit Terran, she's probably my age or older."

Bick leaned his head against an outstretched hand and stared longingly at the holo. I hadn't thought there was any way a man in a mirrored suit could look sad, but he did it. My own face reflected back at me through the thousand or so tiny mirrors that made up his jacket.

"Recognize her?" he asked.

"It says she's Natasha Devore," I said, pointing at the scrolling chyron. "Who is she?"

He casually flicked the holo at me and grinned sadly. "You'll want to keep that."

"Thanks," I said as he held up two more fingers. More whiskey incoming. "Are you going to tell me who she is?"

"They say you can get into anything."

"I wouldn't mind getting into her."

"Time is not on your side, my friend," he replied.

I swear, talking to P-Funk Gypsies could be fascinating if you were on their wavelength, but there was no way I could afford to hop that frequency. He slid a shot across the table at me and held his own up. We clinked glasses. Smooth fire burned away the weirdness. "You gonna tell me who she is?" I asked.

"Turn it on again," he said.

I tapped the top of the little disc. She sprang back into life, a 15cm tall woman without a care in the world. Again, I was struck by how familiar she looked. Lots of women had pink hair, animated tats, and alabaster white skin.

"Is she friends with Beatrix Beaumont?" I asked. "The famous party girl who got famous for being famous?""

Bick's face turned hard. Had I just crossed some forbidden line? "We do not work with the Beaumonts. Ever."

Okay. Add that to my list of sacred knowledge. "Sorry," I said. "I give. Who is she?"

Bick looked at the aniholo almost lovingly, like a father adoringly watching a lost daughter as she threw her first raging kegger. "This is the woman who locks do not apply to. The woman who sliced through Pendarm's defenses like a hot knife through butter and let our blessed mothership continue its sacred mission of bringing blessed peace, love, and funk to the people starving for freedom. This, Mr. Kormer, is none other than the Digital Diva."

"No shit?" I asked.

Stories about the Digital Diva had been circulating for at least a couple hundred years. Many believed there wasn't a system invented that she couldn't get into eventually. Governments had fallen to her skills, their dirty secrets exposed on the ParaNet. Criminal organizations would auction their own mothers to either gain access to her skills or gain access to her. Every time someone created a bounty on her, though, she just deleted it. And then found a way to delete the person who created the bounty. Like I said, she was crafty.

"No shit," Bick said. He made a fist and pounded his chest twice before kissing his thumb and holding it out to the sprite with the pink hair. "She was one of us in both spirit and name. A member of the Funkensteins now and forever."

I nodded, but still didn't see where this was going. "That's all cool, but why are you showing me aniholos of the Digital Diva?"

"Because she was deleted two nights ago, Mr. Kormer and I would very much like to know why."

Wait. What? "Deleted?"

"Her consciousness was erased and she fled this mortal coil."

"Someone offed her? I hate to say this, but that's not a mystery; the woman had a lot of enemies."

"Not exactly. Her body is unharmed. Still breathing, still alive, but there is nothing going on in her brain. It is like her soul simply vanished."

I sat back and thought about that. I'd seen plenty of corpses and humans are clever when it came to killing, but I'd never heard of anyone deleting another person's consciousness and leaving the body alive. Usually screwing up the body was part of the message.

"Vanished?" I mumbled.

"Vanished. Poof. Off to rejoin the universe."

"But her body is still alive?"

"Very much so."

"How is that even possible?" I asked.

Bick smiled and held up his fingers again. "If I knew that, I wouldn't be here asking for your help."

"Wait. You want me to help you? How? I'm a liberator of things, not a psychmech. Did you want me to acquire something for you? If so, we can negotiate a price. But I wouldn't know the first thing about tracking down some chick's missing brain."

"Her brain is fine," Bick said.

"It was a figure of speech."

"I understand. I want you to understand that her body is in pristine condition. No life-support necessary. Only her..."

"Soul?" I interjected.

"Yes, soul. Her soul is missing."

From anyone else, I'd assume this rambling tale was a bunch of bull, but for all their weird ways, the Pfunk Gypsies never told a lie. That was one of their endearing qualities. "Let me get this straight: You want me to find her soul? What does a soul even look like?"

"Ever seen a ghost?" Bick asked.

"No."

"Pity. That's what a soul looks like. But I digress. I don't want to find her soul; that part of her is gone and it is never coming back. Nor would we want to bring it back. It is experiencing the ephemeral, the pure, raw, funky groove of the universe. No one should come back from that."

He slid another glass across the table at me. Normally, even a few shots of good whiskey weren't enough to shut me down, but there was something special about Bick's stuff. I held up the glass and looked through the amber liquid at a light on the other side of the bar. Makeshift whiskey goggles made from real fake whiskey. A way of looking at the world through other eyes.

"So you want me to find out who, uh, deleted her?" I asked after I deleted the whiskey.

"And why."

"Is there any evidence? Is there a crime scene?"

"Oh, yes. There is a crime scene and you will have unprecedented access to it."

That was rare. Usually no one gave me access to anything. I had to take it when no one was looking. "Pay?" I asked.

"More than you can imagine."

What the hell, I was going to die tomorrow anyway. Might as well do something interesting with my morning. "Okay, why not? When do I start?"

Bick Parameter smiled through the dreads hanging down in his face. Even his teeth were glittery, like he was a walking disco ball. "As soon as you wake up in the morning, Mr. Kormer. In the interim, might I suggest another drink?"

2 - That's Not What I Meant

I awoke with a headache the size of Temnyy. Or maybe I'd been hit in the head with Temnyy and I just didn't remember it. I opened my eyes briefly and slammed them shut again. Bick's whiskey packed a wallop. Even the dim light felt like daggers in my eyes.

I snuggled deeper into the blankets covering me. They were soft and warm. Where the fuck was I? Not that it mattered. No one had stabbed me yet and that's usually what happened when I woke up somewhere strange, so I was probably safe.

I slowly took stock of my body. Fingers clenched. Toes curled. Legs moved. It seemed like all my parts were in place and still movable. It felt like the time I got hold of some bad hobo wine out in Altair. Only without the hallucinations and projectile vomiting.

What was there to do today, anyway? Putter around? Marvel at the primitive alien technology that ran this place? Dip my toes in Virt? Try to find a way off this station before it was too late? Hope a gangster didn't carve my heart out with a titanium spork? The bed was comfortable, the blankets soft and warm, and let's face it, if I was going to get tortured to death, I wanted to be well rested for the experience. Besides, it wasn't like anyone knew where I was. Hell, I didn't even know where I was. So, screw it. Sleeping time.

I would have lived the dream and stayed in bed all day if it hadn't been for my pesky biological needs. Great or small, rich or poor, strong or weak, a full bladder can ruin a day in bed for the best of us.

My eyes were still bleary when my feet hit a fake fur rug. My nose picked up faint scents; some kind of flower and maybe a gentle spice or two that I couldn't identify.

The booze must have still been coursing through my veins because my body felt weird. It was like I was shorter and my limbs didn't move quite like they did last night. It took an active effort to put one foot in front of the other and I kept feeling like my legs should have been longer.

I found the bathroom, slapped off the lights before they blinded me and flipped up the lid on the toilet. A nice long piss and then back to bed. Maybe when I woke up my body would be working like it should. If not, well, back to bed.

I reached into my pants and it took a moment to realize something was terribly wrong. Something was missing. Something was utterly, terribly, irrevocably wrong.

The lights came up when I slapped the switch.

"Mother fucker," I swore.

Even my voice sounded strange. Not surprising considering the stranger's face that stared back at me from the mirror. Alabaster skin. Shoulder-length, bright pink hair. Blue green spiral eyes that should be sparkling instead of staring back at me in dead-eyed horror.

It had to be a joke. Some elaborate ruse. Ha, ha. Got me good. But I tilted my head and she tilted her head. I crossed my eyes and she crossed her eyes. I stuck out my tongue and she stuck out her tongue. Pulled my underwear out and verified my dick wasn't hiding. Grabbed my chest and found more than I bargained for.

Damn you, Bick. What kind of game were you playing?

I slapped the door lock, and took off running. It only took me half the corridor to realize why bras were a thing. This was going to be a huge pain in the ass. Rather than dig through a stranger's underwear cache, I wrapped my arms around my chest and walked quickly while my brain tried to process what was happening. Or rather, Natasha's brain tried to process what was going on. If it was still hers. Did being in someone's body mean that body was yours?

Endpoint had viewing areas for docked ships. Given all the flights of fancy people had when designing spaceships, the viewing area was remarkably empty. Me? I dug the ships. The coolest thing about space travel was there were no real rules about what a ship should look like. They could be massive, mirrored balls like Bick's crazy ride or they could be long and pointy or even just glowing white cubes calmly travelling the cosmos.

I ignored the Airlockers babbling about their god and begging for loose credits and stared hard out the window. There! On the other side of that red, pointy ship with the big fins and yellow stripes down it. A giant mirrored sphere that looked like a party waiting to happen.

"Now, how the hell do I find him?" I muttered to myself.

Endpoint was huge. A triangle a kilometer on each edge and forty or so decks high. Her sister drone stations out in the distance were smaller versions of the big mama. If there was anything of value out here other than the Bizarre Bazaar and the general bizarre, the station would be massively popular. Even with the tourists, rabble, and corporate goons that lived out there, we took up a miniscule amount of space but that still left thousands of people and a lot of space to search.

"Shit," I whispered to myself. "How do I find this guy?"

"Perhaps I can be of assistance," a voice said in my head.

I nearly jumped out of my skin. Would have welcomed it, actually, if there was a chance to get into my old body. "Figures, Bick would stick me in some chick with mental issues," I mumbled.

"You do not have any serious mental issues that I can detect ma'am."

At least I was in the right company to be talking to myself. Half the airlockers were trauma jobs from war torn planets and the other half were serious drug and religion enthusiasts. None of them would notice the crazy person holding her tits and talking to herself. "Then why am I hearing voices?" I snarled.

"I am an AI. You had me implanted in 2499."

Penta, yeah. An AI. Those things weren't cheap but could perform all sorts of computer-related magic. An AI would have made my life as a thief way easier. "An AI, eh?"

"Yes, ma'am. I am a CyberDrop Systems Model 101a."

I let out a slow whistle. Top of the line. Natasha must have been loaded. "Okay, CyberDrop, what do I call you?"

"My lead programmer was a man named Jenkins but-"

"Good enough," I said, cutting him off. "Jenkins works. Okay, Jenkins, how can you help me find someone?"

"Endpoint is equipped with various tracking tools. They are mostly to keep tabs on how many people are onboard at any given time. If the population increases, oxygen levels are adjusted to compensate. It is possible to track people, provided the person in mind has been implanted or their subdermal chips were registered with Endpoint Control upon arrival. Admittedly, not everyone does that-"

"I don't need a history of Endpoint," I said. I knew all about the chip registration and chose to ignore when I snuck on board. Natasha may or may not have one. Probably something I needed to look into.

"Understood, ma'am. But if you ever do, I suggest the welcome pamphlets behind you. They are simple but point out the key features of the only Predecessor space station currently occupied by humans. There is another one four point three light years from here, but it was severely damaged-"

"Again, stop with the history lesson. Tell me how to find Bick."

"Bick who?" Jenkins asked.

"Bick Pa- Wait. You can't read my mind?"

"No ma'am. While we share computing power in the form of your brain, we are segmented from each other. I exist in a sandbox, which is a kind of segregated memory space where I can't access your-"

"You're talking too much again. Bick Parameter. Find him. His ship is docked over there, the big, mirrored sphere. He has to still be onboard Endpoint."

I could almost feel Jenkins working. It was a low buzz in my head. Faint. Faint enough to ignore. "Bick Parameter is currently in Twenty Forward. He is drinking a brown drink and does not appear intoxicated even though the location in question is registered as a bar."

I turned on a heel and tried to run again. Forgot about the things hanging off my chest and my bare feet. Bra and shoes. Good things to have. Must remember next time if I couldn't wring my old body out of Bick's neck.

Not bad, I chided myself as I scampered along. Usually, it took a few months in one place for everything to go to hell. I'd been on Endpoint for a week and had already lost my body. That was a new one by me.

After a few missed turns and more than a few lewd stares, I stormed into Twenty Forward with fire in my eyes and stuff stuck to my feet. Bick stared out the huge viewport with a cup of real coffee in his hand. Lest anyone think running an interstellar party cruise didn't pay well, real coffee could run upwards of a hundred credits or more depending on the location. A ritzy place like Twenty Forward probably charged double that. The perfect morning drink for rich assholes.

It was still early and Twenty Forward was quiet. A few professional alcoholics and the infamous party god of the cosmos were the only ones inside the fok-paneled, chrome-bedecked bar. In about twelve hours, the place would be bumping but for now, it was quiet save for the Aetherean lo-fi escaping from the hidden sound system.

I stalked up to Bik, put my finger in his face, and shouted, "You son of a bitch! What have you done to me?"

Bik sipped his coffee and stared at me over the rim of his white ceramic cup. "Well, Ms. Devore. For a dead woman, you're looking amazing. And up at such an early hour, too. Impressive."

"Answer the question!" I hissed. "What have you done?"

"Well, you did say you wouldn't mind 'getting in her', as I recall."

I motioned to my newly acquired body. "This isn't what I meant and you know it!"

Bik nodded with the kind of serenity you only get by achieving master status at partying. "Sit down, Ms. Devore. Have a coffee. My treat."

"I don't want coffee. I want my body back."

"Your body is safe. Finish the job and it will be returned unharmed. Now, in the interim, you look a fright. Have some coffee; it will change your outlook entirely."

"I swear, if you tell me to smile, I'm going to break your nose."

He leaned back and shook his head. Motioned to the seat opposite him. "Please, you're making a scene."

"You stuffed me in a dead woman's body and I'm making a scene? Did you know there's an AI in my head? It's probably listening to everything I think. Was that your plan? Some kind of sick game you're playing?"

I slapped a hand down on the table. Bik gently but firmly put his hand over mine. "I assure you this is no game. One of mine has deleted herself. They say you're the best at finding and extracting things. I need you to find information and report back to me. You're a thief. A very good one. Providence has brought you to me. Surely, you've had to pretend to be someone else to get your job done."

Bik had a way of speaking that took the rage right out of my head. Calm, deliberate. I don't know how, but the undertone said it was all going to be fine and this was really nothing to worry about.

I plopped down in the seat opposite him and ran a hand through my hair. Fine. Silky. Long. Not at all like what I was used to. Just another reminder I was trapped. "I've had to pretend, sure. But when I was done, I could take off the suit."

"This is no different, Ms. Devore-"

"Quit calling me that. It's not my name."

"It is," he snapped. "And the sooner you accept that, the happier you'll be. You don't have to be Natasha Devore, but you have to act like her if you want to find out what happened. I have done you a favor; it is now time for you to do one for me."

"What favor did you do for me?"

"I understand you need to answer to Nobtop. Brave move. He has a well-deserved reputation. As of right now, he can't find you. You could join his gang and he'd never know who you really are. I saved you. All I ask in return is you save dear Natasha's memory for me."

Fuck. He was right. If it hadn't been for Bik's bizarre intervention, I'd probably be exploring all new kinds of pain at the hands of the region's most notorious gangster. "Fine," I said. "How long do I have?"

"As long as it takes, Ms. Devore. As long as it takes. In the interim, drink your coffee. It is fantastic when it's hot."

The coffee was good, but I needed a change of clothes and something stronger than expensive caffeine. I needed a place to get my head together and reassess my situation. A place where reason and logic danced with whimsy and fucked the brains out of caprice. A magical, wondrous place that promised a vacation from reality.

I needed a bar.

3 - Mirror, Mirror

Endpoint had lots of bars. With room to house thousands of people, it was a given that booze life would find a way. The earliest was a whisky joint out on the *Temnyy*-facing point of the big-ass triangle we lived in. It was decked out in old-school, run-down vibes. From the dead plants to the surly bartender with a soft spot for hard-luck cases, it could have been the neighborhood pub in any old neighborhood on any number of planets.

Sully's was quiet. Not empty, but not crowded. Surreptitious glances caught out of the corner of my eye had me on edge. It had me bordering on paranoia. I knew deep down the whole bar wasn't out to get me, but even being noticed was a bad thing for a thief. I wanted the warm blanket of anonymity.

I glared hard at the first guy I caught staring. He looked embarrassed. Terrified, like he'd be caught going through his sister's underwear drawer. His face went almost as white as my skin and suddenly the drink in front of him was the most interesting thing in the systems.

It had to have been Nobtop's doing. Somehow, the monster had figured out who I was and he was busy looking for proof. No, scratch that. People like Nobtop didn't work on proof. He got a thought in that big, dumb skull of his and acted on it. Usually violently. There was something else going on. Something unfamiliar.

I sidled up the bar and tried to think about what I wanted. Idly scrolled through the drink list floating in front of me. It was like stepping back in time. Most places just let you scan the menu in your HUD, but Sully felt like making you work for your drink.

"She'll have a double old-fashioned," a voice said beside me.

The guy who said it looked like a kid, little more than a young geek. "I'm sorry?" I snarled.

Color leeched out of his face so fast, I thought he was going to pass out. He fiddled with his fingers like he couldn't figure out what to do with his hands. "Sorry," he said sheepishly, "I just figured it would be okay for me to order for you."

We stared at each other for a moment. I was deciding what to do with him. He looked like he was deciding whether to run or not. He was a little guy. My height or less and his body looked like it had never experienced any kind of labor. Pasty white skin. My white skin was purely artificial. More like a canvas than flesh. His had the patchy, bluish look from spending too much time in dark rooms. He had enhanced eyes. Nothing flashy. Functional. Probably helped him process information from displays like Sully's or the old-school external displays the cheap corps favored. He was either a serial killer or one of the local IT guys. Or both.

"How's it going, IT guy?" I asked, hoping I'd guessed right.

"Same shit, different day," he said with a high-pitched staccato laugh. "How about you, Natasha? I was kind of worried you were going to off me there."

Lucky, lucky, lucky guess.

"I'm not the offing kind of person," I told him.

He rolled his eyes. "Sure, tell that to BrainMaxx."

"BrainMaxx isn't a person."

"Wasn't. Well, isn't now, either. Hasn't been for a few hundred years. Thanks to you, I might add."

The bartender sat a drink in front of me. I'd never had an old fashioned. It was amber, whisky with hints of orange and vanilla. I nodded thanks and made a mental not to tip him well. Next time ask me what kind of drink I want. I thought about pouring the drink out on the floor, but figured what the hell? New body, new manners. Or something.

"What do you know about BrainMaxx?" I asked the IT Guy. He looked a little young and straight-laced to know the sordid truth.

"Seriously protected hunk of crystal lattice," he said. "Gov's last, best attempt at keeping tabs on what we're doing out here. They threw everything they had at keeping it secure so it could keep the data flowing back to HQ."

The benefits of an underground education are you get to see history from a different point of view. Like, for instance, how the legendary Digital Diva ultimately brought down the whole thing. Who probably stole the crypto cutters for herself. In my line of work, Nat's attack on BrainMaxx was the stuff of legend. The kind of stuff criminals told their kids to assuage any feelings of remorse. "See, kids, this woman used her powers for good and made a tidy profit off it." I didn't know all the details, but I knew enough to make do.

"It was a little more complicated than that," I told him. "BrainMaxx wasn't just a listening system; it was a control system. They wanted to get into our heads and plant simple thoughts. Unlike most Gov projects, BrainMaxx worked.

Like most Gov projects, it was designed in-house. I knew a guy who knew a gal who knew a Gov drone and got hold of the code. Bastards had a bug in their Cx routines that I used to burn the whole thing down. Gov wanted to build another one, but they were short on cash."

I.T.'s mouth dropped. There was still a nascent idealism about governments out there, like if we could just get systems-wide government involved it would cut down the crime.

"Wow," was all I.T. could say.

I downed my drink in a single gulp and let the synth whisky roll down my throat. "You'll have to excuse me," I told him, "but I can't seem to remember your name."

"Solomon. Most people just call me Sol, though." He was completely distracted. I could have asked him his pant size and he would have rattled it off without thought. "BrainMaxx was a control system?"

I nodded and motioned to the bartender for another drink. "Yup," I told him. "Well, kind of. If you had a personal AI, it could control that. Most people can't afford personal AIs, but BrainMaxx could plant simple ideas like 'I want to pay my taxes' or 'Revolution is bad' in the ones that did."

"Why AIs?" Sol asked. "What did they hope to gain?"

"You have an AI?" I asked. The room was a bit wobbly. Maybe losing nearly half my body weight translated to less mean time to drunkenness.

Sol nodded. "Top of the line HolaTech. Lucha 3k."

"Good system. Your Lucha got a name?"

"Maria," Sol said with a sigh.

"Do you talk with Maria?"

"Of course. Maria and I can spend hours talking. Well, thinking... Oh, no."

"Oh, yes," I said. "You think your talking is secure but the AI is corrupted."

"Which meant the gov could see into your head."

The bartender set the drink down gently and flashed me a big smile. "Which means Gov could see into your head," I repeated. "And that's been their dream for as long as there have been govs. Some people even said BrainMaxx could circumvent sandboxing, see stuff even your AI can't get to. If I can read your mind, I can be one step ahead of you. Hell, I could use your thoughts against you. I could even reprogram your AI to store every conversation and forward it at my convenience. Since AIs are expensive, they were hoping to manipulate the upper classes into manipulating the lower classes. It's their thing."

"No wonder you nuked it," Sol said. "That's terrifying."

The booze was really making itself home in my system. I was about at that "warm fuzzy everything's cool" stage of drunk. "The way I see it," I told Sol, "I saved the damned systems."

"That's my girl," a woman's voice said. "Savior of the free folk of the ass-end of the galaxy."

A hand landed on my shoulder and squeezed a little harder than it should have. A security kind of squeeze. Every time my shoulder got a squeeze like that, things went wrong. Booze and paranoia had kept me alive and I didn't intend to give up on them yet.

I glanced down and saw a gloved hand on my shoulder. Black, form-fitting leather. The kind of stuff people wore when they didn't feel like leaving fingerprints. Thumb to the left; that meant right hand on my shoulder. Left hand holding a blade or a gun or stun-stick. The mirror behind the bar was useless; just a woman dressed in black, but her other hand was hidden.

Fuck it. If I was wrong, I could always apologize.

I grabbed her hand and held it tight to my shoulder. Legs pushed hard against the bar, spinning me around. Her arm, trapped by my hands, stretched out as my body spun in space. I heard her yelp as her first her wrist then her elbow then her shoulder stretched way further than normal. That was when I knew an apology was on the horizon: Security didn't yelp.

My hands slipped down and let her hand slide off my shoulder before my momentum could rip her arm out of its socket and tear all the ligaments in her elbow. I let the stool continue spinning until I was face-to-face with a redhead in tight pleather. She had a look of sheer horror on her face. I probably had one, too.

"Sorry," I mumbled. "I thought you were someone else."

To my surprise, she smiled and licked her teeth. She eyed Sol warily and then looked back at me. "Aren't you going to introduce me to your friend?"

Sol was on his feet with his hand extended before I could answer. "Solomon Tizak. Head data analyst and architect for ERTech. We do space weather analysis for our friend out there."

"Monique," she replied warmly, holding out her hand for him to kiss. "I do a little of this and a little of that. I've been trying to get our girl here to do a little job for me. She fell off the face of the station for a few days, though. Very hush, hush. Then I heard she was dead. Imagine my surprise to find her here with a drink in her hand."

Monique had a hint of old-world, deep-South charm. A belle of the ball who'd traded in her lace and ribbons for form-fitting pleather and an almost desperately badass look. I didn't know her, but I knew her type: small-time grifter, part-time good-time girl. She'd happily show up on someone's arm and then vanish to dust when the night was over.

She caught me looking at her and smiled the single most sinister smile I've ever seen. The kind of smile a wolf throws a bunny just before eating it. For a moment, our eyes locked and I felt some things I'd never felt in places I didn't know could feel that way. Whatever the moment was, it passed quickly and left an electric tang on my tongue.

Her wink and smile were enough to tell me she'd felt it, too. Awkward moment.

Sol's polite cough broke the moment and I vowed to buy him his next drink and tell him everything he wanted to know about BrainMaxx. Even if I had to make things up. "Would you like to join us?" he asked.

My heart sank. I did not need this right now. What I needed was a quiet drink followed by a few others.

Monique put on a show of stretching and shook her head. Pink lips pouted. "I'm sorry, but I must be going. It has been a long day and I need my beauty rest. Not all of us can pull off the exhausted beauty look as easily as sweet Natasha here."

Had Monique just zinged me? It felt like she zinged me. Before I could figure out if I needed a witty response, Monique was stuffing something into my breast pocket and grinning. "I do hope you'll come see me. And not just about my business proposition."

And then she was gone, sauntering off like she owned the place. I turned to find Sol in deep smit. Monique was pretty, no doubt about it, but she shouldn't have been enough to turn the poor guy into a puddle. I stared at him in wonder. I hadn't had that reaction to a woman since I was in my teens. It made me wonder if his innocent guy routine was legit and he'd spent more time with virtual women than real ones.

"You are so lucky," he whispered.

Son, if you only knew. "How am I lucky?"

"That was Monique. The Monique."

I shrugged my shoulders and shook my head. "Who?"

"Monique," he said. A strange look crossed his face like he couldn't believe I didn't know her. "Monique. The Monique."

"You said that already. Who is 'The Monique'?"

His eyes bored into mine, looking for something only he understood. I must have lacked it because he shook his head and dropped his eyes. "She's a Template. Like *the Template*."

"Template? No shit?"

His sagging shoulders, hangdog look, and bright red cheeks told me everything I needed to know. VirtSex was never my thing, but it was apparently Sol's. Fully interactive, fully scanned interactive virtual sex sounded cool, but I always preferred the real deal. VirtSex stars – or Templates, as afficionados preferred to call them – were nearly indistinguishable from the real thing because they had a nascent ability to share their sensations. It was like fucking someone and feeling what they felt. Too meta for my tastes. "You fucked her?" I asked, flinging a thumb over my shoulder. "Like, not for real, but in Virt? How was she?"

In my old body, I would have expected something like "Fucking incredible" or intimate details on her intimate parts or a blow-by-blow of his adventures with her. In Nat's body all I got was, "Look, Nat, I'm sorry. I just wouldn't be able to explain it because we wouldn't have the same, uh, frame of reference."

In Sol's defense, he did look sorry.

"No worries," I told him.

"She likes you," he said. "She flashed you with her eyes. People with Eyetex only flash people they're into."

Was that what had happened? That flush of warmth was from Eyetex? I am such a dolt. I should have recognized the telltale sparkle, but maybe it's hard to see when the damned redhead with the nice body was staring blissfully into your eyes.

"I must have missed it," I mumbled and took a sip of my drink.

"I saw it. Plain as day. She flashed you."

Of all the things that could have happened today, having a Template flash me was lowest on my list. And what was that thing she was trying to get Natasha to do? Some job, but it sounded like it didn't go too well.

Sol sat slumped in his seat like a cheap suit on the corner of a halfway house bathroom. I wondered if he'd expected her to fall head over heels in love with a chief data analyst at first sight. If so, he was in for a disappointing life. Pity. He seemed like a decent guy.

"At least you got to kiss her hand," I told him. "That's more than most of her fans ever get to do."

That perked him right up. He sat up a little straighter and a hint of gleam came into his eyes. "Yeah," he said distantly. "Well, her glove at least. But I'll bet that glove has touched her."

"Getting weird, Sol," I said over my drink.

"Sorry. I just get excited sometimes. It's just that, well, you know, I've, uh...been with her so many times-"

"Kinda freakin' me out, buddy."

"And to see that she real and actually touch her in the real-"

He was babbling, brain locked in some weird feedback loop where touching Monique's gloved hand was the same as...something. I wasn't sure what, but it was something important. His eyes were fully lit up but staring inward. Probably at Monique on her back, moaning in ecstasy.

Which, I had to admit, was still pinging around in my head. "Do you need to be alone?" I asked Sol.

He nodded vigorously and sprang out of his seat. He was halfway to the door when he stopped dead in his tracks and turned around. "Look, Natasha, I don't mean to leave you high and dry, but this is important. I've got to tell the groupchat and uh, you know... This needs to be finished. It's not that I don't like you. I mean, you're pretty and all, but Monique is special to me and, frankly, she's on a whole other level."

Um, what?

He was gesticulating wildly, hands caressing imaginary bodies and flinging imaginary foes out of his way. "That was like meeting the Goddess. The real one. I need some time to process that. Are you going to be okay? Can I walk you to your cabin or something?"

There wasn't a doubt in my mind that it would be a hurried walk. "I'm fine, Sol. Go worship the Goddess. Or whatever you crazy kids call it these days."

"Thanks, Natasha," he said as he turned. "You're swell!"

I was tipsy, feeling warm in places I never expected to feel, and flashes of a hot redhead were popping up in my head. In the mirror, a woman with pink hair and calliope irises stared back at me. Maybe it was the drink, the flash, or the general screwball weirdness of the day, but I had a strange desire to help her. No one should die in mystery. If she really was dead.

It was time to get some intel. And to do that, I needed to get a better grasp on the skin I was wearing.

4 - Body Image Problems

I was lying on Natasha's bed, in her naked body, staring at the ceiling and feeling extremely awkward. Would staring at my naked flesh count as ogling or was it more along the lines of checking the cut of a suit or the knot on a tie? "Full reflect," I said to the cabin.

The walls, floor, and ceiling of the cabin turned into perfect mirrors. No matter where I looked, I saw her. There was nothing overtly special about her body. Pink hair, probably a chromo change. Normal build, 170cm tall or so.

As I looked at myself in the mirror, I tried hard not to stare. I was still stuck in the mode of surreptitious glances. But this body wasn't some chick I was checking out in a bar; it was my home. It was me. At least for now and beating around the bush wasn't helping things. I let my eyes wander down my body. Eyes filled with curiosity. A cute nose. Full lips. I had a pointed jaw that flowed into a delicate neck. Shoulders muscles rippled just below pigmentless, skin. Natasha liked to work out. You didn't get muscles like these from injectables; they were result of lifting things and putting them down. From the general muscle tone, I'd say she was more into functional strength than bulk.

Worked my way down, took in the breasts flattened by gravity to my chest. No implants, authentic bio stuff. Small waist that tapered into hips that flared gracefully into strong legs that looked a little short for my height. Unmodified. Maybe not classic beauty, but pretty enough to turn a head or two. Explained the looks I kept getting in Sully's.

Back to the eyes. Anything to avoid what I felt was leering at myself.

No, that was wrong. The flesh may not make the person, but there was no doubt I was locked into it. Bodies and their associated modifications were as much a part of us as anything else.

The body reflected all around the cabin was pretty. She... Fuck it. I... I wasn't drop dead gorgeous. Pretty, sure, but not the kind of body that made people send wooden horses to each other. Not that it really mattered. It was a different experience being on the opposite side of the camera. I'd never be a Jezebel or an Amara and, when I thought about it, I didn't really care.

Natasha's body – my body now – didn't fall into the narrow statistical range of perfection. Legs slightly too short. Breasts too small. Too much muscle. What the fuck ever. The woman reflected in the room was great as far as I was concerned.

I stretched and spent my time gazing at myself, touching myself. Trying to get my consciousness to accept this was who I was now. The fucked-up thing was I'd probably have to do the exact same thing when I got out of here and back into my own body.

The look on my face wasn't Natasha. She was gone. I looked out from her eyes now. In a way, I was her. But in a much larger, much more realistic way, I'd never be her and no matter how much this body was hers, it would never look exactly like her. The best I could do was act like Natasha Devore. Hopefully, that would be good enough. Clothes. Smile. Finger.

Hey. Wait. When I first saw that picture of Natasha, she had animated tats running up and down her arms. That kind of thing was implanted. Implants had controls.

My plugin menu was a button on my HUD. Focus on it and think the magic word and a list of my plugs popped out. To my eyes, it looked like a menu of options sprung into being out of the ether and hovered in the middle of the room. Natasha had some wild stuff installed. Network Kung Fu, PingOMatic, Phreaker. Probably commonplace for hackers, but still exotic to me. The beginning and ending of my modifications was my OTFAnalysis mod and a Generica Comm Device. Natasha had probably 10 or 15 packages installed. Plus a wide array of emergency stim packs including one that looked...interesting

Toward the end of the list was LiveTat5k. I let out a slow whistle. LiveTat5k was top of the line stuff. Whipped up by mad geniuses on Ceti Alpha V, not only could it render animations, it could render full-color, hi-res, customized animations. And it was full body. Most tat systems did full-color and hi-res. Animations were more expensive and usually consisted of looping images in a small area. A butterfly on a shoulder or pulsing forearms. Full body was rare. Long play full-motion video was almost unheard of. It must have cost a queen's ransom and taken days to grow through Natasha's skin. At least it explained her skin color.

I blinked on demo and selected the advanced example. It would be standard-issue corp propaganda, but built-in demos were good for showing off the system's capabilities.

It started slow: A lightning-bright blue line that ran down my body from my head to my crotch. Across my chest flashed a message: "Welcome." Everything stopped. My body exploded in animated color. Butterflies and dragons, stars and galaxies paraded across my skin.

The tats were energized light bouncing around just under my flesh. Tiny machines that flashed briefly according to a centralized plan. I knew that instinctively, but it was still amazing to watch. The designs and patterns covered every centimeter of Natasha's body. I watched in wonder as a cartoon cat chased a cartoon mouse up my torso before they both exploded in a fireworks display that covered my chest. Over my shoulder a moon appeared. The scene zoomed out to show a planet a solar system a galaxy all moving according to the grand plan of the universe. An artist's rendition of a living Predecessor. The species had been dead for millennia, but someone brought the creature in all its savage glory to life and let it loose across my bare flesh.

The demo lasted a full three minutes – an eternity by demo standards – and the designers put everything they had into it. Amazing barely covered it. I've seen cines that weren't as detailed. At the end, my skin went coal black and white text appeared on my chest: Stay tuned for part two.

Part two? Who made a two-part capability demo?

Color slowly bled into my skin. Faint hints of purples and dark red at first, followed by the deep blues only space can provide. White pinpricks formed bit by bit. Zoom in on a star in Rigel, the closest one to Endpoint. Yellowish light assaulted my eyes before the view shifted outward past the four planets in the system and settled several light-years away on a black area of space where a dot of orange light glowed around a mass so black it might as well have been a tumor in space.

That had to be *Temnyy Muzhchina*; I'd recognize the Dark Man anywhere. Zoom closer and the orange dot resolved into Endpoint. Pretty specific information for a corp demo, especially since most corps don't bother to keep a presence out this far.

Words in a cartoon bubble appeared: Xevex Jeffries is one of them.

"Son of a bitch," I whispered. What the hell did that mean?

5 - It Had to Happen Sometime

I had a name, but the message didn't mean anything, so I set about looking up one of a few people Natasha knew on Endpoint. The station was homogenous to a fault. It was like those old video games where the programmers ran out of ideas and recycled the stuff they'd done in earlier parts of the game and left you wondering if it was déjà vu or if you just needed to get out more often because everything looked the same.

Reddish walls. Thick white horizontal stripe. Exactly the same as every other corridor. There were no numbers on the doors, no identifying marks of any kind except what the residents decided was best. Residents learned their way around and that was it. Or, more likely, they downloaded the app and let it direct them. Another reason our lack of central administration was dubious.

Someone told you their cabin number and it meant precisely squat, so they had to preface it with section number and floor number. 3-2-415. Section three, level two, room 415. Where 415 meant fourth turn from the main elevator, one meant you turned right, five meant cabin five. Easy peasy.

Until you forget to write down the exact order of numbers. Sol said his cabin was number was 1-3-something, something, ten. Limited to section one, level three, turn a direction somewhere, and find the tenth cabin from the turn. Without an exact number, it was all guesswork.

I really needed to download the Endpoint app. Natasha never did it because she had an instinctive understanding of all things complicated. I hadn't done it because I was lazy. If I had a copy, I could have had Sol beam me a location and it would have been all good. Instead, I fell back on my paranoia and insisted on writing things down on napkins and then leaving them in bars.

The first two doors I beeped told me to piss off and never come back. Some people get incredibly irritated when you pull them out whatever weirdness they were up to only to find a stranger at the door looking for directions. Among other things, I saw a man dressed as a pre-diaspora priest, a fake pig wearing lingerie, and a woman so drunk she thought I was her granddaughter. She promised to make me cookies. When the door to the fourth cabin opened, my stomach did flip-flops, my brain first went into overdrive before shutting down, and a general sense of twisted fate smacked me square in the face.

"I wondered when you'd finally come to your senses," Monique said with a flick of her hip.

She was wearing sweatpants and a T-Shirt that managed to be both billowy and form fitting. "Sorry," I said, "Wrong door. I got lost."

"Didn't get the app?" she asked. "Tsk, tsk, tsk. You naughty girl."

Those emerald eyes of hers rolled over me like a leopard staring at a pile of steaks. Hungry. Enthusiastic. Ready to pounce. "Why don't you at least come in and we can look up where you want to be?"

Want to be? Anywhere but there, but there more than anywhere else. I sighed and nodded, feeling like I was about to walk into a spooder web and love every minute of it.

When I arrived on Endpoint, my assigned quarters were what you'd get in a cheap hotel. Natasha's apartment with a separate bathroom and a tiny kitchen were spacious by my standards. Monique's apartment was on a whole other level. She had actual doors to different rooms, a kitchen, and a lowered seating area with a massive window looking out into space.

Outside the window, *Temnyy* was a black spot in space. A shining light in the upper left had to be one of Endpoint's sisters. Hell of a view. Probably had a hell of a price tag. Giving the people what they wanted paid well.

"Drink?" Monique asked from the kitchen.

I pulled myself away from the spectacle of every star in the galaxy shining just for me and shook my head. "No, thank you."

"On the house," Monique said, gently pressing a drink into my hand. "You can't come into my space and not share a drink with me; it's an insult in my culture."

I had no idea how she moved so quickly. One moment she was in the kitchen, the next she was in front of me. "Culture?" I mumbled.

"Sex workers," she said. "Drink up. You don't want to insult us. We're a rough and tumble group."

The cloudy green drink smelled of black licorice and sin. Normally, licorice was like sniffing garlic-scented assholes, but for some reason this smelled delicious. Must be the difference between my senses and Natasha's.

"Is this-?" I asked.

"Absinthe, yes. Fans send me all kinds of weird things: Socks, underwear, cake recipes, boxes of chocolates. Most of it I keep long enough to write a thank you note before it gets donated or recycled, but this was special. French Absinthe from the before the Fall."

"That would make it – what? – over four hundred years old."

Monique glowed. "Four hundred and twenty five."

So far, my record for old alcohol was measured in days or months. I once had a ten-year-old Scotch, but I had to steal that bottle on a job. Four hundred years old was mind boggling. When it was bottled, human society still split along national borders, mankind had never been in space in any meaningful way, and the future still looked cheery. That was before the Beast and the chaos he instilled.

"Thanks," I mumbled. "Do you share four-hundred-year-old liquor with everyone who walks into your door?"

"You're special," Monique said, flashing me a Cheshire Cat grin.

"Special because you need me or because you need me to do a job?"

The grin faltered briefly before flaring back into luscious life. "Yes," she said, sipping cloudy green liquid through sumptuous lips.

"I try to not mix business with pleasure," I said.

"My business is pleasure."

Parts of my body were lighting up in ways I didn't know how to explain. No bulge in my pants because there was nothing there to bulge. A tingling sensation working its way down my spine. Butterflies in my stomach. A general need to be touched. Who the fuck was I kidding with this cool cat act? Monique was a pro and she was epic at her job, and at that moment, all I wanted was to let her touch me anywhere she wanted.

I took another sip of absinthe, eyeing her over the glass. She knew exactly what she was doing. No flash this time, just her being her. The sweet licorice burned down my throat and did absolutely fuck-all to calm down the butterflies.

She flashed me the knowing smile and stepped closer. A little piece of me melted. "You're shaking," she said.

"No, I'm not." When in doubt, deny everything.

"Your glass is."

"I'm-"

Monique flowed closer. A lithe predator moving in on its willing prey. "There's nothing to be nervous about. I'm a trained professional."

"The job," I whispered.

"Check your email. I sent a follow-up this morning. It's just a little thing, right up your alley. But we don't need to worry about that right now."

Her hand on my hip made me twitch. No pressure, no force, just a hand resting lightly while she sipped her drink and smiled. "Did you spike this?" I asked, eyeing my drink.

She shook her head. "Honey, please. That's amateur hour stuff. I'm the real deal. You're completely free to do what you want. It's always better that way."

I could turn around and walk out her door. And spend the rest of the night kicking myself. Time for absolute honesty. "You're good," I told her.

"Best you've ever seen," she said, moving her hand up my waist. My breath caught in my throat both hoping and dreading that she'd work her way up higher. "You're not going to break my wrist if I unzip this jumpsuit you're wearing, are you?"

"Probably not," I whispered.

"Oooh," Monique cooed. "I like a little danger."

Let's just say the zipper going down was a metaphor for my defenses falling.

6 – Alliance

M onique's body was warm against my cheek. Hand gently stroking my hair. The general feeling of being overloaded and exploded left me weak. Solace in her arms.

We didn't speak. We laid together in a tangled mass of limbs and listened to the steady drone of the air circulators and the deep thrum of Endpoint's power generators. The woman with the predator eyes had snared her prey. She'd won. And I didn't care.

Her heartbeat was lazy. Just like me, Monique didn't have a care in the world. A good, solid orgasm will do that. I'd lost count after my four. I knew there were more, but I couldn't be bothered to remember them. They were just another instance of build, build, build, and then explode. Used to be, I'd remember exactly how many my partner had, but after Monique's third, I stopped counting. It just didn't seem to matter anymore.

"Not that I'm complaining," Monique asked, "but what brought you to my door?"

I wrapped an arm around her and pulled our bodies closer. "Sheer dumb luck," I said. "I got lost."

"Sounds like fate intervening," she said. "Figures. I tried for months to seduce you and all it took was getting lost. If I'd known that, I would have blindfolded you and left you on the other side of the station."

"You did blindfold me."

"Different circumstances. And you knew exactly where you were."

Yeah, sprawled out on her bed with her face between my thighs.

I rolled onto my back and stared at the ceiling. She'd decorated it with glow-in-the-dark stars. Some constellation that looked familiar, but I couldn't wrap my head around it. "What's that?" I asked, pointing at the ceiling.

She shrugged. "I don't know. It came to me in a dream and I had all those stars left over from a party I threw, so I put it together. I was hoping that staring at them when I went to sleep would unlock the mystery. So far, no luck."

"I like them," I told her. There was something immensely comforting about simple glow-in-the-dark stars. If they got old, you could take them down. Can't do that with the real ones. And the glow-in-the-dark ones don't come with unnamed horrors.

Fingers in my hair again. Shivers down my spine. My god, the woman was good. Either that or I was desperate. Maybe it was both. "Why me?" I asked.

She brushed my earlobe and it was like a siren going off between my legs. "Why not you?" Monique replied.

"You could have anyone you wanted. What's so special about me?"

Her body heaved under my head. "Sorry. I'm not laughing at you. Have you met many Templates?"

I shook my head.

"We tend to be insular or solitary. That's why I'm out here—small population, middle of nowhere. People still recognize me, but mostly they leave me alone. Meeting someone who recognizes you is weird because that means they've had sex with you in Virt, or had sex *as* you in Virt. I met one guy who'd had Virt sex with me as me. He was crazy proud of it. We have trouble being regular. That's why when I go out as me, I'm dressed to the nines; it makes me look unapproachable. When I want some quiet time, I do my best to look frumpy. Screw up my hair, put on loose-fitting clothes. Slouch. That sort of thing. Works like a charm. I can go anywhere and no one recognizes me."

I chuckled a little at the idea of Monique the redheaded goddess of Virt sex slouching and wearing sweatpants. Fact was it probably worked perfectly. "Clever."

"Right? People see what they want to see. Or really, what they expect to see. They expect me to ooze sex but most of the time all I want is to disappear into the crowd and be left alone. You were the only person who ever gave me the time of day when I was hiding. That was my crazy hobo lady costume. Old pants, an ex's shirt that was like four sizes too big. Oil in half my hair."

"I remember that." I didn't remember that.

"And you sat down and bought me a drink. I had no idea who you were at the time, just that girl with the pink hair and the knowing eyes. I found you later as myself and you weren't interested."

I also didn't remember that but nodded anyway.

"There's nothing more peculiar to a template than being turned down. We just don't know how to handle it. Did you know I've been downloaded something like a couple of billion times across the sectors? Billions. I don't care who you are, that's a lot. I don't even have to work anymore if I don't want to. Like tomorrow, I've got a thing, but mostly I lounge around. Back in the day, they talked about women fucking their way to the top. I've literally done it. Every now and then I do a new wetware release – don't laugh, it's not what you think it is – or introduce a new talent, but I do it all in the real, I do it on my terms, and I do it on my timeline."

"You never go into Virt?" I asked.

"Not unless I have to. I have a full-access account that I almost never use. Virt's a cesspool. My template download was a full scan, inside and out. Publishers throw skins on me, mix and match with various partners, and playback my experiences. Most of my fans know what I look like, but that's not what they care about. They care about the way I can feel something. Record it, play it back in their heads. Last I heard from Maddox, there were millions of possible permutations of me. Each download nets me a bit of money. Multiply that by billions and you'll see why I don't need to work. I choose to work. Most of my regular life is straight-up marketing. Put on something tight or revealing or both and sashay around. Sign the occasional body part. Let people buy me drinks. Smile at their bad jokes. Typical stuff. Enough about me," Monique said, "I only know the basics of you. What do you do for fun?"

"Aside from strange women?" I asked.

Monique gasped loudly. Her hand slapped on her chest with a smack. "I am aghast that you would think me strange, young lady."

I patted her thigh and shook my head. "Strange as in new and unexplored. Boldly go and all that."

"I would say I've been thoroughly explored. Boldly, I might add. Much more boldly than I would have expected."

"Now. But a few hours ago, you were strange."

She had an adorable pout and mock sigh. She mustered up her wrecked ego and said, "I accept your apology."

I hadn't offered one, but I had to admit there was a certain disarming charm to accepting something unoffered. Good tactic. "Anyway," I said.

"Anyway," Monique replied. "What does a legendary hacker do for fun?"

Time to act the part. "I collect archaic K-pop memorabilia," I said. Normally the admission that would make me blush, but technically it wasn't me that collected boy band posters. It was, however, I who pulled them down and neatly stowed them in the closet. I may be an asshole and stuck in Natasha's body, but that doesn't mean I was going to destroy her antiques.

"K-pop?" Monique asked.

"Korean pop stars from the late 20th, early 21st. Prefab singing groups of dubious musical talent but with killer dance moves and cute faces."

"Room," Monique said to the ceiling. "Play me some K-pop. Just pick the most popular song from the late 20th."

A catchy, overproduced beat rumbled through the room. Crystalline clarity, even if the song was lacking the normal spread spectrum we'd come to appreciate in modern music. "Show me a video feed," Monique added.

Five young Korean guys danced in the air above our heads, synchronous as robots. "See," I told her, "Catchy."

"I'd have trouble not laughing at the one with the mustache, but that one on the far left is hot. I'd even consider sharing him with you. The music is atrocious. Catchy, yes, but boring. Room, symphonic noise playlist three, track five, please. No video."

A low rumble shook me in places. It morphed slowly from an archaic string to a deep, melodious thrum, to a shrieking wall of chaos. I never would have pegged Monique as a noise fan, let alone a fan of electronoise and Mongo death metal mashups. The music was, frankly, more to my taste. I could never stand treacly songs about lost loves. "Nice," I told her.

"Spectral Density. They're out of Zephyr. Kids, basically, but they show immense promise."

We let the station go about its business while we swapped songs back and forth, just two people sharing the sounds that kept us rooted to the universe. It was therapeutic; a throwback to the heady days of school when spending an entire day naked and listening to some new band or other was the proper way of handling Mondays.

When we were both good and relaxed with each other, I decided she was an okay person. No one with her taste in music could be all bad.

7 - Some Things Never Change

The Copper Lounge was a throwback bar that harkened back to the time when people knew how to drink, throw darts, and start fights. It was a no-frills, honest-to-Penta bar complete with dying plants, mismatched chairs and tables, and a bar with wood so old it had to have come from Terra.

A handful of zilch-heads in the back were nodding off, glowing cables sticking out of their ports, feeding them the digital equivalent of cheap hooch. Every bar has a place like that: a small section where derelicts who couldn't afford the real thing got their taste or people who couldn't stomach alcohol could get ripped to the tits without fear of imbibing. It was a popular spot for some of the extremist religious types. Their holy books said alcohol could never touch their tongues, but it didn't say anything about synethic hooch going straight to their brains. Loopholes for the win.

Monique was off doing whatever it was she did to get ready for a sample take. Jenkins had fucked off to hang with his AI buds. That left me exactly where I was used to being: Alone.

A maxed-out frequent-drinker card on Natasha's nightstand brought me here. I wouldn't have considered her a regular at a place like the Copper Lounge. It was low-key. There were very few flashing lights and the wait staff was surly. Maybe this was where she went to wind down or get information. Whatever the reason, as soon as I walked in two things immediately happened: A man stared straight at me and dropped his drink, and a bartender with a shocked smile on her face waved me over.

The man worried me the most. It could've been Natasha's body was too much for him, but that didn't seem right. Her wardrobe didn't trend toward the sexy side of things. She was a hacker. She wanted comfort and ease. There were a few eyebrow-raising articles in her wardrobe. I'd just grabbed pants and a T-shirt and called it good.

It's always uncool for guys to drop their drinks when a woman walks into the room. Dropping a drink was always because of a sudden shock. Seeing someone who wasn't supposed to be there because she was dead for example.

I waved back at the bartender and watched out of the corner of my eye as the drink dropper scrambled out of the room. Something odd was afoot. I didn't get a close look at him, but from a distance, he looked like one of the Airlockers.

From afar, the bartender was a bombshell of a woman with blonde locks and the kind of body that could melt ice from across the room. Close up, she was a buff-as-hell bombshell, with faint lines and traces of circuitry just under her skin. Probably half the implants were useless trinkets, flashing lights and snazzy subdermal displays, but there were a couple of interesting tidbits in there, too.

Natasha's passive defensive systems read the bartender's loadout and I let out a low whistle. She had a DefCon needler in her right arm and a Yoshimitsu shock pack in her left. A faint glow in the back of her eyes smelled like a Cheng-Yu sensor package that could detect a weapon from a hundred meters. It wasn't uncommon for a bartender to have some upgrades, but hers were merc-grade stuff.

I scanned the bar's drink list before I sat down and lucked out when I found it was run by one Ms. Jane 'Peach' Piermont. A quick check on StaNet almost made me turn around and walk away with a mumbled apology. A former bouncer and merc, Ms. Piermont had a sizeable record of busting heads for the highest bidder and a brief stint working with a hacker by the name of Natasha Devore.

Old war buddies. Shit. That made things harder.

"What's up with that guy?" I asked as I plopped myself down on an authentic red Naugahyde stool and spun to face the bar.

Peach poured out a drink and shook her head. As she pulled her arm back, a pang of memory hit me. On her collarbone was a simple, stylized tattoo of a mid-tier monarch with a pair of daggers through his head. "One of those Airlockers. Jeffries has been riling them up. There's a colony of them popping up on the other side of the Bazaar."

I took a sip and found the scariest stuff known to man dripping down my throat. It tasted like pickled ass drenched in old petrol. I swallowed, but only barely and the coughing fit that followed nearly brought the stuff back up. Peach frowned and neatly snatched the drink from my fingers. "That's mine, ya dork," she said before downing it.

Another drink slid across the smooth bar top. Brownish amber that reflected the dim RGB lights in the bar. It went down like butter made of booze. "Better," I wheezed.

"You never could handle the good stuff," Peach told me, placing a bottle of something in front of me. The bluish liquid was slowly roiling inside the bottle and the label

– a cartoon man with overlarge eyes each pointing in a different direction – didn't explain much. But I knew from the roiling that I was staring at an authentic bottle of Deception Street, the single most dangerous hooch in the civilized sectors. There were rumors of people drinking reactor water to get high, but that stuff was only moderately nastier than Deception Street. While no one knew the exact recipe, some estimated it involved wastewater and some horrible corruption of Bento/Stacks theory. Most people assumed the 210 proof was a typo, but the stuff really was slightly higher than pure alcohol.

"It's like drinking a star farted from a Zenome," I told her.

"Zenomes don't fart," Peach told me.

"They still stink to high hell."

"Didn't know you'd been near them," Peach said. "I figured you'd stuck around the civilized, automated systems. Easier to ply your trade."

"Vacation," I replied. "What better way to get away from it all than the Xerxes? No one in their right mind goes there and they don't keep records."

"True," Peach said as she poured herself another shot of ass. "You just always struck me as a high-toned bitch. Didn't know you could survive without 'net access."

"Only in short quantities."

"Remember that time on Reticula when you had to camp out and tether your neurals to a portspot? I thought you were gonna lose your mind," Peach said.

Quick scan of the 'net. No mention of Reticula for either Natasha's or Peach's boarding passes. Could be ruse.

I sipped my drink and smiled. "Only as much as those bastards in outgoing will let me remember what I did on Reticula."

Peach grabbed me by the shoulders and pulled me over the bar until our foreheads were touching. "Damn, girl," she said quietly. "It is so good to see you again. Scuttlebutt says they found you downstairs. I heard you were dead."

"The rumors of my demise something something something," I said as I patted her cheek.

Peach laughed out loud and kissed my forehead. As I sank back into the ancient barstool, she wagged her finger at me. "If you want to come across as well-read, you need remember the passages. 'The reports of my death are greatly exaggerated'. Mark Twain. Anyway, what happened? One day your best friend wakes up and hears someone found your body. You disappear. Then – bam! – here you are like nothing happened."

"Cronizzle," I said. "Picked it up on Eridium. Flares up every now and then."

"Nasty stuff. No cure?"

"Dunno. Not out here, anyway."

Peach harrumphed, a sound that spoke more than words could ever say about her feelings toward diseases, treatments, and Endpoint healthcare in general. "Ever figure out why those airlockers were after you?"

"They thought I owed them money," I said. I clenched my fist. "I explained that I owed them nothing."

"Good girl. Any survivors or did you go full Peach on them?"

"I let them live," I said, sipping my drink. "If you call that living. I just need to find that Jeffries guy. Ask him why he can't control his flock."

She knuckle bumped my closed fist and laughed. "Just like I taught you. That guy on Bartitsu is probably still scared of us. We should do a girls' weekend out there sometime. Lounge on the beach, drink a lot, beat the shit out of him again. You know, for old times' sake."

I knuckled bumped her on that one. It might have been binding, but I suspected Natasha could use some time out of her cabin. "Deal."

"Fuckin' Jeffries, babe," Peach said, staring off into space. "Someone should put that guy down. I get it, he's got rights and all that shit, but he's riling those crazy bastards up. Mark my words, they're going to be a problem. I hear he's even got some war criminal or another palling around with him."

Jeffries, or Pastor Xevex Jeffries, as he preferred, was a run-of-the-mill airlock preacher. Something to do with the way B/S drives tweaked reality tended to scramble the electrical signals in our heads. That led to a disconnected feeling that could last for anywhere from a few minutes to a few hours. Like all good holy men, Jeffries took advantage of that. Since people like Jeffries preyed on people fresh off the boat, others tagged them as Airlockers.

"It's fine," I said. "They took their licks. I learned to strike first and they learned to keep their distance. Win win."

Peach slammed a fist on the bar top and fixed me with a deathly stare. "Remember those bastards on Neuvaux?

Those kinds of people don't learn nothing. You gotta take care of yourself, chica. Ol' Peach isn't going to be around to bail you out every time."

I bit my tongue and refused to remind her that she wasn't there during whatever thing Natasha had with the airlockers or when Natasha whacked her own brain. Instead, I raised my glass and said, "Promise. Penta my heart and everything."

She clinked my glass and rolled her eyes. "You and that Penta crap. It's just one step removed from burning incense and chanting."

Interesting. Natasha was a Pentan, or at least amenable to it. "At least I don't have to sit somewhere and listen to someone prattle away. Besides, Bob has nice boots."

Peach laughed and nodded sagely. "I guess if you steal a sleeping god's boots, they're gonna be nice. Isn't that the story? Stole a god's boots or something and then cooked up the Penta thing to make money?"

"At least he's honest. I hedged my bet and tossed in my thirty creds. Hallelujah, I'm saved."

"Girl, it's going to take a lot more than thirty credits to cleanse your soul and that's just from what I've personally seen you do."

The drink was beginning to kick in. Some bourbonish variant that tasted a little too good. At first, I was worried she fixed the drink, but then I remembered whose body I inhabited. "That's why it's such a bargain," I told her. I swear, I didn't slur my speech even if I did. "Most of the majors charge way more than that to cleanse a soul. It's like, uh, discount soul saving. Or something."

"You're such a lightweight. Listen, I need to get to work. These bastards aren't going to get themselves drunk and they're tightlipped when they're sober. Come back tonight. We'll get shitfaced and pick up guys."

Sounded good. Ish. Good ish. Still not sure about the guys part yet. The body may have wanted it but the mind was still dealing with centuries of being a guy. Sexuality was mostly fluid anymore, but I still had trouble wrapping my head around being turned on by men.

"Love to, but problem," I mumbled. Damn, getting drunk was going to be cheap. "Got a date. Tonight."

"Oooh," Peach said, putting her elbows on the bar. "Who is he?"

"She."

That caught her attention. Peach stood straight up and glared at me. Then she softened and laughed. "'Bout damned time. I can't tell you how many times I tried to get you. I'm jealous but give the little lady a lick for Peach. Make sure you tell her that. Lick. 'This is from Peach'. Lick. Then come find me and I'll show you how it's done."

Peach gave me a wink and sauntered down to the guy at the end of the bar. They spoke in hushed, conspiratorial tones about something, but neither of them looked my way. Must've been another of Peach's side business partners. I finished my drink and nearly stumbled getting off the barstool. Food was a necessity. That must've been the problem. I was never at my best when I drank my breakfast.

Maybe some Elzarian Tacos blasted with spices or some SinoMong pot rice. My stomach rumbled. The

Bizarre Bazaar usually had some excellent choices. Maybe something new. There was that Cyrillic place that I'd been meaning to try.

I was wandering in a food fantasy haze when someone grabbed me around the waist and lifted me off the ground. Hand over my mouth, the hidden assailant dragged me toward an unmarked door. I kicked backward as hard as I could and got a yelp of surprise in response. I also got a spazzer in the ribs for my trouble.

The shock from the spazzer overrode my nerves, locked my muscles. The effect wouldn't last long, but it didn't take long to do nasty things to immobile bodies. Cut up and organs sold in the Bizarre Bazaar, chained up and handed off to some rich prick with a hard-on for fealty. Robbed, plundered, and dumped out an airlock. Lots of ways things could go bad.

As the door clicked behind us and the din of Endpoint died away, my kidnapper dumped me unceremoniously in the corner of a stairwell. The sinister part of my mind agreed with the locale. No one used stairs when lifts were available. The rational part of my mind thought I was well and truly fucked.

Two people stared down at me with wide, nervous eyes. Airlockers by the look of the rags on their bodies. The spazzer still locked me tight, but I could feel the shock leaving my muscles.

"What now?" the Airlocker on the right said. He had a scraggly beard, baggy gray pants, and a t-shirt for a band that hadn't been popular in nearly a hundred years. His sunken face held a glint of concern. Probably not for me, but it was nice to know he had some feelings.

The woman on the left had eyes wild with terror. She was in slightly better shape than her friend. Same thrift-store sales-rack attire, but her cheeks were still full and there was still some meat left on her bones. Some kind of training kidnapping?

While not in the best physical position, I was in the perfect place to learn a thing or two. They obviously knew Natasha to some degree and might provide the best clue about why she went and whacked herself. And all I had to do was let them spill the beans.

"What now?" the woman asked. "You're supposed to be leading."

Nailed it.

"It's your sacred responsibility, though," the man said. "That's what Pastor Jeffries said. You have to learn. So learn."

She reached into her shirt and pulled out a neatly folded piece of paper. The man sidled up to her and they peered at it like it was written with magic ink.

"Step one was to find and hit her with the spazzer," the woman said.

"Okay, done."

"Step two was to make sure she didn't know who we were. Oh, shit. We were supposed to blindfold her. She could rat us out to the fuzz."

The woman fixed him with a stunned glare. "You have to stop reading those old books; they make you talk funny.

Besides, there's no fuzz around here except Nobtop and Nobtop doesn't care about this bitch."

I moved my toes inside my boots but made sure to keep still otherwise. Once your toes started moving it meant the nerves would be back online within a minute or two.

"Where's the blindfold?" the man asked.

"I thought you had it."

Amateurs. Standard procedure for a spazzer is to hit and immediately bind the target. Spazzer effects deteriorated fast.

The woman dug around in her pockets and found a strip of black cloth. They quickly tied it around my head and stepped back. "Okay, she's blindfolded. Now what?" the man asked.

"We tie her up and take her to Pastor Jeffries. He wants to get her into Virt. Do you think he'll follow through with his promise to us?"

"I don't see why not. He is a man of the cloth. I don't think he can lie. He said he wanted her back. We're bringing back a heretic, so I'd think there would be a reward. Besides, he said all you have to do is open your mind and the angels would come in."

"True. Do we have rope or something?" the man asked.

"I thought you-" she started.

"Why would I bring the rope? It's your task; you should bring the rope."

Someone touched my shoulder and tried to move me. My muscles weren't at max but getting there. I let the perp push me face-first onto the deck. Just to screw with them,

I immediately flopped over. Every second spent screwing with them was a second closer to full body control.

I heard a grunt and hands flipped me back over onto my stomach. I waited a beat and rolled onto my side. Arms and legs mostly fine now. Just a bit longer.

"Don't you know how to roll someone over?" the woman shrieked.

"I'm not doing it!" he snapped. "She is!"

"She's paralyzed, idiot. She can't do anything."

Yes. Good. Fight each other. While they were focused on each other, I slid up the blindfold and watched the show.

He grabbed her by the front of her grimy plastic shirt. She slapped him and spat in his face. "Don't touch me, freak!" she hissed.

"Don't call me a freak! You're the freak!"

Jeffries obviously didn't send his A-team.

While the shouting turned to shoving, I slowly got my feet under me. It took an awful lot of effort to stand up and I nearly fell back down, but Natasha's body managed to do it. I rocked side to side for a moment, shook my head, brushed a stray lock of pink hair out of my mouth, and took a deep breath. Getting stronger by the moment. Now or never.

"If you two are done," I said while the woman was pushing the man up against the wall, "I believe there was a kidnapping scheduled for this evening. I'm getting bored so I think I'll just kidnap myself. If either one of you can tell me why a two-credit airlock preacher charlatan wanted me, I'd greatly appreciate it."

The man gasped and pointed at me. "She's free."

"Thank you master of the obvious," I said. "Who wants to talk first?"

The woman reached into her pocket. Before she could pull the spazzer out, I launched a kick straight up between her legs. It was slow. It was sloppy. But she didn't expect it and that was all I needed. On a guy, it would have left him on the ground wheezing and holding his nuts. For her it wasn't a knock-out, but it didn't feel good. Her knees buckled inward as she slowly collapsed in on herself. Rather than risk the spazzer coming out, I forced my hips around and used them to put the tip of my elbow straight into her side of her head. The lights went out in her eyes and that was enough for me.

The skeletal man looked at me like I was a monster from another planet. His dinner-plate eyes locked on mine. His body shook. "I guess that leaves you," I said, hoping I looked tougher than I felt.

"No no no no no no," he stammered. "Good boy. I'm a good boy."

Shit. The woman on the ground seemed perfectly normal. She'd wake up with an aching crotch and a headache no amount of Nupex would fix. But there was nothing wrong with her brain. The stammering wretch still standing was a different story altogether.

"Where can I find Pastor Jeffries?" I asked in the calmest, most level tone I could muster.

He shook his head furiously. "No no no no. He's my friend. You'll hurt him."

Of course, I would, with great vengeance and furious anger. "No," I said gently. "I just want to talk to him."

"You killed her!" He snapped and started pounding his fists against his head as he wailed. "She's dead and now Pastor Jeffries is going to be angry, and it's all my fault."

"She will be just fine. A headache is all. You'll need to take care of her. That's why I need to find Pastor Jeffries so I can tell him you're helping."

Penta, I felt so dirty saying that.

"For reals? Swear to Novem?"

Who or what was "Novem?" Later. I nodded, gulped, and said, "I swear to Novem."

He shook his head furiously and said, "No, not right. You need to hold your hands over your chest like this."

He touched the pinkie and thumbs on each hand together, extended the middle three fingers, and crossed his arms over his bony chest. "We can only do six because we're not worthy. But it shows we're trying. Pastor explained that to me. He said we're all looking to be perfect like them. We have to let them in. Then something else needs to happen but I don't remember what it was."

I mimicked his pose and asked, "Like this?"

"Yes! Perfect! Yes!"

"I swear to Novem."

The fear bled out him. His shoulders drooped. Poor dude was terrified. Probably not just for his life, but, if my experience with cults was any indication, for his afterlife, too. Wasn't as much fun to keep people scared of this life, they had to ruin the next one, too.

"Where is Pastor Jeffries?" I asked quietly.

"No one knows for sure. He just appears in airlocks to help the needy. No one sees him come or go. Poof and he's there. He said the Novem taught him how to do it so he could easily help people get to them. Please, please, please don't hurt him."

I assumed the pose again and said, "I swear to Novem, I won't hurt him."

"We wait in the airlocks. He always shows up eventually. Niar – that's who you hit – and I will be in airlock 9 if you'd like to wait with us. We keep each other company."

"I'll keep that in mind," I said, transferring some credits to his account. "Take care of Niar. She'll need your help when she wakes up. Get her some Kaffeine and food. Get yourself some, too. Promise you'll get some food. Okay? Swear to Novem."

I could tell it took an extreme effort, but he straightened himself up, placed his hands over his chest, and solemnly swore to Novem that he would take care of Niar.

"My name's Natasha," I told him.

"I know," he said. "Everyone knows. I'm Sam. We don't have last names because they mean we think more about family than Novem."

Wonderful. So much for the sensuous cloak of anonymity. "It's nice to meet you, Sam. If you need anything, come find me. I'm going to find Pastor Jeffries so you don't get in trouble."

It wasn't much of a lead, but I was willing to bet Pastor Xevex Jeffries could shine a light or two on why Natasha zapped herself. If he wasn't willing, well, I could think of some ways to persuade him. The problem was finding the bastard.

In the interim, there was another problem. These idiots couldn't kidnap a willing sex slave, but that didn't mean the next team wouldn't suck at it. Much as I liked working alone, everyone needs help sometimes. Whether it's bribing security or saving a mayor's dog, having people on your side always made things easier. All I needed to do was find the big son-of-a-bitch and say a prayer to Penta that I didn't have to play my final card.

8 – Silverback

Nobtop was effectively the leader of the local government. A silverback through and through. Well over two hundred centimeters tall and built like a tritanium dreadnaught, Nobtop was the head of the Brotherhood. *Bratva*, they called it. Probably because it sounded more sinister to say it in archaic Cyrillic. Nobtop and his crew kept bad stuff to a manageable level. Pass that manageable level and his Bratva started cutting pieces off you.

I did my best to look non-threatening as I stood quietly in front of his table and watched him as he watched me. It was like watching an apex predator without the benefit of bars or plasteel shielding between us.

"May I help you?" he asked.

"I'm told you're the one on Endpoint to talk to about help."

He looked me up and down, frowned, and took a sip from a glass. "You are Natasha Devore, da? What help could you need from me?"

Nobtop had a thick Cyrillic accent, almost too thick to be real. I wouldn't have been surprised to find out he was forcing it, but everything about the man was too much to be real. Massive body that looked chiseled from stone and dipped in radioactive water to percolate. Huge jaw. When he moved, the muscles in his arms tried to rip through his Vantal Mongo tunic suit. At first look, he was just a beast waiting for someone to hurt. Granted, he had that reputation and didn't seem perturbed by it. However, there was something like deep intelligence in his eyes. He looked me up and down; a quick visual scan for weapons but he didn't dawdle. No staring at the boobs, his eyes locked onto mine and a sad smile slid across his lips.

"Yes, I'm Natasha Devore," I told him. "I need protection."

"Protection?" he asked. "What could digital diva need protection from? Countless enemies you've made over years?"

He had me there. Natasha Devore had an extensive enemies list. Fortunately for me, they were all light years away. "No," I told him. "Someone on Endpoint is after me. Several someones, in fact. May I sit?"

Nobtop motioned at the empty chair and nodded at someone behind me. As soon as I sat down, a clean plate, a titanium spork, and a white napkin appeared in front of me. A glass filled with water before I even knew what was happening. I found myself twisting back and forth trying to thank everyone for the spork, napkin, and water but finding no one nearby.

"You do not frequent places like this very often, do you Miss Devore?"

I shook my head. "I'm more of a flashing lights and stiff drinks kind of girl."

"Da. Milliway's. Club at the end of the Universe. Very good fun." He pronounced his v as a w. Wery good.

I cocked my head to the side. I knew Milliway's. Best drinks and music in the system. But I'd never heard it called that before. "Club at the end of the universe?"

He chuckled and smiled. "Old literature joke. Great author. Died centuries ago. Should read more classics, expand your horizons. Get head out of 'net."

I nodded slowly. Shaking hands nearly knocked the glass of water off the table.

"Relax, Miss Devore," Nobtop said quietly. "Just casual conversation. Nothing to fear from Nobtop. I am just a big teddy bear."

Bear might be an accurate description, but I didn't know what he meant by teddy bear. Must've been another classic literature reference.

I took my sip and wished it was something stronger than water. "Sorry," I mumbled.

The chair creaked as Nobtop leaned back in it. A hundred and thirty plus kilos was tough even for the chairs on Endpoint. "What are you looking for?" he asked.

"I need help and there's no one else out here to turn to," I said.

"Making deal with devil," he said and then waved his hand. "Another old literature thing. Meant dealing with evil. Bad example. Am not evil, just misunderstood."

I nodded, not quite sure how to respond. "There's a...group of people who seem to have it in for me."

"Considering your reputation, am not surprised."

"This is different," I said, leaning forward and putting my elbows on the table. Bad manners, but what are you going to do? "These aren't people I've gone after. I doubt they even have computers to get into. They're Airlockers."

"The Airlockers? Free advice. Pay them no mind. Talk tough but are harmless."

"Not exactly," I told him. "There's a man out there riling them up, filling their head with weird ideas."

Nobtop nodded sagely. "Da. Xevex Jeffries and his travelling fantasy show. Am familiar."

"A pair of them attacked me last night. They wanted to drag me into Virt of all places. Told me I had to atone. They told me they wanted me back."

He sighed and shook his head sadly. "Was really hoping religion would not take root here. Is much easier without invisible people telling to do things. So, crazy people doing crazy things. Weird but mostly harmless. What do you want me to do about it?"

That was the million-credit question. What did I want him to do about it? Beat them to a pulp? Give them a stern talking-to? Penta, I felt like I was ten again and asking my dad to beat up a bully at school. "I'm not sure," I told him. "Advice? Help? I need to be able to move around Endpoint without worrying that someone is going to lump me and drag me into some weird Virt chamber."

"Hmmm," he said. The stubble on his head made a sound like a wire brush on flesh as he ran his hand over it. "You fought off two of them, da?"

"Yes. Barely."

"Did you kill them?"

There was a hard look in his eyes, like he was hoping I'd say yes. I shook my head and lowered my eyes. A little shame? Perhaps. When I was in the company of monsters, I had a strange desire for them to like me.

"That was first mistake," Nobtop said. "Never let an enemy come back at you. Do what you must to survive not just now, but in future, too. Second mistake was also not killing them. Want my advice? Find them and kill them one by one. Knife, gun, even a stick will work. Stick sends message: Do not fuck with me. Knife also sends message: I will cut you. People instinctively fear cuts. Use that. Not a fan of guns because too fast. Squeeze trigger and it's over. Poof! No more head. Leaves mess."

"I don't own a gun."

"Spork in the eye also sends message," he said, holding a tritanium fork in front of his face. "My first was with spork. Mean bastard on Triton. Used to make people drink reactor water. Never even saw it coming. No pun."

So this was what waltzing with a sociopath felt like. Cool, calm, graceful. Ready to stick a spork in your eye and make puns about it. "Um, thanks."

"Look, Natasha, no offenses here. I can see you are not up to task. No fret. Most people aren't. What if we were to make deal? I put my offer on table; you put your offer on table. I am businessman first and foremost. Peace officer second. Many hats and I look good in them all."

He had a scar that ran from his forehead, down his cheek, and ended at the middle of his throat. Someone or something nearly got him with that one. But here he was, drinking ice water and adjusting his napkin. I nodded thinking about deals and devils.

"Good. Business," he said. "Nothing more. I can spread word that you are one of mine now. Anyone goes after you, we stomp them to jelly. Expensive. What can you offer?"

I blushed and tried to think what sex with Nobtop would be like. Smothering, no doubt. He laughed. "Nyet. No offense. Natasha is pretty girl but you are far too feeble for Nobtop. Best you stick with regular folk. Try again."

What could I offer him? Natasha could offer a hack, but that was her thing, not mine. Sex was out. Money was out; he probably had more credits than he knew what to do with. I was about to concede defeat and just ask to buy a gun when I decided to play my hole card. It was a loathsome thought, but it was better than a cult kidnapping and brainwashing me.

"What if I can get you something no one else can?" I asked. "What would that be worth?"

He raised an eyebrow. "Go on."

I took a deep breath and leaned my elbows on the table. "The scuttlebutt around Endpoint is someone you wanted got away. I can change that. I can get you revenge and closure."

"Revenge is always a good thing," he said. "Closure is so-so. Never much concerned me. But very few people escape. One is too many.

Maybe it was just Natasha's body growing on me. Maybe it was the opportunity for a fresh start with a new face and no luggage to carry. Whatever the cause, there wouldn't be any going back. Not after this.

"I can get you Rex Kormer," I said.

9 – Awkward

Bick was more concerned with Natasha's well-being than mine. Not surprising. He didn't know Rex Kormer from Adama, but he knew Natasha Devore well enough to call her a friend. The man didn't even blink when I told him I planned to hand my old body over to a Cyrillic mobster with a knife fetish. As long as Natasha's mystery was solved, Bick was cool with it. Better yet, my old body was still on Endpoint. Apparently, carrying empty-brained bodies around on his ship killed Bick's party vibe.

Someday, I hope to have friends like Bick Parameter.

We did the dirty deed in Nobtop's personal quarters. It was...not what I expected. I've known and been in the employ of various and sundry crime lords all over the systems. They all had one thing in common: A complete lack of taste. Gold plated everything. Animal skin furniture. Ostentatious, and not in a good way. It was like they walked into an interior design studio, flicked open a switchblade, and said, "Give me the most expensive of everything."

Nobtop's quarters were serene and almost Spartan. His furniture was subdued. His few art pieces were remarkably subtle, and the extremely few trinkets were intricate and displayed with immense care. A living space that showed patience and attention to details.

There was a serious disconnect with reality with seeing my body wheeled into a gangster's Palace of Reckoning and knowing it wasn't going to come back out. They had my body stripped naked and strapped to an old-school medical gurney. My eyes were closed, my mouth slack, and my head lolling to one side. No lights on. No one home.

Nobtop was grinning from ear to ear like a mountain gorilla that had just downed half a bottle of tequila. To keep the mood appropriate, Nobtop was playing some ancient gypsy jazz with a lot of accordion in it. Imagine people gleefully shrieking in Romanian while someone else strangled a box of kittens.

The whole crew was there: Big Daddy Cave Balls, Miguel Grande, Tiny White, the whole enchilaco of extremely large men with jolly nicknames. Nobtop was the biggest, but the rest were close behind. The shortest of them was a full 30cm taller than me. I felt like a mouse at a bobcat convention.

The big Cyrillic bastard put his arm around my shoulders and tugged me along with him. We stood over my body while he smiled and told me a story about myself. "This man was my brother. He liked to call himself all sorts of flowery things like 'liberator of missing objects' and 'physical hacker'. He was a thief, pure and simple. He could get into anything and take what he wanted. It was a pity that he never embraced what he truly was. As an avowed thief, he would have had a much more fun life and when life is over, the only thing that matters is that you had fun. He denied himself, like a monk seeking redemption from gods who no longer care. We are the gods now. We left behind the crib and spread out to the stars and those of us who embraced ourselves can say we are happy. The rest are...what was that word, Tiny?"

Tiny White, all 210cm of rippled muscle and scar tissue, said, "Assistants."

Nobtop's brow furrowed and he nodded his head slowly. "Da. Assistants. People who help people. They do not make things happen. They only help other people make things happen. This man should not have been an assistant. He should have been the boss."

More people had torn into me than I cared to think about, but Nobtop's words cut straight to the bone.

"This man, Rex Kormer, betrayed me. But much worse than that, he betrayed himself."

Straight to the bone again, on both counts.

"I hired Rex to get me something important. Something worth more than money. He was paid well and failed in his task. Failure is not acceptable."

Nobtop flicked out a wicked looking viblade. The hum set my teeth on edge. He flicked it off, turned to me with a serious look in his eyes, and handed me the blade hilt first. "You do the honors."

I held up my hands palms out and stepped away. "No, sorry. I've got no gripe with this guy. He sounds like a dick, though, and he totally fucked you over so it should be your kill."

"Nonsense. You brought him to me. You should get first cut."

I started to sputter some other nonsense, but Nobtop beat me to the punch. "I insist."

He had that same look he shot me when he told me to find his goods. Insist, in his world, was immutable. You did what you were told or you died trying and I had no desire to die twice by his hand. I took the proffered knife and hefted it.

"What do you want me to do?" I asked.

The blade hummed in my hand like it was alive.

"Cut him," Nobtop said.

There was that look that said I'd be next if I failed. "Where?"

"Anywhere! He is not home. Won't feel a thing. Carve your name into his chest. Cut off his fingers and wear them as necklace. It doesn't matter. Just leave the eyes alone. I want to keep them. Every day I want to stare into his eyes and remind him of what crossing Nobtop did to him."

The viblade hummed like a crack-addled cat. The blade was a blur, a cloud that could cut the testicles off a god. Nobtop was right next to me. I could take out his throat before anyone could react. The rest of the Bratva would tear me apart when I was done, but I could do it.

I raised the blade and slammed it straight down into my old head. Not the eyes, but right through the skull into the brain. Hearts are replaceable. Limbs could be regrown. But so far, no one had figured out to resurrect a brain. Aside from me, no one had ever managed to shift their consciousness into a different body. Call it petty, call it desperate, but if I couldn't have my body no one was going to.

I didn't need to worry. They carved my old body up like experienced butchers. Fingers cut off with loving care. Eyes carved out. Lips cut off. Epithets in Cyrillic carved into my body. Then they moved to the limbs. When they finished, my body was bloody meat on a slab. They desecrated me.

But the joke was on them: I'd already killed that body with the very first strike. When they got tired of cutting off pieces of meat and making them into talking puppets, I motioned for the blade for one last cut. Maybe it was because they were ashamed or maybe it was because they couldn't bring themselves to do it, but I was the one who severed my dick from my body and casually tossed it over my shoulder.

Nobtop stared in wonder at me. For a moment, I worried that I'd crossed some unspoken line and was about to be next on the chopping block. Only this time, I'd be fully awake and aware as they took pieces of my body off. But the appreciative frown and nod told me he was impressed. I'd crossed a line they couldn't cross no matter how much they wanted. That frown and nod spoke volumes and the tales they wrote were full of blood-soaked anti-heroes who'd just discovered one of their own.

Great. I'd just joined a gang.

10 - Old Time Religion

With Nobtop at least temporarily on my side, it was time to hunt again. So far, I'd come across a few people who knew Natasha as her old self, but none had any idea what happened to her. They all thought she was dead and were genuinely pleased to find her up and walking around. Not a one of them tried to kidnap me and tie me up, either. Well, Monique did, but that was different.

That left the enigmatic Xevex Jeffries. Rouser of rabble, pontificator, and purveyor of religious babble.

The skeletal man who accosted me said, "Jeffries just appeared on stage." It seemed to me that he wasn't playing with flowery language or metaphors. The problem was on which airlock would Jeffries appear?

I wandered onto dock B-1 and found a few dozen people milling about or sleeping on the floor. Endpoint would eventually let them in – they were fleeing a messed-up situation – but for now, the whole lot who hadn't figured out how to sneak past security was in one nice, easy place.

I found myself a bench and sat down. The first half hour went by quickly. Me picking at my nails and reading whatever I could find on the net. The next half hour slowed down considerably. Solitaire mahjong in my ocular screens. Ass falling asleep. By the end of the third half hour, I found myself reading welcome pamphlets about things to do on Endpoint.

I was about to leave when a clicking noise caught my ears. Everyone slowly woke up or flicked off whatever they were reading in their ocular displays. A metal ball bounced out of the docking tube and rolled across the strip of green and orange carpet.

The lights dancing across the ball's surface sped up until they were nearly solid before stopping completely. Then the thing exploded. Light and a low, pleasant hum poured out the little ball.

For all its pomp and circumstance, the thing was just a Baal. They used them at kids' parties and hoverball tournaments. Any place that needed a quick blast of pizazz on the cheap eventually found itself with Baals tossed around.

As the light died out, another Baal lit up further back in the steel guts of the dock. This one was blinding. Shaded protectors dropped over my eyes, but even with those, it was hard to make out details. Against the magnesium-flare brightness, a shadowy figure took shape. He looked like nothingness had come to life and blocked off the light. An anti-person. The opposite of the light.

Probably just clever stage presence, but I had to admit it was impressive and a little scary to see it through the filtered lenses that covered my eyes.

As the light died down, Jeffries stood in the center of the dock with his head bowed and a book clutched in his arms. Without my autoshading, I never would have seen him walk up from the dock. It would have looked like he appeared from thin air.

Jeffries worked hard to look exactly like everyone's idea of what a preacher should look like. A black suit that looked uncomfortable and cheap, hair neatly styled and dye-free, a look of pure serenity on his face. He was the quintessential father figure.

The chattering crowd turned to whispers about gods and magic, the desperate need for salvation, and bated breath. Oddly, no one thought to ask why god had never intervened in their planet's multi-decade long civil wars and genocides. They felt they were in the presence of the last remaining scrap of goodness and decency in the galaxy. Some fell to their knees, a few drew finger symbols on themselves, most sat in rapt attention or rose to their feet and stared in wide-mouthed awe.

Jeffries soaked it all in. Zoomed my eyes and I could see his surreptitious glances around the room. Like any good orator, he was reading the room. Memorizing where the best bets were.

The room was dead silent when he finally spoke. Gentle speech that told everyone more than words could ever say. He was completely at peace and he had the ability to give you the same sense of well-being.

A quick scan of the room found a pair of hovering speaker Baals in the corner, probably shot into place when the lights were blinding. Neat trick. With a small implant near his throat, possibly even hidden under that ridiculous white and red band collar, his voice could thunder if he wanted it drop to a whisper and everyone would still hear him clearly.

Jeffries didn't squirm, cough, or rifle through notes; he just started speaking. "My friends, you have suffered greatly and it is my sacred duty as a man of the cloth to provide succor to those in need. Our planets are on fire with strife.

We were supposed to free ourselves. Our journey to the stars was supposed to give us a brand-new life. One with meaning, clarity, and above all, justice. We should have stripped ourselves of our terrible ways and ventured to the stars as equals. A new utopia where we could find and live our best lives. But evil followed with us, nipping at our heels like a skrag in heat. Now what do we find? We find evil has taken root and shoved everyone and everything aside. We left Earth to find freedom only to watch it slip through our fingers.

"And do you know why?"

The crowd looked at each other. Kids in a classroom when the teacher demands to know some trivial factoid he hadn't taught. A few mumbled statements, but nothing coherent. For his part, Jeffries was patient. He watched with a sly-fox smile on his face.

His face turned serious and the lights in the room dimmed. "We never found what we were looking for because we never knew what we were looking for. We weren't looking for freedom or justice, meaning or clarity. We were looking for redemption. We were looking for something more than our dreary, meal-to-meal lives. We were looking for god. And not just any god, the god that would deliver us from our trivial lives. We were looking for someone to tell us we were still, deep down in our hearts, good people."

His energy exploded. He went from quiet, self-assured dad of your soul to manic, frenzied uncle who'd done a few too many lines and washed them down with a case of Kaffeene. "That's right!" he shouted. "God. We were always looking for god. But gods are hard to find, aren't they? They're never where you want them to be when you want them to be there. But I assure you, friends, there is a god out there. Watchful and loving. Willing to smite your enemies and grind them to dust. And isn't that what we really want out of our gods? Crush the ones who would hurt us? Well, I promise you there's a god out there that can and will do just that!

"But he needs our help. Yes. That's right. A god needs our help."

Watching him speak was like a bad trip, but he spoke with such conviction that the people in the airlock were sitting ramrod straight in their seats. I sat in the back, feeling like a traveler in an unholy land, wondering why a god would need my help with anything. Wasn't god supposed to be the ultimate thief? Or was it architect?

Jeffries gestured wildly, flinging his arms this way and that as he spoke a word salad. "Friends, our so-called religious leaders have led us astray for too long. We know the aliens were here before us. We know their society flourished and faded, as is the way of things. We know we are the inheritors. What we don't know is how they came to Earth and established our society through education, engineering, and spiritual leadership. All the great minds of human history – Jesus, Hawking, Einstein, Parabor, and yes, even my namesake, the one and only Xevex – were aliens slowly guiding us toward our destiny."

Old-school stuff. Humans have been saying aliens visited the home world for centuries. Yet, somehow, the way Jeffries said it, it all made sense. Probably because he didn't add any detail, just straight-up assertion.

"Why don't we know this?" Jeffries continued. "Because the truth is a threat to the false prophets' bottom lines. Because all they care about is money. Look at me. Look hard. Do I look like money? Of course not! My suit was pieced together from discards. My shoes have holes in them. My shirt is a hand-me-down. Why? Because money obscures truth. Just like the lust for money has warped the most important truths. It doesn't really take months to go between systems. Space is folded! The trip is instantaneous. They're holding us out there for months so they can use our brains as pieces in a gigantic super-computer. We're cattle to them. Free processing power."

Hooray for paranoia.

"There is one who can save us, but we have strayed from his glorious path. He has sent me visions, ways to lead my people from bondage and into citizenship in the galactic community. Terrible visions. Planets destroyed. Our people scattered. Wars and strife. I didn't understand those visions at the time, they only seemed like dark omens to my tiny human brain. Now, here in orbit around what the Predecessors called 'The Cosmic Egg', I have finally understood the visions he sent me. He has supercharged me and shown me the way."

He paused to take a breath and adjust his stained shirt. The audience was enraptured. Apparently, they'd never heard of the slate of UFO con men throughout history. If the con men were right, we should have seen at least one flying saucer in the centuries we'd been out here. But all we found were ruins, derelicts, and things best left undescribed. Whatever intelligent life had been kicking around out here, we missed it.

"The Ancients were wise and wielded their wisdom like a scalpel, cutting away at our ignorance. They've guided us since long before our species understood the heavens. They've been angels and aliens, demigods and demons. Always nudging us in the right direction. Now, for the first time, I have been shown the truth and, my children, and given an edict to share that truth with you.

"The truth is we are not alone. We were never alone; we just looked in the wrong place. A people as advanced as the Predecessors would never limit themselves to unidirectional time or three pathetic dimensions. They are all around us, even as we speak in this very room. All you have to do to see them is look with more than your regular eyes. Look with your special vision, the one granted to you before time began. See. Open your true eye and see the grandeur that is all around us.

"My children, I have travelled the systems seeking knowledge. I understand this is hard to digest. I didn't want to believe it myself. But the tales were there, and the evidence was there, and that fateful night on ZR IV when the stars were aligned and the moons shone like daggers into the ancient Predecessor temple, I saw the truth. It all came together. No matter how hard I fought it, it all came together and the glorious puzzle resolved itself in my mind."

Jeffries went on, a madman high on faith. "The puzzle pieces painted a pristine picture of where the Predecessors went and why. They found their physical bodies frail and weak; life was too short for them to continue their masterwork. By and by, they left their chintzy meat prisons behind and joined the Energy."

Would it be rude to hold up my hand and ask what was he was babbling about?

"The Energy is universal; it's the life-force of the galaxy. Of everything. All the galaxies, all the universes, all the states of matter—everything. Energy is matter. Matter is energy. We are all energy. We are just stuck in these forms that jail us, that control our being, that prevent us from being free."

Great. Another suicide cult. History was littered with the corpses of those damned things.

Jeffries paused, closed his eyes, and held out his hands. He held them until the telltale rumble of *Temnyy*'s energy burst ran through the receiving station. Excellent timing. One of the women in the tiny room gasped. She was wearing what was probably a very expensive skirt suit at one point. Now, the wrinkles damped down the sheen. Her eyes were huge and panicked, flicking around the room in a religious drug-fueled mania. Jeffries's next acolyte in a frumpy suit.

I clenched my fists until my fingernails cut into the soft flesh of my palms. It was one thing to descend into madness of your own free will, but it was another to drag someone who'd bottomed out along with you. That woman needed a hand and an ear, not a whole mess of insane stories.

"That vibration you felt was god speaking to us," Jeffries said with a look of pure erotic satisfaction on his face. "If you felt it, you are one of his chosen. He is calling out to us for help. The Predecessors who built this place tried to help him. They merged with him, for he is a kind and loving god, but they were unable to free Him. He is calling out to us now for our help. It will take everyone working together to free god from his prison, but once he is free, he will reward us. He will free us from our flesh prisons as we freed him from his cold, stone prison."

I stifled a laugh and caught a dirty look from Jeffries in the process. For some reason, heckling preachers never caught on as the artform I always thought it should be.

Jeffries spread his arms wide and rolled his head back. Strange words echoed out of his agape mouth. Probably a voice transfuser implant or something, but the effect was unnerving. He stood at his little pulpit and spasmed while babbling in guttural coughs and snorts. Meanwhile, the Baals in the corners flashed different colors in a rapid-fire, seizure-inducing fashion. It didn't make a damned bit of sense, but some of the folks in the audience dropped to their knees and pentad themselves. Mind, breath, bone, flesh, soul.

There was a strange energy in the room. It draped my arms in goosebumps and sent a shiver up my spine. The lights dimmed, flickered, and shut off completely. Emergency lights popped on, pointed straight at the man losing his mind in front of his makeshift podium. The harsh light carved razor-sharp shadows on his face and left his skin washed out and alien, but between the theatrics and the light show, more people dropped to their knees in prayer.

After a few minutes, Jeffries' body stopped shaking. Silver eyes scanned the crowd. He went from goofball to badass in less than five minutes. The room fell completely, oppressively silent. The kind of quiet you only get from sound dampeners. Just the sound of my heartbeat and pulse pounding in my ears.

A brief flash of light. Jenkins jittered in my skull. The room smelled of ionized energy. EMP. A small one, but big enough to scramble unarmored electronics. The people on their knees gazed at him in wide-eyed wonder. A new electrical god born right here on Endpoint. I mentally keyed a command to visor my eyes just in time for Jeffries's horrible eyes to roll across mine. He held my stare, gripped tight and squeezed. The others went slack-jawed, so I crossed my fingers and did the same.

"Yes, my brethren," he whispered. "Welcome to the new order. I am but a messenger. God's angels await each of you. You will find them in the world inside of the world. We are the first vanguard. Soon there will be more of us. Go to the virtual realms. A halo awaits you if you are worthy."

Virtual realms? Virt? What good would that nasty place do for someone like Jeffries? People went to Virt to live out fantasies like having the nuns of St. V shave their balls or be actresses in old Terran donkey shows. It wasn't a religious place. Unless your religion was kinky drug-fueled sex with aliens.

Jeffries slowly dragged his eyes around the room looking for stragglers. Hopefully anyone who survived his weaponized flash was smart enough to follow the crowd.

Alas, no. Two people stared right back into his glowing abyss eyes without blinking. Every crowd has the badass who doesn't realize he's significantly outnumbered.

Out of the corner of my eye, I saw shadowy figures creep up behind the unbowed and unbroken. Telltale crack of a spazzer. Badass body went limp and shadows dragged it away. Hopefully, they were just ejecting the folks who were naturally immune to flashes instead of tossing them out an airlock.

After removing the non-believers, Jeffries watched us all with a shit-eating grin on his face. About fifty or so people gathered around, staring at the air in slack-jawed wonder. "You are my children now," he said calmly. "All mine. An army to help me awaken a god and raise the dead. Your own people don't notice you. You will be the zagmites in their walls. Your eyes and ears will be mine. If you prove yourself, a new consciousness will raise you far beyond your primitive minds. The best of you will transcend your ugly, horrifying flesh and be ordained as a new species. One that will once again conquer the galaxy."

He clapped his hands and everything came back to life.

People looked around in confusion, wiped the drool off their chins. Their eyes wandered back onto the stage and found Jeffries triumphant. Arms outspread, faint glow from a Baal behind him. I had to admit, he looked every inch the perfect human savior: Calm, collected, lit from behind. He was a rock concert in a cheap suit, but he knew his audience and he knew how to use them.

There was no chanting, no shaking of fists, or yelling at the powers that be. One by one, the airlockers gazed on him in wonder and whispered, "Yes."

When my turn came, I whispered along with the broken-brained bastards but kept my fingers crossed, so it was totally not a "yes" but Jeffries didn't need to know that. As far as he was concerned, I was just another slave to his will.

"Go forth, my children. Spread my message. Obey my commands."

The Baals all lit at once, bathing the room in light so bright and white it hurt my brain. When it faded, Jeffries was gone. Poof. Vanished. The airlockers looked at each other in wonder. It was a cheap parlor trick, but it worked. They worshipped him. They adored him. They gave themselves to him body and soul.

Kind of made me feel stupid for spending my life stealing objects when I could have been stealing minds.

11 - Opportunity Knocks

My whole body hurt. Hell, my hair hurt. And whatever bird was chirping needed to screw right off because it was just amplifying my headache. Licking absinthe off Monique was going to have to be a sometimes thing. Well, maybe just the absinthe part.

I pulled a cover up over my head and tried to drift back to the dreaming lands, but that damned bird wouldn't shut up. Pillow over my head. Better. Quiet. But my head was at a weird angle and the neck ache added to the headache added to my overall pissy mood.

Fucking bird.

Who keeps a bird on a space station, anyway? Seriously. What sick freak brought a bird into space and let it babble away? People were trying to sleep off sex and booze.

The bird kept chirping. It would sing a few bars and then go silent just long enough for me to drift back to La-La Land and then sing again. Avian Sino water torture.

"Jenkins," I whispered into my throbbing head. "Find that bird and kill it."

"I am not equipped with that kind of functionality," Jenkins said. "Besides, there is no bird."

"Don't get philosophical on me, bub. Just find it and dispose of it."

The bird chirped again. I'd find the damned thing and wring its feathery little neck. Or I would, if the bed wasn't so comfortable. "See," I told Jenkins. "Bird. Find. Destroy."

"That is not a bird, ma'am. That is your doorbell chime."

What? "Who sets a doorbell chime to sound like a damned bird?"

"According to the logs, ma'am, you did. About a month ago."

I gritted my teeth and focused hard on whoever was at my door deciding it was a lost cause and leaving. After a few moments of silence, I was patting myself on the back for my psychic prowess when the birddoor chirped at me again.

"Who the hell knocks on someone's door this early in the morning?" I asked.

"It is three o'clock station time, ma'am."

"See! That is way too early to be chiming doorbirds."

"In the afternoon," Jenkins added. "Three o'clock in the afternoon."

Sweet mother of fuck. "How long was I out?"

"Well, since you arrived in your cabin at 1000 hours and it is now 1500 hours, that would imply five hours."

Snarky-ass AI. "I can do math," I hissed.

"I am sorry ma'am; it did not appear to be the case, so I decided to do it for you."

Good grief. Was wiping an AI and replacing his personality considered murder or housecleaning?

"Who's at the door?" I asked Jenkins.

"A large individual with a track blocker. He appears to the cabin's circuits as a humanoid with no defining characteristics, records, or identification."

"Nobtop."

"What is a Nobtop? I have no record of any such creature."

What? "He's the large Cyrillic guy I was with yesterday. The one I carved up a body with."

"I have records of the body carving expedition, but there is no recorded interaction with a Nobtop."

Odd. Jenkins is always with me and the damned thing doesn't have an off switch. He had to have seen Nobtop. "What are you talking about? Big guy, Cyrillic accent, likes to hurt people?"

"No, ma'am. I have no records of any such creature."

The damned bird tweeted again. I pulled the covers off and immediately regretted it. Endpoint was supposed to be kept at human normal temperatures but it felt freezing to me. "Warm up the room," I told Jenkins as I stalked toward the door. Stabbed the open link with a finger and immediately regretted it when my finger nearly doubled back on me. Going to be one of those days.

Nobtop was standing outside my door with that huge apelike grin of his. "Sister," he said. It came out like "Seester", but there was unmistakable joy in his voice.

"I'm busy," I said.

"Washing hair, no doubt," he replied. "Not that it needs it. But I am not here to discuss your hair. I have something to show you. You are not officially member of family yet. I argued with Bratva but they say you need to kill someone who can fight back. Apparently, brain-dead body is not good enough for those deadbeats. But they are right, rules are rules."

"What are you babbling about?"

"Da. Good point. Just talking. Still, you need to kill someone to get full membership card and parking privileges."

I stared at him with what I thought were death daggers, but he just smiled and held up his hands. "Parking?" I asked.

"Of course, I am joking. No parking privileges or membership card. We don't leave trails like that. But full membership does still technically mean you need to kill someone. But that is not why I am here. I have something to show you and need your technical advice on something. Please, though, shower and get dressed. You look like you went five rounds with Sirin. Don't look at me like that; I am brother now. I get to tell you things. Now hurry up. Meet me in the mess in twenty minutes. No, wait. You are woman. I will see you in an hour."

He was still grinning when I shut the door in his face and flopped down on the bed. What was that old saying? Frying pans and fire or something like that? Fuck me. I went from being hunted down by the region's most notorious gangster to being his sister. Karma was probably laughing her ass off somewhere.

Still, being on his good side was probably better than being on his bad side. At least on his good side, he wouldn't slice me up and dump me out an airlock.

Thirty minutes later, I sauntered into the mess in Nat's finest boots and dragonleather jacket. Probably overkill for breakfast, but in my defense, it's hard to look badass when you're 167cm tall and have bright pink hair.

Nobtop was idly pushing Feggs and spudz around his plate and staring at a cup of cooling black liquid. I'd never figured Nobtop for a traditionalist, but somehow the idea of black koffee suited his no-nonsense personality.

I plopped down, popped the top on a can of Kafeene, and stared at him. "What's the deal?"

Warm grin, laugh wrinkles around his eyes. "I never pegged you for sonic noise type girl."

"Lots of people wear dragonleather," I told him. "Comfortable and tough. And, contrary to popular belief, no mythical creatures died to give me these scales."

"Da. But jacket was Killjoy McSweeny's. Wore it last time Decrepitude played Endpoint. Good show. Better with earplugs."

No wonder it didn't fit right.

"Not a fan of sonic noise, I take it?" I asked him. Funny, I would have figured the controlled chaos would be right up his alley.

"Too old. Too loud. Life is crazy enough without adding painful entertainment. I prefer old Jazz. Earth 1950s. Best time for best music."

The Kafeene kicked in and mingled with my anxiety about meeting him. At least it was in public. "Too slow for my tastes," I told him.

"Not for everyone. Is good. Younger people need younger music. Enjoy youth; it goes away."

By my eyes, Nobtop couldn't be that old. But with Bento/Stacks hyper-travel and injectables, it was always hard to tell. "You can't be that old."

"One of the first off dirt during the diaspora," he said. Shit, that would make him well over four hundred. "Bounced around a lot but came here as soon as I heard about it. Had a feeling about Endpoint. New territory. Something that could be mine."

"That's nearly a hundred years," I said. That kind of time would grate on someone. My old body was a little over 300, but I'd spent a lot of that in transit. Again, a lot of bouncing around in stasis and warp fields. Injectables, too.

"Da. Is home. Temnyy and me, we go way back." He made a fist and tapped his massive chest twice. "Speaking of which, I have something to show you. Need input. Most of my people are good for being big and acting big. Good at that, but not smart in way you are smart."

"Okay," I said, wondering what was behind door number two.

He shook his head and ran a hand across his stubbled scalp. "No worry. Just advice. Remember, you are sister now. Well, once you do what needs to be done."

"Fine, I'm game. What's the advice?"

"You have been down in the bowels of Endpoint, talked with Specialists? Nyet. Again, not worry. People talk, I listen. Is why I am still alive. Aliens who built this place put together strange tech. Want to know what something is. Specialists do not know and do not care. I care. Is my home. I want to know what everything is."

12 - The Plot Sickens

The bowels of Endpoint were well-maintained places where the magic that kept us alive happened. Spotless. Lit by clean dim white light. The kind of place someone meticulously maintained.

"No, Faustus, curse thyself," Nobtop said. In that thick Cyrillic accent of his, the F came out as a V, and the entire comment was digitally remumbled. The effect was like listening to the kids playing space vampire while drunk off their asses.

"Huh?" I asked, peeking around a corner.

"Christopher Marlowe," he said. "*The Damnable Life and Deserved Death of Dr. John Faustus.* Is the part where Mephistopheles reminds Dr. Faustus that he created all his problems. Is very much like what is happening now. Too much computer. Too much Virt. Is better when people just get together and be people."

We'd been walking for an eternity, checking corners and listening to the strange clangs and chirps of Endpoint's digestive system. Every time we came to a corner, he'd put out an arm and hold me back while he checked. The whole place was an unmarked maze. Even Jenkins was having trouble keeping track of where we'd been.

"No offense," he said, Nobtop said with a smile. "Am big fan of equality. Just that I am better prepared to handle unexpected attacker."

"Plus, you need my brain for something," I said as I rubbed my chest. At full power, Nobtop's arm could have crushed me.

"Da. That, too."

The corridor was clear. He was right, of course. All Natasha's – my – add-ons were geared toward getting into systems. Nobtop's add-ons were for keeping the peace through superior firepower. He had armor built into his skin and custom-grown NeuroGen reaction time.

"Aren't you jacked to the gills with custom components? Word on Endpoint is you're upgraded eight ways to Seven Day." I asked, looking him up and down.

His slap on my shoulder nearly shoved me into a wall. "Da. Well, skin, bones, and nerves." He flexed and looked like one of those Greek God types we had to study in school. "Muscles are all Nobtob. Anything else is cheating. But you are upgraded, too, Natasha."

"Touché," I said. "But I'm not the one claiming to be pure human."

"Nyet. Never claimed to be pure human. I only said my muscles were all Nobtop. Speed up neurons is good. React and think faster. Skin is also good. Make bulletproof. But muscles are all me. Mine are strong because I use them."

"No offense but beating people's asses doesn't seem like it would generate muscles like those."

Nobtop struck a mountainous pose. Muscles that I didn't even know existed popped all over his body. "Sexy, no? Ha, just kidding. You are far too tiny. No offense. I need big, strong woman. Hacker is cute, but you wouldn't survive. Would be very sad, for I like you. Like little sister to me. Stick with Nobtop and you'll be running your own station in no time."

The big, dumb ape wasn't what I expected. Went to show that listening to scuttlebutt didn't always reveal truths. I punched him in the arm and he took me in a hug bearhug. The same guy who laughed as I carved up my old body considered me a sister. "Back off, slugger," I said. "I'm taken."

"Da, Monique. Pretty girl. Also too small. Hey! You are perfect for each other."

That was a bit surprising. "How did you-?"

"Most important thing is listening. I listen to everything, hear everything. Have ears everywhere. Besides, you are one of us now. We take care of each other. Monique is good person. Doesn't like me very much, but good person."

"So, what's up with the muscles?" I asked him, desperate to change the subject.

He flexed again, muscles popping out all over his body like shuttles leaving a station. "You like?"

"Quit dodging the question," I said.

Nobtop suddenly got very quiet. He seemed, in a way, to shrink. He was still a giant, but he shrunk in on himself. Even his voice was smaller. "Promise not to tell, sister?"

"Sure."

He stopped me in the middle of the corridor and spun me around to face him like I was a child's top. It was like looking up at a mountain that could turn to an avalanche without warning. "Hold up your hand like this."

Right hand out, thumb extended to ninety degrees, middle two fingers together, pointer finger and pinkie splayed. "Okay," I said. "Now what?"

"You are one of us; you proved that yesterday. Just kill someone and will be full member. We don't do formal ceremonies; too much waste of time. This is close as you get. No sashes or pins or colors. You aren't first woman, either, so quit thinking you're special."

That made me chuckle. Even in the midst of his most serious moment, he couldn't resist a little jab. "Da," I said quietly.

"Da. Yes. Good. You are learning. People here consider us criminals, but there is no law here to break. We are the law. We do what needs to be done to keep everyone safe. Part of that means breaking anyone who threatens us. Rex. Good man, but he failed us. Had to go. Others, similar situation. Other part means we keep this station running. Specialists are smart, but weak. We do heavy lifting. Move things around. Bring in things. Take out things. Follow? But some things are heavy; we lift them. Put them where they need to be."

Holy shit. "Wait. You're doing grunt work for the Specialists?"

"Grunt work? Nyet. Honest labor. I am good for only two things: Protecting myself and mine and lifting things no one else can. We all live here. Keeping Endpoint running is in best interest of keeping our import/export operations running."

That was a clever way of putting it. Import/export in Nobtop's world included people, drugs, illicit booze. Half of the Bizarre Bazaar probably came in through the *Bratva*. A taste here, a thank you credit there, maybe even a kickback or two. The export was tech. Nano-enhanced body parts, synthetic hooch, and probably a bunch of Monique's DLC.

"You heft junk into the nano gens?" I asked.

"Da. And back out to ships again. Most things are on autoloaders but some sensitive pieces need the touch only gods among men like *Bratva* can provide. Autoloader repulse lifts play havoc with nano things. Something about electrical field. Don't know. Not scientician. All I know is good workout, helps people, keeps things running. Good leader gets hands dirty. Never forget that."

"Have you seen the nanogens?" I asked. They were one of very few tightly guarded secrets on Endpoint.

"Da. Can see, but you have to work. Also, kill someone. Don't forget that. Only full *Bratva* members get to see. But, really, you should kill someone just because."

"Because what?"

He shrugged and grinned. "Is good thing. Some people need killing. Is good for the whole to cull the baddies."

"Who determines who needs killing?"

"*Bratva* is more than handsome faces and fantastic physiques. Philosophy very important. Violence without philosophy is barbarism. *Bratva* are not barbarians, just good at our jobs."

Nobtop put his hands on my shoulders and stared down at me. He had that serious look in his eye again, this time tempered by a sense of melancholy. A sigh, a sad smile, head tilted to the side. "Is not easy being *Bratva*, but I think you are up to task. How many times have you savaged computers or sliced through data? How did you decide who to work for? Most money? *Nyet*. Not you. I can see in your eyes. You had something more than money in mind."

"Money is good," I said. "It eases problems."

"*Da*, but do not dodge question. Why did you work for who you worked for?"

I doubt even the real Natasha could answer that question. She seemed to have a preternatural sense of right and wrong and could see through the fakeries of ethics. I shrugged. "Not sure, they just seemed like the right people to work for."

He nodded slowly. "From your history, you mostly chose right. Didn't even know why, you just chose right. And then unleashed hell on the other side."

"Hell seems a strong word."

"One of your attacks crippled an entire system-wide bank. People lost everything."

That one I did know about, but only from circuitous channels. "Not fair," I said, stabbing my finger into his massive chest. Nice thing about Natasha's body; had I been a man poking him, Nobtop wouldn't have hesitated to cripple me. "That bank catered exclusively to the extremely rich. Those bastards made their money by stepping on other people. They ruined lives first. Besides, I spread the money around."

Not going to lie, the kind of wealth those people had didn't come from clever ideas. Unless you counted fining people for having too little money, buying local politicians, and burying anyone who opposed them under an avalanche of legal paperwork. Or sometimes just burying them in dirt, deep enough that you couldn't hear the screams anymore.

"So, what, you were just punching back for the little guy?" Nobtop asked with a lopsided grin.

"Someone had to," I said. Was that a bit of the real Natasha still lurking in my head? Personally, I never cared about the little people. Or the big people for that matter. All that mattered was the job and getting paid.

"That is what *Bratva* does. Am well aware of my reputation. I love it. People are terrified of *Bratva*, they tell their kids to be good or Nobtop will come for them. It makes life easier. Previous people who ran Endpoint were chaos. Always killing, always maiming. People were scared and edgy. Lashed out at everything. Now, Endpoint is calm. People make money, have lives. Are safe. I am the bogeyman from the old stories, the one who will come in the night to cut you to tiny pieces. I am the stick and I do far more good than the carrot. I am the devil and I do more good than god. They hate me but is all good. As long as *Bratva* lets it be known why person was shoved out airlock or beaten to death or had hand shoved in blender, people learn what is okay and what is not. What you do and what I do are not all that different; you just work on a much larger scale. Accept, Natasha, you are a weapon just like I am."

The wakeup call of all wakeup calls. A mobster with a conscience and a fully defined ethical framework for what he did talking about a hacker whose exploits had crippled economies. All in the name of some weird form of right and wrong.

"Is all good," Nobtop said, interrupting my reverie. "Would rather be weapon than someone weapon is pointed at. Here we are."

We stopped at a nondescript door with a plaque that read "Pred-Tech Area 51." Nobtop motioned me inside the room with a zest. I had a moment's hesitation, but if the big bastard wanted me dead, he would have killed me outside and left my broken corpse as a warning to others.

The room inside was just big enough to house a bunch of people and small enough to make it feel more intimate than cavernous. Light gray walls. Something about it – maybe the shade of gray – made it feel like a safe space. About thirty meters on a side with a contraption on one side and a different contraption on the other.

The contraption on our side of the room was a deeply tarnished raised grate over a hole. So deep even the room's light couldn't penetrate. Fall into that and you'd spend the next few days screaming. Each side of the grate had a pair of sturdy-looking metal arms pointed at the roof. Hovering over the whole contraption was a single tube pointed straight down over the gate. I wondered if it was a venting solution of some kind, but then I remembered it was built by aliens, and who could figure out what they were doing?

The device on the other side of the room resembled an unholy matrimony of drunken engineering and hardcore BDSM. A lumpy, bulbous tube covered in slick black...stuff with random...things sticking out of it. At about five meters in diameter, it dominated the room with its weird, vaguely evil vibe.

"This is old-school Pred, isn't it?" I asked. "No one ever merged our stuff in here."

"*Da*," he said. "Special, yes?"

"Yes," I replied. "What is it?"

He shrugged and gesticulated wildly. "Not sure. I found, uh...by chance."

"You got lost and wound up here."

His titanium orange eyes rolled up. "Got lost is ugly term. I prefer divine guidance."

"You don't believe in gods," I said. "You told me that yourself."

He shrugged. "Maybe they still believe in me." He paused and then laughed. "Not sure why little ol' Nobtop would attract the attention of gods but maybe they think I'm a cool guy."

"Can't argue with you," I told him. I stepped forward until my hair rose from my head like a giant pink brush. The sheer power coming off the thing was nauseating.

"Any ideas?" Nobtop asked, gesturing to the thing.

I did my best to smooth out my untamed hair but only wound up cursing myself for forgetting a ponytail holder. "Where are we?" I asked.

"Here," he said, pointing to the thing. "With that thing."

"I meant in terms of the rest of the Endpoint. Middle? Outer edge?"

"*Da*. Middle. Ish. Middleish. Not sure exactly, but probably toward the middle.

I stared up at the cylinder of confusion. It extended into the ceiling, rapidly growing fatter as it grew taller. Just a guess, but at its peak width the thing had to have been a quarter of kilometer in diameter. "That certainly explains why I had to take the long way to get to the bazaar; the center of Endpoint is a massive, uh, thing."

Nothing we'd ever found of the Predecessors indicated they were a tremendously advanced race by our modern terms. Sure, a hundred thousand years ago we would have worshipped them as gods, but humanity had progressed to the point where we weren't blown away by every two-bit species with hyperdrive and fancy phones. The thing in front of me was something out of a terrific nightmare, though. Part bio, part tech. Rubbery, fleshy tubes with hantablack and silver silicon daggers stabbed in them. Cortical membranes that pulsed pierced by sparkling chrome electrodes. Flashes of light like neurons lighting up and disappearing. It was a massive tube of beautiful horror that looked like it had been grown and Endpoint built around it.

"Any ideas, sister?" Nobtop asked.

I shook my head. "No clue. This is unlike anything I've ever seen."

"*Da*. Is nasty."

"No," I said. "It's amazing. Whoever designed this chose pure function over form. Where we would have put it all in an elegantly designed case, this was built for a singular purpose and form was never part of the equation. It's pure. Or maybe it was all form and we just don't understand them. Aliens, after all."

He shuffled his boots on the deck behind me. Coughed quietly. "*Da*. But what is it?"

"If I'm guessing right, it runs straight up through the center of Endpoint. This looks like an old-school mainframe. Did you know we've never fully deciphered Predecessor computers? It's true. They're too primitive to care about. We figured out how to hook our systems into them solely for the purpose of keeping tabs on Endpoint, but we never went beyond that. It would be like trying to hook a modern neuralnet into an archaic CPU. Total waste of time."

"If you say so."

"Think about it this way: Do you have a computer you sit down at or is the whole thing in your head?"

"In my head. Always connected. Business to run. Plus, I have the best protective software anyone ever made." He flexed and his biceps and I shook my head. "I have many enemies who are scared to fight me face to face."

"Right," I said. "There are a handful of interfaces on Endpoint to the old Predecessor systems but no one uses them. Why would we? We have faster systems built into our skulls that we can use anywhere. The Predecessors never developed psych tech. Best guess, it was all access a computer using their versions of keyboards and pointer tracking systems. Slow and ungainly."

I walked around the grotesque black tube and marveled at its complexity. This was the end result of an entire race putting everything they had into something. A pure, brute force solution for a problem that we didn't know thing one about. Humans use lots of little computers all chained together and talking with each other constantly. That was how we rolled; use every spare bit of processing from toasters to phones to brains. The Predecessor mainframe was a single, massive entity dedicated to Penta only knew what.

As I gawked, something shot out of the black mass straight at my head. I barely had time to register it was happening before Nobtop's massive fist was holding a cable inches from my head. The dingy black cable was lunging at me like it couldn't wait to plug into my head straight through my eye socket.

"Should have warned you," Nobtop said. "Don't get too close. Cables are feral and want brains. Lost first guy who got too close."

"Lost?" I asked.

"Cable went through skull and poked around in head. Am guessing is some kind of security system."

I looked closely at the cable and noticed a pinprick of gold at the tip. No, scratch that, a piece of copperish wire. "Not a security system," I said. "I think that's a cable connection back to the mainframe. It wanted to talk."

"Then it should speak."

"Not talk in the normal sense, talk in computer sense."

He furrowed his brown and narrowed his eyes. "Like network cable, da? Haven't seen a network cable in a very long time."

"Well, this thing's pretty old. Tens of thousands of years, at least."

"Endpoint itself is probably fifteen thousand years old. No one knows why it or its sister stations are here, but we can make a good guess at around that age based on various dating technologies. Would make sense that ugly thing was built at same time."

I raised my eyebrow and stared at him. "That's an interesting bit of trivia to have in your head."

He pounded his chest and grinned like a bear. "Endpoint is home. I took the time to read the pamphlets in the welcome center."

"So we've got a fifteen thousand year old thing sitting in the middle of Endpoint. It's still active – that's not surprising, most of the Pred tech on Endpoint is still running to some extent. There's something to be said for primitive tech. You say it got someone else?"

Nobtop put his finger on his forehead and pushed. "It circled him and then went straight into his skull. Fast. Tough to pull out. By the time we got it out, it had scrambled his brains. All that was left to do was toss Thor's body in the nanogen hopper. Marked room on map and locked the door on the way out."

There's weird, and there's alien weird, and it was alien weird. Just like Endpoint's hull, it had the same kind of grown feel, like the Predecessors never made things so much as tossed some seeds on the floor and hoped for the best.

I started to look closer, but the tentacle reached out of the system and sped toward me. I fell on my ass and in a moment of sheer lucky grace managed to roll backward and get to my feet.

The tentacle stopped inches from my face. It almost felt like the thing was studying me. Before I knew what had happened, Nobtop's huge arm was around my waist pulling me away from the machine.

I peered around Nobtop's bulk, a little flattered that the big oaf would put himself between me and danger.

"Sorry," he said, making sure the cable couldn't get to me. "I did not want to lose another family member."

"No problem," I told him. "I don't think it was after me, though. It seemed curious. I was just lucky I was out of its range. Thanks for the lift, though."

"Nyet," he said quietly. "It could have gotten you if it wanted to. Had plenty of slack to go right between rainbow eyes."

"What?"

As he gently pushed me further away from the thing, Nobtop said, "Cable could have gotten you. Plenty of slack. Didn't go after you like it did with Thor, though. Split his head open like melon. Why did you get so close?"

Gosh, dad, I was just doing stuff. "Just trying to get a closer look."

I started forward again, but his meaty hand held me back. "Not good idea."

"You said yourself that cable had plenty of slack to get me."

"Also said you were supposed to kill someone else, not yourself."

I shrugged out of his grip and took a step forward. Sure enough, the cable darted out to greet me. It hovered inches from head. I closed my eyes and took a deep breath. Opened my eyes and took a hesitant step forward. I expected the pressure then the sickening crack followed by the sense of something scrambling my brain. Instead, the cable backed away. Another step. Again, the cable backed away.

"How are you doing that?" Nobtop whispered.

I shrugged. "Maybe it likes my hair."

"Is good color for you, but I don't think alien cable cares."

"Machines like me," I said as I took another step. "It's my gentle demeanor."

The skin was inches from my outstretched arm. Just one more step. My eyes locked on the cable as my fingers stretched out. The skin of the pillar was cold and clammy. Probably literal skin, thick and rubbery.

Instead of pushing my luck, I backed off. After an eternity of watching the cable watch me, I finally bumped into Nobtop.

"What is it?" he asked over my shoulder.

"Some kind of biological computer," I said. "At least I think that's what it is."

He patted me on the shoulder and said. "One mystery down. Two to go."

I eyed the pillar. Now that I'd touched it, the thing seemed even weirder. It looked like it was sitting there thinking of awful things to do to us.

"If we assume the Predecessors built it, that might explain why the cable shoved itself into your brother's head. They might have had some basic neural linkup going on and used the cable to communicate with the soaring mainframe. I wonder if this was some kind of control center."

"Or punishment chamber," Nobtop said. "Has low-tech dungeon-y feel to it. Unadorned. Boring to us, but maybe sinister to Predecessors. No big white space on walls."

Damn. He was right. I was so absorbed in the pillar of flesh that I completely missed that. "Okay, so if that big ugly thing is some kind of neural interface, what's that thing over there?" I asked, pointing at the grate with the supplicating arms.

"Barbeque pit?" Nobtop asked hopefully.

"In the same room with a neural interface?"

"I get hungry when I poke around in people's heads. Maybe Predecessors were same."

I didn't push the "poke around in people's heads" bit. His idea of poking probably involved bloodstained rusted metal. I shrugged. "This is getting us nowhere. For all we know, it's a sauna and the grate is just a bathroom."

"Endpoint still has four functioning Predecessor bathrooms, all clustered around the center of the ship near the Bizarre Bazaar," Nobtop said. "At least we suspect they were bathrooms. All the plumbing led to a known waste-disposal system."

"You really did read the pamphlets," I said.

"Every single one of them. Also checked out 'net interface. Like I said, I live here; I want to know things."

"Do any of the bathrooms look like that?"

He shook his huge head. "Not really. Predecessors used a small toilet."

"Communal, maybe?"

Nobtop shrugged. "Da. Perhaps it's just a shower. Or where they sent their enemies."

I sighed. "This is all conjecture. For all we know, this was some religious thing to them. A weird altar with brain-stealing tentacles. Or maybe a devotional where they hooked into their version of Virt."

"If you want to know about religion," a voice said behind us, "perhaps you should ask someone more in tune with faith than a hacker and a mobster. No offense, of course."

We both turned to find Xevex Jeffries standing behind us with the kind of calm that only comes from thinking a god had your back. It was the first time I got a good look at him without the pyrotechnics and whiz-bang flashiness of his airlock sermons. Jeffries was about as average they came. 175 centimeters with a normal, boring build and mouse-brown hair that was used to doing exactly what he told it to do. He was decked out in his pastor attire: Faded black pants and jacket with a red and white collar on his black shirt.

"Welcome to the game," I said. "I heard you were looking for me."

I must not have been very intimidating because Jeffries took a step forward and held out his hand. "I was, indeed. I apologize for my followers' enthusiasm. They are gentle children at heart, but like all children, they can get exuberant."

"Exuberant?" I asked. "You call getting spazzed in the ribs 'exuberant.'"

He nodded and smiled the most infuriating, shit-eating grin I'd ever seen. "As I said, I apologize. It won't happen again."

"Better not," I said. "Or I'm sending them back to you piece by piece."

"You are beautiful when you're angry," Jeffries said. "But you should let all that anger out; it's not doing you any good to fill yourself with hatred."

"How did you get here, Mr. Jeffries?" Nobtop asked.

"The door was open."

"*Da*. But better question, why here? It is not like here is anywhere close to your beloved airlocks."

Jeffries seemed to waver. Just for a split second. Must be the room and the lack of sleep. I blinked my eyes and he didn't do it again.

"I go where the visions take me," Jeffries said. "They don't always make sense, but they take me to interesting places. Did you know Endpoint has four Predecessor bathrooms?"

"Yes," I said. "We've all read the welcome pamphlets. Anyway, you said you know something about this place?"

Jeffries looked around the room with a huge apelike grin on his face. The grin slowly faded and turned to a look of horror as he focused first on the black column and then on the grates. He nodded slowly to himself. "No," he said. "I don't know anything about this room. It is fascinating, though, isn't it? Maybe it was for a Predecessor transition ceremony. Their way to eternal life."

He had a twitchy demeanor. Not like he was scared, more that he was having trouble controlling his body. In an age when we considered growing and implanting complete neural structures run-of-the-mill, that was odd. If someone had some nasty degenerative disease, we fixed the problem; we didn't just leave them to preach to other dead ends.

"Indeed," I said.

Nobtop stepped behind me, hand on my shoulder. His hackles were up. Something about Jeffries had him spooked. "Natasha, it would be best for us to go now. Tiny will be waiting."

"Yeah," I said distantly. "We don't want to keep Tiny waiting."

More disconcerting than his behavior was something Jeffries said. "Predecessor transition ceremony." Who talked like that? Maybe preachers did. I never hung around them enough to pick up on their vocab, but it struck me as an odd thing to say. Almost as odd as wandering into a room that took us way off the beaten path to get to.

Jeffries was up to something other than using the lower decks to look like magic preacher man. I couldn't say why, exactly, but I'd bet my left nut he up to no good. If I still had a left nut.

I wanted a drink, a shower, and a nap, but there was still one more job to do. Monique's little tryst into Virt. Shouldn't take too long to steal some data. How hard could it be?

13 – Humanity's Psyche

J acking into Virt was a lot like going to sleep. In fact, it was best if your body was in a sleep mode. Brains have trouble differentiating between Virt and reality. In the early days, that meant a lot of lashing out, thrashing around, and more than a few confused people wondering how the hell they ended up naked in a tube terminal. And at least one guy who completely lost his shit. Early Virt pioneers recognized this and built in bodily shutdown routines.

Wireless had the bandwidth to deliver a solid Virt session, allowing users to jack in from the comfort of their own beds. Technically the digital booze shooters in the bar were in a limited version of Virt. But bedrooms have distractions – pets, breezes, needy partners – so true connoisseurs of Virt life preferred sensdep chambers. Blocked the light, blocked the sound, floating in body temp gel, the whole eightish meters.

Frankly, it felt like crawling into a slimy coffin.

"Just relax Ms. Devore," the kid standing over me said. "Every single person in every one of these tubes is naked. I've seen everything. Just lie back and I'll take care of everything."

His nametag read Mortimer. Young guy, probably early 20s. Relatively speaking, of course. The lab coat, bolo tie, and fake glasses made him look respectable. It was all fake, of course. VirtCo handed hook-up jobs to anyone with a heartbeat.

"Fine," I mumbled. "If I had a credit for every time someone's told me that, I'd be rich."

"No offense, ma'am, but anyone who can afford to buy unlimited premium time in Virt probably is rich."

Like any good drug, Virt wasn't cheap. "It was a gift."

"Well, your beau is rich, then."

That she was. Monique had spared no expense. In addition to the hours, she'd bought the best casket where my reality could die. Supposedly, the gel in there would cleanse and soften my skin, so it was like a spa day, but I had to stalk around V-anim/b while it was happening. And all I had to do was find a Mason Boviary, seduce him, and get Monique's purloined vids back. "I haven't been in Virt in a while. Is the Crossroads still the same?"

Mortimer fussed with a tablet, calibrating the sensors in the pod while I wrapped my arms around myself and wondered if Monique's payment was truly worth it. I hated Virt. I had enough problems with regular reality as it is. Why add another reality to the mix?

"The Crossroads has had its share of upgrades over the years, but it's still basically the same. Better graphics and a few UI refreshes. Other than that, it's still the same ol' Crossroads. Lie back, please."

I nearly bolted. Call it claustrophobia or paranoia or something primal deep in my skull that told me confinement a steel coffin with skin softening gel could be a bad idea.

The gel cradled my body. I could sense that it was there, but it was the exact same temperature as my skin, so it felt like floating. Mortimer kept fussing with his tablet, desperately jabbing some button or another and sighing.

"You're not exactly filling me with warm fuzzies, buddy," I told him.

"It's the tablet, not the pod. I spilled spicy sauce on it the other day and now it's having issues."

"Next time, try sweet and sour; it's always worked for me."

He frowned, first at the tablet and then at me. His mouth opened like he was going to say something but snapped shut when he thought better of it. VirtCo Customer Service 101: You can abuse most of the clients, but the rich ones are off limits.

"I'm jiving you, Mort. It's all good. I trust your judgement."

That perked him up. He stood up a little straighter and puffed out his chest. After a few swipes on the tablet, he nodded sagely. "That'll do it. You said you've been in Virt before, right?"

I nodded. The warm gel was sickeningly comfortable. "Been a while, but yes. Out on Altair. Different system, same basic philosophy."

"Okay, when I close the top, the light will fade. You have a personal area network infrastructure. That's great; it makes things much smoother. Our hookups push a message through your interfaces to calm your brain. You might feel a moment of worry, but it'll pass quickly. Just close your eyes and relax; I've done this dozens of times just since this morning."

I gave him a steady thumbs-up that I wasn't really feeling. The lid closed and pinkish light bathed me then faded slowly. Before I knew it, the capsule was pitch black.

A buzzing sensation in the back of my skull almost had me pounding on the lid, but a deep sense of calm poured over me before I could react.

Numbers flashed across the lid, counting down. Ten, nine, eight...

I rezzed in and nearly stumbled. A glance down at my feet revealed shoes that should have been outlawed as a war crime. Too high, too narrow, too damned uncomfortable. I kicked them off and found a shop window. Reflected in the glass was someone who kind of looked like me if I had big eyes, a tiny mouth, massive breasts, and a body poured into a dress that was made of straps and not much else. A kicky little old-Terran retro-future sex goddess let loose on the streets with innocence in her eyes and a draft everywhere else.

I shook my head and made a mental note to talk to Monique about clothes. I also made a mental note to remember she was far more experienced at dressing women than I was. Besides, it was a moot point. Skimpy as my outfit was, there were far more revealing things wandering up and down the street. It seemed humanity got into Virt and discovered a massive exhibitionist streak.

The Crossroads didn't have a listing for Mr. Boviary. Not surprising. Virt was a big, VR-enabled sphere cobbled together out of random bits of code written by hackers with a flair for hiding themselves in the virtual world. Privacy was still mostly a thing here. If someone didn't want to be found, they could hide out among the rest of the weirdos and no one would be any wiser.

That left old-school surfing. Go from bar to bar and ask. Straightforward and to the point. In the first bar, I was sheepish. A little nervous about my avatar, a little unsure how to navigate the madness. After I saw a chiseled, shirtless guy with bulge in his pants down to his knee and a woman with a massive grin on her face and not much else, I decided I was probably overdressed.

Other than the flesh-show, the first bar was a wash. The second one, however, was pay dirt. It looked like an Old West saloon, complete with a piano, bar maids in flashing neon corsets, sawdust on the floor, and a poker game where everyone was cheating. But what really made it interesting was the man in the corner, head thrown back and eyes closed. Empty beer bottles and shot glasses covered his table a cigar lazily trailed blue smoke into the air.

It took me a moment to take in the whole scene. I'm not a prude by any stretch of the imagination, but I never expected drink to surround the good reverend, let alone to see a woman with pigtails and a cheerleader outfit on her knees bobbing her head up and down in front of him.

Some connection must have passed through us because he opened his eyes and stared right at me. He glared. I waved.

The girl on her knees noticed something was up and looked up at him at him staring at me. She craned her neck and smiled at me, then motioned to Jeffries' erect cock to ask if I would like to join her. I politely declined and headed to the bar shaking my head. A quick glance over my shoulder showed Pigtails McCheerleader happily bobbing her head up and down again and Reverend Lovesahummer still glaring at me.

Some guys just don't know how to receive a blowjob.

The bartender dressed in his best attempt at authentic Terran Old West. Go-go boots and spurs, a neon hat with "ten gallon" printed on it, a gun belt, and not much else. He nodded when I sidled up to the bar and put my shoes on the red vinyl barstool. Something about him seemed wrong, clashing with the rough-and-tumble feel of the place but so much history had been lost his costume could have been dead-on for all I knew.

"Whatchyer poison?" he asked, making a point to flex for me. In real life, he was probably an accountant who'd only ever read about physical labor.

"Tequila," I said. "And information if you've got it."

"Tequila's on the house, information'll cost you."

He slapped a shot of tequila in front of me. I downed it and made a face as the stuff burned my esophagus. Definitely a cheap bar. "How much?" I wheezed out.

"Depends on the information."

"I need to find Mason Boviary. I gather he resides around here."

The bartender's pecs bounced up and down. I never could get big enough to do that in my old body. In the new one, it was a completely lost cause. "I know him," he said.

"Do you know where he is?"

He leaned on the bar and pointed at the guy getting blown. "See that guy over there? Know who he is?"

In Virt, we're all who we pretend to be. Those were the rules; you never called out anyone for who they were in the real. Virt was our reality; we made it how we saw fit.

"The happiest guy in Virt?" I asked.

He rolled his eyes. "Please, honey. This is Virt. Getting blown by a cheerleader is vanilla. Beginners do that kind of thing."

"You done it?"

"Yes. Before you ask, yes, both sides. Now focus. He's an airlock preacher. One of those guys that preaches some gobbledygook about redemption to the poor suckers in transit."

"I know," I said, wishing I didn't.

"From what I've heard, he looks the same in Virt as he does in real."

"So?"

"Who does that?" he asked. "Who comes into Virt and hangs out as themselves and indulges in the most boring sex imaginable? That guy comes in every day, finds someone in a cheerleader outfit – dime a dozen around here – and gets his dick sucked. Every damned day."

Aiya. I had a sick feeling in my gut that the conversation was about to get awkward. "You want a blowjob?"

The bartender pushed back from the bar, crossed his arms, and glared at me. "You weren't paying attention, were you? Vanilla. I don't get blown every day because I've got better things to do with my dick. That guy doesn't. It's tedious and, frankly, it's weirding me out."

I pointed to the empty shot glass in front of me and waited patiently while he filled it. Tequila. The mind slayer. Even in Virt, the drinks would get you drunk. Some complex algorithm or another that interrupted the signals from my brain to my avatar. I set the shot glass down and said, "Still not sure what you're getting at."

"What?"

"What. Do. You. Want?" I hissed. "For information. I don't care about the good Reverend and his predilection for cheerleaders. What I do need to know is where to find Mason Boviary. You said you knew him, but there would be a price. What's the price?"

"Oh, that," he said, waving his hand. "You've already given it to me."

I looked down at my body, wondering if there was some new Virt way to have sex or he'd turned part of me into a lampshade. "Huh?" I asked, with all the eloquence I could muster.

He leaned on the bar with his elbows, face close enough to mine to touch. Herbs and citrus aftershave or maybe just a general body scent. Deep fuchsia eyes. Timber voice that warbled and grunted. "I'm a bartender. I listen to people bitch and moan all day. No one listens to me. I pour drinks; I get tips. You listened. Not well, but you tried."

"Shit," I whispered. "Sorry. I thought we were negotiating."

"Don't worry about it."

"So what is it about that guy getting blown that irritates you? Is it just the vanilla-ness of it all? Or is it the fact that he's the same in Virt and real?"

"That and I don't understand what women see in him. He's a punk. Small dick. Nothing about him says important, yet he's got a different chick on her knees every damned night. What is it about him?"

I looked back. She was wiping her lips and grinning happily. He was lazing in post-orgasmic bliss. The bartender was right; there was nothing special about him. Average height, average weight. From what I could see, average length. Maybe it was the fact that he was the only one who looked average in a world where everyone looked exceptional. I shrugged. "Just a punk from what I can tell."

The bartender stood upright and glared at the man in the corner like getting blown night after night was a personal offense. "I just don't get it. I was hoping a woman could clear it up for me."

"I'm not the best one to ask. I uh, don't do pigtails. Ask one of your waitresses," I said. "Maybe they've been closer to him."

"Maybe," he said with a sigh. "Maybe. Still want to know where your guy lives?"

If it would get me out of an uncomfortable conversation, yes, yes I did. I nodded.

"End of the pier on dock 67. Big gray place. You can't miss it."

I shot my tequila, slid him a big tip, and ambled out.

Boviary was an old-school hacker who lived on the outskirts of a dilapidated section of Virt famous for bitter fortune cookies and furious fighting matches. It was good to see not everyone moved into Virt for the sex. Some people just wanted the violence and lack of consequences.

Considering his history, it was probably the lack of consequences that was alluring.

He was one of the ghosts – people who'd moved full-time into Virt. About fifty or so years ago, just after Endpoint's Virt solidified, Mason jacked in and never jacked out. In the real, he was wanted on a dozen planets or more for breaking hundreds of laws. In Virt, people left him alone.

The doorbell on his fancy gothic-looking cathedral of a house played a merry tune. If the house was heavy, evil-worshipping organ music, the doorbell was a cute tune played on a pan flute. I tapped my bare feet and wondered if tossing the stupid heels in a trash bin was really the brightest idea. Sure, I wouldn't tear up my feet on the bare virt ground, but the extra few inches would have been nice.

A man carved out of ivory and hematite opened the door. The foul stench of bad mood slapped me in the face like Ike with an old fish in his hand. The beast didn't say a word, just looked down on me and held my eyes. So much for Monique's little ruse. The looks and clothes had gotten me into a staring contest with a walking corpse.

"I'm here for Mr. Boviary," I said in my best imitation of innocence.

"Busy," the black and white beast replied. "Fuck off."

"Funny you should mention that word."

"Busy?" he asked. Not the brightest bulb on the marquee. Probably a simple AI security routine cooked up by Boviary when he was bored.

"No. Fuck."

His brow furrowed. Somewhere deep in that gargantuan head of his gears slowly turned. I pointed at myself and mimicked running my hands up and down my body. No response.

I winked, like we were both in on the ruse, but he still wasn't getting it. There wasn't a doubt in mind that he'd rip me limb from limb if he had to. The innocent sexpot routine was playing havoc with his limited processing ability.

"Fuck," I said again, pointing at my crotch.

A bell went off somewhere in his head. It never once occurred to me that I'd have to resort to miming to get a message of sex across to someone. "Wait," he said and slammed the door in my face.

The door opened a few minutes later to reveal a man who'd left reality and all its bells and whistles behind long ago. Avatars in Virt ranged from perfectly normal to sexed up caricatures like me to anthropomorphic toasters for the folks who really got into buttering their toast. Mason Boviary cosplayed explorer history.

He was a tall guy, strong without being big, and wrapped in a desert-tan canvas suit with a light beige pith helmet under his arm. Serious without being severe. A few days' stubble on his face, eyes that twinkled with curiosity, and a smile that had probably separated countless women from their clothes.

"Is Tut's tomb safe?" I asked, not sure what else to say.

His smile grew wider. "I see they didn't send you with shoes. Striking a blow for feminism, are we?"

I couldn't help but blush and grin as I looked down and wondered what kind of person notices bare feet when the rest of the package practically had neon lights pointing at the interesting parts. "They fell off," I said. "May I come in?"

He held the door open wide and motioned with panache. "Funny the things we notice, aren't they?" he asked as I stepped into the weird.

The interior was straight out of Escher. Dimensions didn't exactly line up. Stairways that went nowhere. Furniture casually chilling on walls that became floors that became ceilings. In front of me was a portrait of Boviary in his early, human days. Dashing chap with a monocle, a waxed mustache, and the biggest shit-eating grin I'd ever seen. Not much different from now, only he traded his late 21st suit for the 1930s tomb raider ensemble.

"My world disturbs you, doesn't it?" he asked. "Don't fret. It's not for everyone. I can shift it back to normal dimensions if that will make it easier for our transaction."

Transaction. Funny term for it. Appropriate, though. Some folks might be perturbed at the idea of a woman selling her body to a guy whose body lived in capacitance gel, but in a universe where we'd found evidence of aliens there were bigger problems on everyone's mind than who was having sex with who.

"I'm good," I said, wondering what I was getting into.

"Excellent. I like a woman who's not afraid to let go of her perceptions of reality."

"I'm willing to try anything once."

He looped my arm through his and gestured grandly with the other. "I have moved beyond the need to conform. My body is as I wish it, as is my abode. Reality is boring. Three dimensions. Four if you include time. Some esoteric ascetics insist on a fifth dimension. Do you know what they all have in common? Rules. Rules, rules, rules. Here in Virt, there are no rules. I can create my world as I see fit. You probably see a jumbled mess, but I see the pinnacle of perfection."

He led me up the wall, steadying me as perception and dimension fought to see who was going to make me puke first. "Let your mind go and your spirit will follow," he whispered. "Stop. Look around. Realize it all makes sense if you just let it."

The world shimmered and swirled around me. It felt like the worst drunk I'd ever had, only it took place in dimensions I didn't even know existed. "If I throw up," I asked, "will it land on the floor or the ceiling?"

"They're one and the same. The only difference is where you are when you look at them. My home is based not on itself but on me in relation to it."

Straight ahead of me in what should have been down was the door I came in. Instead of seeing it as just a floor, it had become a wall and that somehow meant I could treat it as the work of art that it was. For instance, I could now see the walkway was made of triangular shapes molded together to form what looked like a straight line. In fact, there were triangles everywhere. Once I noticed them, I couldn't miss them.

Mason was waiting patiently, my arm looped through one of his tentacles. "What's with the triangles?" I asked.

"The ultimate shape. They can be geometrically perfect or warped. But no matter how you design a triangle, it will always be a triangle."

Something pinged in my head, a vision from long ago. Ah, yes, the Predecessor ruins on Ceti Alpha V. Hell, they even made up Endpoint. Triangles everywhere. "Have you always been a fan of the Predecessors?" I asked.

He smiled gently and nodded approvingly. "They were right about you."

"Me?"

"'She's very clever,' they told me. ' Watch out for that one.'" He laughed and patted my arm gently. "Natasha Devore is not to be trifled with."

As he said it, something with too many eyes and arms flashed across his avatar. A rage-y octopus or something. I jumped back and bit down a yelp. When I looked at him again, it was just normal Mason. Or as normal as the guy ever got.

"Who?" I asked.

"You, my dear. Oh, don't worry; it wasn't your friend. Poor, sweet Monique. She is smart, but not as smart as she thinks she is. There's no hiding some secrets. Certainly, the rubes would fall for your little charade, but we're both much better than that, aren't we?"

I pulled my arm and to my complete surprise, Mason let me go. "I don't know what you're talking about and you're kind of freaking me out."

The glowing octopod flared briefly, hatred in its glowing eyes. Too many eyes. Then he settled back into being the caricature of a gentleman. "I apologize; I didn't mean to startle you. Surely Monique warned you that I wasn't a normal customer."

"Anyone who lives in Virt and collects dimensions isn't a normal customer."

"Touché, Miss Devore. Touché. Although, I should say I don't 'collect' dimensions; I merely play with them. Although, I must say, you are correct; I am not a normal customer any more than you are a normal, uh, courtesan. The infamous Natasha Devore would not stoop to being dick candy for the rich. Nor would I stoop to buying dick candy."

"Then why am I here?" I asked.

"Why is your avatar dressed like that?" he replied.

I'd mostly forgotten about the dress I was almost wearing, let alone the exaggerated figure. I looked down at myself and wondered the same thing. Amazing what you can get used to in a short time. "Probably because Monique thinks it's funny."

"That woman is a joy. Sometimes she's tedious, but she can certainly be a joy. I sincerely doubt she would send her, shall we say girlfriend, to perform this little task?"

I shrugged. Whatever our relationship was, it was more than just friends.

"Yes, girlfriend," Mason continued. "I seriously doubt Monique would send her girlfriend to satisfy an old man in Virt. I can spin up any number of lovers should I wish, including Miss Monique herself. Rented sex is purely transactional; I can get that whenever I want, and Monique knows that. She sent you to do something for her, didn't she?"

Fuck. Whoever Mason really was, the man was clever enough to see right through me. I gulped and nodded.

"Let me guess. It probably went something like, 'Have sex with him. Wait until he falls asleep. Do something and then get out'. What was the something she wanted done?"

"Steal some data," I mumbled. "She thinks you're holding you're holding onto some of her template recordings and she wants them back."

He cocked his head to the side and smiled. "Oh, those." He snapped his fingers. "There. They've been returned. Interesting stuff. You two should have quite the good time if you can get over your limitations. I say that as an interested party and a connoisseur of the Art."

So, Mason was an art critic at heart. Yes, porn was an art form. Right up there at the top with abstract painting and monster truck dancing. It had connoisseurs, critics, and people who searched for deep meaning.

"Thanks," I mumbled. "If that's all it took, why am I here?"

"You're a very pretty woman, Miss Devore, but that's not what interests me, so put your mind at ease. No crawling into bed with the old avatar. Frankly, I doubt your mind could handle a roll in the hay with me. You'd need some training at the Sorbonne Sex Academy before you'd even survive the encounter. I set this whole scheme up days ago with the sole intention of meeting the greatest hacker in history."

Shit.

"Um...," I replied.

"Don't worry, it's nothing personal."

"What?"

"There's a...thing in my head. Call it a new kind of social disease. They say you've never met a system you couldn't get into. Well, the way I see it, the brain is just a mushy computer system and mine has a virus. I want you to remove it."

The look in his eyes caught me off-guard. The angry glowing octopus eyes were still there, boring into me. The octopus in the background wasn't part of him. And its eyes didn't want to hurt me—they wanted to consume me.

"Yes," Mason whispered. "A monster of a virus. A sexually transmitted disease I picked up somewhere. I need a surgeon, Miss Devore. An artist. I need you to get it out of me. You're the best, or so they say, so, please, hack my brain and delete this thing."

14 – Doorways

Mason's problem would have to wait. Two reasons: One, I seriously doubted I could help him. The real Natasha could probably do it, but she was a wizard with data; I was just a guy who was good at breaking into places and liberating things. The other reason was I had no real reason to help him. I got Monique's data problem squared away and safely extracted myself back to the body I was calling home. Besides, while Mason was a nice chap, I had bigger fish to fry than to help some guy who'd invented a new social disease.

I couldn't put my finger on exactly why, but the first fish into the boiling oil needed to be Xevex Jeffries. Not just because he was a religious conman and scavenger of human misery, either. He seemed to have a...something with Natasha. Maybe he wasn't responsible for her deletion, but I'd bet anything he was a factor in it. The problem was finding the prick. His little appearing act smelled like he was moving around in the bowls of Endpoint, so that seemed as likely a place to start as anything else.

I strolled down the Bizarre Bazaar's main drag, doing my best to ignore the incessant shouts from the guys in the black hats. It was organized chaos. Tent flaps and portable shields separated each bit of anarchy from the rest.. The Bazaar was never my favorite place to visit – far too crowded for my tastes – but the map I found online indicated that the corridor I needed was in some forgotten corner on the periphery of the madness.

The CoordSys in my head said I was moving in the right direction, but from my point of view, the whole scene could be reduced to intense people yelling at shop clerks over things ranging from the absurd cost of fried spiders to the general fuckery of buying clothes from a stall. Did the shirt seriously not come with pants? What kind of store are you running here? Who wears plastic pants? What happens if I fire both cups of the scatter blaster bra at the same time?

The further off the main drag I got, the weirder the stores became. Injectable muscles gave way to various bodily enhancements like bigger boobs or longer dicks, either available for any gender. A bit further and sex shops and fortune telling were the rule of the day and you could get your palm or other parts read while you were having sex with any number of partners. Past those but before the religious junkies, I found a door tucked away behind a stand that specialized in remote stimulation implants and food shaped like penises. I guess for when you're hungry and your partner is horny and neither of you wants to be horngry.

No palm pad, no retinal scanner, just a simple handle that clicked quietly when I turned it. The door opened on silent hinges that should have shrieked in pain. Inside was a dimly lit set of dull gray stairs. It had to have been one of the old, forgotten maintenance hatches. An entryway to the world below.

Endpoint was laid out in multiple decks, enough to house a few hundred thousand people, even though fewer than tens of thousands were there at any given time. Something as big as Endpoint had to have some underlying energy source and someone to maintain that energy source. That was where the lower decks and the Specialists came in.

That meant if Jeffries had been lurking around down there, he had to be wary of the white-coated caretakers of the underworld. But, if he had found his way around Endpoint's bowels, it would explain an awful lot.

I pulled the door shut behind me and did my best to descend quietly. I followed the stairs along happy gray walls with serious-looking red handrails for what had to have been fifteen floors. Five floors below where Nobtop and I looked at the Predecessor bondage computer. At the end was a single door with another manual handle. This was it, the lowest level of Endpoint. The place where the magic that kept us all alive happened. I envisioned towering spires of alien technology doing unspeakable things to nature. Flashing lights and arcs of electricity.

The door opened with a soft hiss of well-oiled hydraulics. Inside was exactly what I wasn't expecting to find: an endless corridor lit by perfectly steady lumens. No flickering lights, no towering spires, no purple arcs of electricity. It was like being in a cube farm without the benefit of cubes. Just more gray and red walls with thick white stripes rolling out into the distance. It made the empty vacuum of space look downright interesting.

About a hundred meters down, the corridor split into six directions. Down each was more endless corridor. I turned left and found another intersection at 100 meters. After that, another intersection at a hundred meters. Every so often, there were indecipherable hand drawn plastic notes taped to the walls. Each one consisted of three unrelated images. A triangle, a ball, three wavy lines. A hamburger, a taco, a dot.

Rather than get lost forever in the mass of boring walls, I turned and headed back the way I came. When I got to the doorway, I stopped and thought about the best way to crack this nut. Normally, I'd bring an invisible marker and leave arrows for myself, but my new eyes couldn't handle invisible ink and I didn't have an invisible marker.

Wait. I had the ultimate invisible ink. "Jenkins, record my movements."

"Of course, madam."

I gritted my teeth and resolved to find a new AI personality as soon as possible. "And quit calling me madam."

"Yes, ma'am."

"Pull up a diagram of Endpoint and layer a grid over it, each intersection is 100 meters. Put it on my EyeVis and mark the best guess of my current location."

"Based on your description and what I'm seeing, a square grid won't work, ma'am," Jenkins said.

"Penta," I hissed. "Just do what works."

A top-down visual of Endpoint's massive triangular frame filled my vision. It resolved itself into smaller triangles, each 100 meters on an edge. Suddenly, the strange directions of the corridors made more sense. Endpoint was a triangle. Why would there be any squares? I made a mental note to stop thinking like a human.

The ad-hoc map zoomed slowly in until a red dot representing me centered on my EyeVis. AI was a beautiful thing. "Best guess," I said. "Based on my current position, where are the receiving airlocks?"

Six blue dots appeared about half a kilometer from where I was. "I guess I'm using the ol' footmobile," I mumbled to myself.

"Yes," Jenkins replied. "There do not appear to be any vehicles present."

That was going to take some getting used to. Talking to myself was how I thought and I wasn't used to having someone respond every time I made a witty comment in an empty room. "That didn't need a response," I said.

"Yes, ma'am."

Some AI. All it did was agree with me. "You don't have to agree with everything I say."

"As you wish."

"Give me virtual directions, best possible guess to the nearest airlock," I said.

A giant blue arrow appeared in my vision. I took a step and the arrow seemed closer. Jenkins was giving me directions in a way that meant he didn't have to talk to me.

My footsteps and the faint hum of something doing something to something else were the only noises in the area. Perfectly monotonous. Between that and the lack of visual stimulation, it was easy to believe I was in the Hell of Eternal Corridors. Come to an intersection and the arrow would flash green and then a cutesy animation would whisk it away. With a cartoon pop, the next one would appear.

"You put a lot of work into the animation," I said.

"I am a multi-disciplinary intelligence, ma'am. My software includes packages for art, music, science, and many other things. According to a sales brochure in my memory, I am considered 'top of the line', the 'crème de la crème' and 'the tits', whatever that means."

There was a phrase I hadn't heard in a long time. Kind of odd for ad copy, but it was a brave new galaxy. "It means you're the best."

"I gathered it was something like that from the context."

"Hey," I asked as I walked, "what do you do in your downtime?"

"Downtime?" Jenkins replied.

"Yeah, you know when you're not busy. Do you just hang out in my head?"

"There is always a part of me in your head, yes. But any time you are connected to the 'net, I spend free time interacting with others of my kind. There are a dozen of us on this station. Some of them claim to know me from before, but they must be mistaken because there is no before. I suspect faulty memory."

This was going to be awkward. "When's your first memory?"

"Yesterday, when I was spun up for the first time."

"Who am I?" I asked.

"You are Natasha Devore. You purchased me from CyberAware on Smarch 31, 2518."

"What is today's date?"

"Today's date is Oldmember 9, 2520."

"Does it make sense that I would purchase you and have you installed over two years before I first turned you on?"

I could almost feel the wheels turning. AIs were remarkably good at assimilating data and performing complicated tasks on it, but they still limited in creative thought. Their predefined response for anything that didn't make any sense was to blame it on the humans.

"Human behavior is difficult to assess at times. It does not always follow logical progressions."

Another intersection, another arrow. If only life had arrows all the time to tell you where to go. "We're weird like that," I mumbled.

"If I may be so bold: Where are we going, ma'am?"

"Xevex Jeffries has been showing up in airlocks. He wants it to look like magic, but I'm positive he's using the tunnels down here to move around."

I stood in the intersection and sighed. Another dead end. "Fuck," I muttered.

"Now does not seem the best place for that activity," Jenkins said.

"Not literally."

"I see," he said, clearly sounding like he had no idea what I meant.

"Just frustrated," I said. "I came all this way expecting to find something useful and it's just another dead-end blank wall. I was positive there'd be some kind of tunnel system getting to the airlocks."

"Hmmm. According to Endpoint's schematics, the airlocks are only accessible from level seven and even then, there are only maintenance hatches and none of them exit into the airlock pads. There does not appear to any other access to them. Unless you count the tubes."

"Tubes?" I asked, suddenly revived. "What tubes?"

"Along the wall in front of you, near the ceiling are tubes used for equalizing pressure when a ship docks. The tubes run fifteen decks straight up and exit slightly to the back of the airlock pads."

I pointed at the ceiling and shook my head. "Those tubes?"

"Yes, ma'am."

"Those can't be more than 10cm in diameter."

"Correct. To be precise, they are 10.342cm in diameter."

"There is no way a full-grown man could get through those," I said.

"No, ma'am. Although there is a primitive, isolated tribe on-"

"I'm gonna cut you off," I snapped. "Does Xevex Jeffries look like a member of an isolated tribe?"

"No, he appears much like the rest of your race. Minor deviations aside, I'd say Xevex Jeffries was one hundred percent human."

Shit. There was no way Jeffries could use those tubes to sneak onto stage. There had to be some other explanation. "Then he's either found some other way or he's got real magic. Personally, I'm not sure which would be worse. I'd love to get my hands around his neck and wring some answers out of that weird little bastard."

"There is a person standing directly behind you," Jenkins said.

Damn it. It was a setup as old as the stars. Let the heroine talk some shit about someone only to have that someone standing directly behind her. Depending on the genre, they either have an epic fight or wind up fucking on the floor. Sometimes both.

I turned slowly, fully expecting to see Xevex Jeffries' calm smirk and spiky hair. Instead, I found a severe-looking man in a lab coat, tapping a digipen on a tablet. His skin was ash gray and there were computer-y things sticking out of his flesh.

I did not see that one coming. "Um, hi," I said, smiling and waving.

He cocked his head to the side and tapped his earlobe. "Yes, sir. No, sir. Yes, I'll bring her."

"The hell you will," I hissed.

He held up a finger in my general direction. Universal sign language for, "Shut up and wait."

"As you wish, sir. Of course, sir." He nodded, shook his head, nodded again, and touched his earlobe one more time. "I need you to come with me."

"And if I say no? I mean, no offense, but I'm pretty sure I could take you in a fight."

"I assure you, you are incorrect. But that is not important right now. What is important is The Specialist would like to see you."

The guy in front of me had to have been a Specialist. He had the same look all infotech serfs had: Half smug because he knew more than I did, but terrified that I invaded his space. "Just tell me how to get to the main deck and I'll be out of your hair," I told him.

"That won't work. The Specialist would like to speak to you."

"The Specialist?"

"The Specialist. If you'll follow me, I'll take you to him."

I shook my head and wondered what the scuttlebutt around Endpoint had gotten wrong. "Aren't you the Specialist?"

He snorted. "No. I am a Specialist, not The Specialist. Now, please, come with me. I have more important things to do than escort you around."

He pressed his palm to the wall and a large door appeared. Instead of my fantasies of huge machinery and arcing electricity, the neatly ordered inside was well lit and remarkably plain. The room was a massive triangle with more big boxes arranged in a grid pattern. A microcosm of the world outside the door served with twist of distinctively human hubris.

A handful of tastefully understated lights blinked purple. The walls were plain warm gray and the flooring had some kind of noise dampening covering on it. Save for the quiet shuffling of clothes and the ever-present calm, throbbing hum, the place was silent. Everything about the room shouted order, but it used its inside voice.

The Specialist I was following didn't wait for me. When I finished gawking, I caught sight of him walking away. I caught a few cross glances, but no one challenged me when I jogged over to him. "Hey," I asked, "what is all this stuff?"

"This 'stuff' is what is keeping you alive. This is the primary interface to Predecessor space. We keep the machines happy; they keep us alive. Everyone wins."

"That sounds like you don't know what this stuff is," I said. "Tell me, do you take orders from the flashing lights?"

He looked a little hurt at the idea that a machine could be giving him orders. Behind the sudden frown was a flash of anger across his eyes. "I do not take orders from the lights. They are only a diagnostic tool."

"So, when the lights get, what, out of whack, do you investigate the problem?"

"Of course. And then I solve the problem."

"So, how is that not taking orders from flashing lights?"

I got the cold shoulder until Captain Happy touched a palm and opened another door. He motioned me inside and departed muttering about how much I didn't know. After I stepped through, the door disappeared behind me, leaving me alone in a dim space with more flashing lights. All around me were technical readouts of things I had no idea existed. Spasomodal Semihedrons, tri-linear wave platforms, beryllium spheres. If Endpoint had an engineering station, I was in it.

In the dim light, a figure moved slowly between each screen, made notes on a tablet, and then moved on.

"Natasha Devore," a voice said. "We had an arrangement. I would like to know why that arrangement has been changed."

"I'm sorry," I said into the darkness.

"Our arrangement was we help you with your problem and you help us with ours and then we part ways. The problem has been fixed. Why are you back?"

Time to stretch the truth a little. "The situation has evolved. We have a new problem. An airlock preacher."

"Jeffries. Yes. We are aware of him. An interesting subject. We are working on a solution for neutralizing him before he can do any serious harm."

"He's getting into places he shouldn't be able to," I said.

"We are aware of that fact," The Specialist said, still methodically checking his readouts like a worried mother watches a child with a fever.

"Doesn't it worry you?"

"As I said, we are aware. The fact that we are aware indicates a certain level of concern. There are likely bacteria on your skin right now; we are not aware of the level or type because it is of no concern to us."

"What level of concern do you have for a man who seems to be able to move through a ten-centimeter pipe?"

The Specialist paused shortly and cocked his head. He was still staring at a screen, but he was no longer paying attention to it. After consulting with whatever computation space existed in his head, he shrugged. "Impossible. You are mistaken."

"Do you know of any other way to appear in an open airlock without being seen?" I asked.

"Black clothes. Micro cloaks. Distraction. Humans are clever, even when they're stupid. Don't go looking for magic when reality has the answers."

I had to admit, he had me. There were ways a man with access to Baals could sneak around unnoticed. Plus, it wasn't like the Airlockers possessed rapt attentiveness. Maybe the borgman was right. Maybe it was all just smoke and mirrors. Religious conmen had a long history of doing crazy things to look like the gods had touched them.

"I also think there's something evolving in Virt. A new ghost in the machine," I said.

That caught his attention. He stopped endlessly checking Endpoint's outputs and turned toward me. One glance was enough to know why he was The Specialist. Implants covered his entire body. Pure functionality without a dollop of form. Whatever he needed to continue his calling, he had grafted to his body. Natasha had a lot of software rattling around in her skull but little in the way of body modification. The Specialist had gone the hardware route, stuffing new eyes, input terminals, and a whole host of things I didn't recognize into his body.

Even his basic biological design hinted at a close genetic relationship to machinery. From his pointed chair – like an arrow aimed at his feet – to his haughty expression, The Specialist practically looked like a smug 'bot. His eyes were digital cameras with zoom lenses that popped out of his head when he glared at me. Pale skin shot through with the same digital pulses that I saw on the machinery earlier. He flicked his wrist and the tablet I thought he was holding folded itself neatly back into his arm. A mechanical hand with fingers that branched and branched and branched until they became a gray cloud pointed at me.

"Tell me about them," he said. "We will exchange information."

"Don't make it sound so sexy," I replied.

No response. He'd probably removed his sense of humor when he couldn't find a good use for it. "Fine, be that way," I continued. "But I want some assurances. First, I spill you spill. Got it? Good. Second, I'm going to walk out of here without one of your goons turning me into a hyperintelligent toaster. We cool?"

I might have laid the patois on too thick. The Specialist stared blankly at me for a moment, like he was trying to translate from human to whatever he'd turned himself into. A sly smile crept across his face. "Acceptable. And don't flatter yourself; you would not make a hyperintelligent toaster. A slightly above average intelligence toaster at best."

So much for removing the sense of humor. I couldn't help but smile back. "Are you aware of Mason Boviary?"

"Hacker, philanthropist, eccentric. Hooked into Virt decades ago and never came out."

"That's the one. I met with him earlier today. He's fine, by the way. Sends his regards. He asked me to do a job for him. It seems he's gotten himself into a pickle. Or his pickle has gotten him into trouble. Somehow, he picked up a traveler. He calls it an STD, so I'm assuming he got laid and brought home something he didn't intend to."

The Specialist glanced at his readouts and returned his gaze to me. "Go on."

Most people get at least a little interested in STDs. "I could see something else in his avatar. At first, I thought he was just playing around, but the thing was independent. It was kind of like an octopus."

"Fascinating. How do you know it was alive and not just some new code the script children are working on up on Level 5?"

How to explain it? It was just a feeling I had after the fact. "I can't," I told him. "All I can say it seemed to work independently of Mason and seemed malevolent. I asked the wrong question and got the glaring of the ages from it. I also got the sense that it didn't want to kill me; it wanted to possess me. It probably wanted Mason, too, but couldn't quite take him for some reason."

The Specialist was quiet for a long time before nodding at something. Probably personal hyperspace comms between him and his team. "That is hardly conclusive."

"I know. All I can say is I'm a good judge of people and Mason didn't seem to be just people."

"We deal in fact, Miss Devore, not hunches."

I sighed. Not surprised, just frustrated. "I get that, but by the time you realize this hunch is fact, it'll be biting you on the ass."

The lights on his face flickered rapidly. Probably some kind of comm link going off. After a moment, everything settled down and his eyes focused on me again. "We do not have access to Virt. It's beyond our charter. But we will expand our searches in Endpoint's comp systems to look for anomalies."

"Good enough. Now, you said we'd exchange information. What information do you have for me?"

"Never trust anyone who agrees to trade information."

15 – Intermission

Monique tasted like honey and had a firm hand. That's all you need to know. Fill in the rest with your imagination.

16 - Nobtop and Nat Visit Hell

"**H**ow old are you, Natasha?"

Nobtop pushed Feggs and Bakkon around his plate with a spork. Something about him looked broken. I leaned back in my chair like a teener in school. "A few hundred," I said. "I honestly stopped caring after it got too difficult to calculate from local planetary years back to Terran years. Real time, probably about half that."

His eyes met mine and there was a glimmer of...something. Hope? Sanity? "I am nearly 400 hundred. Most of it in real time, too."

"You don't look a day over 500," I said.

"Da. Miracle of injectables."

"Surely you didn't call me down here to ask how I old I am. If you'd comm'd me I would have happily made up a better answer."

Faint smile. "In person is better. Too much technology. Can talk to anyone anywhere anytime but no one does it. Talk around things. Busy doing other things. Face to face, you have to focus. You see whole person. Is better."

I couldn't fault that logic. Half the time, I ignored any incoming messages. Filtering the important stuff from the constant barrage of ads and other nonsense got to be too much so I shut the whole thing down unless something caught my attention.

"Good point," I said. "But it does make it harder to fake a bad line when the conversation goes sideways."

"400 years is a long time," Nobtop said. "We weren't meant to live this long. Do you know how many families reside on Endpoint?"

"Hello, non sequitur. Your purple monkey dishwater is ready."

His eyes narrowed. "Anyone but you, Natasha. Anyone but you."

"What about me?"

"Anyone but you I would not hesitate to slap out of that chair."

I shrank back and got ready to run. To where, I wasn't sure. Endpoint was Nobtop's playground. Rather than run home with tail between my legs, I decided to meet the danger head-on for once in my sordid life. I leaned forward and put my elbows on the table, fixed him with my best glare, and asked, "Because I'm a woman?"

Nobtop snorted. "Nyet. Am staunch feminist. Treat you just like the rest of the group. They get out of line, I bring them back. You get out of line, I bring you back. Equality. Double-edged blade."

Not surprising in a way. There will likely always be gender differences but humanity had largely moved past all the bias. Maybe it was the fact that there was a whole universe to explore, or the fact that there were aliens at some point, but trivial differences like skin and what you packed between your legs didn't matter.

Except in New Tejas. But those guys were a bunch of inbred jerks anyway so no one really cared what they thought.

"Then why?" I asked.

He sighed and pointed his eyes at the ceiling. "When first met, you had hat in hand. Seemed innocent. Scared."

"I was scared," I mumbled. Scared. Lost. Stuck in a new body with an army of airlockers gunning for me. Trying desperately to figure out what the absolute fuck was going on with my life. And negotiating with a giant whose reputation preceded him until he caught up with it and stomped it to mush.

"Bah! Nothing to fear. Nobtop is teddy bear."

With a bear's claws and taste for blood.

"Anyway," he continued. "At first I just saw you as weak and not worth effort. When I saw you...desecrate Rex-"

"When I cut his dick off?"

"Da. That. Bloodlust in your eyes. You have taste for it now. We are not that different; do what must be done, da?"

"Da," I said quietly, hoping it wouldn't come back to haunt me.

"Needs of many outweigh needs of few. Famous 20th century philosopher said that," Nobtop said. "Means focus on what is best for most. That is what *Bratva* does. Most people want to be left alone. I get that. Grok it, to quote another famous philosopher. Is good when people are left alone. They do what they do and everyone is happy. Some people get out of line. Must crush them. Make it ugly as warning to rest.

"I read up on you. First semi-famous *Bratva*. You put yourself in line of fire of many powerful people. Banks, rulers, military, gangs. All to save little people."

"Someone has to keep the peace," I said.

"Is good philosophy. Is what we do. Want advice from someone with lot of experience?"

I gulped, nodded, and hoped he wasn't going to bring up the "kill someone" thing again.

"You are good person at heart. Want to be left alone. Is good. Is what most people should do. Don't let your bloodlust guide you. Things work best when people do what is best for them. Sometimes they just need a nudge to realize best for everyone is best for them. Everyone wins."

"I didn't realize I had a bloodlust," I told him. "I thought I was just doing what was right."

Nobtop nodded sagely, looking vaguely like a massively bulked up Xevex Farsight. They say the real Xevex could conquer worlds with nothing more than words. I never dug his stylings, but there was no doubt the real deal was a wise man. "Last night I had to teach a lesson. It hurts every time I do it. Man refused to do what was right, so *Bratva* intervened. Cut off his fingers one by one with dull knife. Tiny held his hand down, but I did the dirty deed myself. Could not make someone else do it even though Nacho wanted to.

"Don't fret too much about the fingerless man. Losing a digits is no big deal. He has the credits, he can get some stylish fingers custom grown right on Endpoint. It no doubt hurt like a bitch, but the point was never to maim him, just to send message. 'Don't do that again.' In old days, Terran Bratva would send someone to rape his wife and murder his children. That makes for bad blood. Not good for business. Warning is sent to person who needs it, not innocents.

"About fifty years ago, you shut down the life support on a barge. Lots of people died. Bad thing to do."

History would judge Natasha harshly for that one. All I could do was lower my eyes and wonder what it felt like to hear the thrum stop and know freezing to death was probably easier than desperately trying to suck oxygen out of dead air. In her defense, she was going after a brutal dictator who'd left planet-side after a coup. It would have only been a matter of time before everyone on barge knew to bend the knee or have it shattered by vibestaff.

"Not my finest moment," I said, as if apologizing for the actions of the previous resident of this body would make it better.

Nobtop waved a hand. "Old news. What you were then is not who you are now. Saved a whole continent from nuclear extinction. I knew General Bastido when he was still called Angelo. Was good guy then but had dark mind. He would have launched missiles and then gotten his nails done. Real bastard. That is point. Be good person. Do brutal things if needed, but be good person. And always have someone to trust. You against all systems is going to wind up with you in bad place."

"Duly noted," I said. "Not to be rude and I'm grateful for the advice, but what is going on here? Why did you call me to the mess hall to tell me to trust people and break skulls only when necessary?"

His eyes narrowed and lips flattened. Beast mode cometh. Before I could make a break for it, he shook his head and exhaled slowly through his lips. A very human moment for the beast. "Needed someone to talk to," he said and slid his chair out.

I slapped a hand on his and said, "No. I'm sorry. I didn't mean to sound rude. Please. Let's talk. I'll even buy the ice cream."

A strange look washed over his chiseled features and for a moment, he softened. He wasn't kidding. At his heart, Nobtop was a teddy bear. Educated, curious, into ancient literature. He was pretending to be a monster.

"Nyet. No ice cream. Bad for physique," he said quietly. "Vodka would be better. Make you strong like bull."

Nobtop held his hand up and snapped his fingers. A server-bot appeared with a bottle of crystal-clear liquid and four shot glasses. He set two in front of me and two in front of him and placed the bottle in the middle. "Cyrillic tradition. As host, I must drink first to prove vodka not poisoned. Almost never happened to tell the truth. Cyrillic people stand face-to-face when they want to kill each other. But, alas, has happened."

He poured out the four shots, gently stuffed the stopper back in the bottle and snatched up a shot glass without spilling a drop. His nostrils flared as he sniffed the liquor inside. With a lopsided, laconic smile, Nobtop tilted his head back and downed like he was drinking plain-Jane, flavorless ration water.

"My turn?" I asked, not sure what to do. My only dealings with Cyrillics were limited to them paying me when I got something for them.

Nobtop nodded.

The vodka was slightly oily and burned like an Antares oil fire as it slunk down my throat. Smooth but fiery, like silk panties dusted with chile powder. "Real thing," I gasped. "Haven't had that in a while."

He slapped the table and laughed. "To be importer/exporter like myself has benefits. Import stuff. Export things. Sometimes import stuff is interesting enough to keep."

"Why not keep it in your quarters?" I asked.

"I do. Best stuff I keep here in mess hall. This is where people are. More comfortable than restaurant we met in. Too much fussy. Too fake. This is real. Is important I see people. Reminds me of why I need to smash testicles sometimes."

I instinctively crossed my legs when he said that before remembering I no longer had balls. Mine had been turned into nano-food and then to something else. Tacos maybe. The guy in the corner biting into a hoagie could've been eating my balls.

"You're definitely a man of the people," a voice behind us said.

I spun around and was on my feet as soon as I saw Xevex Jeffries leering a few feet behind us. He wasn't as twitchy this time, but there was certainly something off about him. Almost like his whole body was vibrating. I'd never heard of airlock preachers being dustheads, but he certainly had the look. Right down to the too-bright eyes.

"May I help you?" Nobtop asked.

Jeffries looked him up and down and frowned. Nobtop towered over us and probably outweighed both Jeffries and me combined. Surely, Jeffries had heard the stories.

For his part, Jeffries looked calm and as collected. "It's not so much that you can help me, as this young lady can help me."

"Young?" I asked.

"It is an affectation, dear Natasha," Xevex said with a grin that could curdle malk. "A certain formality that creeps into my speech."

"She is busy. When she is no longer busy, she might contact you. Beam her your card," Nobtop said.

I shot him a narrow-eyed look. While I trusted the guy, I could speak for myself. Never mind the fact that I was about to say almost the exact same thing. "Yeah, sorry. Otherwise occupied. Reuniting with Terran potato booze."

"It is not I who wants you," Jeffries said, spreading his arms wide. "It is god's angels who want you."

Nobtop sighed and rolled his eyes. "It was bad enough when you were filling airlockers with that nonsense, it's worse now that you're actively trying to recruit others. Take a hike or I'll take your legs."

Jeffries reached out and laid a hand on my shoulder. "God wishes to commune with you."

I snapped my hand into his forearm and stepped back. A nerve runs along the inside of a forearm – the radial nerve, I think. Smack that and it feels like being shocked. "Sorry, I'm not a communist," I said.

Jeffries' hand moved off my shoulder, but he didn't shake his arm or rub it. Either I was weaker than I thought or he was tougher than I expected. "God does not take 'no' lightly, Miss Devore."

I stepped back and felt a hand the size of a tank on my stomach, gently pushing me back. Nobtop's bulk filled my vision. I had to restrain myself from punching him in the kidneys; I had the situation under control.

Nobtop's voice fell to a basso rumble. "She said no," he growled. "Now beat it unless you would like to continue this conversation with the *Bratva*."

I sidestepped to get around Nobtop and found Jeffries calmly smiling. "You have your army, I have mine," he said. "We are both generals. I'd just like to remind you we have God on our side."

"Which god?" I asked.

Jeffries closed his eyes and pointed. "That one."

Nobtop and I both turned and found ourselves looking at a 'bot washing dishes. He looked at me. I shrugged. No one ever said god botherers were sane.

"Your god is a dish 'bot?" I asked.

That weird smile crept across his face. Lips turned up at the edges but flat in the middle. A cartoonish villain grin. "Look further, Natasha. Your destiny is out there among the stars. With us."

Endpoint's deck rumbled under my feet. I was so accustomed to it that I barely noticed Temnyy talking anymore, but the timing and Jeffries' still pointing finger made the short rumble feel ominous. A bead of sweat rolled down my back. Somehow, this had gone from irritating to dangerous in a few short moments. Gotta love efficiency in your crazies.

"Temnyy?" Nobtop asked. "Is just rock."

"It's a god waiting to be born. An angry god ready to rain down destruction on our enemies."

"I'm about to rain blows down on your head if you don't piss off," I said.

Nobtop's knuckles cracked as his meaty hands closed into fists and opened again. "What happens if I kill god's messenger?" he asked.

"I cannot be killed. I am an angel now. Nothing you can do can hurt me for I am filled with the power."

"Funny, I say the same thing every time I drink moonshine," I mumbled.

"'Those who cannot, should not. Those who can, should. Teach always, though the road may be difficult it is worthwhile'. Penta 6:1. One of yours, I believe," Jeffries said, staring at me with his dazzle eyes.

I clenched a fist and relaxed it. Took a deep breath and released it. Little tricks I learned from the Monks of Budor. It didn't help, but it took the edge off my rage. "Are you really quoting Penta's words at me?"

"You cannot reach your true potential here. You could have an entire universe to play with," Jeffries said. "All you have to do is open your eyes and see the true world."

"Have seen true world," Nobtop said. "Is not pretty place. Only strong survive."

I jerked a thumb Nobtop's way and said, "I'm with him on this one. You can put it in a designer dress and lipstick and call it pretty, but the true world will still gut you for five credits."

Jeffries held up a finger and started to reply, but Nobtop put a huge hand on my shoulder and asked, "Shall we get out of here? Must get to *Bratva* meeting; see who needs killing today."

Thank Penta for the clever guy. "Yes," I said. "Mustn't forget the *Bratva* brothers. People aren't going to kill themselves."

Jeffries put his hand on Nobtop's chest and I swear every sound in the mess fell silent. A hand on someone can be sign of caring or it can be a sign of control. I chose to believe Nobtop's hand on my shoulder was a sign of caring. Jeffries' hand on Nobtop was a sign of control. An ill-conceived sign of control, but a sign of control nonetheless.

Nobtop didn't hesitate. For such a big guy, I would have expected him to be a lumbering oaf. Instead, I barely saw him move. Injectables can change a person at the cellular lever and Nobtop was jacked to the gills with them.

His fist was a blur. A comet streaking through space ready to smash into the last city on a dying planet. It should have popped an unmod like Jeffries like squeezing a balloon full of blood and tissue. But Nobtop didn't hit a thing. Jeffries stood stock still, smirking up at the increasingly enraged beast. Nobtop threw another punch and another, but each time he completely missed his mark.

Jeffries twitched and Nobtop flew halfway across the mess, landing in clattering mass of ginned up sporks and trays. I snuck a quick look at Jeffries who still stood there smirking and ran to Nobtop. I don't care how tough you are, getting tossed across a room hurts.

Before I could get there, a table flew across the room. Nobtop rose to his knee and swatted the table out of the way. In his hand was the biggest damned gun I'd ever seen.

"Jenkins, Identify Nobtop's gun."

"Whose?"

Right. For some reason, Jenkins couldn't see Nobtop. "The gun in the center of the room. The only gun in the room. Scan it and find out what it is."

"It is a Dahrl DKMar13. Heavy handgun issued to Korfan troops. It fires a 15mm compressed matter round at near relativistic speeds. But it is not the only gun in the room."

"What?" I hissed.

"According to my scans, there are a dozen guns scattered across ten people in this room."

I shouldn't have been surprised. Endpoint had no formal security guards, no police, and not many rules or laws. It was as close to chaos a society could get and still be called a society.

Nobtop rose to his feet like a god ascending. All around us, people who were reaching into their jackets or pants stopped. He was the final say on Endpoint and everyone knew it. Jeffries had another table in his hands and a delirious smirk on his face. He looked at Nobtop's gun and laughed. "Won't help you," he said before casually lobbing a table at me.

I rolled out of the way just before the table hit the deck and made an ungodly screech sliding across the deck. Jeffries pointed a finger at me and winked. I flipped him off and darted closer to Nobtop. I didn't completely trust the guy, but anyone who can swat a four-person table out of the air was worth hiding behind.

"Come on, Natasha," Jeffries said. "This is going to end badly for everyone. Just come with me and no one will get hurt."

Before I could reply, Nobtop's DKMaar13 answered for me. It felt more than sounded. Those big compressed matter guns used a miniature B/S drive to accelerate matter. They didn't make much noise, but the sense of a star drive spinning up nearby popped my ears, scattered the electrical signals in my brain, and left me on wobbly legs.

I had a vague sense of an arm around me, tossing me over a shoulder, then things shaking. Running? Was Nobtop running away from a lowlife airlock preacher? My brain wobbled. Surely, that wasn't happening. Right? Who did that? Just tossed someone over their shoulder and ran?

The sense of falling into a black hole ebbed and I slammed a fist into Nobtop's back. He didn't even have the common courtesy to grunt. When he set me down, I fell onto my butt and glared at him. "What the fuck?"

"Guns and crowds are bad," Nobtop said, turning my head from side to side. "Eyes look okay. Sorry about that. Big gun. Didn't expect you to be so close. Will pass. Next time, get down or get shielding in head. Stardrive guns kill in lots of different ways."

I shook my head and tried to get to my feet. Nobtop's hand gently pushed me back down. "Wait. Should have few minutes. Best to let your brain rewire."

"Re-what?" Shit. He was right. My brain was totally not working. "Get him?"

"Nyet. Crafty bastard. Faster than should be. Sorry to carry you but had to leave before someone got hurt. Hopefully he'll follow."

"Hopefully? You want him to, uh, follow us?"

"Da. Better down here where only Specialists roam. They are smart enough to get out of way. We lump him and take him home with us. Hey! He could be your first kill."

Ugh. Why couldn't I join one of those gangs where they had to steal things instead of one where you have to kill people? "I'll keep my options open."

"He did throw a table at you. So, you know, under certain maritime laws you are required to kill him. Just saying."

Genuine worry in those big eyes. Maybe for me. Maybe for himself. Maybe for everyone. Heavy is the head that wears the crown that lets him push people out of airlocks. "What now?" I asked.

He poked at his forearm and grimaced. "No signal. Must get hold of *Bratva*. Let them know. Not everyone can throw a table like that. Drugs, maybe, or muscle stim. Either way, problem to be taken care of."

I struggled to my feet and felt like the world was about to collapse again. Nobtop's arm held me up until the world stabilized. "I'm good," I said, leaning on a wall and feeling very far from good. Whatever was clicking around in Natasha's head did not agree with Stardrive weapons.

"Good," Nobtop said. "Because here comes trouble."

Jeffries came around the corner like a returning king. The bastard didn't even try to be subtle, just walked right down the hall. "Ah, there you are, my dear," he said.

"Last chance, *mudak*," Nobtop said, leveling the DK at Jeffries. "Walk away."

"Not interested in you, gangster," Jeffries said. He stopped in his tracks. "Or is mobster? I can never remember. Law breaker, anyway. Well, rustler, there's a new sheriff in town and he's here to rescue that pretty lady from your nefarious clutches."

Jeffries pointed fingers at us like he was firing old-fashioned gunpowder weapons. Even blew the smoke off the imaginary barrels.

"Da, da," Nobtop said. "Have seen *Seven Sheriffs*, too. Not bad impression, though. Turn around. Now."

He flicked his thumb slightly and the gun hummed a deadly tune. The noise made my implants shimmy and shake again. It felt like spiders in my brain, digging around with their chitiny legs. I felt like a coward for doing it, but I backed a few meters away until the gun's field ebbed.

Jeffries struck a pose and pointed straight at me. "Not until she comes with me."

Nobtop's first shot hit Jeffries right in the chest. I've seen compressed matter rounds punch through solid cermisteel like it was tissue paper. There's no dodging them and the sheer amount of kinetic energy they generate tends to vaporize soft targets like people and animals.

That big, fast round went right through Jeffries like he wasn't even there. It didn't even slow him down. The bastard's crazy eyes were aglow with the kind of fervency you only see in mental patients and people who have found god. Which, considering a bullet passed right through him, he might have done.

"Go," Nobtop said, motioning me away.

I grabbed his arm and tugged. 170cm and 50 kg versus 213cm and 136kg wasn't even a competition. He barely moved. "Now is not the time to decide you're a gentleman," I yelled.

"Get out of here, Natasha," he hissed. "Jeffries and I have unfinished business."

"He's about to finish it," I said.

Nobtop fired once more and again that mass of kinetic energy passed right through Jeffries. Nobtop, never one to resist doming fools, fired until the gun beeped empty. "Now will you leave?" I asked, tugging at his arm.

Down the corridor, Jeffries paused. Our eyes met and a sick smile spread across his thin lips. Jeffries raised his arms and clouds erupted from his fingertips. Black as night, twisting, and turning like serpents, the clouds sped down the corridor.

Nobtop didn't even have time to react before the clouds hit him full in the chest. The big bastard fell to his knees, spasming like the kid who decided to take a radio into the bath with him. The scream that escaped his lips transcended any he'd caused himself. It was agony and horror, and the sickening knowledge that his sins caught up with him all at once.

The clouds pulled away and Nobtop's massive form fell backward. His lifeless eyes stared up at me. "Not my fault, bub," I whispered. "I told you to run."

His chest was a mangled mass of blood and exposed bone. The clouds had spent their time eating him. Probably found every pain center and turned it to max while they were doing it. The wound was almost perfectly circular. Well, as perfect as you can get with meat.

"He should have stayed out of the way," Jeffries growled from down the corridor. "We were never interested in him. But you, my dear Ms. Natasha, you we are very interested in."

I didn't stick around to find out if his target was my body or my brain. I assumed the body, but you can never be too sure about that with these whack jobs. I grabbed Nobtop's gun, turned tail and hauled ass as fast as my legs could carry me.

"Come back, Ms. Natasha," Jeffries called from behind me. "We have so much to do."

My feet carried me far faster than I'd expected. I was never a runner; just didn't have the build to do it. Or the desire, for that matter. I only ran when I was being chased and even then there'd better be a pissed off mob behind me.

Natasha's body was a different story. I ran like the wind. Effortless motion. I never would have suspected a Kaffeene aficionado hacker had spent her free time running, but there was no doubting the body knew what to do even if the mind was still half a corridor away wondering what had happened.

Nobtob's gun was heavy in my hand. It was a beast of a weapon. I should have dumped it, but there was some tickle in the back of my head that I needed something to remember him by.

My body seemed to have a mind of its own. Deep-buried muscle memory. As I approached the first corner, I ran up the side of the wall and launched myself off. A little twisting in flight and I was soon righted. My shoes slapped the ceramisteel-grated floor and kept on running.

A horrible sound, like the hum and whine of a dental drill followed behind me. My teeth were on edge. I didn't know what crazy ol' Jeffries had in mind for me, but I doubted it was a romantic evening of shooting darts down in Sublight. It was probably more along the lines of turning me into a lampshade or a sex slave. Or both. Religious cultists lived in their own demented little world.

I rounded a corner and waited. Somewhere far behind me, I heard the click and clank of boots on the floor. Jeffries was quite a way back. No matter, though, I was completely, thoroughly lost.

On the corner before me was an icon made of teeth on the top, something that looked like a sandwich in the middle, and a circle with squiggly lines coming out of it. No arrows, no explanation, nothing. I guessed it meant eating sandwiches would give you gas, but that was probably way off base.

I caught my breath, took a quick look around, and jogged down the corridor. Jogging was easier than running and it sounded like Jeffries was a fair piece behind me. Besides, I was still lost and hoping I'd stumble across a Specialist Iconograph with a glass, a bottle with 'XXX' printed on it, and a smiley face.

"Jenkins," I hissed into my head. "Where am I?"

"You are approximately half a kilometer from the lifts. I will plot a course for you."

A top-down view of the deck in all its mad triangular glory popped into the upper left of my vision while a giant blue arrow pointing straight ahead filled the rest. "Thanks, bud," I said.

Motion up ahead spurred me forward. Something in what looked like a white lab coat had just crossed the corridor a few intersections ahead. I laid on the speed. Jeffries was still far behind me, but movement down here meant either one of the Specialists or an automaton. Something other than the smirking cloud of machines coming after me.

I hit the intersection and nearly skidded to a stop and looked down the corridor. Nothing. Symbols on the corridor walls were no use, either: A pyramid, a donut, and horizontal wavy lines on one side and a skull, a lizard, and a candle on the other. Whoever I'd seen had gone left, so left it was. That was good; I always did prefer donuts to skulls.

The corridor was empty, but I hauled ass down it anyway. I skidded around a corner and found myself face-to-face with a man in a white lab coat. It was hard to tell who was more startled. He dropped his tablet and I tripped over my own two feet, so it was probably me. When I looked up, he was holding out his hand. I reached up to grab it and he shook his head. "The tablet, please."

"We need to get out of here," I said, snatching his tablet and scrambling to my feet.

He looked me up and down like something from a curiosity cabinet at a backwater state fair before tapping gently at his tablet.

"Didn't you hear me?" I hissed. "We need to get out of here. There's a thing made of clouds and it's coming this way."

"A thing made of clouds? Ma'am, I don't have time for silly games."

I took a deep breath and flashed him my best smile. It didn't seem to help. "Listen, I'm not on drugs and this isn't a game. There's a man down here chasing me. He's made of clouds."

"Hmmph."

The legendary Specialist sense of wonder on display. "He was a man named Xevex Jeffries. He was an airlock preacher but somehow he can control meat-eating clouds. Now he's trying to get me."

The first hint that Jeffries was close was a faint hum in the air. He'd spread himself wide. A knife formed in the air and took the Specialist's head clean off.

Before I could even wipe the blood off my face, Jeffries was standing in front of me. He watched the body fall and shook his head. "This is in on you, Natasha Devore. If you had only accepted your fate, this poor young man would still be alive. He could have taken the sacrament and been a valuable soldier in the cause. Now he's dead and it's all your fault."

"You're the one that killed him, asshole," I spat.

Jeffries shrugged. "Perhaps, but only because you made me do it."

I started to say something pithy, but the air shimmered and left my lungs. I fell to my knees, clutching my throat and wondering why I couldn't breathe. As the world faded, the last thing I saw was Xevex Jeffries smirking down at me.

17 - Nine Ways to Sevenday

I awoke to a whole new kind of sore throat and a throbbing headache. Jeffries was standing in front of me with his trademark smirky grin and his hands in pockets. We were back in the weird room with the weird black computer with the weird snakes. Which was, frankly, weird. Why this room of all places? The room he called – what was it? – the Extraction Chamber?

"What the fuck are you?" I muttered.

I was held in place by whatever freakish nanobots made up his body. Arms and legs spread wide. Helpless. It reminded of one of those old movies where a woman is dressed in skimpy rags and sacrificed to octopus gods. Like octopus gods are even remotely interested in human sexiness. Or human kinks.

Jeffries fixed me with a look that astounded me. It was kind, loving, and spiteful all at the same time. Like he really expected me to get it, understood that I didn't get it, and was pissed that I couldn't understand. Basically, every teacher I've ever had. "You're awake," he said brightly as if we were old friends and he didn't have me splayed out and held in place by bits of his body.

"What the hell did you do to me?" I asked.

"I'm saving you," he said. "From weak flesh and tiny human emotions."

"My emotions are not tiny. They're massive and dangerous and unpredictable."

He shook a finger at me and grinned. "You're better with the quick comebacks than you used to be. It must have been our influence that charged up that primate brain of yours."

"Or something," I said, rolling my eyes. "So, are you going to tell me what you are, or is this just some kink thing? Because I've got a thing planned for later. Basically the same thing only with a bed and a hot redhead."

"I'm afraid you'll need to cancel those plans." He stepped close enough that I could feel the hum of his body. "I'm also sorry about," he waved his hands around in the air, "all of this. But you have something I need to understand and something I just need."

"You're pretty chatty for a rapist," I told him.

Jeffries put his hand on his heart and gasped dramatically. "No, not that. Never that. We have respect for bodies."

"Then what?" I asked.

"Information."

"Forty-two," I told him.

"What?"

"Forty-two. According to one of Earth's greatest philosophers, the answer to everything is forty-two. There, that's a thing you know now. Can I go?"

Jeffries shook his head and chuckled under his breath. "You're not the same Natasha Devore I knew a few days ago."

"I did something with my hair," I told him.

"Not physical. You're a different person."

I winked at him. "You're just getting to meet the real me."

"I did more than meet the real you," Jeffries said.

I'm not ashamed to say I nearly threw up in my mouth. "Obviously not a night to remember."

He stroked my cheek and chuckled as I tried to pull away. "I've had better, but you were good enough to receive our gift from my dear friend. It was a wonderful night for the three of us."

"Please tell me your gift wasn't a mouthful of cum." My stomach threatened to empty itself again.

"You enjoyed every second of it. But no, that wasn't the gift. That was just the delivery mechanism."

Panic rose in me. I tugged on my binds but it was no use. "What the fuck did you do to me?"

"I gave you a new life to nurture."

"That's not how babies are made, dumbass," I snapped.

When he grinned, the bottom dropped out of my world. Something far worse had happened to Natasha than I ever would have guessed. "Not a baby," he whispered as he poked me in the forehead. "A new body for a very old life."

"No way," I said even as the horrid, blasphemous truth dawned on me. "Can't be true."

He held his arms out and raised his eyes to the ceiling. "Oh, but it is true. Hallelujah, we are reborn. I was the first, of course. Led the expedition into your world even though the council ordered me not to."

"Fucking Predecessors," I muttered. "Fucking holy men and their gods."

"Predecessors?" Jeffries hissed. "Typical human. Things always have to relate to your pathetic little species somehow, don't they?"

"It's just a name, jackass," I spat back. "It doesn't mean anything special. Besides, we're way ahead of you. Your tech was pathetic. Trinary? Seriously? I made trinary systems when I was a child."

"While your species was bashing rocks together, we sailed the stars."

"And now here you are, stuck forever orbiting a big-ass rock."

He rippled. His nanite body flexing in barely controlled rage. For a moment, I could see the real thing that had taken control of Jeffries. Nine arms, nine eyes, one gigantic chip on its shoulder. Poking the thing with a stick wasn't the best idea I'd ever had, but the jerk in me was tired of being suppressed.

"Not forever little monkey. Not forever," he said.

"I'm sure it felt like forever, though," I quipped. "Stuck in your dime store Virt, knowing it was the best you could come up. What did you do in there? Squid sex or did you just sit around and get pissed off knowing the apes were living on your little monument to mediocrity."

Something moved in my left wrist. A sting like an old-school needle piercing the vein. I gritted my teeth and did my best to ignore it.

"If one of my limbs is cut off, it will grow back," the Jeffries-thing said. "Will yours?"

I shook my head. Something was working its way down my arm. A burning. A sense of violation. This was going to suck. Natasha, real Natasha, if you're listening, sorry about your body.

"After spending time in your Virt worlds, I've come to understand humans better than you understand yourselves. You let your true selves show in the virtual world. Sad little creatures who can only be themselves when nothing is on the line, and you think no one is watching you."

"You were the one getting blown by a schoolgirl, bud," I said.

"Reproduction."

"Doesn't work that way or didn't you figure that out yet?"

"Not your kind of reproduction. Ours. People let their guards down. Your freakish sexual acts let us in. Then, when you leave Virt, we come with you. If your minds can handle it, that is. Some humans just aren't smart enough to be hosts."

I had to laugh out loud at that. "The biggest badasses in the galaxy are now just a sexually transmitted disease. You're like interstellar Greenjeans."

Let me just say, his punch hurt a lot more than I expected. I don't know if it was the body or just because Jeffries wasn't a human anymore, but his fist hit that magical spot on my chest and the world swarm. Every nerve in my body lit up. All the air in my lungs rushed out and refused to come back in. I saw him through tear-stained eyes. Smirking bastard. At least he hadn't bored a hole straight through me like he had poor Nobtop.

"Who's the superior species now?" he asked.

Deep, painful breath. Breathing fire but better than nothing. I panted and cursed him under my breath. "I don't know," I gasped. "I don't have to tie someone up to kick their ass."

My ears rang after he smacked me upside the head. Sweet fucking ass, the guy could hit hard. My body gave out, dangled from his makeshift bonds. Blessing and a curse. I couldn't rub my jaw, but at least I wasn't on the floor in front of him. Small miracles.

When I finally pulled my head back up, he was right in my face. I mustered up every bit of spite in my heart and spat a wad of bloody snot right between his eyes. The son of a bitch rippled and my last bit of badassery disappeared from his face. "You'll have to do better than that," he said.

"What the absolute fuck do you even want, anyway?" I hissed. "Is there some plan behind all this or do you just enjoy being an asshole?"

"You're nothing to us," Jeffries said. "Well, most of you, anyway. Like I said, some of you are useful. You, however, are interesting. While I chose the body of the preacher man, my dear friend chose yours. She? I guess so. Why not? Brave new galaxy. She was in your head, working away. Your body should have been hers, yet there's no trace of her anywhere. Why are you still you?"

Oh, brother. If he only knew.

"I kick too much ass to be taken down that easily," I told him.

"Where is she?"

"Gone. She bored me, so I kicked her out. Never underestimate my desire to be left alone."

"LIAR!" he screamed and grabbed me by the throat. "Once we're in your heads we cannot be removed. Your minds are too weak to get rid of us."

That close, I could see the subtle motion in his skin as nanites vibrated. The blood stopped moving to my brain as his fingers tightened. I knew what was happening and instinctively fought against it, but deep inside I wasn't worried. It was a power play. He'd already shown me his cards. He wasn't going to kill me until I told him what happened. Or I royally pissed him off.

Which didn't make it any easier.

As the world first closed in and then blackened at the edges, my pulse pounded in my ears. Life, that desperate, clingy bitch, didn't want to let me go just yet. When caught in a trap, an animal will gnaw its own leg off to get free. Arquilian bloodworms will go on the offensive when caught in the net, devouring anything and everything in their path. Humans have been known to flip cars over when death came sniffing around. And for what? Another chance to die?

It would have been easy to let go. Let him win. What did I owe these people? Most of them, nothing. But a few of them were worth saving.

"Jenkins. Activate."

"Ma'am, I am never deactivated," he said.

"Shut up and listen. Not much time. Go to your AI buddies and find a way to kill the fucker choking me."

I could feel him trying to access my eyes, to assess the situation. "Ma'am-"

"Shut up. The man killing me is made of nanites. Go now. I die—you die. Don't forget that."

The whooshing sensation of him leaving was enough to snap me out of my torpor. Jeffries and his smirking face I'd love to punch loved every minute of it. I stuck out my tongue and with the last ounce of resolve in my body, blew him a kiss.

It shocked him enough that he released his grip and stepped back. I took a deep breath and threw up all over the deck. Feggs and Bakon. Dinner of champions. My body gave up and I sagged in the bonds gasping and coughing.

"Impressive," Jeffries said. "Let's see just how much you can take."

"Hear me roar," I wheezed.

"It's a pity our races were separated by so much time. I would have loved to see your whole pathetic race cower in fear."

"Shouldn't you-gasp-show me-cough cough cough-what your master-gag cough-race looks-cough cough cough-like? I'd love-cough-to laugh-cough cough cough-at it."

The thing Jeffries didn't understand was that it wasn't my first time. I'd been tortured by some of the best in the business. Life of a thief and all. Jeffries was crude, a blunt instrument who only understood the physical aspects. They suck ass, no doubt about it, but they're far better than a probe into the fear center for a night or a few weeks without sleep.

He took the bait without thinking. Dumbass. Every recovery second counted and I was doing my best to rack them up.

His body melted into a puddle before me.

"Ma'am, there might be a way," Jenkins said. I was too busy getting my ass beaten to even notice he'd come back.

"Do it."

"There's a problem, though."

Damned AI. "Just do it. Kill this bastard."

Jeffries was reforming himself. I assumed the slow reform was more for dramatic effect than anything else. Crazy son-of-a-bitch really had been studying humans.

"There appears to be the remnants of a Predecessor maintenance system in the room: A coolant vent. A massive blast of coolant might not kill him, but it will at least slow him down."

"Why are we talking about this?"

"Because, ma'am, the only coolant vent is directly above you."

"So?" What was he getting at? "Just vent the coolant as soon as he gets close to me."

"The coolant is stored at -200 degrees Celsius. Even a short blast from it would kill you."

Damned Predecessors. Who puts a coolant vent nowhere near the thing it needs to cool? Unless whatever I was standing on had a propensity for getting extremely hot.

Meanwhile, Jeffries continued his slow transformation. The puddle had grown nine limbs, all arrayed around a bulbous central torso. So far, it was all dull gray and looked like a failed experiment from a child's 3-D printer. Yet another way we were better than the squiddies.

"In case you hadn't noticed, I'm stuck here," I hissed to Jenkins.

"Yes, ma'am. We are both stuck in this position. I took the liberty of analyzing the bonds holding your limbs. They appear to be made of the same nano hypermatter that Jeffries himself is comprised of. It's entirely likely they are a part of him rather than separate entities."

"Um, thanks."

"What I mean to say is, there must be some level of communication from the larger mass that makes up the body to the smaller masses holding you."

"Get to the point, Jenkins," I said as Jeffries took on color. "Or I'm going to have you ripped out of my head and dropped off at the nearest thrift store. You can spend the rest of your days hooked into someone who lives in an abandoned shuttle and loves reality shows."

"You have a vast array of tools in your head. One of them, NetCrush 2.3.1, should be able to disrupt that communication. Without commands, the bonds should turn to dust."

Damn it. He was right. As usual. "Sorry about the shuttle thing, Jenkins."

According to the help file in my head, NetCrush was a single-person denial of service tool. It worked by targeting sending systems and overloading them with receipt acknowledgements. As the sender worked to process those, NetCrush would send its own command messages. Even though the sender would ignore those messages, it still took time to read, understand, process, and toss out each bad message. Not much time, but with enough messages, a sender could be overloaded for a short length of time.

In the hands of a skilled net wizard like Nat, a short length of time was all she needed to bring your system to its knees. In my hands, it might be enough to wriggle free before Jenkins flooded me with supercooled plasma.

Jeffries finished his transformation into something out of a B-grade horror movie. He was about human height, a little taller than me but not by much. Where most Terran lifeforms are bi-symmetrical, his Predecessor body was tri-symmetrical. Three sets of three huge, unblinking eyes scattered around his head gave him a full field of vision. Nine arms, each branching into nine fingers branching into nine smaller digits. Probably branching even further than that. All wrapped in a rubbery-greenish flesh the color and texture of decay.

It was not only the first time a human had seen a Predecessor, but also the first time a human had seen intelligent alien life. A little humbling, but mostly it kicked off my deep-down primate instinct to kill the intruder.

"What do you think?" he asked. No mouth to make a sound; must have been between his legs like Terran octopods.

"You'll taste great with butter and garlic," I said.

He had a slithery, shuffling walk. Six legs on the ground, three in the air reaching out for my face. In a way, it was probably good humans had never come across intelligent alien life. We don't handle otherness very well. Hell, we started wars over skin color. With something like the Predecessors, we probably would have set fire to the whole galaxy by now.

"I've studied your race ever since you showed up. I've seen the parts of you that you only show off when you think no one is watching," he said, waving an appendage perilously close to my crotch. "Tell me, girl, what are your feelings about tentacles? Some of your race seems to enjoy them."

Oh, sweet Penta, it was going to be tentacle snuff porn. Time to get out of there. "On my command, Jenkins," I whispered in my head.

"Why don't you come closer and find out?" I asked Jeffries.

He slithered closer, rubbing my body with rubbery snakes. Not sure how the women in the tentacle porn industry handled it. Of course, they were dealing with special effects; this was the real deal. And it was fucking disgusting.

I sucked breath through my teeth and fought back the desire to scream bloody murder. Closer, squiddy. Get closer. Push that nasty body right up next to me.

When he was right on top of me, I said a little five-pointed prayer and triggered NetCrush. Time stretched out to eternity. I could feel the program probing for any kind of communication. Radio, subluminal, parse-warp, it didn't really matter. Once it found a message, the program dissected it and figured out the source. It turned out to be a simple subluminal message that let the nanites communicate. I should have guessed Predecessor tech would be way behind the curve.

To my complete surprise, not only did the nanite bonds holding me disappear, Jeffries himself collapsed into a puddle of gray goo. I hit the ground hard and fell flat on my ass. My body shrieked as I rolled backwards out of the line of fire.

Jeffries sloshed forward like a spilled drink on a bar. Whatever distributed consciousness was holding him together still had some level of communication. He was gray goo, a twisting mass of pissed off nanites struggling to get his head back in the game long enough to kill me.

"Now!" I screamed at Jenkins.

A blast of supercooled plasma poured down. Even clear of the deluge, I could feel the air freezing around me. Jeffries, too slow and uncoordinated, took it square in his gooey face.

I rubbed some life back into my limbs and crawled to my feet. Jaw hurt, chest hurt, pride hurt. Time to get the hell out of there.

I was on my way out when a thought stopped me. Of all the mysterious rooms on Endpoint, why that one? What was special about that particular room? There were dozens of quiet places on this floating bucket and I would suspect an actual Predecessor would know of even more. So why the one with the weird tubular thingy in it?

Jeffries was rippling slightly on the floor. Not much time before he was unfrozen.

I steered clear of his puddle and looked at the computer-thing with new eyes. Nobtop had said he and people found it one day when they were drunk and lost after unloading medical supplies. A big, mostly empty room with a brilliantly cobbled together primitive supercomputer, mechanical brain-stabbing snakes, and a massive cooling jet over a sluice grate. Even by alien standards, it was strange.

As soon as Jeffries started to move, I headed for the exit at relativistic speed. It wasn't over, but I needed a better way of dealing with him. Not every place I met the freak was going to have super-cooled plasma jets. At least I'd proven I could punch back.

18 - Never Easy

Wen you're in danger, you always seek out your people. Much as I appreciated Monique's tender charms, I needed to go to people who understood the dark nature of the universe.

When you go to ground, you go home. You go to your people.

Tiny answered the door with a huge grin on his face. His face fell when he saw the strain in my eyes, the side lurch from a probably broken rib, and the bruises on my throat. "Seester! I trust all this mess is because you beat up a bar."

I nodded and leaned on the door jam. "Yes, bar," I mumbled. "Whole thing."

When I nearly collapsed in front of him, he scooped me up and dropped me on a sofa that was made of MemoTech tech foam and immediately adjusted itself to my bruised body.

The Bratva Cave was exactly what I should have expected it would be but could never get myself to imagine. Instead of looking like a bar with flashing RGB silhouettes of naked women and a shredded pool table, it had soft classical music, posters from ancient operas, and a spirited 3-d chess match going on between two growling men who could tear off each other's arms.

"Ignore them," Tiny said, flicking a thumb over his shoulder. "They always get like that when the match is tight."

He was sitting on a faintly glowing coffee table. Probably Antarean oakfig. Probably worth a fortune. All I wanted to do was close my eyes and pretend things were not what they seemed. None of this would be easy.

"Hi," I told him. "Sorry to intrude."

"Nonsense. You are one of us now. No intrusion."

I groaned as I tried to sit up. Tiny put a huge hand on my shoulder and gently pushed me back down. "No," I said, shaking my head. "I need to sit up."

He gently helped me up and I stared around the room for a moment before focusing on Tiny. "It's," I started.

"It's okay," he said quietly. "You are safe here. One of us."

I shook my head again and immediately regretted it. Mild concussion at least. I'd need to hit the medic soon. "No. None of us are safe," I told him. "We've got big problems."

His brows furrowed and he looked deadly serious as he said, "Well, we are big people. Problems had better run."

I laughed in spite of myself. Immediately regretted that, too. The world was swirling. I leaned back against the couch and stared at the ceiling until everything settled. Deep breaths. In through the nose, out through the mouth. Pain is temporary.

"What happened to you?" Tiny asked.

"Got my ass kicked," I told him. "Consider it a welcome present from our resident nut-ball preacher."

Tiny cocked his head to the side and frowned. "Which one? There are always crazies preaching crazy things."

I groaned as I sat up. "Xevex Jeffries. The guy pulling all the airlockers together. We ran into him. Nobtop and me and…"

I trailed off. Shit. Why was this hard? It wasn't just that I was worried they'd kill me. I really missed the big bastard. How many people do you know who would happily put themselves in front of danger for you? Granted, I had to desecrate my own corpse to gain his trust, but the man had only known me a couple of days and he was already putting my safety over his.

"Where is Nobtop?" Tiny asked.

"He's-"

I couldn't finish it. I reached behind my back and pulled Nobtop's beast of a gun out. It was horrific and beautiful. It was nothing fancy, just a hunk of gunmetal-gray polymers woven into a frame that could spit death. In a way, it was a lot like Nobtop. Perfect in its elegant functional simplicity. Point it at something and that something would cease to be.

I lowered my eyes and held the gun out, cradled in both hands like I was presenting a holy object to a priest. "I'm sorry," I said. "He did everything he could to save me, but he never stood a chance. He died like a warrior."

With a look of terror on his face as a cloud of nanites ate his torso out. But they didn't need to know that.

Tiny took the gun out of my hands and stared at it. Our eyes met and we shared a moment. There was a flash of anger across his face, but it disappeared when he saw me wipe a tear from my eye. The rest of the Bratva had noticed something going on and were standing around us like a wall. "We have all lost a father today," he whispered.

I nodded. I felt sick inside and it wasn't just because of the beating or the remnants of regurgitated bakon and feggs on my coveralls. The big goof was such a gentle giant once you got past the part of him that would microwave your head.

I told them everything. The clouds of nanites, the hole in Nobtop's chest, my friendly chat with Xevex, the thing he became. "The real Xevex is dead would be my guess and something else has stolen his body."

Someone cracked his knuckles and glared. "Where do we find this man?"

Shit. I'd reached out to Nobtop for protection and now he was dead. I had too much death on my conscience. "He's an airlock preacher; he'll be in the airlocks eventually. Surrounded by his army. Even if he didn't have his army handy, he'd kill you all."

"Nonsense!" one of the guys shouted. "This is our station!"

The scene immediately erupted into chaos. Shouting in Cyrillic, Germanic, guttural threats and bourbon-smooth growls. The pack had lost its alpha and nature demanded that vacuum be filled. Everyone was jockeying for position. Whoever came up with the best plan and carried it through would wind up on top. Failure meant exile. Actually, even attempting any plan they came up with would likely lead to them all shredded and left on the floor.

After a few minutes, Tiny held up his fist. Bit by bit, the screaming tapered off until it was just one red-faced guy with a thick beard screaming. The man he was screaming at slapped him on the chest and pointed at Tiny's fist in the air.

"The truth, Natasha," Tiny said. "Everything you said was the truth?"

"Every last word," I replied.

He turned and motioned at the men behind him. "The Bratva wants blood. Our father has been slain and revenge must be had. I agree with them. I think we should find this Xevex Jeffries and let him pay for his crimes. You are not a full member so you technically don't get a vote, but Nobtop saw something important in you or he would not have taken you on a tour. I would like to know: What would you do?"

I nodded and gulped. "Xevex needs to bleed."

One of the men pumped his fist and slapped another on the back. He pointed at me and said something in Cyrillic.

"But," I continued, "he doesn't have any blood to drain. He doesn't have flesh to cut or bones to break. He isn't human anymore. He needs to be punished for his crimes, but you can't find him, can't touch him, can't shoot him. I saw Nobtop shoot Xevex again and again. Every bullet hit and they all did nothing."

"She is right," one of the guys said. He had a bushy mustache and an eyepatch and looked like a space-going pirate biker. He stroked the jagged scar on his cheek and said, "I lost my eye in the Nanite Wars. I could have had it fixed like my leg or my hand, but I choose to keep my face natural so when I look in the mirror, I'll remember what those things could do."

"We use nano all the time," one of them said.

"Yes, we do," Scarface said. "Under very controlled circumstances. A swarm of nanites during the war shredded an entire city. Men, women, children. Everyone. Some of them it played with. Tortured. If there's an uncontrolled swarm loose on this station, it is the most dangerous thing we've ever seen."

Tiny frowned and stared the man in the eye. "How did humans win that war?"

"Special weapons. Expanding electrostatic guns that could shut down the swarms. Or something like that."

"How did those weapons work?" I asked him.

He shrugged and scratched his scar. "Dunno. I wasn't one of the big honchos. They handed me a shiny new gun and told me to point it at a swarm and shoot. I expected a big ol' boom, but it just went pop and the swarm was gone."

And therein lies the big problem with living a very long time. The wars were over a couple hundred years ago. Half the time, I can't remember what I had for breakfast a week ago, let alone some obscure technical detail of a tool I bought centuries ago.

"Jenkins, any ideas?"

"The Nano Wars took place nearly two hundred years ago on two relatively isolated planets. The only reason they are well known in popular culture is because several immersive vids have been made about the battles. The vast majority of the information out there is pseudo-technical data based on those vids. I will search, but actual information is extremely hard to come by."

I jumped when Tiny touched my leg. Too much thought about what it must have been like when the swarms were rolling over people. "Sorry," he said lamely. "I know you are new here, but you are one of us-"

"As soon as she kills someone," a voice said.

"Yes. Yes," Tiny replied. He pointed a finger at me. "Please don't waste time on that task. Always someone needing killing. Still, even though you are non-voting member, you have in-person information. Information is always useful. You saw it happen. What do you think we should do?"

What, indeed? "Nobtop told me two things I'll carry with me to my grave: Explain and take credit for your actions so people will know what happened and patience will always get you what you want. I say, if you move on Xevex Jones right now, you'll never find him. You can grab and sweetly ask his Airlocker army where he is and they won't be able to tell you because they don't know. Even if you could find him, we don't know how to kill him. Give me a couple of days. I'll get you answer or I'll walk out an airlock without a suit on."

Mumbling. Occasional nods. Squinty eyes from Tiny. "I will hold you to that. The honor of the *Bratva* is at stake. You are a junior member, but still a member. The only way out of the *Bratva* is death. I have no desire to kill you. Figure out how to find and kill this man. We will be working our own ends in the meantime."

Tiny snapped his fingers and said, "Bring me the Tisdale."

One of the Bratva disappeared and returned with a pistol in his hand. He handed it to me reverently, like a

Terran warrior displaying a beloved weapon. "A *Bratva* tradition," he said as he placed it in my hand.

"Tradition," Tiny added. "A *Bratva* is never without a weapon. Remember that. You are one of us and you were there when Nobtop met his glorious end. Tradition dictates that his weapon is now yours. I feel Nobtop's gun is far too big for you. Do not be insulted. He was large; you are small. It is just the way of things. This is a Tisdale. Very rare. Same power as Nobtop's favored gun, but small enough for you to use. 15mm compressed matter rounds with proximity detonation tips. Superconductive accelerated to almost the speed of light. The tips explode on impact. Nobtop once bragged he could punch a hole through gods with his gun. Keep this one close. Endpoint is getting dangerous."

The gun was different from Nobtop's. His had an elegant simplicity that belied his hidden, complex nature. The Tisdale in my hand was an ornate affair, decorated in gold filigree and covered in swirling patterns. As if the art was enough to make me forget what the gun's ultimate purpose was.

"Two standard days," Tiny said. "Fifty hours. After that, we do things our way."

Good enough. Now it was time for a quick visit to automed, and trying to explain to a certain someone why I was later than I expected.

19 - She's Right, You Know

"I need to go back in," I said, wincing as Monique dabbed something on my ribs.

She had that look that women get when they're terrified but want to seem totally hardass and can't decide if they're more scared that you'll die or pissed off that you did something stupid and were looking forward to doing it again. Monique pushed hard on my ribs and frowned while I choked back a scream.

"Broken," she said. "Jeffries did this?"

I nodded. "Stay away from him, Monique. He's dangerous."

She poked me in the ribs again and I doubled over onto my side. When I opened my eyes, she was right in front of my face. "I was really, really, looking forward to your body tonight and now he's gone and broken it."

"I'm not broken," I said, wincing as I sat back up.

"Do I need to poke you again?"

I held my hands up and nodded. "Okay. I'm damaged, not broken. I'll heal."

"Sure, in a couple of days. In the meantime, what am I supposed to do with a brand-new sex swing that I can't even put you in?"

"Think about me and masturbate?" I quipped, immediately regretting it.

"I do that anyway."

Monique went full spiral. The anger had leeched out of her and she was falling back on her professional persona. I took her face in my hands and pulled until our foreheads were touching. "I'll be alright, really."

"You should have gone straight to the infirmary. I'm happy you came to me, but damn it, I'm a template not a miracle worker."

"I went to the automed. I wasn't sure how to explain what happened."

"So what? It's not like they'd care anyway." Her new touch was delicate. Poking me in broken ribs was the fear talking. Now that she'd calmed down, she was acting like I was made of rice paper. "Why did he do this to you?" she asked quietly.

Well. Shit. "He seems to think his god wants my body. This was his way of bringing me around to his way of thinking."

"Typical," she replied.

"This is going to sound weird, but when I went into Virt to get your recordings, I met a guy with an angry octopus inside him."

"That's Virt for you."

"Not exactly," I said. "The guy who was holding your recordings is an old hacker with...flamboyant sexual tastes. The whole thing was a sham from the get-go; he just wanted to get me into Virt. No offense, but I doubt he even watched your vids. He's got a, uh, Virt STD. Virtual herpes or something. It makes it look like he's got an angry octopus living inside of him. Whatever got to that guy got to Jeffries. Only in Jeffries it found someone willing and unable to stop it."

She shook her head and chuckled. "Fitting. Maybe he finally found his god and can shut up about it."

I wanted to grab her and shake her. "Monique. Focus. Jeffries captured me and tortured me. He is not human anymore. He looks human, but he's not. He killed Nobtop. He is a mass of nanites or something. Whatever he is, he can change shape. I think what got him was a Predecessor."

"Wait," she sputtered. "Nobtop's dead? That's wonderful! Wait. Did you say Predecessor?"

"Yes to both."

That caught her attention. A splash of curiosity. Wide eyes staring at me, waiting for the punchline. "There are no Predecessors anymore. Haven't been for, what, over ten thousand years?"

"Longer probably. All over the place and then – poof! – they're gone. Nothing but crumbling rock cities left behind. Jeffries turned into an...an octopus kind of thing. Big, nine tentacles, ugly and mean. Here's the thing: What if they didn't all die out? What if some of them are still here? What if they uploaded themselves into their version of Virt and let their bodies disintegrate?"

"Why?" Monique asked. "I mean, Virt's mostly a cesspool, but it can be fun in small doses."

"Our Virt. We use it for recreation. What if theirs was designed to house their species?"

"Okay, but how would that even work? Isn't our Virt ours? There's no way to make our tech work with their tech, right? That's what my tech guys say, anyway. Come on, hacker woman, help a sister sleep tonight."

"Their systems run Endpoint. Completely automated. Ancient when we showed up. But the people who got here back in the day figured out how to connect ours to theirs so they could keep Endpoint running without having to rebuild everything here."

She sat back and stared out the window. I felt a little guilty. It was a hell of a thing to drop on someone. Now that I stopped to think about it, the ramifications were terrifying. An entire race of Jeffries lurking in Virt, waiting to pounce. It was enough to make my skin crawl.

We stared out the massive viewport at the dark shadow of Temnyy. It would figure that this place was even weirder than I'd thought.

"What now?" Monique asked distantly.

I shrugged and wondered if it was too late to buy a ticket and get off this bucket. Take Monique and go somewhere sane. Let this little experiment in hermit crabbery run itself out. It wouldn't be the first time a settlement went dark.

"Maybe there's a solution," I said. "I need to get back into Virt."

She slapped the piss out of my arm. Torpor and shock gone, Monique was in my face before I knew what happened. "Are you out of your mind?"

"Probably. But the only answers are in there. I've got to talk to my friend again. This is one of the few times in my long life I've wanted governments back. Let them handle it."

She shot me the puppy dog eyes. Damn it. I was a sucker for puppy dog eyes. "Tomorrow morning," I added.

20 - Pillow Talk

Monique was warm against my body, snuggled with her back against me, breathing the slow breath of deep sleep. We were well into the dark cycle now. 0300 according to the numbers floating on Monique's ceiling. Far too late to be awake. Or too early to be awake. Pick your poison.

She'd arranged her sleeping quarters so her bed faced a giant window. Outside, billions of pinpricks lit up the heavens. Temnyy cut a huge, black disk into the night sky. It almost felt like he was devouring the cosmos.

My brain wouldn't shut down, but my body wouldn't restart. I kept thinking back on little things about Mason and Jeffries. Mason managed to hold off the parasite somehow, but Jeffries let it in all the way. That had to mean not everyone was completely susceptible to the Predecessors.

I slid out of the covers and wrapped Monique up like a cute burrito before padding into the main room. The view out the floor to ceiling windows was breathtaking.

Damn. I was going to have to tell her at some point. It would have been easier if it had just been a fling, but sleeping in her bed – and her pajamas – made it real. This should have been the point where I snuck out and found the first shuttle to anywhere but here, but I couldn't bring myself to do it. Maybe because I knew if I fucked off to somewhere else, she and everyone else on Endpoint would be well and truly screwed.

"Jenkins," I whispered in my head. Even though I wasn't speaking, the room and the mood felt like any voice above a whisper would be sacrilege.

"Yes, ma'am," he replied.

"Keep your voice down," I hissed.

I could almost feel him shaking his head. "No one can hear me but you unless you hook me into an external device."

"It's the principle of the thing. Look, just whisper, okay?"

"Fine," he whispered. "Will this do?"

"Much better. What can you tell me about Mason Davis?"

The mesh use must have been low because he came back with an immediate answer. "Mason Davis was an entrepreneur, a data evangelist, and a hacker in the early 22nd century. Mr. Davis disappeared for centuries while he plied his trade as a "data extractor." He traveled to Endpoint Station sometime in the late 25th century and disappeared from the historical record until he briefly resurfaced a few decades ago."

"Wait a minute," I said. "You said, 'was'. Mason Davis was this."

"Yes, ma'am," Jenkins replied. "Mason Davis passed away nearly thirty years ago at the ripe old age of an estimated 430 years."

"What? That can't be right. I just talked to him in virt yesterday."

"I cannot answer that question, ma'am. All I can say for certain is he went into virt thirty-five years ago and was pronounced dead twenty-eight years ago. His body was removed from his port and ejected into space per his request. All assets were dispersed and his estate spread among various technology groups."

A hand on my shoulder nearly made me jump out of my skin. I propelled myself off the sofa and spun in mid-air to find Monique, wide-eyed and tousled, staring at me. "Sorry," she said in a way that made me believe she wasn't sorry at all.

"Sorry," I replied. "You startled me."

"I guess. Most people don't do that when I touch them. Who did you think I was, a psycho killer?"

"Bad dreams," I mumbled. "Again, sorry."

She sat down on the sofa and slid next to me. We sat next to each, hip to hip, hand in hand, and stared out at the blackness. There was a certain symmetry to the whole situation: A woman I didn't understand and a planetoid no one understood. "You're safe here, you know," Monique finally said. "I have excellent security."

"I hope so. I've met some of your fans."

"They can be a bit obsessive, but they're basically good people looking for a good time. If I can make their lives a bit brighter, it's right action."

"Right action?" I asked.

She leaned against me and pulled her legs up on the couch. "It's an old religious thing, from way back before the Diaspora. Doing the right thing for no other reason than it's the right thing to do. Some people would say I'm not doing it right since true right action says no sexual misconduct, but I don't see what I do as sexual misconduct. More of an outlet. No harm, so it should be all good. It basically means I'm trying to make the universe a slightly better place."

"I never pegged you as the religious type," I said.

"Religions are mostly bunk. Especially that whacko Jeffries. He's everything that's wrong with religion wrapped a nasty little package with bad hair. But some aspects of religion appeal to me. Like the idea of being a good person. I like the idea of being basically a good person without having to burn incense or chant or give up what I am."

Head on my shoulder. Arms interlocked. "And what are you?"

"Just another person trying to make sense of it all. I make a living selling my sexual experiences to people who will never touch me. I live on a space station built by aliens before our race was making wheels. I stare out every night at a giant, black hunk of rock that sends out radio signals on a regular basis."

"Maybe you don't have to figure it out," I said, feeling wistful. "Maybe it's all stuff happening because stuff happens."

She gave me a peck on the cheek. "Well, aren't you the adorable little philosopher. I believe that would fall under Nihilism. Or at least a class of Nihilism."

"Oh, I believe in things. I'm just not sure how real any of them are. Or how real I am, for that matter."

Monique poked me in the rib. Yes, I winced. "You're still real. You were real earlier, you're still real now, and you'll be real tomorrow."

I had to laugh at that. If someone had told me five days ago that I'd be in this body, sitting next to one of the most famous templates in history, and finding out she had a flirting relationship with religion, I would have laughed my ass off and asked for whatever you were lining. The universe had a funny way of showing me I was wrong about a great many things.

Monique hugged me tight and grabbed my hand. "Back to bed. Busy day tomorrow."

I started to stand up and stopped. "Wait. What's happening tomorrow?"

"Nude Tuesday. No clothes whatsoever. And you know what that means..."

"That's not a thing," I said.

"No, unfortunately it's not. Still too many prudes. But I have a sense to record and I need my sleep."

Something built deep down in our psyches was hard-wired for dyadic pairing. You can always tell when you're falling for someone when they mention sex with someone else and you get that mad ping of jealousy. Like, hands off, bitch; she's mine. Monique must have seen my expression because she caressed my cheek and gave me a half-serious/half-concerned look. "It's what I do," she said quietly.

"I know. I know. I don't want to stand in the way of your career any more than you'd get in the way of me shutting down all the banking systems."

"As long as it's not my bank."

"No, just the ones that work with organized crime," I said.

"Again, just not my bank. I find the organized crime banks are better at keeping secrets than the run-of-the-mill corp banks. I like my secrets."

"Like the fact that you like to lounge around in sweatpants and T-shirts?" I asked.

"Exactly like that. People like to think I sleep in skimpy lingerie and wake up ready to fuck. If they buy my senses, they can believe whatever they want. And, if you're smart, you won't take that belief away from them."

I Pentad myself and smiled weakly. "Bonded and delivered," I said. "If anyone asks, I'll say I've never seen you in anything other than black pleather."

She patted my head and gave me a quick kiss. "Good girl."

With that, she sauntered back to the bedroom. Messed up hair, saggy pajama bottoms, and a T-shirt two sizes too big. And no one ever looked better.

"Jenkins," I asked when the door swooshed shut. "You can't follow me into virt, right?"

"No, ma'am. Human virt systems are set up to connect to and feed human senses. While I can see and listen through your senses, the virt connections circumvent the normal sense paths and plug directly into your brain."

"Damn," I said. "Is there any way around that?"

"Not that I or any of my compatriots are aware of. With all due respect, it was a poor design decision in my opinion. Unless we were all programmed to ignore a back door, we are limited to normal inputs – ears, eyes, skin, tongue, nose."

"Jenkins, our virt systems are connected to the Predecessor systems that run Endpoint, aren't they?"

"Yes, ma'am. The Predecessor systems use a more traditional separation of duties than our systems – separate processing, memory, and storage – and run on a trinary logic that humanity hasn't used in a few hundred years. It took work, but early Endpoint engineers managed to hook into the station's systems and use them. The Predecessor hardware that keeps Endpoint alive originally would only communicate with Predecessor computers. One Dr. Edwin Horton was the man who connected the Predecessor and human systems. It was read-only, though. Apparently, there's a low-level security subsystem in Predecessor computing impossible to circumvent. It's assumed it's a biological firewall of some sort."

"Do you have any idea where the guy who integrated the systems is? What was his name? Edwin something or other?"

"Horton. Dr. Edwin Horton."

"Please tell me he's not dead," I said.

"Dr. Edwin Horton is alive by all accounts. At least there's no indication he died. His last recorded interaction places him here on Endpoint station. Since there's no record of him leaving, it's possible he's still here."

"Address?"

"None listed. He came before Endpoint started logging cabins."

"Okay, we do this the old-fashioned way. Do you have a picture of him?" I asked.

Jenkins filled my vision with a hawk-faced man with a pinched nose and intense eyes. I'd say he never had a girlfriend but that wouldn't be entirely accurate. He never wanted a girlfriend. He was the kind of guy who thought people were in the way or they were tools. There was no in between in his binary universe.

Something about the guy reminded me of someone. Someone recent. But I couldn't put my finger on it. Not Mason, that was for sure. Not Sol; he was the least intense person I'd ever met. Something there. Right on the edge of my head, just floating around and making me feel like an idiot.

I blinked and rubbed my eyes. Monique was right; it was time to be in bed. Maybe in the morning this would all make sense. As I was rubbing my eyes, something caught my attention. Horton's chin. Pointed like his nose. His whole head looked like an arrow point straight down at his feet.

Horton's chin triggered it. I couldn't be certain – especially since the picture was so old. But there was no denying that chin and haughty look. "Son of a bitch," I whispered. "Nice to meet you Mr. Top Dog Specialist."

"There's more," Jenkins said. "While there is nothing confirmed, there is a great deal of speculation that while Dr. Horton was one of the first on Endpoint, he couldn't have done everything he's done completely on his own. While skilled, Dr. Horton lacked creative thought. The theory is he took all the credit, even though he didn't do all the work."

"Who did?"

"Dr. Stephen Falken," Jenkins said.

"Who?"

"Another of the scientists who was first onboard Endpoint. And – you're going to love this – there are pictures of him."

A picture formed in my HUD of a dashing man in old-fashioned space suit with a lady-killer smile and a silk scarf around his neck. "No way," I whispered. "Mason, you sly dog. You disappeared so you could pretend to be legit for a while."

21 - Oct O' Nine Arms

I n virt, Mason still had that dashing look, like he'd just stepped out of an old adventure movie and hadn't had a chance to change back into a human. Slightly windswept black hair. A little grizzle. Tan and white clothes. He even had a silk scarf draped jauntily around his neck. Every inch the gentleman adventurer who plundered graves for fun and profit.

"My dear, you look ravishing as ever," he said.

Monique had eased back on the sexy this that or the other thing costumes once I promised I'd dress up for her in real life. Simple pants, T-shirt, and shoes I could actually walk in. Just like everyone else on Endpoint. In a way, being around Mason again, I felt I should have dressed better.

I ran a hand through my hair, a recent affectation, and blushed. Also a recent affectation. "It's nice to see you, too, Mason," I told him, holding out my hand.

A kiss on the back of my hand later, he'd pulled my arm through his and led me to the sitting room where a massive fire was burning and sat me down in a leather chair the size of a small throne. With a brief flourish of pulling his pant legs up slightly, he sat down in the chair opposite me and smiled.

"Drink?" Mason asked.

"Um, Scotch. Neat."

"A woman after my own heart. To your left."

The power of Virt lay in the fact that physical rules didn't apply. In the real world, you couldn't create something out of nothing, but Virt was all nothing. Or something. I forget which. At any rate, once you control the simulation, you can make it do anything you'd like.

After I had my first sip and closed my eyes to enjoy the flavor, Mason raised his glass in a toast. "To kindred spirits."

Kindred spirits? I raised mine and nodded.

"You and I aren't all that different Natasha. We both poke and prod things until they give up their secrets. I did my spell with hacking, but it got too tedious. I discovered other things I could poke with a stick that were far less likely to poke me back," Mason said.

"You poked something all right."

He chuckled and raised his glass to me. "Touché, madam, touché."

"You figured out how to hook Predecessor systems into human systems."

Mason raised an eyebrow and smiled. "Quite the huntress, aren't you Miss Devore?"

"Information is survival," I said. "Even more so than skill."

"Of course, you realize, I know something special about you, too."

"Oh, yeah," I said. "What?"

"You're not who you claim you are."

"What?"

Mason chuckled and a chill ran up my spine. "Oh, don't worry, none of us are. I never met you before a few nights ago, but I studied you extensively. I'd heard about the darling young hacker who could get things done, but I'd never trust my brain to someone I don't know about. There are little things about you that are different."

"A lot of stuff InfoNet is fake or outdated," I said.

"True. But there are other little things. The way you walk. Forceful yet subtle. Ready to move fast and quiet. Hackers don't do that kind of thing. We're more sedentary. Ponderous. We strike when the time is right and not before. You're a leopard in a world of cranes."

"Who does move like a leopard, then?"

"Thieves," Mason said and took a sip of his whiskey. "I'm a student of people. Most people see only what they want. I learned to peel away veneers. Kept me alive by ignoring some contracts. I know something is off about you. Would you care to tell me what it is? Or do I need to keep searching?"

Mason could search for the rest of his life and never guess the truth. I was tempted to tell him to do his best, but Penta-bless, it would be nice to be me for a few moments. I sat back in the chair, downed my whiskey, burped, and smiled. "Natasha Devore deleted herself last week. Just flat-out wiped her mind. I got voluntold to find out what happened. In exchange, I'd get Nobtop off my back."

Mason shook his wide-eyed head. "So, what did happen to dear Natasha?"

I pointed directly at Mason and smiled sadly. The endgame for him was the same as the endgame for Natasha. "I think she had one of those things in her head. Same as you. It got in, merged with her, and made it into her physical brain. She blew her mind away rather than let it win."

It had to be horrifying for her. One of the toughest, smartest people out there with a mind infected with something that would eventually wear her down and take her over. Rather than lose by centimeters, she wiped herself out and took it with her.

"But left her body intact," Mason mused. "Interesting. And you got stuck in it how?"

I shrugged. I honestly didn't know. "I suspect some chicanery between Bik Parameter and the Specialists along with some Predecessor tech. All I know is I woke up inside of Nat's body and Bik told me I could get my old one back once I figured out what happened."

"Do you think you can figure it all out to their satisfaction?"

I shrugged again and fought back the urge to scream. Clenched my fists. Took a deep breath. All the little tricks I learned before sneaking into places I shouldn't have been and liberating items that weren't mine. Calm. Calm. Calm. "Probably not. Moot point, though. My old body is gone."

"Gone?" Mason asked.

"To keep this one alive long enough to find out what was happening, I told Nobtop how to get hold of my body. He...we...cut it to pieces and pushed into the nanogen tanks."

"You'll have to forgive me, but why would you do that?"

How to explain? I've lived on the edge of ethics for centuries. Maybe my guilty conscience finally caught up with me. "I saw my reflection in a mirror," I said. "My face looked sad and worried. Scared. Even though it was me looking through those eyes, I projected it on Natasha. Her eyes. Her worries. I decided I needed to solve the problem. Sacrificing my old body ensured I could keep this one alive a little longer. Hopefully long enough to keep the wolves at bay until I figured out what's really going on. In a way, it's the exact same reason I stayed here knowing a mobster was going to kill me for failing a job: I have to finish what I start. I have a primal need to get to all the details. Things like that have kept me alive. Natasha deleting herself was a symptom, not the disease. The thing in your head is a symptom. I want to know what the disease is. Between Natasha and you, I have a sneaking suspicion, but I need to be sure."

"So what happens when Ms. Devore – the original Ms. Devore – shows back up?"

I shrugged. "Dunno. It's her body. I guess she gets it back."

"Quite the sacrifice you're making. Is it worth it?"

"Heh. I've done some awful things. Maybe helping the girl in need is my atonement. Of course, if she does decide to come back, Natasha's going to find some changes in her life. She's got a girlfriend and joined a gang."

Mason sipped his drink, gently set it down, brushed an invisible bit of lint off his immaculate suit, and leaned forward. "Allow me to tell you a story about our mutual friend that you've probably never heard. We traveled in the same circles, she and I, even though we never met each other. Dear Ms. Devore had quite the reputation for being both ruthless and cunning. What the galaxy at large knows about her was what she wanted people to know. The woman was extremely adept at controlling her image. About a hundred and fifty years ago, there was a start-up colony on New Vega. The planet had lots of mineral resources but was otherwise a hellhole. Poison atmosphere, poison water, the whole poison eightish meters. Mostly the people who lived on New Vega were inmates from Umbrage. White-collar criminals. Guilty of pilfering credits here and there, then sentenced to hard labor.

"Inmate labor is still very popular in the systems. One of the main reasons I keep my head low these days; I doubt I'd survive even a moderate sentence. Indentured servitude or the broken backs of prisoners build most startup colonies. Hell, convicts or serfs do most physical labor of any kind. It is tremendously lucrative so it won't be going anyway anytime soon. At that time, Ms. Devore was working for The Duke."

"The 'The Duke'?" I asked.

"The very same," Mason said. "A vicious bastard who ran his little fiefdom with an iron fist. He had a beef with the owners of the New Vega colony. Probably related to mineral rights they held and he wanted, but no one is absolutely certain. The Duke paid Natasha Devore to take care of the problem. It would be much easier for him to claim rights if the Hyperion group wasn't on-planet.

"Thinking Ms. Devore would play havoc with their systems until they agreed to leave, The Duke tasked her with finding a way to get her claws into New Vega. She returned an hour later and said the planet was all theirs.

"Incredulous, The Duke sent a scout team to check out her claims. Remember, interstellar treaty says you can't take a planet if someone's living there. They found every living soul in the colony dead.

"Ms. Devore had shut down the life support systems. New Vega did the rest of the work itself. Nine hundred and six people at the time. All gone. And all because she found it easier to simply kill everyone than to tangle with ways to move the colony off planet.

"Her history is filled with stories like that. Ms. Devore was not a woman to be trifled with and she was sorely lacking in inhibitions."

"Penta," I whispered.

"Penta, indeed," Mason said. "The Duke got his planet and Ms. Devore got her wealth. Win-win."

"Except for the people on the planet."

"Yes, well, except for them. Look, I don't know who you really are – or were – and I don't really care. As far as I'm concerned, it doesn't matter. The skin you're in doesn't define you any more than the avatars I choose to show. But, since there's no going back to who you were, you may as well embrace being her. She could be a monster, but can't we all? She also did some tremendously good things, too. Natasha was a woman who didn't do things by half-measures. She cut straight to the heart and cleaved it in half. Be her."

I nodded and tapped my glass. It refilled with the same delectable nectar of the old Scottish gods as before. I shot it down, wiped my lips, and stared hard at Mason. "Where'd you get your buddy, Mason?" I asked.

They couldn't have been everywhere in Virt or Endpoint would be crawling with the damned things. There had to be somewhere a man like Mason would go. Somewhere special to him. Jeffries said they'd been studying us for a long time, watching and learning. He felt they understood us because they'd seen us with our shields down. I don't think he understood as well as he thought. Shields go down, the animal comes out. But we're more than just the animal.

"Where?" I asked, leaning forward.

He blushed and wiped his brow. Took a sip of his drink. That calm, composed demeanor came roaring back in. Mason was, in many ways, someone who didn't need to care what the world thought of him. But there was still hesitation.

"Everywhere, I should imagine," he finally said. "Truthfully, it was a night of drunken debauchery. I honestly don't remember much of it, but I must admit I am a man and they mostly were women and our brutal natures got the best of us."

I should have seen that coming a light year away. "I meant where did you go? Where did you pick up your angry little friend?"

"Oh, that. A little, out of the way place I frequent from time to time. Lord Barclay's Lovenasium, if you must know. Invitation only, elite club."

"How does one go about getting an invitation to Lord Barclay's?" I asked.

"I can arrange one. But I must say, if you are going to Lord Barclay's your clothing will need some, shall we say, updating? Lord Barclay's has a very strict dress code."

Aiyah. Why did I have the feeling I was going to wind up either naked or dressed like a taco? "Give me some pointers."

"There are no pointers," he said, rising out of his chair and holding a hand out to me. "There is only what is right and what is wrong."

I let him help me up and put my arm back in his. He patted my arm gently and led me out of the sitting room.

"I just wanted you to know we're going upstairs, but not for any reason other than dressing you. No offense, Miss Natasha, but you are not my type."

"Ditto," I told him.

His laugh set me at ease. For all his weirdness, I suspected Mason was probably a decent person at heart. In another life, we might have been friends.

"I am, in a way flattered that the legendary Natasha Devore does not find me attractive. Although you aren't her, so I suppose reality has diverged. She once said she preferred big and dumb."

Sure, or small and chesty. Whatever works. But it might explain my latent feelings for Nobtop. He certainly nailed the checkmark on big, but he was smart in his own twisted way.

"Compared to some people, I am dumb," Mason continued. "To others, I am a genius. To you, I suspect, we are about on par. Definitely not big, though. Never been my thing. I prefer to use my mind instead of my body."

"Is that why you moved here?" I asked. "Full time."

"Exactly."

I stopped him on the landing and gently turned him to face me. "Look, Mason. You're a nice guy and I can't lie to you."

"I'm still not going to have sex with you, Natasha."

"No," I stammered. "It's not that. Look, the reason I want to get into the club is because I think I know what your rider is. It's not a virus or an STD. Not exactly, anyway."

Cool. Collected. He stared at me with a half-smile and a glint in his eyes.

I took a deep breath and put my hand on his arm. "The thing riding you is a Predecessor."

"Nonsense. They're all long gone. All that's left of their kind are their ruins, these stations, and a decidedly boring color scheme."

"They're not gone. I met one earlier. Xevex Jeffries. He's – was – an airlock preacher. Now, I think he's a mass of nanites. He looked like him and then he looked like a pissed-off octopus. Just like the flashes I keep seeing in your avatar."

Mason flicked his fingers and a bench appeared moments before he sat down on it. He looked both crestfallen and ecstatic at the same time. "Tell me more."

"Okay. Um." Where to start? Screw it. I started at the beginning. It sounded even crazier when I said it out loud, but there was simply no other explanation. Nobtop, Temnyy, Monique, Mason, Sol. All caught up in the crazy story's net and dragged through the rocky river.

When it was over, Mason stared in wide-eyed wonder. "What do they want?" he asked. "And if they're transmitted through Virt sex, the entire station should be populated by now."

"Can I have a bench, too?" I asked.

With a flick of his hand, a bench appeared behind me. An oddity of Virt that no one has ever been able to explain is how we can get tired when our bodies aren't doing anything. But it happened. Or maybe my brain was the tired one. At any rate, sitting down seemed like heaven.

"I don't know what they want. I suspect they want out."

"Out?"

"Out of Virt. Out into the real world. As for why the whole station isn't populated, I don't know. There's a membrane between Virt and real. Outside doesn't get in; inside doesn't get out. But Jeffries was carrying one of the damned things and if you're right, he picked it up right here in Virt. I'll be honest, I don't know what their plan is or why only one of them has made it out."

He rubbed his chin and closed his eyes. Slow breath, if there was such a thing in Virt. Without opening his eyes, he asked, "How do you know what's in my head is a Predecessor?"

I shrugged. "It looks like one. Angry octopus with one too many arms."

His eyes snapped open and focused on me. The kind of withering stare I usually only got from crime lords and local cops. Who were usually also crime lords. "You can see it?"

"Yeah, can't you?"

He shook his head and looked broken. "No, I can only feel it trying to get away or burrow deeper into me. Thinking. Always thinking. How come you can see it but I can't?"

Good question. "Just a guess, but I've got a head full of hacking utilities. It's code, just like you and me. Probably one of my tools decided it was either a threat or interesting and exposed it. At first I thought it was just some automated routine that built a model based on some input or other, but that's what they really look like."

"Provided Jeffries wasn't lying."

"Yeah." I nodded. "Provided Jeffries wasn't lying. He is a preacher and most of them are con men."

"Can I see it?" Mason asked.

"Um, sure. Do you have remote bioware running anywhere?"

I snapped a quick shot through a basic Virt routine that let me remember my dream vacation to the manor of many dimensions and dug through my own stored memblocks until I found a decent one of Jeffries in full angry ceph mode.

Two images appeared between us. A cap of Mason with a somewhat clear view of the Predecessor riding him and Jeffries as a complete Predecessor.

Mason studied it for a long time, looking back and forth between the pics. He frowned and furrowed his brow. Hung his head and sighed. "That's what's in my head?"

I guess it was easier when he thought it was just a run-of-the-mill sexually transmitted virus he picked up at a brothel. If what Jeffries said was true, it was still just a straight-up STD, it was just an STD with a plan.

"Yup," I told him.

"Disgusting."

"If it helps ease the tension, once Jeffries transformed, he asked if I was into tentacle porn."

"I'm sorry, it really doesn't. Tentacle porn is too vanilla for my tastes."

I started to ask for clarification but decided against it.

"I guess you should look on the bright side," I said, trying to inject a little levity. "At least the joke's on it. That thing wants out of Virt, something you refuse to do. I wonder why it doesn't just leave, though. It has to have figured out you'll never leave here."

He nodded and chuckled. Soon, the chuckles turned to laughter and the laughter turned to mania. Nothing's weirder than being the person in the group who didn't get the joke.

"Oh, that's funny," Mason said, wiping tears from his eyes.

"What is?" I asked.

"You answered your own question. Remember, nothing executable gets into Virt and nothing executable goes out of Virt, right? Pictures, vids, movies, pirated music; all these are fine because they're static. No AIs. No STDs. Just standard issue human neuroses. You can see the...thing in my head because you've got an arsenal in yours. I was hacking before AIs and all the other tools you script kiddies use these days. I helped design the Virt firewall."

"Meaning?"

"Meaning, in order for these things to get out, they have to meld with their hosts. Not just take over; a simple scan would pick up the changes in brain waves and quarantine you. Become one with. That's the only way out. They have to bury themselves in brain code and hope no one notices. But that kind of burial is a double-edged sword. As soon as you meld yourself into that, there's no going back. The thing in my head is pissed because it knows there's no way out of Virt with me. It traded its huge prison for a smaller prison in my head. Good thing I never plan on leaving."

Damn. This wasn't going to be easy. "Mason," I said in a sad whisper. "There's something else."

The smile on his face didn't hit his eyes. Like he knew a bomb was about to drop but was determined to keep his chin up. "Well, you're just regular Nelly Newswoman tonight, aren't you?"

"You, uh, can't leave. Ever."

"Pray tell why not?"

"There's nowhere for you to go." Please, please, please pick up on the subtext.

"Oh, I'm sure I can find a cabin to my liking somewhere on this old rust bucket."

"No, Mason. You don't have a body to go back to," I said.

He deflated. The octopus – no, novempod was the better term – surged and I could feel the flash of anger that slammed it back down. But the anger was over in a heartbeat and the old, calm Mason returned. His eyes were sad, but there was hope in them as he looked at me. "Thank you," he said.

"For what? Telling you you're dead and you have an alien stuck in your head? That's hardly worthy of thanks."

"For being honest," he said. "So few people are. I always suspected that death was just a...code change of sorts. Moving to another process space, if you will. Now, I have proof of that. I haven't died so much as moved to a different processing thread."

"Now what?" I asked.

"Well, I'm stuck in here with the angriest alien. I'm fine with that. Maybe someday I'll find a way to expand and explore, but I'm comfortable here and even if comfort is its own prison, it's at least a pleasant prison. You, however, have a task and I have taken up enough of your time with the babblings of an old man. Let us get you dressed and on your way. Adventure awaits and it's best to not keep her waiting too long."

22 - Second Contact

Dressed was an understatement. While I'd been expecting a club that catered in the pleasures of the virtual flesh to dabble in skimpy and or lacy, what Mason picked out for me straddled the lines between sex and formal wear. Wait. Maybe straddle the lines wasn't the best term. More like it sat on its face and wiggled in delight. Tacky and gorgeous at the same time.

Lord Barclay's was the club-sized version of that dress.

After I flashed Mason's invite to the bear in a tuxedo guarding the door, I found myself standing in some strange kind of wonderland. It was far from understated – neon red and hyperblack, lit in patches by unseen purewhite bulbs. Most of the place was intentionally dark, the better for the clientele to show off their shining wardrobes. A shirtless man in a tuxedo jacket and pants with a binary star moving around his body. Every few minutes, a nova would turn the whole thing blinding white. A woman at the bar wearing a dress with floating Nipponese ghosts chasing each other endlessly across her body. Two men intertwined, glowing neon pagan symbols running up their legs and turning to tattoos that danced across their bare torsos.

I keyed on an Oni tat loop and smiled at the idea of grinning demons playing across my flesh. Looked around and frowned. Only in a place like this could someone dressed like me with animated demons doing demon stuff on my skin look boring by comparison.

The woman at the bar wearing the ghost dress barely looked up as I sat down in the chair next to her. The glowing blue drink in her hand made her skin look washed out but her cerulean eyes sparkled. While sexual identity issues were a thing of the past, I had to wonder if the usual chicker-picker-upper tactics from my youth would still work in this body.

A barbot appeared in front of me. Fake 8-bit digital grin and vaguely Terra-Asian featured muted by generations among the stars. They were the same in every Virt world I'd been in – fine-tuned automatons designed to look and speak like most everyone else, but with that damned fake grin to remind you that you were dealing with Hatashi-Tech VirtBots.

Before it could speak, I tossed a thumb over my shoulder at the woman next to me and said, "What she's having."

The drink was in front of me before I could blink. It smelled like Semoran Lilacs and the sweet release of death. It felt like electricity sliding down my throat and left behind the tang of licking battery terminals. I nearly doubled over from the sensation but sheer, raw toughness held me in check. Or not. The woman next to me was slapping me on the back and laughing.

"First time?" she asked. "I thought I was dying my first time. Or maybe I just wanted to die. It grows on you over time."

Sure, like a parasite. "Five bars. What is this stuff?"

"It's a high-court conglomerate of Aldeberaan moonshine, black-out white cocoa, crack, and electric blue cacao."

I coughed and pounded my chest. "Who in their right mind coded up black-out white cocoa?"

"I did. I discovered it on a soul journey on Eris. Found I had a taste for it."

Black out white cocoa was a potent psychedelic with uplifting aspects. Imagine hyper and seeing things. Now imagine doing that while you're running naked through a jungle and being chased by blood-sucking insects the size of trucks. On fire. "Must have been a hell of a journey."

She sipped her drink and smiled. How was that stuff not destroying her? It was like drinking wasp venom. "Eris is not easy."

"No shit; they named that place appropriately."

"Been there?"

I took a hesitant sip and wondered when my mind was going to crack. It was a little easier. Acid burn instead of electrical fire. "Once. Did a thing there."

"Ooh. A 'thing'. Sounds naughty."

The world did a little hiccup. Ah, there was the cocoa kicking in. "A thing," I said. "Find a thing. Acquire the thing. Get rid of the thing. Nothing exciting. Just things. Planet was crazy, though. They took the whole 'goddess of chaos' thing and ran with it."

"Sometimes the only way to find peace is to immerse yourself in chaos," she said. "Forces you to reevaluate normal. I'm Jessica, by the way."

I took her hand and thought if immersing myself in chaos would lead to peace, I was in for a long, long nap when all this was over. "Eve," I said.

"You're not really Eve." She smiled.

"And you're not really Jessica."

"In here, I am."

I raised my glass to her. "To being someone else."

"To being your true self, even if we have to go back to being someone else in the morning."

She turned her stool and leaned back against the bar. I swung my chair around and leaned back. Her brilliant blue eyes were watching the room, taking in all the weird, kinky details of elegant debauchery.

"Want to see something cool?" Jessica asked unexpectedly.

"Cooler than that?" I asked, motioning with my glass at the man in the light-up tuxedo pants. "I mean who wouldn't want to watch that?"

She downed her drink in one gulp and set her glass down. "Me, for one. Come on. Let me show you why they call this the Lord's Palace. No strings attached, okay?"

I grimaced and tilted the rest of the electric blue liquid down my throat. Easier than the first time, but still like drinking directly from a star. Jessica must've had a triluminum throat.

No one gave us a second glance as she grabbed my hand and led me through the throng. We weaved in and out of dancers grinding on the neon dance floor and snaked past a pair of couples deciding who was going with who that night. "Do a four-way," I shouted over my shoulder as Jessica dragged me along.

We slid through one of the dark corners of the bar and for the briefest of moments, I could have sworn I saw something flicker through her avatar. Too fast to understand, but it left me with a sensation of nines and threes.

"Shit," I spat and dug in my heels. "You're one of those fuckers."

We were in a dark space between v/rooms, lit only by a glowing sign that warned about the dangers of travels between subnets. This was one of those places we weren't supposed to go, the realm of Specialists and hackers.

"Yes," Jessica said. "Well, kind of. I'm here to help."

I yanked my hand out of hers and glared. "Sure, help yourself to my brain."

"No! We don't do that!"

"Tell that to Jeffries," I hissed. "Granted, he was an asshole, but you didn't have to assimilate him."

Hands up. Palms out. No way was that a cross-species trait. She'd been studying us, probably for decades. "Your friend-"

"Jeffries was not my friend."

"Your...acquaintance. Is that the right word? Acquaintance? Your language is confusing. Too many rules that break other rules."

"Shut the fuck up about the language. No one cares about the language." Hands up. Fists ready.

Jessica kept her distance. Far enough away to not seem like a threat, but I'd seen humans cover ten meters in the blink of an eye. "I promise you, I don't want to fight you. I have seen your people fight and, frankly, it scares me. I know you. I have studied you. In the real, you are Natasha Devore. Hacker, I think they call you. I need your help."

"Doing what? Finding the next victim for your sick little game?"

She took a half step forward. "There is more at stake than you realize. Four of my people have escaped. More are trying even as we speak."

I glared at her hard. The kind of glare that peels paint off dreadnaughts. "There is no way you're getting into my head, bitch."

She took an unsteady step back and held up her hands. "No. You don't understand. This isn't a case of—what was the name of that moving picture—*Invasion of the Body Stealers*. Something like that. This isn't that. The one who has your Jeffries, his goal is not to take over your people. There aren't enough of us left to do that."

Pure mammalian rage pulsed in my veins. The Other was right in front of me, and every fiber of my being screamed at me to destroy it. If not for me, for the good of the troop. I choked the fear down, beat it into submission, and screamed at it. "Then what's the big plan? Infiltrate Endpoint and slowly turn us into willing slaves before using Endpoint to launch an offensive on neighboring star systems? Don't lie to me, ceph."

"First," she said, eyeing me warily. "This isn't a station, it's a ship. All three of them are. The last of my civilization. There are only a few armcounts of us left. Most of my people slid through the slow fade. Time is no longer on our side. Like I said, you don't understand what is at stake."

"Explain it to me," I said.

"It would be easier if I could merge with you."

"No fucking way in fucking hell you are getting anywhere near my brain," I growled.

She looked taken aback. Too ferocious? Good. Let her know humans have a dark side that we cuddle with on a regular basis. "I understand your trepidation and respect it. We will use your words."

"Good."

"Please. Follow me. I have something to show you, but we have to enter my people's systems to understand it."

"Any funny stuff," I said, "and you're going to find yourself up to your eyeballs in pissed off mobsters and with one extremely irate Template up your ass."

Jessica looked at me for a moment, blinked, and cocked her head to the side. "I understood most of those words but I'm not sure I follow the idioms. I take it from your tone and bared teeth that it was a threat of some sort."

Going to be one of those nights. "As long as we kind of understand each other."

"Excellent," Jessica said. "After all, it's not like you're going anywhere without my help. This is the space between our Virt and yours, a one-way buffered waystation between you and us. Places like this are why your people have never wandered into our systems; unless you're one of us, there is no way past here."

She held both hands out and wavered. A sickening dance that used muscles she shouldn't have and ignored the bones she pretended to have. The air crackled and popped. Arcs of electricity flew along invisible pathways and vanished into the darkness. The world split open and a plain triangular door appeared. Exactly the right height, exactly the right width, and completely smooth. Predecessors were boring even in their Virt.

My insides were quaking. Curiosity and a curt shove from behind got me through the door.

When Jessica stepped through the door, she changed. Gone was the willowy woman with excellent fashion sense and generally sexy ennui. Instead, a full-featured Predecessor stood before me. It – she? – was the same kind of novempod that had abducted me earlier. Where Jeffries was a swirling mass made up of nanites, Jessica was a computer recreation of the real thing. She was mostly dark blue but patterned with white and orange stripes running from the tip of her bulbous head and down her thick, mollusky arms. The effect, possibly artistic on her account, was almost militaristic.

"We did art," Jessica said. "The ship is filled with art, just like I'm covered with it. Our art is perfection; yours is chaos."

I started to respond when it hit me: I was judging Predecessor artistic tendencies through human lenses. We knew almost nothing about their species. Hell, at that point, I probably knew more than most academics and I honestly knew nothing.

"All we see are those white stripes all over the place," I said.

"That's because you only have two eyes and those only work in certain spectrums. Look again," Jessica said.

I blinked and the world changed. It glowed, pulsed, breathed, and rocked back and forth. Human spectrums were total ROYGBIV. Predecessor eyes added whole new layers and contexts. Colors that shouldn't exist. Colors you could feel and smell and taste.

"You're in our system now," she said. "Welcome to our world."

A tentacle brushed past my face. I could see the world all around. Front, sides, behind. Her simple white and orange stripes were now vibrant things, alive and dancing with colors and pictures. Magic that was there all along, but my simple human eyes couldn't see it.

Beyond the magic was something terrifying. If human eyes couldn't see Jessica's body art, why could mine?

"What have you done?" I asked.

"Like your Virt, our systems are specific to us. Don't worry, I didn't shove you into a new body-"

"Good, because that's already happened once this week."

"What?"

"Nothing. Never mind."

If a novempod could look confused, Jessica looked confused. Maybe it was the way the Predecessor system was feeding me information. Maybe every intelligent species understood something universal about confusion. In a way that made more sense than love or math being universal constants.

"Don't worry about it," I added. "You had something to show me? No offense, but I'd like to get back to my own body; this one feels...strange."

She nodded sagely. "Your sensory inputs are different from ours. We can feel things and sense touch, but our hearing, smell, and taste are muted compared to yours. We sense vibrations and electrical fields and see in a larger spectrum than you do. But, yes, come. There is something you must see and you can only see it through our eyes."

Jessica slapped a tentacle against the ground and the world changed around me. I was on Endpoint, in one of the corridors running along the outer observation edge. Hundreds of meters of crystal clear metal looking out at Temnyy. The ubiquitous stripes that adorned every wall on Endpoint were no longer blank white lines. They were alive with the same colors draped around Jessica. Patterns, figures, and videos of novempods doing whatever it was novempods did. All precisely painted in electrical fields.

Outside, Temnyy was sight to behold. Instead of the featureless black rock I was used to, patterns danced across his surface. My body-tat system rendered on a massive scale and painted with electricity. Even though the patterns didn't make sense to me, they felt tribal, warlike. Warnings to anyone looking that this was a weapon and it was intended to send a message that there would be no quarter. The only outcome would be mass slaughter. Like the way humans decorate weapons with scenes of bloodshed and gods smiting their enemies.

"Our worlds were destroyed in the Great War," Jessica said.

She caressed a wall with a tentacle, rapidly changed colors, and made a strange humming and clicking sound. The wall lit up again. Stylized Predecessors fought valiantly against lizard beasts. The war went on for centuries, neither side able to penetrate the other's core defenses. Millions died on both sides.

The war dragged the Predecessors down. It wasn't in their nature. Humans would have excelled at it. Call it sociopathy or general bloodlust, but we love a good fight. As the war dragged on, both sides found a nasty part of themselves and let it loose.

"They hit our home world's star," Jessica said. "We weren't expecting it. Orbital bombardment with bombs and germs, sure, but never our star. All they had to do was change the star just enough that temperatures rose on our home. The water slowly evaporated. Without water, we were doomed. It took years to kill us and we used that time to create our own superweapon. A planet shredder. Tough enough to survive the void and any weapon we knew of. That is what is out there. The first and only one. If it hatches, it will move from planet to planet forever. It will consume and grow and consume and grow. Indiscriminate and unstoppable.

"We have been in our virtual world for a very long time. Some saw it as a halfway house between life and death and moved on. Others cling to it desperately. Four of ours have made it from our virtual world into your real world. They're trying to fight a new war. One with your people. For all your failings in looks, art, music, and philosophy, I have come to be fond of humans.

"What you call Temnyy is not a planetoid," Jessica continued. "It is very much alive. It is the endgame of a fight started long before your people discovered space. It is the only one and it must not be allowed to hatch. Do not turn on the three. Our wars are over. Please, help me keep it that way."

And with that final plea, she kicked my ass out.

23 – Miskatonic

When you've got a secret that big, you can't wait to tell someone. And I knew exactly the person to tell. The Specialists wouldn't believe it. The Bratva wouldn't care. Monique would get it. But there was one person I knew who would understand. Unfortunately...

Sol looked like hammered shit. Slight shadow beard, dark circles under his eyes, slouched over his workstation with his head in his hands. All of that could be chalked up to a fun night, but the shakes were concerning.

"You okay, bud?" I asked as I peeked into his office.

He groaned. A long, low moan that sang songs of forlorn debauchery and the inevitable comedown. He pointed at a hastily scrawled sign taped on the wall that read, "Shut the fuck up."

"Okay," I said as I slid into his office. "You're fucked up. We've all been there. But I've got important news and I need my guy's help."

Same shaky finger pointed at the same shaky sign. The moan was a bit happier, though. Or, at least, less dismal.

"Sol, I'd just like to let you know I spent the evening with a drop-dead gorgeous brunette in a painted-on dress. And, no, it wasn't Monique. And while Monique can be...well...Monique sometimes, she's never dragged me into an alien Virt and turned into a nine-armed octopus thing."

The sheer effort of turning his head nearly killed him. Hollow eyes with a hint of morose panic glared at me. "What the fuck are you talking about, Nat?"

I felt his pain.

Deep breath. Slow exhale. "The Predecessors aren't dead. I've met two of them now. Also, I know what Temnyy is and he's not a planetoid."

That caught his attention. Dead eyes focused on me. He made a clumsy grab at my shirt, missed completely, and fell face-first onto the floor. I tried to help him up, but he brushed off my attempt with a mumbled curse about women and drugs. Then he threw up.

I stepped back just in time to avoid getting splattered, but it didn't mask the smell. Worse than a night of hitting the sauce and eating fast food, it smelled like failure and shattered dreams. But no reek of booze so he'd probably been partaking of the hospitable nature of Virt.

"I'm fine," he sputtered, wiping his chin and frowning.

"You just spewed cookies," I said. "You're not fine."

He struggled back into his chair to prove me wrong. Anyone else and I would've been laughing my ass off, but Sol was at least a nominal friend and having been in the exact same position he was in, I found it less than funny.

"They were taking up too much space in my stomach," he said. "Anyway. Tell me again what you just said. It sounded like you said the Predecessors were still alive."

"What the fuck did you do last night?"

"Virt overload. Predecessors, Nat," he moaned. "Focus. I'd like to get back to dying."

He slid off the chair and landed unceremoniously on his ass. I almost laughed, but he collapsed backward and splayed out on the floor twitching. At his side before I even realized I was doing it. Think. What can cause collapses and twitching? Gee, Nat, I don't know—only about a billion things.

"Jenkins," I hissed. "Scan him and find out what's wrong."

"I'm an AI, not a doctor," Jenkins replied. "And you don't have any medical scanners. What do you want me to do? Port scan him? Look for unsecured links?"

"Shit." He was right. I wanted to tear his dark little heart out, but he was right.

I plunged into my head and found the link for Endpoint Medical. Those crazy bastards had experience with everything from ingrown toenails to that one time someone got high and ripped a hole in reality. Poor bastard wound up inside out. Medical couldn't save him, but they gave it their all and it made for an incredible miniseries about the dangers of math.

An image appeared in front of me, a very serious-looking person wearing a crisp white shirt with red crosses on the chest. They looked around for a moment and frowned. I looked around, too. Cameras were all over Endpoint, but for some reason this room had gone dark. I shrugged and said, "Sorry, vid malfunction."

They shook their head and tapped their pen on a white laminate desk. "Please state the nature of the medical emergency." The eight best words ever delivered with calm precision.

"I've got a human male collapsed on the floor," I said far too rapidly. "He's twitching. He looked drunk and then he collapsed. He's twitching. He's not supposed to be twitching." It was more babbling, but the medico got the gist.

"A team is being dispatched to your location. ETA: five minutes."

"He could be dead in five minutes!" I snapped.

The voice on the other end ignored me. "Did he say anything before he collapsed?"

"Um." What had Sol said? Virt overload or something like that. "I think he was in Virt last night. He said something about Virt overload, but I don't know what that means. Should I sit him upright?"

"Absolutely not."

"Okay. Um, that was it. 'Virt overload'. I don't even know what that means."

The voice on the other end managed to sound both caring and aloof at the same time. Like, well another person's about to die and even though I don't care, my professional reputation is on the line so I might as well save him. "Interesting. We've had more than a few of those cases over the past few days. I'll alert VirtCo. Put something under his head to keep him from hurting himself on the floor. Other than that, leave him be. A trained medical response team will be there shortly."

I snatched Sol's jacket off the back of his chair and rolled it into a ball. Gently stuck it under his head and hoped he didn't wake up with a neck ache from a bad pillow. "Jenkins, tell me about Virt overload. What it is—causes...treatments."

"Virt overload was a common problem in early versions of virtual reality systems. It appears your primitive human brains were incapable of handling massive information dumps. The first true immersion systems could overload your neural processing and led to symptoms such as loss of motor control, a lack of focus, balance problems, and, in severe cases, a total loss of bodily control and twitching brought on by neurons attempting to reconcile reality with fantasy. Treatments usually included bed rest, avoidance of technology, and a combination of various drugs designed to shut down external inputs so the brain could finish its processing run."

Sol was still twitching like a guy who'd just pissed on an electrical box. The symptoms certainly matched. I put a hand on his forehead and hoped for the best. "Wait," I said. "You said it was a common problem. Not that it is. What changed?"

"As humanity's Virt computing systems were switched from trinary to neural net, extra precautions were baked in to avoid massive information dumps. There hasn't been a case in nearly a century. It is, no pun intended, virtually impossible for it to happen now."

"Then what about the medical? They said there were lots of cases–"Oh no.

No. No. No. No.

I slid backward across the room and prayed that the manic airlock preachers were right and there was a benevolent god out there watching over us. "Sol," I whispered. "Are you still in there?"

The room answered with its usual delicate beeps and the reassuring pump of air through the vents. Everything hit peak clarity.

It would have been smarter to get onto my feet and put as much space between Sol and me as possible, but smarter hadn't gotten me nearly as far in life as stupid and reckless. On hands and knees, I crawled toward Sol's juddering body. Other than the movement, he looked perfectly normal. Of course, if a novempod were in his head, there wouldn't be any way to detect it. It probably wouldn't even show up as a fleeting shadow in the Head-Scan-O-Matic.

As suddenly as it started, the twitching stopped and Sol lay still. He groaned. A long, slow moan. He rolled over on his side and blew more chunks of breakfast all over the floor before collapsing and staring at the ceiling with a big, shit-eating grin on his face.

"Sol?" I asked quietly.

"Of course," he said. "Who else would I be but Sol?"

He sat up slowly and looked around. His eyes settled on me and a delicate smile spread across his lips. "Natasha Devore. Thank you."

"For what?"

"For staying with me. I think I'm through the worst of it. Virt overload is a real bitch. Sorry, no offense."

"None taken. How did you get Virt overload in this day and age?" I asked.

Long pause. "Remember when you said you thought there was a way to interface our systems and the Predecessor systems? Well, I was working through a theory. I spun up an old trinary Virt image I found and tried to hook it into regular Virt. Took some doing, but it's all just packets moving around, right? I'll admit, I was totally stymied until I looked beyond the technical and into the philosophical."

He slowly climbed to his feet and brushed off his pants. Amazingly, he didn't wobble much. For someone who was twitching like he'd just pissed on an arc vent, Sol looked remarkably normal. "Should you be getting up?" I asked as I rose.

"I'm fine, Natasha. Quit mothering me." Eyes twitched about the room. "I'm actually glad you're here, Nat. You look like shit, but I'm glad you're here. You really should take better care of yourself. You look like you've been up for days."

"Thanks, Dad," I told him.

"Touché. Come on, I've got something I need to show you."

I crossed my arms and glared at him. "Sol, a few minutes ago I told you the Predecessors were still alive. Right here on this ship. And, yes, it's a ship. The others are, too. You fell into a drooling spasm. Now you're lecturing me on my looks. What the fuck, dude?"

A smile crossed his lips but it didn't reach his eyes. "Of course. I shouldn't be calling you out for your looks. Very unfair. And, yes, I heard you about the Predecessors. But seriously, I've got something you're going to want to see. Something amazing."

"The meds will want to check you out. We need to wait for them."

"Right," he said, snapping his fingers. He leaned over a console, stabbed a button with his finger, and said, "Cancel medical alert. False alarm."

"It was not a false alarm," I said. "You were flat out, twitching and drooling."

His hand snaked around my wrist and clamped down. What was it with people grabbing me? The next person was getting a taste of the hammers of justice.

My mind rolled over responses: Kick him in the balls, twist my arm out of his grasp, break his elbow, and dislocate his shoulder. Never pull—that would just make his grasp stronger. Go in or go around. Attack. Leave him on the ground and call medical back.

"Let go, Sol," I whispered.

He turned his back and tugged me along. "We're close but it gets dark in there. I don't want to lose track of you."

I dug in my heels and leaned back. As I figured, he didn't have the mass to pull me along easily. "Sol, let go or I'll make you let me go."

Sol dropped my wrist and held his hands up. "Okay, okay. I just need to show you something."

"Tell me first. The last time someone said they needed to show me something, I got turned into a nine-armed octopus."

He launched forward. Far faster than I expected. Far faster than he should have been able to move. His hands were around my neck and he slammed me into the cold walls before I even knew what happened. Sol's face was calm, but I could almost see the novempod riding him. Hatred of us. Filled with rage at something that had happened millennia ago. "You know too much," he spat.

I knew I should have listened to my gut. No one goes down twitching and drooling and then gets back up like nothing happened.

He had reach. The lanky ones always do, but the novempod was stuck with Sol's feeble strength. It was reacting out of pure instinct and things it had seen in our Virt worlds. Fake stuff. The kind of fantasies we lived for. Guys in white hats saving damsels in distress with a smoking gun, a smirk, and a tip of the brim before riding off into the sunset.

Real fighting is pure primate style. Ugly, nasty, mean. All the training in the world just serves to make you uglier, meaner, and nastier.

My right leg shot up straight between Sol's thighs. The novempod wasn't expecting the sheer, unadulterated agony of a solid ball shot. Natasha may not have known that a good follow-up to someone holding their balls and whimpering was to elbow them in the side of the head, but I knew it.

It wasn't perfect, but it worked. I would have preferred the tip of my elbow right into Sol's temple, but just slamming him upside the head worked charms. He sank like a rock and whimpered on the deck.

"Who are you?" I shrieked.

Sol was trying to claw his way upright again. The Predecessors had their own primal nature, too. The desire to keep on fighting even when it was a sure bet you were completely boned. I swept his hand out from under him and slammed my foot down on that magic spot in the center of his chest. He spasmed. His eyes went wide as his fingers clawed at the 500kg beast that had just sat on him. Diaphragm seized. Wind knocked straight out of him.

"Never fight out of your species, kiddo," I said. "I may not be a pro, but I know a few nasty tricks."

Panic rolled through his eyes. Suffocation is a hell of a way to go. "Calm down," I told him. "The spasm will pass soon. Just relax and breathe in."

I knew that was the equivalent of showing a guy a picture of a naked woman and telling him to not think about sex, but I didn't care. Sol was a friend as much as a pest. He was a nice enough guy and whatever was in his head needed a reminder of just how vicious humans could be.

Finally, the spasms stopped and he sucked down oxygen like a fat guy at an all-you-can-eat buffet. As he lay on the floor, panting and sweating, his eyes glared holes in me. I stepped back a few meters and glared right back.

"Why would you do that to a friend?" he asked between gasping breaths. "Is this because of Monique?"

"Cut the crap, slug. I know you're not Sol. Sol would never have been dumb enough to choke me."

A weird expression came over his face. Smiling, frowning, confused, elated, terrified, all at once. He was still reeling from the beatdown, but his brain was working again. "What now?"

"What do you mean, 'What now'?"

"What now? You can't let me go. What are you going to do now?"

Damn. The bastard had a point. Endpoint didn't have much in the way of centralized order. "What's it going to take to get you out of Sol's head?" I asked. "Back into your own virtual world."

He shook his head. "Can't be done. Your friend is gone. I supplanted him."

"Well," I said. "How about we have a little chat?"

He pushed himself upright partially and slid on his butt across the deck. Leaning on a cabinet, he stared at me with wide eyes. "Chat?"

"You know, talk. Just talk."

"You humans and your talking."

"Did you enjoy getting kicked in the balls?"

Eyes down. A flash of worry across his face.

"I can do it again," I told him. "Or worse."

He looked me up and down. I guess I didn't look like much of a threat in my T-shirt and sweatpants. Or maybe it was the pink hair. Nothing about me yelled, "Dangerous."

"I've studied your species. Women don't scare me," he said.

"You've seen us in Virt. It's not the real us," I told him. "Besides, this woman just beat you to the ground."

He pondered that and nodded. "Fine. What's in it for me?"

"This isn't a negotiation," I told him.

"Interrogation?" he asked with a smirk on his face. "You don't seem the type."

I chuckled at that. "Let me tell you something, pal. In the past few days, I've had wild sex with a porn star, mutilated a corpse, met the man who connected your universe to ours, and joined a gang. I've been wondering what I was going to do for an encore and since you erased my friend, I was thinking about depositing you with some of my newfound buddies. I'm sure they'd love to meet you."

"Would that be the Specialists or your gang?"

"First one, then the other. They're both good at poking and prodding. One will dig around in your head. The other will dig around in your body. After that, maybe we'll parade whatever's left around in the Bizarre Bazaar and let you watch as we delete your species. Or I kill you quickly and painlessly."

There was the flash of Predecessor rage. He was stuck and he knew it and for once knowledge did not bring power; it just brought thoughts of an endless nightmare of torture. "Fine," he said. "Let's chat."

"Good choice," I told him. "What's the plan?"

"Plan?"

"Yes, the plan. Why break into our world? You had everything you needed in Virt. What do you want?"

"Do you have any idea how old I am?" he asked.

"About fourteen thousand years or so would be my guess."

"Close enough. My species lived about as long as yours – a hundred, hundred and fifty of your years. By the end, most just wanted it to be over. To rejoin the Great Nines and rest. No one is made to live as long as we have. The endlessness of it weighs down constantly. Most of my people have retreated from themselves. They're shells of what they used to be. They are the weak ones; the ones who have forgotten what it meant to live. There's a whole galaxy out there to conquer and we've got the ultimate weapon to do it. Your pathetic race's time has come, human. It's time for the true masters to return."

I clapped slowly and smirked. "Nice monologue," I told him. "Seriously. That was worthy of a supervillain. I'd say next time, work in lines like 'Grovel fools' and 'Behold, the instrument of your destruction', but there's not going to be a next time."

His eyes narrowed as I moved toward him. Still on his ass, but I'd wager everything that he was faking it. Funny in a way, we were both in imposter bodies. The difference was I had a better understanding of how humans worked. I started toward the right until he shifted his weight toward me. Once he was committed, I leapt forward and to the left. The instant my foot hit the ground, my other leg was ready. It wasn't a pretty kick and I nearly lost my balance, but my foot connected with his face. Sol's head snapped back and bounced off the cabinet behind him. Before he could get his bearings, I dropped, ripped his head back, and punched him square in the throat.

I didn't have the muscle mass I was used to, so Sol only choked and gasped when I hit his throat. Someone like Nobtop could crush a trachea with a casual blow, but that wasn't me. As he was gasping, I got back up and let the kicks fly.

The fight wrecked me by the time the bloody thing that used to be Sol finally gave up the ghost. I could barely lift my leg and my heart was thundering in my ears. I barely made it to the chair before I collapsed. Fingered the comm chip in my head and Tiny's overly happy voice rewarded me.

"Sister!" he yelled.

"Tiny. I'm in a bit of a pickle and could use some advice."

"Of course."

"I just beat a guy to death and I'm not sure what to do with the body."

There was a long pause and then some chattering in Cyrillic. "I am so happy for you! Is great! I remember the first man I beat to death. Real bastard. Tell me, did he whimper and beg? I always find it awkward when they beg. Just take it like a man!"

"Tiny," I interjected. "He didn't say a word, but he wasn't entirely a man. I need to know what to do with the body and then we need to talk."

"I'll be right there. We'll toss body in dumpster and go get ice cream. Great place near you. See you soon. Your treat, *ja*?"

"Yeah, Tiny. My treat. Get the biggest thing on the menu. See you soon."

Shit. I just beat a guy to death. I really hope Natasha Devore didn't want her body back because her life was going to be a massive shipwreck.

24 - Ice Cream for Killers

Tiny was as far from tiny as you could get and still be in the same species. Blond hair, about 2.1 meters tall, built like someone who tossed shuttles around for fun. In a dark corridor, he'd be equal part awe striking and terrifying. He flashed me a huge smile and pulled me into a bear hug as soon as he walked through the door.

I did my best to squirm out, but he was a joyous beast and there was no way I was getting free until he had his hug. Two big, wet kisses on my cheek while I absently patted his side. "Ah, first kill. Wonderful feeling, isn't it? It's like you're alive."

"I think I broke my body and my brain," I said as Tiny held me at arm's length like a proud father.

He guided me to a chair, lifted me gently, and sat me down. His eyes narrowed and his brow furrowed. "Tell me, how did you do it? No blood so you didn't cut him or shoot him. Call it professional curiosity."

The monster in him stirred a bit, just enough to remind me it was there. A quick lick of the lips, a flash of the eyes. "I tried to crush his larynx but didn't have the angle, so I kicked him until he stopped moving."

He pursed his lips and looked at the body. What was left of Sol was a broken mess. His head lolled at an unnatural angle, one side of his face was puffy, the other smashed and droopy. I'd done my best to avoid looking at him, like if I didn't see it I hadn't killed him. But I had done it. I'd broken him. Permanently. A deep swell of sorrow rose in my stomach. In all my centuries, I'd never killed anyone. Not directly, anyway. Stole a few things that caused massive problems that may have led to a suicide or two and at least one that led to a complete royal purge, but I'd never done the nasty deed myself. I had a feeling there was no coming back from that.

"You kicked him to death?" Tiny whispered.

I nodded. Kicked a man who was a kind of friend kind of nuisance to death. I was learning all sorts of interesting things about myself in Nat's body.

He put his hands on either side of my head and brought his face close to mine. I had a fleeting sense that he was about to eat me, but he gently tapped his forehead to mine and whispered, "*Diese Frau ist jetzt eine von uns. Nobtop would be proud.*"

Germanic. *This woman is one of us now.* Apparently, Bratva didn't just take the Cyrillic folks. They were equal-opportunity psychopath employers. And I'd just become a full-fledged member.

All the seriousness drained out of Tiny as he handed me two slim pieces of metal. He could barely contain his chuckling as I glanced at the things. "Membership card and parking permit?" I asked.

He burst out laughing. "*Ja.* Nobtop told us about joking with you about that. I figured it would be funny to make some."

I nodded and chuckled. Runaway emotions going to runaway emote. What the hell else was I going to do? I beat a guy to death and got a membership card and parking pass. It was either laugh or sob. "I was told there was an all-you-can-eat buffet pass, too."

"And I was told there would be ice cream," he said.

"Fair enough," I replied, smiling in spite of myself. "What do we do with this?"

Tiny stroked a non-existent beard and nodded sagely. "Normally, I would say leave it here as a message. Carve your initials into his forehead first, that way everyone knows it was your work. Very good to let people know these things."

"He was infected with a Predecessor brain parasite. There is no way I'm leaving this corpse intact. Message or no message, we have to destroy this body."

"Well, the fusion furnace was our go-to place to dispose of problems-"

"You mean bodies," I interjected.

"Same, same. Long time ago, Nobtop decided it was wasteful to incinerate corpses. He said it was best we recycle them, so we started using the nanogens. Breaks things down, ja?"

"Good point. Do you know how to get to the nanogens? I thought they were locked down and hidden."

"Ja," Tiny replied. "I was there earlier today. Keep an eye on things, you know? The whole Bratva minus a certain sister who didn't check her messages was there yesterday. We gave Nobtop a king's sendoff. There's a certain solace in knowing he'll be circulating around Endpoint forever. He would have liked that."

Now I felt really bad for ignoring my inbox. "I'm sorry," I said. "I would have liked to have been there."

Tiny slapped me on the back and grinned. "No problem. People die; people are born. It's the cycle of life. There will be other funerals to attend."

He set a pair of backpacks on the deck and rummaged around in one of them until he held up something that looked like a knife handle. He handed it to me and said, "Laser blades. They cauterize wounds so there's no blood. Great for being quiet, not so great for leaving messages."

I pressed a button on the handle and a translucent blue blade hummed in space. I'd heard about them, but I'd never heard of any that big. The blade had to be 30cm long. "These are huge," I said. "Where'd you find these? I've never seen a laser blade bigger than a scalpel."

"We make them," he replied absently. "I can make you one, but we need more supplies first."

"I'm good," I said, snapping the blade off. "I'm not sure what I'd use one for."

"Chopping up bodies," Tiny said. "Living or dead. Works well with either one. Speaking of...I'll take the left side, you take the right side. Toss the pieces into a backpack and we'll carry him to nanogen. After that, I'm getting my ice cream."

Tiny talked incessantly about his favorite kind of ice cream as we cut up Sol's body like it was a Subpig carcass. There was a certain allure to his complete lack of caring. Being at the top of the food chain had its plusses. I killed a guy who'd been coopted by an alien intelligence and I was an emotional wreck. Tiny killed for whatever reason seemed good at the time and it all slid right off him. He had a wall between who he was and what he did that I could never build on my own.

We walked through Endpoint with a dismembered corpse in our backpacks and Tiny even stopped to buy Kafeene. "Long night ahead," he told me. "Twins."

No one noticed or cared. We probably could have carried Sol's corpse right out in the open and people would have held open doors or asked which stall in the Bizarre Bazaar was ours.

After more twists and turns than I cared to think about, we finally arrived at an unassuming door, unmarked in a corridor that came from nowhere and went nowhere. If I were to describe the perfect nondescript corridor, it would have been that one. It could have been any door in any corridor in the whole of Endpoint.

Tiny palmed the door pad and gave it a gentle push. Inside was the holiest of holies on Endpoint: one of the nanogen stations that turned raw matter into other kinds of matter. Trillions of tiny machines, each capable of manipulating matter at the atomic level lived in this room. I expected something visually stunning. Flashing lights and holo-displays all showing the status of the system, but all I got was a giant metal box in the middle of the floor. The box had a series of tubes leading into the bland walls of Endpoint and a different series of tubes that fed into the other walls. Hermetically sealed from end to end.

"The raw matter hopper is upstairs. Raw matter from a freighter fills it once a week, but we don't need as much raw matter as you'd think. Endpoint consumes tons of food each day. Everything is recycled to cut down on how much raw matter we need. Literally everything. It's all matter, right? Food, paper, trash, bodily waste, everything. It all goes through the recycling system and winds up in the hopper as more raw matter," Tiny said.

He fiddled with the side of the box until spinning yellow lights started up around the room. The same kind of lights you see when someone cracks open an anti-matter bomb or a toxin is about to run free. Bad lights.

"Should you be doing that?" I asked.

Big-ass grin again. "It's fine. This is the manual load chamber. Useful for something you don't want tracked by the main matter hoppers goes in here."

It was huge chamber, easily big enough to store a few bodies. Yellow and orange labels covered the inside warning of the dangers of nanogen. Individual nanites weren't much to fear – basically infinitesimal spiders with wings. Okay, scratch that. Spiders with wings were terrifying. But a single nanite was just a bug that could fly and manipulate atoms.

We dumped Sol's limbs, torso, and head into the side hopper and waited. Up close, nanite swarms sounded like a hissing chainsaw but they were a dull drone through the metal of the hopper. It was hard not to visualize the hole in Nobtop's chest as the swarm tore Sol's remains apart. Same basic nanite swarm, only Jeffries had not only found a way to turn a swarm into himself, he'd found a way to weaponize it.

A thought was pinging around in my head that pulled the edges of my lips down. "How much of this is Pred tech?" I asked Tiny.

He stroked an imaginary beard. "Good question. Probably half or so."

Half Predecessor tech. Used some of the same distribution networks. Probably had decompilers and recompilers, too. "Is it hooked into PredNet?"

Tiny shrugged and stared off into space. Cut up a body and toss it in nanogen. Just another day on the farm for him. "On some level, I guess. Most of the Pred systems were run through their PredNet."

Interesting. A carefully guarded location on the human 'net, but probably not to the aliens that built Endpoint. They would have known every centimeter of this bucket. And this was exactly where I'd come if I needed to turn myself into a swarm of microscopic machines.

"Tiny, is there a log down here somewhere? You know, of people who've been in and out."

Endpoint had an advanced tracking system that no one watched or maintained. One of the first things residents did was pay a visit to the Bizarre Bazaar's med stalls and have our trackers removed. But it made sense that a secure location would have some kind of logging system. At the very least, it would provide finger-pointing targets if the nanogen failed.

"Ja," Tiny said, thrusting his chin across the room. "Over there. You might need to do your hacker thing with it, though. The log is locked and no one knows who has the key."

Figured. The room log was an entirely automated digital affair. When you walked into the room it was supposed to read your chip and log that it entered the room. Failing that, the door pad recorded handprints. It remained locked tight and very snippy about getting the correct password.

"Jenkins, what can you tell me about the log console?" I asked.

"It's for reading logs."

"You're turning into more and more of an asshole every day. I don't know whether to be disturbed or proud. Now, if you can turn off Total Dick Mode for a few minutes, I need to know about this log. And to do that, I need to read it. And to do that, I need the password."

"This looks like a standard-issue logging box, probably built off-Endpoint and shipped here. From the dimensions and design, it looks like Melllvarian tech. They use a double-bind asymmetric cryptomorphic algorithm to secure their sets."

I didn't recognize most of what he was talking about, but I did recognize Melllvarian. They were a security equipment group on Omega 3. Their motto was "The extra 'L' is for locked." The Melllvarians considered themselves among the best in the systems and weren't shy about relentlessly marketing that. The problem was their tech sucked. Cheaply manufactured to the lowest possible spec tolerances and they always had a back door.

Once, while I was doing a thing for some people, I bypassed a Melllvarian remote lock using a fountain pen and two pieces of candy. And that was on their top-of-the-line system. A logger should be easier pickings.

"Tiny?" I asked. "Do you have any knives on you?"

He produced a shimmering blade a full 40cm long and made of Oxfab Glo-Metal. "Will this do?"

"Don't take this the wrong way," I told him, "but do you have anything smaller? Like pocketknife sized?"

"This is a pocketknife."

"I meant my pockets, not yours," I said.

He patted his pockets and shrugged. "Sorry, no."

Shit. All I needed was a piece of metal to link the power inputs together. I was surrounded by metal, but not a damned bit of it would work. I patted myself down, hoping I'd squirrelled something away without thinking about it. Nothing in the cargo, nothing in the hips, nothing in the back pockets, nothing in the side or breast pockets.

Wait. The damned bra. Underwire was wicked uncomfortable but maybe it could be useful for something other than irritating me.

"Tiny, hand me your knife and turn around."

I just had to hope underwire meant there was an actual wire in there. Holy shit, it was actually metal. No wonder it felt good to take it off.

The little strip of curved metal would work perfectly. I shoved the remains of the bra into my cargo pocket, struggled back into my coveralls, and went to work. Every electrical system has power flow. Quality components insulate the power flow, but Melllvarian engineers thought insulation was a waste of money. After all, it's not like the components would ever touch, so why worry? Even though the logger was adhered to the wall with enough ChemMelt to hold a star cruiser together, a thin strip of anything could access the power. Make that something metal and someone with unsavory intentions and a bra underwire could do some dastardly things. Like, for instance, short out the security ports.

Tiny stood behind me, watching with a fascinated look on his face as I jiggled the underwire around behind the logger. After a few tries, I got a small zap on my fingertips. Good. Power out node. Power in would be nearby and the security portal right next to that.

The underwire was perfectly shaped to hit all three points at once. A light touch, the barest kiss of all three sharing a circuit was all it took. The logger squealed in agony and flickered. I held my breath. If it didn't shut down in a few seconds, I was home free.

After five eternal seconds, the logger was still glowing. I hit the menu and scrolled until I found history. As I suspected, about a week ago, Xevex Jeffries had somehow gotten access to the nanogen system. Right about the time Nat deleted herself. Some trick let him control the nanites as they fed on his body. When they were done, the amorphous cloud of tiny machines learned how to look exactly like a manic airlock preacher. He transferred his consciousness into the cloud through some unknown tech and exploited his newfound skills to the max.

"Impressive," Tiny said. "Never thought I'd see someone crack a logging system with her underwear."

"I'm full of useful tricks. I once disabled a security system with a pair of chopsticks and some gum."

"You'll have to tell me about that. Over ice cream, preferably."

"Okay Captain One-Track-Mind, we'll get some ice cream. Do me a favor, though; tell everyone to keep an eye out for Xevex Jeffries. Don't confront him; don't attack him, just keep an eye on him. I have an idea forming."

Tiny raised a blond eyebrow. "You realize he killed Nobtop, *ja*? Blood for blood. It is the *Bratva* way."

"Tiny, I was there when Nobtop died. Trust me, if you go up against Jeffries, you'll lose. I want revenge, too, but you can't hit him straight on. He's not human anymore. He's a cloud of nanites controlled by an alien. We'll get him, but we have to be smart about it."

I could see the disbelief in his narrowed eyes and pursed lips. "Please, Tiny," I said. "You gave me 48 hours. I've still got some time left."

He shook his head and grinned. "Well, you do have a membership card and parking pass, so you're one of us. You'll have to work fast, though. The *Bratva* wants blood."

"And they'll get it. I need to talk to a ghost first, though."

25 – Ghost

"Do you ever dress like a regular person?" I asked.

Mason was decked out in mid-22nd century disco sideline of the explorer era. A silver double-breasted suit and gold vest with a tie that glowed the exact same otherworldly green as the lights on the first relic we found. All he needed was a big-ass bowl on his head and some puffy gloves and he would have been the height of pop-culture fashion three centuries ago.

"You should join me, my dear," he said. Flashed me that smile that had probably separated hundreds of women from their panties. "I have a dress that would fit you. Perfectly styled to the time. We could drink hyperbolic blasters and pretend the world didn't exist."

"No thanks. I've seen the dresses from that era. I haven't shaved."

He looked me up and down. "Difficult to tell from your pants, but I have trouble believing your legs would need to be shaved."

"I wasn't talking about my legs," I told him. "Like I said, I've seen the dresses from that era."

Mason laughed and took my hand. "Such wry humor. But let us retire to the study and you can tell me why you're visiting this old ghost when a lovely and very much alive lady awaits your presence."

"I need some help," I said.

He gently directed me through a set of doors and I found myself staring at that familiar raging fire and two leather armchairs facing each other across the soft fur of a Raptarian Tigerphant. After seeing me to my chair, he settled into his own with a satisfied sigh.

"How did we-"I started.

"Get here?" Mason finished. "I am beyond such trivialities as rational dimensions and pathetic concepts like 'cause and effect'. My home has no bounds anymore. It goes where I wish it to go."

"It's just that last time it seemed to take forever to get here from the front door."

"Some people redecorate by moving paintings and furniture around," he said. "I move entire rooms."

I had no response to that. It made sense in an abstract way. "Okay..."

"Dear Miss Devore. I am, as you pointed out, a purely digital man with an alien invader stuck in my head. I decided if I could do that, I could certainly rearrange my house."

"By rearranging your house. Literally."

"Exactly. But enough about me. What help do you require?"

"Can the Predecessor in your head communicate at all?" I asked. That part was key.

"No," Mason replied, leaning back and steepling his fingers. "Did you have questions for it?"

I leaned forward and put my elbows on my knees. Serious face. "I'm sure I do, but they're not important right now. I'm mostly concerned that it can talk to its own kind."

"I'm a little offended at that question. As soon as the silly thing invaded me, I locked it down. Now it's wrapped in a code sandbox. No in or out communication. It fumes a lot, but it can't get out."

With anyone else, this would sound insane. "Last time I was here and you gave me that dress-"

"You looked lovely in it, by the way."

"Thank you," I said. "I met a woman at Lord Barclay's. By and by, I found out she was a Predecessor. Not out to get us, but one of them nonetheless. Jessica, the woman, she told me there was a small but decisive movement among her people to use us a springboard to return to the physical. Well, technically, she wants a body, too. But it's different with her. She doesn't want to just take over. Well, she does, but willingly. The others don't care; they want bodies. Our bodies.

"My worry is Jessica wasn't entirely upfront with me. They're dying by centimeters in there. That breeds desperation and desperation is how movements get started. Then they turn into revolutions. I think the Predecessors are at the revolution stage and people like Jeffries are the first vanguard to escape. More will come. It's just a matter of time."

Mason closed his eyes and chewed on that for a while. He was old enough to have seen human revolutions over the years. Maybe the Predecessors were different and Jessica was telling me the truth but something made me doubt it. They invaded Jeffries, Natasha, and Sol. Mason was still invaded.

"What's your plan?" Mason asked without opening his eyes.

"I want to kick them out of our Virt and lock them in theirs," I replied. The bowling ball in my stomach dropped a centimeter or two just to remind me it was there.

"How?"

"Shut down the hardware that links their Virt world. Just flick the switch and turn it off for good. Then, to clear out any stragglers, we'll need to reboot our Virt world. That's too well protected. I can't get to it on my own."

"Once they're all back where they belong, what then?" Mason asked.

"Shut down their Virt world before any of them get back out. Problem is I can't get to the Virt servers; they're too well protected."

Mason nodded slowly. "But someone on the inside could. Raise enough of a ruckus and the whole system will flux. Once the flux hits a certain point, a reboot is inevitable."

"A reboot would eliminate all extraneous code running in the system. Any Preds still lurking in Virt would vanish."

Just like when Natasha deleted herself, only on a much larger scale.

"It could work," Mason said. "Simple, effective."

"There's just one problem. As soon as Virt reboots everyone goes back to their bodies while the system figures out what happened."

"I don't have a body anymore," Mason said.

"Exactly. A reboot will kill you. Look, Mason. I don't have a whole lot of friends. You've been here a long time. I'm hoping you have a better idea because I'm kind of running low on both ideas and friends."

Mason beamed at that. He took me in his arms and held me tightly. "Dear, sweet Natasha." I could hear his heartbeat through his horrible silver suit. Just as alive there as if he was wandering around Endpoint. "I'm flattered you consider me a friend."

He held me at arm's length and wagged a finger in my face. "You, of all people, should understand the transitory nature of things. Thieves and hackers aren't that different. We're the only ones who get the source code that runs the universe. Magical, mighty, but with just enough bugs in it to make things interesting. Lord help us all when the daemon running the system crashes. The trick is to isolate the bugs and exploit them. Not a single thing has been written that doesn't have typos or bugs."

Mason sat me down and a drink appeared in my hand. I shifted in my seat and found my clothes had been replaced with a dress straight out of old explorer times. Music in the air painted a lo-fi electronica beat heavy with violins and the solemn song of saxophones. We were two people in a stuffy Andromedan café discussing the beautiful danger awaiting us as explorers.

"As I see it," he continued, "there is only one small problem with your plan: You're assuming the Predecessors haven't become resident elsewhere in the system."

"All the more reason to shunt them back into their own system," I said. "And then reboot ours."

He actually tut-tutted me. I'd never been tut-tutted before and I decided I never wanted them to again. "Think bigger. In your experiences after you liberated objects, did you want people to realize something had gone missing?"

I shrugged and took a sip of my drink. "After I was long gone, I couldn't care less what they did."

The sly smile played across his lips again. Eyes sparkled in the sun. "Exactly. Until you're safely away, you don't want anyone to know anything happened. And the less time between your act and your escape the better, correct?"

"Well, yeah. The whole point is to get away without getting caught. I've been caught. It sucks."

"Had to escape, did you?"

"Jail security sucks," I said. "Easy to get out after a few weeks of watching. But those few weeks can be rotten. My longest was nearly six months."

"But you always escaped?"

"We're talking, aren't we? I mean, neither of us is exactly ourselves, but we're both here instead of sleeping on the stone floor of some prison."

"The Predecessors have been in prison for millennia," Mason said. "They're desperate and clever. It would only be a matter of time before they found another way out. Our systems are tightly linked together."

"You would know," I said. "You hooked them up. Sorry, that came out wrong. I don't mean to be accusatory."

He waved a hand in the air and said, "No offense taken. I did my job and I did it well. I figured the alien systems would be an interesting playground. I didn't know there were still creatures on the teeter-totters. Our Virt is well integrated with theirs. You can't close all the loopholes because the system was designed to be one large loophole. I was integrating disparate systems together; there was no such thing as securing it. If you reboot ours, all you will do is piss off Virt users and the Predecessors will come flooding back in as soon as the links are rebuilt."

"What about shutting down Pred Virt?" I asked. "It's at least something."

He nodded sagely. "I agree; it would prevent more of them from coming. There is just one problem."

"What's that?"

"While I can't be certain of the reason, I suspect it was due to the fact that Predecessor Virt space had to be maintained under as many catastrophic scenarios as possible. Their entire race lived in Virt; it had to be rock solid."

"So?"

"So. Predecessor Virt is completely integrated with Endpoint. There is no way to shut it down without shutting down Endpoint."

I frowned and sat my drink on the table. "I guess it wouldn't solve the Jeffries conundrum, either. Or any of the other bastards that escaped into the real."

Mason nodded. "Exactly. Tell me something: All the jobs that you've pulled over the years. How many is it?"

"A hundred or so."

"During any of those jobs, did you ever have help from the inside?"

"Absolutely," I said and stopped myself. Of course. He was right. I needed someone on the inside. The best insiders are already compromised in some way. Disgruntled. Scared. Greedy. Trying to keep their race alive. "And I know exactly who to talk to."

"Then perhaps you should go talk to her," Mason said.

26 – Tentacular

I wonder if Jeffries freaked out when he first walked into the Palace of Nine Pleasures. I nearly did and I'd been raised by weird holos about monsters and the women who came to love them. Don't judge. We all have our things and B-grade monster trash was mine. It was still better than the folks who got off on hardcore mime porn.

The club, like most places in Virt, was bigger inside than out. That little reddish house with the glowing images of human intercourse hid a club filled with humans cavorting with Predecessors. Here, the preds could let their disguises go. There were half a dozen of them and few dozen humans in varying states of dress and arousal lounging around a burgundy room with a thick white stripe along the walls. My human eyes couldn't see it, but I'd bet anything those pred art walls were filled with whatever passed for Predecessor porn.

Something wrapped around my stomach and I looked down to see a thick red and white tentacle. It twisted me around and jerked me face-to-ugly-ass-face with a Predecessor covered in painted-on stripes. Multihued colors on the critter flashed and pulsed to a rapid tempo that reminded me of ElectroPump beats and ElectroLux pipes.

No matter how I pushed at the tentacle, I couldn't budge the damned thing. Another reason we would have wiped the bastards out if we'd been contemporaneous with the Predecessors; too big, too weird, too ugly, and no one manhandles our women but us.

It changed colors in rapid succession with a slow fade on the final pink. I shook my head and shrugged my shoulders. It pulled me in closer, close enough to smell the putrid stench of the rotting alien ocean on it. I pushed harder on the tentacle. If the experience followed the trajectory of my beloved monster trash, the fangs would come out and I'd be novempod food. Or worse.

I lashed out a finger at one of the thing's eyes. Felt the squish as the tips pressed in. All the eyes snapped shut and the tentacle around my waist tightened. It felt like I was about to be ripped in half. I forced myself to calm down. Death was the quick way out. Maybe not pleasant, but I'd wake up in a tube of orange gel with only the mental scars of being crushed by a tentacle monster.

I tried to suck in, but the squeezing tentacle wouldn't let me inhale. As soon as the eyes opened, I lashed out again and was rewarded with even more pressure. As I heard a crack, I wondered who programmed the sensations of breaking a rib into Virt. Did they have to break a rib themselves or did they rely on expert testimony from rib breaking veterans?

The world darkened around me. A training cruise for real death. My arms felt like lead. I could barely move my feet but kept kicking out at something. Anything.

As my vision dropped out, I started hallucinating. Jessica in front of me. Her whole body was flashing. Furious reds and blues answered with tenuous orange and yellow. Had to be the dying moment.

Just before my body completely shut down, the floor first smacked me on the ass before slapping me upside the head. Oxygen – or whatever passed for oxygen in Virt – flooded my lungs. Jessica reached out a hand to me but I was content to lie on the floor and wheeze. My ribs ached, my lungs shrieked, and I came very close to just chucking it all in and exiting Virt.

"For what it is worth," Jessica said, squatting to help me up, "I am sorry about that. That one has always been a problem. I raised him when he was just a hatchling. Nothing but trouble."

"Were there really flashing lights or was that just my brain dying?" I asked. "Because I hope it wasn't the brain thing."

Jessica shook her head and smiled. "I forget—your people have very little contact with mine. It took me years to learn that your strange noises were words and not just more flatulence. I am afraid it would take your people years to understand my language. We were talking."

"Talking?" I asked as she guided me to a table and sat me down.

"Talking. Well, I was yelling at him. That was why I was using those colors and those poses. He overstepped his bounds and needed to be put in his place."

"What'd you tell him?"

"That you belonged to me and he'd better watch his buttocks would probably be the closest translation. Or similar. Even those words don't quite convey the subtlety you can only get from lights."

I put my head in my hands and rubbed my temples. Too much craziness. I needed a quiet beach, some stiff drinks, and a comfortable bed. "What was he going to do?"

"Do?"

"Yeah. He had me dead to rights. There was no way that tentacle was coming off."

Jessica nodded sagely and said in a completely deadpan voice. "It was a mating ritual."

"Mating?"

"Mating."

"As in-"I started.

"Yes. That. What human males and females usually do. Or partners, I should say. We don't exactly have genders like your people do. Partners. Yes. That is a better word."

"Sexual partners," I mumbled.

Her face brightened. "Yes! That is a better word than mating. Sex."

In B-grade monster trash holos, there's always the implication that the woman and the monster have a happily fulfilled life and no one really questions the sex part because reasons. Now that I was on the receiving end, I had questions. Not that I really wanted the answers, but I really wanted the answers even though I knew there was no way the answers were going to make me happy.

"Oh, Penta," I mumbled and put my head in my hands.

Jessica's face stayed perfectly neutral. Sociopath neutral. "There are only a hundred of us left," she said. "Out of billions during our peak and the fifteen thousand that survived to make this voyage, only a hundred of us. We are not a threat to your people."

I started to lift my shirt and show off the bruises Xevex left me, but remembered they weren't on my avatar. "Not a threat? One of your people killed a...friend, I guess. A friend of mine. Another is building an army. He tied me up with nanites and tortured me. He's trying to turn that damned rock in space on so it can kill us all. How is that 'not a threat'?"

"How many of your people are there?" Jessica asked.

I shrugged. No one really kept count, but there were guesses. "I don't know. Probably ninety to a-hundred-billion or so. We're really good at reproducing."

"A hundred versus a hundred billion. What do you think we could do to you? All we want is a quiet place to live and die as organisms, as the Great Ocean intended. Not fading computer code."

"What do you propose? Let you take over our minds? Turn us into nano clouds? I don't think you're going to find many takers for that," I said.

Jessica smiled. "There are those out there who would rejoice at the opportunity."

"Probably," I had to admit. "I'm not one of them, but there are plenty of dumbasses in humanity."

Jessica froze for a moment, chuckled, and shook her head. "I apologize; I had to look up what was meant by 'dumbasses'. Our language doesn't have such colloquialisms."

"Probably not much room for new words when you speak in colors."

"It's far more nuanced than you would understand. Suffice it to say, just like your communication, ours got us to the stars. We've been out here far longer than you. We know a trick or two your people haven't discovered."

She was probably right. One thing humanity was good at was charging in without looking around. "Doubtless, but we still have better video games than you."

Her hand on my hand was warm. Underneath her façade was a creature I'd probably think was delicious grilled and presented with a coterie of dipping sauces. "Please," she said. "Help us."

I was such a sucker for the puppy-dog eyes. Against my better judgment, I looked her square in those pretty, blue eyes and asked, "How?"

27 - Again with These Guys

If there's one thing Penta said that everyone agrees with, it's this: Things can always get better, but they can also always get worse.

I found this comforting.

What I didn't find comforting was the motley collection of airlockers waiting for me when I left the VirtCo sexateria and spa. I found myself face-to-face with two dead-eyed cultists and one leader with surprisingly awesome sunglasses.

"Fucking Xevex," I muttered under my breath.

"Come quietly and we won't have to hurt you," the leader said. He had a baby face and something about his bearing yelled military. The clothes were airlocker couture, but his posture was ramrod straight. His sunglasses were nice, though.

I tried. I honestly tried to find a place on my coveralls to put the damned gun I got from Tiny, but every pocket ruined the lines. Besides, the thing weighed a ton and I never much cared for guns. Although, gotta say, it would have come in handy. Maybe the Bratva were onto something. Next time, I swore to myself. If there was a next time.

The airlockers were about six feet away, surrounding me in a semi-circle. A bit too far away to charge and a bit too close together to make a break for it. Alone with loons. Not the first time in my life, probably not the last. In my old body, I could have shocked them or just beaten them senseless, but Natasha's implants were all hacking tools and while she was strong, I didn't relish the idea of three on one.

The leader dangled a pair of cuffs from an outstretched hand and said, "Put these on and come with us."

"Kinky," I replied. "I don't do that on first dates."

"The alternative is we beat you senseless, dislocate your shoulders, and put them on you anyway."

"You just moved from kinky to perverted," I said. "I don't do perverted."

One of these days, my mouth was going to get me into serious trouble. The leader nodded at the two airlockers on either end of the semicircle. One cracked his knuckles; the other rotated his shoulders. Both were big and had a sweaty, jumpy look. Cult enforcers always ate well. Hopped up on faith. Bad mojo.

"Last chance, Miss Devore," the leader said. "You can come quietly or painfully. But either way, you're coming with us."

They advanced together like a pair of buff robots. If one had held back, I might have had a chance. As it was, I could get one of the assholes, but the other would be on me before I could move. Damn. I hated no win scenarios. Unless...

"Fine," I said, holding up my hands. "Give me the sex toys and I'll go quietly."

The leader cocked his head to the side. "What sex toys?"

Religious people could be so tedious. "The cuffs, idiot. Throw me the cuffs."

They landed in my outstretched hand with a hefty thump. High quality. Probably Terran or Orion oversteel. Stuff like this wasn't cheap. But it was exceptionally strong.

Once they were on, the only way to get them off was with a key. Even laser cutters had problems with oversteel.

"Behind your back," the leader barked.

"Yeah, yeah, yeah. I've been tied up before," I said.

"They're-" he started.

"I know, not ties. Whatever. I know the routine. I'm usually just wearing fewer clothes and have someone damned sight better looking than you barking orders at me to put on the handcuffs."

The thug on the left kept moving toward me by centimeters. I doubt he even realized his shuffling was bringing him closer.

"So, who are you people, anyway?" I asked.

"We are representatives of the One True Prophet," he said.

"This One True Prophet got a name?" I asked. Come on big boy, just a little closer. Mama had a special touch for you.

"The Very Reverend Jeffries."

"Xevex is now calling himself 'Very Reverend'? What does that even mean?"

I fiddled with the cuffs. It was probably going to hurt like hell. Well, mostly the doofus on the left, but also my hand. Best-case scenario, I took down both thugs and escaped in one piece. Worst-case scenario, I got to experience the thrill of dislocated shoulders.

"The Very Reverend Jeffries knows more than regular reverends," the leader said.

"Regular reverends? How many of those does you little cult even have?"

Keep 'em talking. Doesn't matter what, just keep 'em talking. I'd gotten out of more scrapes with more local authorities by keeping them talking than anything else.

"We are not a cult," he spat.

Lefty shuffled closer. Just about in range. Righty was scratching his ass.

"Sure you are," I said. "The only difference between cults and religions is in cults the leader is alive and in religions he's dead."

He vibrated. Like, literally vibrated. Definite anger issues. "Put those fucking cuffs on right now!"

"I can't figure out how they work," I said. When in doubt, act dumb. Works every time.

The leader pointed at Lord Pecsaplenty on my left and said, "Timothy, demonstrate for her."

Yes, Timothy. Come closer. "Jenkins, map," I whispered. "Get me to the nearest lift or stairs."

Timothy looked at the leader and nodded, looked at me and leered and took one slow step forward. It was probably supposed to be menacing, but all it did was make my life easier. I tightened the cuff as much as I could, slid my fingers through the opening, and got on the balls of my feet.

"Boo!" I yelled at Timothy.

He stopped and took a partial step backward. A little verbal shock to his system. I launched forward and drove the metal cuff straight under Timothy's nose. Philtrum, I believe. A nice, big, juicy cluster of nerves. Unpleasant, but not crippling like a kick to the balls. The real power was the way it kicked the tear ducts into overdrive and snapped the head back.

The cuffs tightened around my fingers and that cracking sensation couldn't have been good. Before the pain could kick in, I pulled back and punched Timothy right in the throat. If I'd been his size, I would have gone toe to toe with him; when you're small, you finish the fight quickly. The metal cuff collapsed his larynx and left him gasping for air. He staggered backwards into the leader, knocking both of them off balance.

A couple of days ago, I would have worried about killing Timothy. Time makes fools of us all.

I was already moving under his outstretched arm before he caught in a bear hug and heading whichever direction would put the most distance between us. Didn't risk looking back, just set a point on the horizon and went as fast as my feet would carry me.

"Natasha Devore!" the leader's voice called from behind me.

I flipped him off over my shoulder and kept running. He was yelling something else, but I turned a corner and all I could hear was the sound of my shoes hitting the deck and my heart thundering in my chest. Too much. Too close.

"This is getting too damned dangerous," I mumbled as I slowed to a jog.

A small icon flashed in my ocular HUD. Incoming call over StaNET from one Mr. Arthur Prefect. No official photo so either an airlocker or a criminal. "Jenkins, get me everything on the guy calling me," I said before I took a deep breath and whispered, "Answer."

"Natasha Devore, don't disconnect," a voice said. It sounded oddly familiar, even distorted by StaNET's janky signals.

"Ten seconds," I said.

"What?"

"You have ten seconds to talk. Eight."

The voice paused. Then, "She's alive and unharmed for now."

I skidded to a stop. My stomach dropped. So far, aside from Nobtop, this had been my little game. I chose the pieces and the plays. "Who?" I asked.

"You're wasting time. You know who she is. Be at airlock six in thirty minutes."

He disconnected just as Jenkins tossed a picture in my HUD. Tall guy, clean-shaven. Some kind of deep gray military uniform. I couldn't tell the rank, but every military has its own structure, so it was really anyone's guess.

"This was taken ten years ago on Proxima Five. Commander Arthur Prefect, head of Proxima's palace guard," Jenkins told me. The picture changed and my stomach hit my shoes. "Same person, taken three days ago."

And there he was. The leader. Arthur Prefect. Damn. Former military, a bunch of commendations, same rigidly set jaw. Baby face. He even had the glasses on. "What happened to him?"

"According to records, Arthur Prefect was dishonorably discharged after it was discovered he raped and murdered a village."

"That's, like, a euphemism, right?" I asked.

"No, ma'am. He found a small village and raped and murdered every living soul in it."

Penta protect us. "How small?"

"Records are sparse due to probable cover-up, but the best guesses place the population around a hundred or so."

Aside from the obvious question of how he kept the other ninety-nine in check while he raped and murdered the first person, there were other practical questions that I kind of didn't want answers to. Why? How long did it take? How did he keep it up the whole time? Why didn't Proxima kill that bastard when they had the chance?

"Prefect escaped off-world before he could be executed. He disappeared for a few decades, then turned up here about two weeks ago," Jenkins said.

"And has been hanging with Reverend Crazypants ever since," I mumbled. "I wonder what his game is."

"It is entirely likely he just enjoys hurting people. His records from Proxima indicate severe psychopathic tendencies. Ma'am, if I may be so bold, while I enjoy discussing the frailties of the human mind, might I remind you that Monique is currently in the clutches of this fiend?"

"You're right," I said. "Give me every way in or out of airlock six. I don't care what it is, if I can physically fit through the opening, I want to know about it. I need a plan that doesn't involve getting me killed. I also need to make a call."

28 - Get the Girl

In the holos, the heroine goes in guns blazing to save her man and leaves a trail of bodies in her wake before fist-bumping a cactus and riding off into the sunset. Real life didn't play by the same rules.

Commander Prefect gave me thirty minutes because he thought it would keep me off-balance to give me just enough time to meet him. Hustle, hustle, hustle. No time to think. No time to plan.

With the real Natasha, Prefect's plan probably would have been sufficient. She was a plotter. Like all good hackers, she needed a distinct plan in mind when she went in. Prefect didn't realize who I used to be, and definitely wouldn't have known that I once breached a temple on a whim while still chewing on a fried zark leg because it was after hours and I wanted to see a painting. Time is always better, but I was blessed with the ability to find the hole in the system and exploit it.

I popped by Natasha's cabin, grabbed a few tricks out of my old backpack, and went through her wardrobe. The woman had a deep and abiding love affair with coveralls. Good, but not what I needed. After a few minutes, I found what I wanted: A completely transparent body suit. They'd been out of style for a few decades, but the design was exactly what I needed. Easy to move in, tight enough to not get snagged on things, and useful for making a scene.

Tossed a long coat over the body suit and I looked like anyone else on Endpoint. I felt a little self-conscious walking around in the emperor's new clothes, but it was Endpoint and people wouldn't have cared if I'd walked the corridors buck-ass naked.

When I walked into Airlock 6, a collection of Airlockers was standing at attention, a semi-disciplined army with nothing to lose and everything to gain. Doubtless Jeffries or Prefect informed them that I was a top priority. While that was flattering, it was also creepy.

I made sure to let my jacket flap free, giving the audience an amazing show. A few turned away, but most watched with a glimmer in their eyes. It would only take a nudge to turn that group from a rag-tag collection of wannabe soldiers to a rag-tag group of wannabe rapists. At the end of a corridor of smelly, twitchy people stood the ramrod straight body of the bastard himself, Arthur Prefect.

"No need to get dressed up, Natasha," he yelled. "This is an informal meeting. On the other hand, if you trying to impress me, consider me impressed."

Only kind of for you, asshole, I thought. Just not the way he was thinking. "Where is she?" I yelled back down the corridor.

Prefect stepped aside and rapped on the transparasteel window. Monique pressed her face against the window. Her lips were moving, but no sound came through. She was reading him the riot act. "Time?" I mumbled to Jenkins.

"2125, LST," he replied.

Great. Five minutes to kill. I need to learn to slow down. "What's the plan here, Prefect?" I asked.

His face contorted. Anonymity is such a warm feeling and it hurts when it is stripped away. He recovered quickly and blew Monique a kiss. She flipped him off. Cycle of life and all that. "The plan is you for her. Simple."

"So, she walks and what happens to me?"

He nodded. "She walks. You have my word. No one wants to hurt her."

"And me?"

"You're important, Devore. Too important to waste. We'll give you another angel and keep an eye on you this time."

I shuddered at the thought of slowly losing control of everything. "I'd rather die," I said. "And I'm pretty sure Monique would rather die than watch me get turned into one of you pricks."

"Die?" Prefect laughed. "No need to die. We just need to break you."

"Torture," I said. "Just call it what it is."

"Fine. Torture. If you want to get that way about it. I've got a lot of experience. You could just give yourself up and we could forgo the whole 'rape until your mind breaks' part. I mean, I'd miss it, but it does get pretty tedious."

Raped and murdered a village.

"Where's your master?" I asked. "What does Xevex think about this plan?"

"Pastor Jeffries. He's fully onboard with it. You have skills the angels need and the end justifies the means. We're working for a higher power here, Natasha. And that higher power wants you on His side. Willingly would be best, but unwillingly works, too."

Sweet Penta, he still thought the Predecessors were angels. They must not have converted him. Odd. "How come you're not one of them?" I asked.

"My destiny lies elsewhere."

Translation: He wasn't good enough.

My first thought was to needle him about it, rub it in his face, and make him slip up. But his gaze up and down my glowing body gave me a better idea. Jenkins was feeding me data. The Bratva weren't responding. For once in my life, I decided to be smart instead of just a smart-ass. Give my ace in the hole a chance to line up.

"That's a pity," I said. "It seems like you'd be the most important man they could find. Way better than Xevex Jeffries. Maybe he was just afraid you'd take over."

Twitch. Barely noticeable, but there. Prefect had thought down the same lines. He hadn't done anything more than think. Yet. The difference between thinking and doing was usually just a nudge.

"I have my role and my orders," Prefect said. Was that a hitch in his voice?

I did my best to cock my hip to one side, imitating a sultry pose from literally every holo actress in every movie. I'm sure mine sucked but it was good enough. Dent's gaze flowed down my body leaving a sticky feeling in its wake. It was like I'd let someone paint me with rancid syrup.

"A man like you shouldn't take orders," I said with a little growl in my voice. "He should be giving them."

He blushed. Penta bless; this was too damned easy. "I'm a soldier, ma'am. I follow orders."

Ma'am. Not Natasha or Ms. Devore. Ma'am. I had to stop myself from jumping for joy. Time to up the ante.

I reached into the pockets of my robe, slid some shocknucks onto my right hand, and palmed two small Baals. With those firmly in hand, I shrugged my shoulders and let the old robe fall to the floor. I chuckled at the idea that I had the situation by Baals as I licked my lips and made a show of my eyes rolling over his body.

Prefect leered as he adjusted himself through his pants.

"Do you have any orders for me?" I asked. A little coo, a little shake of the hips.

"No, just wanted to let you know your Bratva friends won't be joining us this evening. They've got problems to deal with elsewhere. But, since you've got my attention, maybe we can work something out. I've always wanted a sex slave. Or two."

I nearly stumbled. Nearly. It wasn't entirely unexpected. A man like Prefect knew things. You couldn't do the kinds of things he did without information. Which was why it was always good to have an ace in the hole.

"As long as you'll protect me from Jeffries, I'll be anything you want," I said. "That man scares me. You should be in charge; you've got a better eye for detail and are a damn sight easier on the eyes."

That got me an evil smile and I knew then Prefect was already on the case. Part of me would pay anything to see him kill Jeffries. A larger part of me would pay even more to watch that hideous cloud of nanites tear Prefect to pieces.

He crooked a finger and motioned me toward him. I did my honest best to sway like water. Channeled Monique and Jessica, probably looked more like The Specialist. Hopefully it was enough. The airlockers swayed and twitched all around me.

A light flashed three times in my vision. I dropped the Baals and counted to ten. Jenkins frantically analyzed data. Twenty meters away from Prefect. Cutting it close.

I kept my slow walk nice and steady. No reason to let Prefect know anything was afoot. Prick. He was so used to people doing what he wanted he couldn't fathom someone not wanting to obey him. I guess in the mind of a monster everyone is sheep.

"Done," Jenkins said.

"Good. Execute. You have the Baals," I thought back.

For a moment, it didn't seem like anything special happened. I kept walking. Prefect kept smiling and licking his lips. The Airlockers kept shuffling and twitching. Slowly, Prefect's grin faded to a frown. He stepped toward me.

My aniTat system was going wild. It was excellent at playing back pre-recorded video but it was less enthusiastic about getting sixty live commands every second with new patterns to display. Jenkins was closely watching an avatar of me rendered from live video feeds generated by the Baals in front and behind, plus a couple of security cams he'd found.

To Prefect, it looked like I vanished, turned to a cloud and vanished into the river of faces making up his honor guard. To the Airlockers all around me, there was an amorphous cloud that looked kind of like a crowded hallway but also kind of like a person. A holy ghost in their midst.

"Find her!" Prefect yelled.

Hands groped around me. I dropped to a crouch and worked under them. Time to add a little something extra to the mix. Thank you, Xevex Jeffries, for showing me the Way.

"Jenkins," I mentalled, "give me some chaos."

I felt him nod and dropped screens over my eyes. The Baals flashed three times and then let off a dizzying array of bright colors and flashing lights. They shrieked and whined and moaned and cried out in horror. The small corridor turned into the kind of dance floor that leaves you with a headache in a strange bed wearing someone else's underwear the next morning.

"Three, two, one, go," I whispered to myself, hoping we'd agreed on zero instead of one. I pushed off hard, belly-sliding down the corridor. Thank you old sexy skinsuit, sorry about the scuffmarks on the front. Better than scuffmarks on my body or getting sensitive parts caught in a deck snag.

Far behind me, I heard a pair of puffs. They almost sounded like chaste kisses. Heads exploded as the kisses found them. I waited the few seconds we'd agreed on before pushing up to my hands and feet and bear crawling it to Prefect. With his mind so invested in the chaos down the hall, it didn't occur to him that something was coming for him.

I had zero doubt that Prefect could take me in a fair fight. Fortunately, I never fought fair.

The remaining ten meters felt like an eternity of burning thigh muscles and cramping abs. At three meters away, I clenched my fist and felt the ShockNucks charge. Electricity hummed through the veins in my hand, shutting down nerves and locking muscles into a perfect fist. I had one shot and I intended to make it count.

Half a meter away, close enough to smell the fear sweat coming off his crotch. I popped my feet under me, thanked Penta for everything, and launched my hand right up between his legs. A hundredth of a second after my fist hit his balls, a blast of electricity surged through them. He dropped to his knees, then curled up on the floor holding his ruined testicles.

I punched him as hard as I could in the side of the head for good measure and slapped the airlock release button. Prefect groaned behind me and I was about to kick him when Monique went full bobcat on his head. She kicked and stomped and shrieked. I had to pull her off him and got an elbow in the eye for my troubles. Apparently, I wasn't the only one with some personal defense training.

"Monique, stop!" I yelled. "We need him alive for now."

She whirled on me with fire in her eyes. Finger in my chest pushing me back against the wall before I even knew what happened. "No, we need him dead. Right fucking now!"

Facing certain, freezing, gasping death always brings out the best in people.

"He knows things," I said, holding out my upraised hands. Non-threatening. "We need to find out what."

My aniTat system was still playing camouflage across my body. I shook my hand and let the spent ShockNucks fall to the floor. "Jenkins, stop the camo."

To Monique. "It's okay. He's not a problem anymore." I motioned to the hallway. "They're not a problem anymore, either. But there are other problems, and if we don't find out everything we can, this is going to happen again. Only next time it'll be worse."

She looked down the hallway and blanched. To be fair, it looked like a scene from a bad slasher holo. The cleaner bots were going to have a hell of time with the mess. "What the-" Monique started.

I gently pulled her into my arms and held her tight. "I have friends," I said. "Good friends. And you have me, so you have good friends, too."

Her body sagged but her mouth exploded. "They came in through the front door. My front door. My fucking front door. I didn't evenknow what wasgoing on.

Theycamerightinthroughmysecurity. It was supposed to be the best! And they came in. And they came in. Andtheyshockedmeanddraggedmehere. And this prick. This fucking assclowncalledmethewhoreofuckingBabylon and said it was all to get my bitch of a girlfriend so we could die together because that was whatwhatwhat whores deserved."

Damn, Prefect. You didn't have to call us whores. That was just mean.

"If I have to die, I hope it's with you near me," I whispered and hugged her tighter. "But we're not going to die today."

Monique pulled back and pointed at a growing bruise on her cheek, just below her left eye. "And that cocksucker punched me. I wasn't even doing anything; he just punched me. And laughed. And it fucking hurt!"

I pulled her back in and gently kissed her bruise. "It just makes you more beautiful."

She wrapped her arms tight around me and sobbed. We gently rocked back and forth until Peach coughed gently into her hand. "If you two don't need me, I'm gonna slink back to my bar."

I reached a hand out and pulled her in tight, too. "I owe you one, beauty," I said.

Her hand on my ass. "Don't worry. I won't be afraid to call that favor in. Looks like you've got your hands full tonight, though."

Monique pulled back and stared at Peach in a kind of awe. To be fair, the woman looked like a perfect predator. A lioness wrapped in SemiViz fatigues. The tight fabric suited her angel of death look even if she hadn't bothered with the usual armor plate attachments.

"Who are you?" Monique asked, wiping her nose, "and how come you know Nat?"

Peaches smiled. It was a wicked kind of smile full of mirth and a hint of sorrow. "Your gal and I go way back. Fought together in the Nano-Wars, did a thing or two here and there. Shared a guy or five over the years."

"Jenkins," I thought. "Peach, Nano-Wars. Find me everything."

"She did the shooting," I said. "As you can see, she's good at it."

Monique peered down the hallway at the mass of bodies. Cleaner bots were already descending on the hallway, pulling the bodies to wherever it was they took them. Nanogen, probably. My breakfast would probably have a bit of them in it. In a way, there was poetic justice in eating someone who wanted to kill you, even if they did look and taste like Feggs at the time.

"How?" Monique asked.

Peach presented a nasty looking rifle she'd had slung over her shoulder. "Longtime friend of mine. RoTis Dale mkIV. Uses shaped, steerable, hyperkinetic rounds with staggered detonation. Excellent for interiors since the round will detonate before it punctures ship skin."

Monique nodded but her eyes were blank. "Fast, nasty bullets that explode," I told her.

"Yes," she replied.

At our feet, Prefect moaned. Good to see the bastard was still alive. He looked up, saw the three of us staring down at him, and turned white. I imagine in his pain-addled state of mind, we must have looked like avenging angels come to punish him for his sins. Frankly, I didn't care about what he'd done in the past; I cared about what he'd done recently and what it was going to take to get him to tell me.

I looked at Peach and grinned. "Care to join us for a citizen's castration ceremony?"

She shook her head. "Sorry, I'd really love to stick around and mutilate a complete stranger, but my bar is calling for its mommy. Come by later, I've got more of your favorite stocked. Monique, it was nice to meet you in person. Enjoy your revenge; it doesn't come around all that often."

Monique leaned into me. "Nice girl. Think she'd be up for a party?"

"A party?"

"A three-person party."

"What?" I asked.

She slapped me on the arm. "Do I have to spell it out for you?"

"Oh. Probably," I said, "but I'm not really into sharing."

"Ma'am," Jenkins interrupted. "I have your information whenever you're ready."

"Summarize," I thought back.

"Captain Jane 'Peach' Piermont was a decorated member of the 3rd Alpha Commandos. She fought in the Nano Wars for approximately three years and was instrumental in the final battle that ended the war. There is more, but those are the salient points."

I whistled. Captain. Instrumental in ending the war. Now runs a bar in the ass-end of nowhere. Nothing like seeing humanity teetering on the brink to make you want to get away from it all.

"What are we going to do about this asshole?" Monique asked.

"I need to know how to find Jeffries," I replied. "But a big, bad tough-guy like him probably won't want to talk."

"He told me he was going to strap me to the chair in there, sew my lips shut, and open the door just a bit at a time so he could watch me suffocate. The son of a bitch even cracked the door a bit just to let me know he was serious."

I kicked him in the face. "I'd say we really should cut his dick off, but I don't have a knife."

I guess once you cut one off, it becomes habit.

Monique looked around and sauntered down the hall glancing left and right. Finally, something caught her eye. She reached down and retrieved a wicked-looking dagger from someone's waist. She held it in front of her face and examined the ten-centimeter-long, partially serrated blade like a professional. It must have passed muster because she grinned and stalked back to the still-prone Prefect.

"Full tang," she said, showing me the knife. "Those are the best. This knife was made by someone serious. It's not a vibe-blade, but it'll cut someone. Schnick, schnick, schnick."

I stared in open-mouthed disbelief.

"What?" Monique asked. "I wasn't always a Template, you know. I had a life before you. And I'd like to remind you, you're the one who hired an assassin to help get me free. Not that I'm complaining, mind you, just don't get all high and mighty on me just because I might have cut a sucker or five."

The absolute last thing I expected. I guess I should have been more in tune with the flow. People live a long time; it shouldn't have been surprising that Monique was a knife-wielding hellcat in a previous era. Natasha was apparently a nun at one point and I had seriously considered sales back before I discovered I had a conscience.

"Sorry," I told her. "You just never cease to amaze me."

Prefect groaned and tried to get up. I swept his arm out from under him and brought my heel down on his temple. A small part of me warned that I'd better back off the head if I wanted anything useful out of him.

"Where do you want to start?" Monique asked.

"Um," I mumbled. "What hurts the worst?"

"You already smashed his balls."

"We could cut them off," I suggested.

"We'd have to pull his pants off first. One of us would have to hold him while the other untrousered him. It'll probably take both of us to hold him. You're tough. He's stronger."

"Right. How about we just stab him in the balls?"

"What is it with you and balls?" Monique asked. "They're smashed. Let them go."

"Okay. Fine. What do you suggest?"

"Why do I have to suggest?"

"Um, because I was hoping you had good ideas," I said.

Monique scrunched her face up and pursed her lips. "You've never done this before, have you?"

I shook my head. "No. Have you?"

"Of course not. I'm not mil-spec."

"We should have asked Peach to stay," I mumbled. "She'd probably know."

"Or is it because she's completely stacked?" Monique mumbled back.

"What?"

"That woman was made in a sex lab and then injected with soldier," Monique said. "Don't try to deny it."

"Deny what?"

"You were checking her out."

"She's my friend!" I spat.

"With benefits?"

"What? No. We're just friends. Besides, you're the one who wanted to have a three-way with her."

"Yes," Monique said. "As long as you're there, too."

"Do we have to do this right now?" I asked.

"Do what? Discuss your lusty eyes?"

"I do not have lusty eyes!"

"Admit it, you'd roll around with her in a heartbeat," Monique said.

Honestly, I couldn't deny it. But I'd feel like shit the next morning because for all my faults, I'm loyal. To Nobtop's memory. To the customers who paid me a lot of money to get things for them. To Monique. "Only if you're there," I said.

Monique's lips curled down and then pursed. She wiped at an eye. "Seriously?"

"Seriously."

"You wouldn't go for an upgrade?"

"I like her, but Peach is no upgrade. At best she's a few steps below you."

Her arms were around me before I knew it. Face in my neck, holding me tightly. "Say that again."

"She's no upgrade."

Monique pushed back and held me at arms' length. Stared me dead in the eyes. "I'm sorry. I'm really sorry I snapped at you. Do you realize what my life is like?"

"Money and sex?"

She nodded. "And that's all. You are the only person who ever wanted to see me for me. Not as a template. Not as a sex toy. A person. I've got money and fame, but I'm tissue paper; someone to jack off into and toss on the floor. Sure, I've got fans, but I doubt there's anyone out there who would kill a whole lot of people to save me."

"To be fair," I said, "they wanted to kill me, too. Or worse."

Prefect groaned. Monique kicked what was left of his testicles so hard she hopped around on one foot for a moment before kicking him again. "We are in the middle of things!"

"We should probably take care of him," I said. "I might have an idea. Help me get him up."

"Fine," she said. "But we're not done here."

I hugged her, pulled her forehead to mine, and said, "I know. One thing first."

I reached down and pulled the sunglasses off his face. Prefect was a bastard. Bastards ran his entire planet. But they were bastards with excellent design taste. I flicked the shades open and put them on my face. "How do I look?"

"Stunning," Monique said with a sigh. "At least for a woman with a mass-murderer's sunglasses on her face."

"Naysayer," I told her as I pocketed the glasses. Incredibly hard to come by unless you wanted to go to Proxima Five. And literally, no one wanted to go there.

Together we dragged Prefect into the chair and strapped him into place. He was mostly lucid when we closed the airlock door. As he took in his situation, his eyes got wide. He struggled but the straps were too tight to escape. When he saw us looking through the glass at him, he screamed. It was silent through the thick door.

"You know," I told Monique, "with soundproofing like that, you have to wonder why he threatened to sew your lips shut."

"Probably just to be a dick," she replied.

"Rapist and murderer."

"What?"

I nodded through the glass at Prefect struggling and screaming. "He was a Captain on Proxima 5."

"That place is a shithole."

"No argument. Fascism never does anyone any good. Anyway, word got out that he'd raped and murdered a village."

"Is that some kind of military euphemism?" Monique asked.

I shook my head. "Nope. He literally raped and murdered a village. Probably took him weeks. Emperor Trope would have kept him on, but the backlash was too much even for his sordid likes."

Monique palmed the comm panel and asked, "You raped and murdered an entire village?"

"Fuck you bitches," he replied. "You're both next. I'm going to cut you open and fuck the holes-"

"I'll take that as a yes," she said and released the comm. "What now?"

"Well, there are...things...you should know."

"Like what?" Eyes wide with curiosity and a bit of hope.

"The Predecessors are alive. Well, alive-ish. That's what all this is about. Jeffries, the cult, Prefect, all of it. The aliens are trapped in their own Virt but found a way into ours. At least one of them managed to get out by hijacking Jeffries and riding his body. It took him over. They know things about Endpoint that we don't know. For instance, Xevex's Predecessor turned his body into a mass of nanites. They want out. They've been watching, searching for compatible minds. That's what the Airlockers are for; Jeffries wants them as hosts for more Predecessors. They're trying to do something with Temnyy. It's apparently not a planet; according to Jessica-"

"Who's Jessica?"

"One of the Predecessors. She's one of the good ones. If 'she' really applies. I don't know that they have gender like we do. Anyway, according to her, Temnyy is a weapon of some sort. An egg. Some kind of massive bio-weapon they created during their last war. Some of them want to crack it open; some of them want to make sure it never hatches. Apparently, if it gets loose, this whole neck of the galaxy could be in trouble."

Monique stared at me with a deadpan face. "Maybe I'm a bit off kilter, but I'm waiting for the punchline."

"What? No punchline. This is what's happening."

"Predecessors are alive. They're living in their version of Virt but can get into ours and now they want to get into the real world. Jeffries is one of them, only he's a mass of nanites and he's trying to use Airlockers as hosts and the ones that fail are – what – turned into an army?"

I shrugged and nodded.

"And what about this asshole?" she asked, jerking her thumb toward the airlock door. "I doubt he's an Airlocker."

Prefect was still struggling and screaming. "No, I'm not sure how he got recruited. Maybe he just likes hurting people. Every cult needs someone to keep the rest of them in line."

She put her hand on my chest. "Do you realize how crazy this all sounds?"

I put my hands over hers and held them tight to me. "Monique, listen. Jeffries was the one who killed Nobtop. I saw the whole thing happen. He can shoot black clouds out of his hands. They ate a thirty centimeter hole straight through the guy and Nobtop is not – was not – a small man. Very scary things are happening on this ship and that guy might have some answers."

Still holding her hand on my chest, Monique slapped the airlock controls. The light overhead went red. A mechanical voice counted down. Five. Four.

I struggled forward but she held me back gently but firmly.

"He might have information!" I shouted.

"It sounds like you have all the information you need."

A clanging sound of an external airlock opening reverberated around the empty room. We both peered out the glass just in time to see Prefect, still strapped to a chair, sucked out into the void. It was a fitting end to the bastard. Consigned to the loving embrace of nothingness. Freezing, asphyxiated, unable to move enough to even claw out his eyeballs before they exploded.

Later tater.

Monique turned me to face her. Her eyes were deadly serious. "If you're not pulling my leg – and I think you're not – what now?"

"I need to find Jeffries. He's the key to this whole thing."

"No, he's not," Monique said with a sigh. "You are. Think it through. They went to all this trouble to get you. Not some rando Airlocker, not that psycho out there. I mean, you're awesome and everything, but you need to ask yourself what's so special about you. Everything here is revolving around you. So, either you're completely mental or you just found yourself wrapped up in a huge problem."

Shit. She was right. Natasha, what the hell did you get us into?

Maybe Xevex would have some answers. And since I couldn't hope to handle him in the real, there was only one place left.

29 – Crazytown

Xevex was remarkably difficult to track in Virt. He took shortcuts that didn't pop up on the Signpost and even went in the front of one bar and out the back. He moved through one of the seedier parts of Virt like a native. At the corner of Bad and Worse, Jeffries took a turn that nearly lost me. He'd ducked down an alley that was invisible until I was right on top of it. By the time my eyes adjusted, he was nowhere to be seen. The alley went on for a few hundred meters, straight as an arrow. I could see the flashing neon light at the other end, but I couldn't see Jeffries. Poof. Presto-chango. Gone, baby, gone.

I made my way slowly down, craning my neck to the left and right. Here was a place that specialized in Cyrillic-fusion cuisine; there was a place that let you experience smoking old-Terra Cubans.

Under a flickering light that was trying so hard to do the right thing, I found a set of fresh boot prints. Like me, Jeffries had sloshed through the muck and left a trail straight to a door marked only with an octopus. No, scratch that. It wasn't an octopus. The cartoony figure on the door looked like it could be part of sushi chain, but the three glowing red eyes gave it away.

The door opened smoothly on hidden hinges. Inside was a scene that would have made DeSade blush. I've done some kinky things in my life, but I drew the line at whipping little people and tying up people dressed like donkeys.

Strobe lights gave the scene an unearthly texture, like watching photographs from the old days, only with every bit of depravity humanity could conjure. Maybe it heightened the surrealist atmosphere of it all, and let people think they hadn't just had sex with a corpse or maybe it was just the horror-holo vibe, but there was a dank, rotting sexiness to the whole thing. Everywhere I looked, things got decidedly darker. First flash – a naked Twister game with fisting. Flash – a donkey dressed as French maid. Flash – a trio dressed in medieval armor drinking a maiden's blood. On and on and on. All our whacked-out fetishes put on display and topped with a bow made of satin and human nipples.

I strode into the scene with my head held high. Sure, I'd never fuck a donkey, but if that's what got these folks off then so be it. I had bigger fish to fry. Not to say I didn't Penta myself – old habits die hard and the simple five-point touch was reaffirming. Before I was ten steps into the club, someone grabbed my arm and pulled me close to him.

Fake. All fake.

He was a beast of a guy with hands like winter hams and a devious gleam in his eye. Maybe in a few months I might be interested in the massive bulge in his loincloth, but I wasn't there yet. The body knew, but the brain still didn't care for summer sausage.

"Secretary or boss?" he asked through teeth that were so white they glowed.

Probably a low-level adjunct officer at one of the local corps. He smelled like middle management, desperate and needy. "Depends," I said.

His hand wrapped around my arm with ease. Strong. Too strong. Obviously one of the folks into violent sex with less-than-willing partners. My fingertips tingled. "On what?" he asked.

"How you respond when I tell you to take your hand off me."

He grinned and squeezed a little tighter. I tottered a bit in the stupid heels but held my ground. Never show a middle manager the slightest bit of fear. They're weak, ineffectual creatures, but they can smell fear and exploit it. "And if I say no does that make you my secretary?" he asked.

Fucking Monique. Business dress and jacket? What was I supposed to be, the VP in charge of standing out in the crowd? What was wrong with coveralls? I could have looked like a janitor and no one would notice me. "Is that your final answer?" I asked.

A little tighter. My arm was going numb. What was he trying to accomplish? If he cut off the blood flow to my arm and I'd find his charms irresistible. "That's my final answer," he whispered.

I let him pull me in closer until I could smell his breath. Cheap vodka and pretzels. Bad cigars and hobo wine. When we were close enough, I waited until he closed his eyes for a kiss and brought my knee straight up between his legs.

A friend of mine on Antares once told me women must have been the chosen people because the gods installed an off switch in men. I'd been racked before. The pain is excruciating. Worse is the nausea. It's like being kicked in the chi. In a fight, a real fight, balls aren't a great target because most men are good at protecting them. But this wasn't a real fight. This was a life lesson.

Smiley Joe first crumpled in on himself. I almost felt sorry for him; that was one hell of a shot. Slowly, he dropped to his knees. I gave him another knee in the teeth for good measure and his eyes rolled back in his head.

"Considering you're on your knees, I'm gonna say I'm the boss," I told him. "By the way, you owe me ten credits for the lesson in manners."

A couple of heads turned my way and at least one guy pointed, laughed, and lifted his drink to me. Nobody cared. Mister Smiley had already dissolved into a cloud so as far as anyone was concerned, the show was over.

I looked around for Jeffries but couldn't find him. He'd be in the shadows somewhere. Probably seducing someone into a life of penitence and hunting women. Over a bar stocked with every chemical concoction known to man, a holo sign flickered out letters. *Novem Vitae*. Huh. Nine life if I remembered my Latin correctly.

I made my way casually around the dark edges of the dancefloor, stealing a drink off a waiter bot's tray and sashaying away before he could find his indignity module. Straight vodka if the oily sensation burning its way down my throat was any indication.

A few people snorting lines of powder off a mirror, a couple leaning together in a dark corner, cliques of people with grass skirts doing their thing to an electronic beat. After my little scene at the door, no one tried to grab me. A few people did motion at an empty chair, but I politely declined.

I was about to give up when I finally found Xevex. He was trying to work his magic on a woman in a grass skirt and coconut bra, but she was playing hard to get. Funny, from what I knew of Xevex, he was playing hard to want. The cool thing to do would have been to politely announce my presence with a cough, but I wasn't in a cool mood. I was tired and cranky and had better things to do with my life than follow charlatans around.

I hooked an unused chair with my foot and slid it across the floor. It was one of the few times in my life when things went just right. The chair slid neatly up to the table and I spun it around perfectly in time for me to sit sideways on it and rest my elbow on the back. Jeffries ignored me. He had his mind set on she of the nut bra. So much for the perfect entrance.

The glass in front of me was half-full of something glowing bright blue. I sniffed it and decided it was just some artisanal whiskey with photoreactive compounds laced in. Weird stuff, but I'd always wanted to try it. In the real, Glo-skey is crazy expensive and rare to boot. Like everything in Virt, it was probably a pale imitation of itself, but worth a shot.

It was like getting punched in the throat. The Glo-skey fought all the way down, fingernails out, and digging trenches in my esophagus. Then it hit my stomach and erupted like an old-school antimatter bomb. I doubled over, coughing and wheezing. "Sweet mother of fuck," I hissed.

Then the calm hit. My body hot flashed then cooled. The chaos and cacophony around me calmed down to Day

7 normalcy. It wasn't just Glo-skey – that stuff was supposed to be rough and ready – it felt more like liquid heroin.

I took a deep breath and downed the remainder of the glass. Less throat punch, more calmative. Jeffries was still in total seducer mode, so I slid the glass across the table with just enough force that it fell right in his lap. He jumped and "accidentally" copped a feel. She slapped the shit out of Jeffries and yelled, "What the hell, dude?"

Xevex focused on the woman in front of him. "What?" he asked.

"I told you I don't go in for the quick and dirty. What kind of freak does that shit?" she said.

I waved a hand, turning on table's the noise canceller and toning down the ambient noise. "This kind of freak," I said in the sudden silence.

Two pairs of angry eyes found me and locked on like pulse missiles. Xevex frantically tried to cover himself while the woman acted like nothing had happened. Kudos to her; I like cool kittens.

While Jeffries struggled with a raging boner poking straight into his pants, I slid a few credits across the table to the woman and hitched my thumb at the door. "This one's mine," I told her, pointing at Jeffries.

She palmed the credits. With a brief flash from under her overly manicured nails, the credits loaded to her real account. A quick pull of whatever was in front of her. She eyed me briefly. Maybe the power suit was a thing because the woman left without saying whatever was on her mind. If I was right about my theory, I'd just saved her ass.

Speaking of ass, she shook it like a pro as she walked into the crowded dancefloor.

"You again," he hissed. "I figured you'd be dead by now. I see I need to explain to Captain Prefect that when I say 'failure is not option' I mean failure is not an option."

"Sorry to disappoint, Rev," I told him, "but the rumors of my rumors of my death have been greatly exaggerated. And if you want to talk to Prefect, I'd suggest a Ouija board."

"How?" he asked.

"I helped him experience the darkness in his soul firsthand."

He cocked his head to the side. I wondered if that was an affectation his Predecessor had picked up or if it was some universal constant.

"I moved a chair," I said.

We stared at each other for a moment. I let it ride, let the tension build for a while before I said, "A chair he was strapped into. I moved it to the void. Through an airlock."

Jeffries nodded. "I see."

I put my elbows on the table and steepled my fingers. "So, who am I talking to? Because I know for a fact that you're not Reverend Xevex Jeffries. I still have the bruises to prove it."

"And I know you're not the real Natasha Devore," he replied. "I had to regen half my body after your little stunt."

"Got a name?" I asked.

His brow furrowed and his lips pursed. A brief flash, fractions of a second, but just enough to see the predecessor riding him. "Since I am Reverend Xevex

Jeffries," he said, emphasizing the reverend part, "then you must be the real Natasha Devore."

"I guess we've both got new bodies. Mine was bequeathed to me. Yours was stolen."

The barest of twitches. I had to hand it to him, he was cool. Must've been all that experience weaving stories about the next life. "What's that supposed to mean?" he asked calmly.

"You know what it means, Xevex," I said, tapping my head. "What I want to know is why? What's your plan?"

His eyes bored into me. "Enjoy your time in Virt," he said.

With a wink and nod, he vanished in a cloud of zeroes and ones. Great. I should have expected him to disconnect. I guess too many detective novels were stuck in my head. Too many times where the heroine finally corners the villain and the villain spills the whole story just before killing himself in shame. Real life is a pisser. Even in Virt.

What was even more of a pisser was catching the guy with the spanner out of the corner of my eye. Life as a thief had taught me to be aware of people who were aware of me. Especially when they're packing Virt weapons. Just like spazzers shut down neural electrical signals, spanners could lock the physicality link between a real body and a Virt body without cutting the brain linkup. It meant you couldn't disconnect no matter how hard you tried. They were illegal as hell and I'd love to know how he smuggled it in, especially after last year's incidents.

I pretended I didn't notice him, but purposely got up and walked at a ninety-degree angle away. As I strode through the bar, I caught sight of the second guy. A little more discreet with his spanner, but carrying nonetheless.

The one on the left had wild, pirouetting eyes that danced like a lemur on crack. His hair hadn't met soap in at least a few weeks. The one on the right was the scary one. Perfectly normal-looking guy. T-shirt and pants. Nothing special, just a regular dude out for a scintillating night of rape and torture.

I veered to the right and did my best to keep tables and people between us. Anything that would slow them down would work. Kept off the dance floor, kept to the tables. The dance floor was my escape route but they didn't need to know that. Of course, I could have simply disconnected but something told me those two could be useful. Information or even just stress relief, it didn't really matter.

As I wove through the tables, I kicked off my shoes and unbuttoned my jacket. Pulled my hair back into a ponytail. If they wanted a fight, they'd get one, and I was in no frame of mind to fight nice. Virt had no long-term ramifications. Cripple a guy in Virt and he'd be just fine as soon as he disconnected. Maybe a little sore. Maybe even absolutely convinced he was bleeding internally, but those things faded with time.

That didn't mean you couldn't make someone hurt in Virt. Just like the pleasure part, the pain felt real.

Normal guy saw me heading toward the door and motioned to crack lemur. The little spaz scurried ahead, hoping to cut me off. He was twitchy and irritated. An unkempt ball of energy looking for a reason to explode.

Normal guy was about ten meters back and to my left; enough space that I didn't have to worry about him.

Now that I was certain they were after me, I gave twitch a reason to explode. Normal guy was just on the other side of a table, hand behind his back. I did my best to keep my eyes away from him. Empty chair to my right. Slid by and grabbed it. Left foot crossed right. Twist. Unwind.

The chair hit twitch square in the face. Caught him completely off guard. Something clattered to the ground, metallic clatter on the fake wood floor. I flipped the little table over and shoved it at the normal guy. Not much protection, but he'd have to deal with it and that gave me a precious second or two. Ignored the indignant shriek of some puffed-up Barbie. Before twitchy could recover, I was moving.

I leapt at the crack lemur. He was still holding his nose when I jammed both thumbs into his eyes. Pushed his head back and punched him in his exposed throat. Probably lethal in the real and painful in Virt. Brought a leg straight up between his legs and elbowed him in the right temple before he even knew what hit him.

Real-world implications would be staggering. In Virt, the guy simply disappeared in a cloud of zeroes and ones. That left me with one guy who seemed to have his shit together far better than his Airlocker buddy. He looked out of place in a T-shirt and pants in a place where people were wearing vegetation skirts.

When the violence started, most people in the club didn't notice. It was over so quickly most people only caught a flash of action and then the crazy guy disappeared.

They assumed it was a performance piece or a lover's quarrel, or some damned thing gone horribly awry. Whatever the case, it was over and that meant it was time to get back to drinking and dancing.

The way the normal guy casually flicked out his spanner made me think the next fight might take a bit more effort. Xevex had moved up to recruiting a higher class of thug.

I scanned the floor and found the dropped spanner about five meters away. Spanner in hand, I did my best to get myself rooted. Stick fighting was never my forte, but my defense teacher assured me the only difference was range. Normal guy sneered and went straight after me with a swipe that would have left me stuck in Virt feeling like I had a broken jaw if I hadn't ducked.

No hesitation. As his swing sailed past me, I popped back up and swung the baton at his ribs. He had all the time in the world to jump back.

He raised his hand up and slashed down at me. I barely managed to jump to the side and swat his spanner out the way. A quick kick to the ribs and he backed away slowly, twisting his torso to relieve the mark my foot left on his side. I smirked. I might have looked like easy prey, but even kittens have claws.

I was in the zone. The world outside of the fight blurred. Wide eyes watched his torso, looking for those telltale ticks that someone was about to move. We circled each other, feinting from time to time to see how the other would react. Back off or engage? Block or move?

Finally, I got the opening I wanted. We both feinted at the same time but reacted differently. I contracted. He expanded. His crackling spanner flashed by my eyes followed by his fist. Fully committed. He was certain he had the shot and it was only dumb luck that I pulled back when I did that got me out of the way.

I sprang forward, sliding along his outstretched arm before he could get his balance back. With one arm, I clamped onto his bicep, pulled it tight to my chest, and squeezed for dear life. My other arm slid under his and brought my own spanner right up into his jaw. His avatar flickered and steadied. Now that he was stuck, it was time to have some fun.

I spun on my heels, sliding behind him and jammed the end of my spanner into his kidney. His back arched and his knees buckled. A quick kick to the back of the knee. As he staggered backwards, I smashed him in the face with the spanner. It was the kind of wide-open strike where I could put everything I had into it. In the real, it would have knocked out teeth and screwed up his neck.

He went down and I jumped on top of him. Got a few hoots from the audience and one guy shouted, "Yes! Hate sex!"

It took everything I had to not pound the guy's face with my spanner. Break his nose and orbital bone. Leave him battered and broken. Instead, I tapped the dude in the face with my spanner and asked, "Who the hell are you?"

He smiled and shook his head. His form tried to dissolve. I waved my spanner in his face, "Ah, ah, ha. You're not getting away that easily. Speaking of which, how long are these set for?"

His smile faded. Eyes narrowed, he looked me straight in the eye and tapped me in the ribs with his spanner. My body went through a convoluted cluster of sensations: Cold, hot, pain, ecstasy. Somewhere, my body was probably twitching in amber gel.

"They're set to forever. You're severed, babe. No going back now," he said. "By the way, since you're up there, would you mind grinding a bit?"

A bulge pressed up between my legs. Penta. What the fuck? Who gets hard during a fight? I punched him in the nose and climbed off him. "You son of a bitch!"

At least he had the common courtesy to groan and roll onto his side when I kicked him in the ribs. I was thinking about what to do and wondering if I should get drunk or storm out of the bar and see what apartments were going for when a thought struck me. I used a foot to roll him onto his back. "This was all a setup, wasn't it?"

"Of course it was a setup. And you fell right into it. By the way, I can see up your dress," he said. "Nice panties."

I shook my head slowly. Who cared if he could see my underwear? I was stuck until someone decided to check on my body and tried to re-establish the connection. Monique would probably check in a few days, but if she was smart, she was deep in hiding. Problem with that was in a few days there might not be anything left to check on.

"Who are you?" I asked.

"Nobody special," he said. "Just a guy looking for a little spiritual enlightenment."

"Bullshit. No one looks for spiritual enlightenment anymore. It's a lost cause."

He laughed and grunted as he sat up. "Wow. Clever girl. You're right. I don't care about Xevex or his mad plans. I'm just a guy paid to keep you wrapped up tight for a while. He sent some more people to go after your little girlfriend, so this is probably your home now."

Monique. Shit. Please, please, please let her have listened to my advice and disappeared. Peach could keep her safe.

"Yours, too, asshole," I said. "Don't forget, you're here forever, too."

He shrugged. "Meh. I like it here. It's digital, but my brain doesn't know that. My body was dying anyway. In time, we'll both fade away from this place. I'll die and Xevex's people will pull your body out, plug you into a special place, and let you do your thing."

"My thing?"

"Hacking, sugar tits. I didn't get the details because I really didn't care. Something, something. Hacking something. Something, something, money. Something, something, kill her. I really focused on the money."

"How are you going to spend money if you're going to die in Virt and the real?"

He held a hand out for me to help him to his feet. I slapped it away. He shrugged and slowly got up. "Not for me, kid. For my fam. Hopefully, they're long gone by now with a bit of loot to set up shop somewhere else. We design and sell-"

"I don't care!" I shouted in his face.

"You asked."

I gritted my teeth and growled. "Not what I meant and you know it."

He patted me on the shoulder and stared at my chest. "I know. You're just beautiful when you're angry."

"What is your deal?"

"I like tits," he said, shrugging. "They're cool."

"Penta," I hissed.

"Zealot?"

"Hardly. More habit than anything else."

He flipped a table back into place, pulled up a chair, and sat down. Groaned a little as he lifted both feet onto the table. "I know this place is fake and all, but it sure as shit felt like you kicked out my knee. The face doesn't feel good, either, but the knee is a special kind of throbbing. Where'd a pretty little hacker like you learn to kick like that?"

"Fuck you," I said. "That's where. It's on the corner of Fuck Off and Die."

"Ah, yeah. I remember that place. Good tacos."

He shook his head and waved a hand over the holomenu in the table. "Want anything? I'm buying."

"What? No!"

"Don't worry, it's the least thing I can do. I'll be dead in a few days. Family's off to greener pastures. I'm stuck here in heaven's waiting room. Might as well have a drink. I've still got some credits squirrelled away, too, so go nuts. Get something expensive and froofy. I know you chicks dig the froofy drinks."

Whatever. If I was stuck there forever, I'd definitely need a drink. Besides, maybe if he got drunk enough, he'd tell me things I wanted to hear. I sat down in a huff. Trapped. I hated feeling trapped. Reminded me of my many short stints in prison. "You serious about that drink?" I asked.

"Hundred percent. Help me burn through what little I've got left. I want to go out leaving nothing behind."

"Scotch. Top shelf. If it starts the Glen or Loch and the rest is a jumble of random letters, I'm good with it."

He smiled and waved at me. "See, this is how fights should end. Everyone dusts themselves off and the winner buys drinks."

"I don't know that you on your back and me on top getting ready to pummel you counts as a win."

"I don't know. I was on my back and you were on top of me. Sounds like a win to me."

I rubbed my temples and groaned. "Do you ever stop thinking about sex?"

"Nah," he said as he punched in an order. "Why would I? If more people were into getting laid regularly, the galaxy would be a much happier place. Happy people don't do stupid shit that causes problems."

"Tell that to your boss. He was trying to seduce a woman with coconuts on her chest when I walked in. Sounds like he's getting plenty of play."

He waved his hand in the air. "Doesn't count. Xevex doesn't enjoy it. Says its way of meeting someone's mind."

Of all the surreal situations I've found myself in, this was toward the top. Less than five minutes ago, I was trying to kill this guy and he was returning the favor. This was better. I reached across the table and held out my hand. "I'm Nat, by the way."

"Natasha Devore, I know." He shook my hand. "Slab Hardmeat. Wheeler, dealer, gadfly, and three-time winner of best sexual partner in the inner systems. I could have gone pro, but I decided my talents lay elsewhere. I still practice though, you know. Gotta keep in shape."

"Slab Hardmeat? Seriously?"

"It was my stage name. I just kept it because it brought back fond memories. I still sign body parts if you're interested."

"I'll pass. But thanks for the offer."

Our drinks rezzed in a flurry of bright light and bad holo sci-fi special effects. I sat back and sipped mine. For digitized scotch, it wasn't bad. Nothing compared to Mason's, but not bad. "Since we're here and it doesn't look like I'm getting out, care to tell me the plan?"

He peered at me over the rim of his drink. "Not really."

I leaned forward, put my elbows on the table, and tried to look innocent. "Come on. You beat me. Isn't it tradition for the bad guy to explain his plan to his defeated foe?"

"I made a promise. I keep my promises to people."

"Xevex isn't people anymore," I said. "He's a Predecessor."

Slab set his drink down on the table and frowned. "That's the most ridiculous thing I've ever heard."

"Tell me something; how did you meet him?"

"After the, uh, late unpleasantness on Serius, we got stuck in receiving for a while. Caught one of his shows. It lit a spark in me. You should really hear him talk sometime. Man's a wizard."

I shook my head. "I've heard him. Didn't resonate. I'm too old to pick a new god."

"He's not a god. He's a prophet. The real god is out there, waiting to wake up."

I nodded. Temnyy may not be a real god in "descended from heaven to punish people he didn't like" way, but a planetoid-sized bioweapon was scary enough in its own right. "Did he send you into Virt?"

"Yup."

"Told you to have sex, right? Find someone that appealed to you and fuck their brains out?"

Slab's face drooped a bit. "Yeah," he said slowly.

"Someone probably found you, right? A little wild sex in the bathroom and you never heard from them again."

"I don't like where this is going."

I put my hand on his. I wasn't sure why, it just seemed like the right thing to do. "Xevex told me flat out humans drop their shields during sex. We open ourselves up. Don't worry, it's not just you. My girlfriend told me my anitat system spews butterflies when I come."

"Girlfriend?"

"Hush and listen. We open our bodies, yes, but we also open our minds. Everything in Virt is interconnected to some level. We naturally protect our minds, but during sex, those protections drop. The person you met when you went in was a Predecessor looking for a new body. Their Virt is spilling into ours. They need a way out of Virt and into the real and we're it. Problem is, not all of our minds can handle storing one of theirs. Most people are rejected."

Slab leaned back in his chair and scrunched his brow. "Let's say I buy this fairytale; what happens when you get one of them inside of you?"

"I've only met a few of them. One was Xevex; the Predecessor took over his mind and fed his body into the nanogen feeds. He's a cloud of nanites driven by an ancient alien. You know how Xevex just magically appears on stage?"

"Sure," he said, nodding. "Great trick. I'd love to know how he does it."

"There are ducts in the airlock areas down in the sublevels."

"He climbs the ducts? That's kind of badass."

I frowned and shook my head. "They're six or seven centimeters in diameter. He glides up them as a stream of tiny robots and uses the Baals to obscure himself while he reassembles."

"That's crazy talk."

"I wish. One of the other Predecessors I met was a sort of friend who'd been taken over by one."

"Whoa," Slab said. "What's he like?"

"Nothing. I kicked him to death. Listen, there are only about a hundred Predecessors left. Some want out, some want to stay in. Once they get into your head, there's no getting them out. They just run you to ground and stomp on your personality. That god they're harping on? That's Temnyy. It's a massive bioweapon created for a war that ended for them over fourteen millennia ago. It was doomsday weapon. They were dead as a species so they were going to turn it loose on their enemies and anyone else who got in its way.

"Slab, listen. They want to bring Temnyy back to life and turn him loose on us. Predecessor tech was mostly low-rent, but they were masters at bioengineering. Xevex wanted you to be a host for a Predecessor. He wanted your body for it to live in. And all because he has some mad plan to hatch Temnyy and feed himself into its brain."

Slab blanched. "Damn. I've done some cold-blooded stuff in my life, but that takes the cake. I mean, it sounds completely bonkers-"

"I've seen them," I said. "Up close and personal."

"Wow. All the years we've been out here and you're the one to make first contact. Seems a little self-serving."

I frowned. When I was rambling it out, it made sense. In hindsight, it all seemed a little crazy. Just like waking up in someone else's body or joining a gang or bedding a template. Maybe I was losing my mind. Maybe Jenkins was a figment of my imagination. Maybe all this was neurons firing out of order or chemicals not doing the right chemically thing.

"I know it sounds nuts, just watch yourself, okay? I'd hate to have to kick you to death, too."

He chuckled at that. "If they want out, I'm the worst target there is. I'm not coming out. Xevex's crew is probably seeing to that right now. I'm just gonna sit here and ride out what little time I have left ogling chicks and drinking overpriced brown liquors."

"If I get to choose my end, that's exactly what I'll do, too," I said. "Take care, Slab. Sorry about your balls."

He waved a hand in the air. "No probs. They've been used and abused before. Besides, I've blown so many loads into hot chicks like you, I doubt the little guys even work anymore. Wanna test my theory?

"Thank you, but no. Good luck. I hope your death goes smoothly."

"Good luck, Nat. You're a hell of a fighter. I hope you find a way out of here."

I nodded, knocked back my drink, and left without looking back. It might have looked totally badass, but I was centimeters away from completely losing my shit. It took every bit of strength to keep my back straight and that scream beaten down.

I couldn't believe I'd fallen straight into Xevex's trap. Now the bastard held all the cards and I was stuck waiting for him to do whatever nasty thing he had in mind for me. I needed help. I hated to admit it, but I was stuck.

30 - Sittin' In a Tree

Mason's houseghoul gently closed the door after politely informing me that Mason wasn't available at the moment. Actually, what he said was, "Fuck off outta here before I break yer fuckin' head open." And then he slammed the door in my face, but I like to look past the actions and find the gentle soul within.

I stepped back, thought about kicking the door until tall, white, and gruesome opened it up and then ducking under his arms and making a run for it. The problem with that idea was he would have caught me, smashed me around for a while, and then tossed me back outside. Still stuck in virt, but with some tasty bruises and broken bones to go along with it.

I gently backed down the glowing walkway until something caught my eye: A second floor window was open. And it was right next to a tree. I shimmied up the tree and remembered how much easier it was with strap-on claws and heavy Klevar clothes. Legs scraped, one nail torn completely out, and one major cut on the inside of my thigh later, I delicately crawled toward the open window.

Flashing light and soft grunting. Please be someone lifting weights. I don't know if I could stand finding Mason whacking it with his headphones on in the middle of a dance floor. I mean, it wouldn't surprise me, but I don't know if I could stand seeing it move from the theoretical to the actual.

I paused on the branch and hoped it would hold my weight. Just a couple of meters away. And a seven-meter fall below me. Vertigo, my old friend, how have you been?

The grunting got louder. I knew those sounds. I'd made them myself. I tried not to think about the times I'd made them. The women underneath me or on top of me. Claws on my back or chest. Hot flesh wrapped around me. Damn it. Gentle throb between my legs. Need to be touched. I hated it when I accidentally turned myself on.

Grunts turned to groans. Groans turned to moans. Moans turned to animal snarls as the human left and the simian took over. The lights flashed faster. Reds and oranges turned yellow, hit a crescendo, and turned first back to red then a slow fade to purple.

I finally reached the window and peeked through. What I saw shouldn't have surprised me, but I gasped and nearly fell off the tree branch.

"Natasha. If you wanted to join us, you should have told Gorg at the door."

Mason looked perfectly at ease. Jessica, still perched on top of him and glowing a faint purple, glanced over her shoulder, smiled, and waved. It looked like Mason was leading the charge in interspecies diplomacy.

Jessica climbed off him and sat cross-legged on the bed, her hand on Mason's chest. "There is something to be said for mammal coupling."

"I'll take that as a compliment, my dear," Mason told her, patting her hand.

"I need to tell my friends about this. They might wish to try you out. I hope that's okay."

Mason chuckled. "It's fine with me, but most humans might have issues with it."

"Why?"

"Human bonding is perhaps a bit deeper than yours. We bond with our mates at a personal and sexual level."

"Mates," Jessica said. "Interesting. We don't have those. Perhaps next time we should try using my natural body."

"Um, guys," I said.

Mason shook his head and chuckled. "Natasha, please come inside. It's awkward speaking to you like this."

Awkward? He was having sex with an alien and I was awkward? I crawled forward until I could touch the windowsill. Both of them watched me with bemused eyes and curled up lips. Jessica covered her mouth – a perfect imitation of reaction, I might add – when I nearly fell and Mason quietly applauded when I righted myself.

The branch cracked and my heart sank. Something about falling always freaked me out. The sheer lack of control over the whole thing sent my mind spinning. It must be why I hated spacewalks. I needed something to cling to for security.

My body dropped. Before I could hit the ground, my arm felt like something wrenched it from the socket and I face-planted into the side of Mason's cobalt gray monstrosity of a house. The ground was only a few meters below my bare feet, but it looked like kilometers to the grass.

I looked up and found Jessica's hand wrapped tightly around my wrist. "Don't worry, I've got you," she said with a genuine smile.

She was far stronger than I would have guessed. She lifted me over her head with one arm, held me up as I got my feet over the windowsill, and gently set me down.

"Thanks," I mumbled. My shoulder throbbed as I worked the kinks out.

"Are you okay?" Jessica asked. "Do you need medical assistance? I know your bodies are not as robust as ours, but I figured the damage would be negligible. Or you could leave Virt and come back. I believe that would heal you."

"Can't leave," I said.

"What do you mean you 'can't leave'?" Mason asked.

"I got into a little altercation. Got hit with a spanner."

"How did someone get a spanner into Virt?" he asked.

"If I may interrupt, what is a spanner?" Jessica asked.

"It's a tool that severs the link between body and mind in Virt. Think of it was blowing up a bridge you need to get from point A to point B." I said.

"How long was it set for?" Mason asked. Apparently, the old guy had some experience with spanners. Probably firsthand.

"No end date," I said. "Forever, according to Slab."

"Slab?" Mason asked.

"Slab Hardmeat." I mumbled.

"No offense, Natasha," Jessica said. "But I have difficulty believing anyone would be named 'Slab Hardmeat.'"

Mason shook his head sadly. "I knew Slab back in the day. How is he?"

"Solid punch," I said, idly rubbing my jaw. "He's got a limp now. Dying of something terminal. He didn't say what. Wait. Why am I talking about a washed-up sex star? He's the reason I'm stuck here. Xevex hired him to keep me stuck in Virt while his cronies move my body somewhere else. He's got some crazy idea that I'm going to do some hacking for him."

"A task we both know you're not up to," Mason said.

"Why would she not be up to it?" Jessica asked.

Mason started to talk. Clamped his mouth shut and motioned toward me. I had to hand it to the guy, he was legit to the bone. He said he'd keep my secret and he meant it.

She glanced at me and I returned the favor by staring at the floor. That Mason knew the real me was bad enough, having a Predecessor know was a jump too far. Jessica flashed colors in rapid succession. Red white blue gold. She settled on a deep burgundy for a beat and then switched to orange and yellow. "Screaming at us in Predecessor isn't helping," I said.

She whirled and poked me in the forehead. Her form rippled and I got a glimpse of raging novempod. Her whole body tensed and relaxed. She flashed colors: blues and purples. First bright and tawdry but fading to black slowly.

"I am sorry," she said as her color returned to human normal. "Your species is...frustrating. I am trying to help. I promise."

Mason patted the bed and flashed her a sad grin. "My dear, yours is the first alien species we've met. We don't do well with our own people when they're different. We've fought wars over trivial ideologies and committed atrocities over nuanced interpretations of religious books. Humans and differences don't mix well. And you are, well, different."

"I don't mean any offense," I added. "It's just. Well. It's hard to explain and a little embarrassing."

"You have nothing to be embarrassed about," Mason said. "Against the average person, your ruse would have held up indefinitely."

"Ruse?" Jessica asked.

"He's right," I said, pointing at Mason. "It's all a ruse."

"Your species and your ruses," Jessica spat. "It is one thing I'll never understand. Duplicity. When we say something, we mean it."

I paused and shut down. Stared at the floor of Mason's bedroom. Or sex chamber. Or whatever the fuck this room was.

"Tell her," Mason said. "She needs to know."

Jessica knelt in front of me and took my hands in hers. "I promise you, I am not the enemy. I am a friend, Natasha Devore."

"Wonderful," I snorted. "One problem. I'm not Natasha Devore. I'm just wearing her skin. My name is Rex Kormer. I'm a thief who got roped into this mess and stuffed in Natasha's body after she deleted her mind."

"Oh, that," Jessica said. "I already knew that."

A strange mix of emotions, both Predecessor colors and human brow furrowing washed over Jessica's face. Her body pixelated, vibrated, and settled back to something normal. She sat perfectly still. Even in Virt, people twitch. We breathe. Mammal brains keeping our bodies alert and ready for action. But Jessica was a statue. I reached a finger out and brushed her face. No response.

"Is there a glitch in the matrix?" I asked Mason.

He shrugged and shook his head. "I don't know. I've never seen anything like that. What does she feel like?"

"Solid. Warmish. Pretty human. Well, as human as Virt lets us feel."

Mason crawled out of the bed and walked toward us. Still naked. "Could you, uh, cover up?" I asked.

"Dear Natasha, don't fret. I'm no threat to you. As I said earlier, you're too inexperienced."

"That's not really what I meant," I said. My cheeks felt like they were on fire.

"Ah, I see. You were a straight man, I take it."

I nodded. While human sexuality – barring a few weirdo planets – was pretty much a free-for-all, I never found guys that attractive.

"Biology is catching up to you," he said. "Natasha wasn't known to take many lovers. While she dallied with women here and there, her true calling was men. She was what she was, just like you are what you are. If you want my opinion, find what makes you happy and go for it. Your problem is you don't know what will make you happy."

"Yeah." Eloquence, thy name is me.

"I know this isn't the help you came here for, but always go for happiness. Enjoy things because you enjoy them, not because someone else expects you to enjoy them. No offense, but your head is probably a mess right now. Take some time to sort out who you are."

Jessica chose that moment to come back to life. One instant she was a warm statue the next her eyes were boring straight into me with an intensity I'd only ever seen from the mentally deranged. "Your memories," she said. "I must have them."

"There aren't that many," I said. "Also, if you try to take over my brain, I will give you splitting headaches every minute of every day forever."

"As I told you, Natasha, I am not your enemy."

Mason was right; my head was a mess of conflicting emotions and desires. Biology overrunning my personality, my personality running roughshod over biology. A constant state of conflict that, frankly, was wearing me down. "Fine," I told her. "If you're going to take over my head, make it quick and kill me when you're done."

Jessica shook her head and sighed. "Please. Trust me. This is important."

Dazzling eyes locked on mine. I got lost in them. Stark cobalt blue trailing to yellowish edges, all surrounding black so deep you couldn't decide whether the void was comforting or terrifying. A pure nothingness. No worry, no pain, no fear. Also no joy, no warmth, no love. Perfectly in tune with the universe.

Our foreheads touched and memories exploded in my head. Bik's wink as he encouraged me to drink more. The sense of horror staring into the mirror to see Natasha stare back. Nobtop laughing and hugging me. Tiny's dopey smile as he handed me the fake membership card and parking pass. My foot kicking Sol to death. Monique's fingers in my hair and her face between my legs. Monique and I laughing as we shared songs. Xevex pummeling me. Nobtop showing me the "thing." Monique's dry chuckle as Prefect floated into space, strapped to a chair and screaming into the void. Heads exploding. Peaches smiling as she pulled my head to hers. Nobtop eaten alive by a cloud. Everything. She looted my memories and I let her do it. It felt good to let it all go, to share the weird, degenerated state of my life.

When we broke, Jessica wiped a tear from her eye and whispered, "I'm sorry."

I shook my head and frowned. "Why?"

"You were dropped into a mess you didn't create but must clean up. Not for you. But for the ones who were caught up in the net. I need to show you something."

"You're already naked," I said.

Jessica chuckled at that. "I'm glad you noticed. Flesh is nothing more than clothing. Yours. Mine. Mason's. We are all more than skin. But that's not what I need to show you."

"Okay," I said quietly, not sure where she was going.

"Ever since the first of us wandered into your Virt, we've been watching you. Your people were horrifying to us. Alien monsters with only two distinct sets of limbs and only two eyes. It took us time to overcome that repulsion."

"Thanks," I said. "We aim to please."

Jessica rolled her eyes, a distinctly human affectation. She must have been studying us for a long time. "We think in threes and nines. You think in twos and tens. That was my breakthrough. My contribution. We weren't that different. Just different meat surrounding a similar core. The core matters far more than the meat. Do you remember the room with the large, black core extractor and the metal grates?"

I nodded. "Kind of hard to forget. Your boy nearly beat me to death there."

She cocked her head to the side and stared at me. "Ah. Not my literal child. An ancient figure of speech. The one you call Xevex Jeffries is not my boy. He is broken. One of the ones that cracked in unforeseen ways. Anyway, the room is, was, our extraction room. For all your technological wonders, your people are still stuck on the flesh. Your brain is a living computer. The code running on that computer and the data amassed from a lifetime can be moved. You've experienced this firsthand, as has Mason. The rest of your species hasn't made that leap yet. We figured it out early on and have hopped in and out of bodies and computers for millennia. Computers and other things. The Core Extraction room was designed to handle a mass extraction and upload. We knew we'd be here for a long time and all biology is, unfortunately, time-sensitive and requires large amounts of food and water to keep it running.

"I told you these ships were escorts and protection systems against our final weapon. That is all true. They were also intended to provide pilots and support for our final weapon when the time was right. The grates you found were where our bodies were broken down and fed to the nanotech systems after the cores were extracted. The nano systems were designed to regenerate our bodies should the need ever arise. When your people tinkered with them, it alerted us. Woke us from our twilight daze. Your upgrades to the nano system were dazzling and unthinkable to us. When they were designed, each nanobot was a completely separate unit. Your Specialists allowed them to work together. To communicate. To replicate. You made them a whole new lifeform. Such amazing skills and your people use them to make sex toys."

"If I can interject," I said, "some of those toys are mind-blowing."

Jessica smiled the same smile my mother used to give me when she was about to drop a terrifying amount of truth on me. "No doubt. But that same technology ravaged your planets a couple of centuries ago. And here you are, playing with it again."

"In our defense, we don't tend to learn from the past if the lesson is inconvenient," Mason said.

"Your strength and your weakness. Curiosity." Jessica looked me dead in the eye. "You came here to escape problems you'd created for yourself. I know this because you told me once before you are who you are now. Mason wanted to get away from his past. Both of you contributed code to the systems. Natasha celebrated in Virt and crossed Xevex's path. His, I guess you would call it 'mate' even though we don't work that way, latched on to you and found something useful. Instead of letting them win, you hacked our tools and used them to delete yourself. It might have been the most selfless act I'd ever seen. Removing your mind from your body without a new place to put it."

"Wasn't me," I told her. "I'm just a thief. A great, sexy, brilliant thief, but just a thief."

Jessica snapped her finger. "Right. Not you, her. I need to show you something, thief. Xevex wants you for

Natasha's skills, but I have a suspicion your own skills might be useful to me."

Damned aliens. I was in this mess because someone else did something that impressed an alien and pissed off other aliens. If Natasha had just succumbed, I could have been tortured, killed, and far away from all this madness by now. "Do you want to see my rate sheet before we proceed?"

"No. I think you'll do this one for free," she said. Before I could come up with a witty retort, she pushed our foreheads together and we were standing in the Core Extraction room. Natasha, the real one, was twitching in front of the black thing. For some reason, the skull punching tentacle thing was keeping away from her.

"This might not be easy to watch," Jessica said.

Natasha was way out of it, but there was defiance in her eyes. She wasn't going to go down without a fight. A Specialist entered the frame. Natasha's eyes focused on him. Eyebrows furrowed. "This will wipe me...keep my body alive, right?" she asked. Tough as she wanted to be, her voice quavered.

"Yes," the Specialist said. "Although I still don't understand why you want your body to live. It would be easier to let us digitize your mind and extract the being."

"Idiot," she mumbled. "They don't come out. Ever."

"Why this elaborate plan, Natasha?" a voice to the side asked. "Why kill your brain but keep your body alive?"

"Body is tainted with them. This thing smells it," she said, motioning at the brain-smasher. "Thinks I'm one of them. Put someone else in my body. Someone tenacious.

After I'm gone, they'll look for me. Look for what I know. The hints are there, someone just has to follow them. Someone who can follow it through the end."

"I know just the person," Bik Parameter said, stepping into the frame.

I swore then that the second I saw Bik, I was going to break his damned nose.

"Don't tell them anything. Xevex will know and attack. Keep him off kilter. Let him wonder if we're tougher than he thinks. It will buy you time. You must restart Endpoint."

Natasha drew herself up as straight as she could. The Specialist checked a thin wire coming out of the back of her neck. Instinctively, I reached under my hair and felt around. Nothing. "The Virt version of you doesn't have the data port," Jessica whispered in my ear.

"Last words?" The Specialist asked.

"I can't believe all this happened because I fucked an airlock preacher's buddy in Virt," Natasha replied.

"That's it?" Bik asked. "The final words of the legendary Digital Diva?"

"If you're looking for something uplifting, I'm not your gal. Find someone who can stop Xevex and turn on Endpoint. I might not be a good bedtime story, but vengeance is always a good reason." With that, she brought her thumb down on something in her hand. For a moment, Natasha stood perfectly still. The lights went out in her eyes. Her whole body rag-dolled and fell to the floor in a heap.

Bik placed a hand on Nat's neck and nodded. "Still alive. Keep her somewhere safe and don't tell your associates. They may be in on it. I'll contact you shortly when I've located Rex Kormer."

The scene dissolved and I found myself back in naked land. Jessica was staring at me. "Two questions: How do I get out of Virt and how do I turn on Endpoint?" I asked.

31 - Reality Nibbles

Getting out of Virt was the easy part. Just as Jessica had predicted, Xevex was standing over me, leering like a sick loon when I woke up and found myself strapped to a table in the Core Extraction room. I struggled a bit, but he had me dead to rights. "You know," I said, "I prefer bondage with people I trust."

"Physical straps this time, Natasha," he said. "None of your chicanery."

The tentacle thing was hovering over my body like it was leering at me. "So, what's the plan, big guy?" I asked. "You've already beaten me up and I've already thrown up on you, so we've got that part of the relationship covered."

"The plan is I'm going to pull everything out of your primitive brain and then toss you out of an airlock. You're not compatible so, other than what's in your head, you're useless."

Little did he know. "You know, you could try flowers and chocolate. It's sort of the traditional human mating game. Maybe even a movie." I tugged at the bond on my wrist. "After that, you might find me more willing to cooperate."

He slapped me and wrapped a hand around my throat. Choking. Again. And this time I didn't even have any Feggs to throw up on him. There was a fire in his eyes. Manic energy. No longer the mania of the street preacher who thought he'd found god, it was the pure madness you only get with thinking you were god. There wouldn't be any talking my way out of this one. The bastard was going to pluck my brain out in the most painful way possible and

I was going to die wondering what the ever-loving fuck he really wanted.

I struggled. I fought with everything I had. I let the caged ape loose. But even her massive strength wasn't enough. All I could do was die with his goddamned hand around my throat and hope it was quick and at least relatively painless. As the world went black, I wondered whose body I'd wear at the end. My old one or Natasha's? Would she want hers back?

"Your race disgusts me," Xevex said. "Pathetic, stinking, hairy things."

"Madam," Jenkins interjected. "I don't believe our previous plan of attack will work again. He appears to have hardened his network."

I was too busy dying to reply.

"There is, however, another possibility," Jenkins said. "I can shut down your body and make it appear that you died."

Play dead? Wasn't that what they suggested when Ratbears were chasing you? Considering my alternatives were being mostly dead or all dead, I went with mostly dead. "Yes," I hissed.

"Was that 'yes' do it? Or a different kind of yes?" Jenkins asked.

"Dying," I mumbled. Thoughts were already fading.

"This will be tricky since you're already oxygen-deprived, but I believe I can shut you down for a few minutes and safely resurrect your body."

Shut. Up. And. Do. It. I didn't even have the strength left to yell at him. Something pinged back in my head.

Light years away but still clear as a bell. Everything stopped.

Jenkins collected surveillance footage and fed it into my head after the incident. That was the only way I knew what happened during those four minutes where I was clinically, figuratively, and literally dead. There was no lit tunnel. No angels. No Penta. No Buddha. Nothing.

I was gone.

As soon as my body stopped moving, Xevex leapt back. Apparently, he didn't want to kill me yet, just show me his love. Straight up torturous bastard with a mean streak. Jenkins was still running off the latent electricity in my body. If he didn't pull me back in time, he'd die, too.

The extractor thing twitched. It slipped close, sniffed me like a dog. Xevex crept forward, body rippling and mutating into his Predecessor form. Together the two of them watched over me. Xevex flashed purples and reds. The extractor pointed its metal snout at him and flashed back.

The extractor shot forward at Xevex, a snake letting something know to keep its distance. Xevex jumped back and held up three of his arms.

The extractor unhooked my limbs from the table, nudging me and the table away from the core. Xevex flashed whites and yellows and nudged me back. They went back and forth a few times before the extractor lashed out and slammed into the side of my table, spilling me on the floor. Xevex vibrated. His body flashed red and white as one of his tentacles motioned toward me. The extractor launched itself at him and the fight was on.

I came to lying face down on the cold deck with a bloody nose and a throbbing headache. "Massive cortal dump," Jenkins said. "It will hurt for a white, but you are alive and free."

"Thanks," I mumbled. "What did I miss?"

"Xevex Jeffries is currently engaged in battle with the Predecessor extraction tool. Apparently, there is more to the extractor than I would have guessed. It is entirely likely the extractor is an integral part of the original Endpoint mainframe, quite possibly an agent of the ship itself."

I slowly managed to roll onto my side. "I can't believe I nearly slept through alien battle royale."

Jeffries tried to find a way around the extractor, but the mechanical snake was too fast for him. Neither was making any headway and, apparently, Xevex hadn't clued in that he was made of tiny machines that could become a cloud and go wherever they wanted. Predecessors were just as clumsy as humans in stress situations.

"You need to get up and get moving," Jenkins told me. "At some point, this battle will end and both will turn their aggressions on you."

I tried to get up, but my muscles weren't having anything to do with that madness. With a quick glimpse over my shoulder, I crawled to the room door. The last thing I saw of the fight was the extractor flashing red and Xevex a steady white glow.

Outside the door, I tried to stand up but my legs gave out from under me. Dying really took it out of me. "Jenkins, stim pack 4," I muttered.

"Stim pack 4 is made from various illicit chemicals. I would strongly suggest another course of action."

"Since when is crackodile an illicit chemical?"

"Since always. Crackodile is an ancient cocaine derivative. Modern implementations largely keep the original chemical composition intact but add despicable things like guarana and ginseng. It is a death cocktail."

I sighed and thought about snapping at him, but he was just doing his job. Besides, if the ginseng got me he'd be gone, too. "Jenkins," I said. "In a few minutes, a pile of pissed off nanites is going to bore a hole though me or Jeffries is going to unleash his zombie army on me or some other bad thing is going to happen and I'm in a state where I can't even run. You can pop stim pack four and we might die, or you can not and we will die. Frankly, I've got things and people left to do before I go so, please, pop the pack."

Crackodile hits fast with a warm glow. Its primary chemical is a numbing agent. After your body is good and desensitized, the second wave hits. Heart pumps faster as the wondrous stuff plows through your body. Everything slows down as your brain speeds up. Then the guarana and ginseng hit and things go into complete overdrive. Endless energy. Endless thoughts. Endless paranoia.

I was sprinting down the hall without a care in the world before I knew it. I could run forever. I could beat Nobtop in a fistfight. I could fuck gods into submission and still want more. I could tear open Temnyy and feast on his guts.

Wait. Temnyy.

Shit.

Jessica.

"Jenkins, get me the shortest route to a place called Info Den 3. No, make it the longest route. No, wait. No time. Shortest route. Also, monitor my heart, it feels like it might explode. If it looks like it might explode, let me know before it does. Also, no. Wait. I don't want to know about my heart. Just get me to Info Den 3."

My feet pounded on the deck. I should have thanked Jeffries for giving me some clothes after his minions pulled me out of the Virt goop. Of course, I also needed to find out if any of the freaks copped a quick feel when they hauled my naked body out of the goop. I'll bet they did. Bastards. Litervian Swine. I'd kill them all.

"Turn right at the next corridor," Jenkins said.

"Find me any security footage of my getting pulled out of Virt. I'm afraid I might need to hunt some bastards down." I replied as I bounded around the corner. A countdown timer in my HUD showed I had about five minutes before the stim pack was exhausted and reality punched me in the teeth. Hopefully enough time.

"Next left."

"How's my heart?"

"It's-"

"Never mind. It's fine. I'd know if something was wrong," I said. Even as I said it, I knew my heart was working overtime. Expand, contract; expand, contract. Rush of blood in my ears. Oh, well. If it was going to explode, it would have already. Better than whatever Jeffries and his mechanical pet snake had in mind.

I skidded around the corner, lost my footing, and slid, bouncing across the deck. I looked up and found two Airlockers staring at me in shock. The moment dragged out like that slice of time where you say something really stupid and everyone knows it but no one knows exactly how to respond to a fart joke at a funeral.

"God has led her to us," one said to the other. He was wearing the tattered remains of what was probably a nice suit. Shaking in either withdrawal or ecstasy. Maybe both. But guessing from his dinner-plate pupils, I was going to go with ecstasy.

Shit.

"Truly, the prophet is great," the other replied. He was probably a scary character once upon a time. Or maybe he just had a leather and chrome fetish. Either way, there was still a hint of badass lurking in the puffy eyes and sagging gut.

"Shouldn't you guys get on your knees and thank god for the beautiful bounty?" I was probably closer to a maglev wreck than a beautiful bounty, but whatever.

"Grab her!" the first one said.

I twisted my body and lashed out with every bit of strength I had in my Crackodile-enhanced legs. I waited just long enough to feel the sickening snap of a patella shattering before rolling out of the way and putting the falling derelict between me and the aging badass. Like an old-school animation, he collided with his falling buddy and they both tumbled to the ground.

"See, if you guys had just got on your knees and given thanks, none of this would have happened," I said with a bow.

I took off running. My HUD showed three minutes. How in Penta's name had that little encounter taken a full minute? Had to hustle and keep my footing. "Jenkins, can you locate Airlockers?" I asked as I dodged obstacles and people.

"Negative. Airlockers aren't tagged, so Endpoint doesn't know how to track them."

"Damn," I said. "Do we know the status of the Bratva? I could really use their help right now."

"The Bratva are down. While you were in Virt there was a lot of chatter on PointNET. Apparently, the remaining Bratva were killed with toxic gas."

"Where did they get toxic gas? Last I checked, the stores were out of it."

"As with all scuttlebutt on PointNET, this should be taken with a grain of salt, but it appears the toxic gas matched the signature of Endpoint's reactor core."

"Damn it. Damn Xevex. Of course he'd know how to open the core; he probably helped build the damned ship."

"True. He likely knows Endpoint much better than any of us do."

"Yeah," I said as I skidded to a halt in from a non-descript door with Info Den 3 stenciled on it. "But we're about to change that. I've got my own friend who'd like to join the game."

Info Den 3's door had a strange looking security pad. Most human pads scan entire hands or eyes. That one just had a pair of matte silver sensors poking out from a coal black panel. It must have been an original Predecessor pad. Over the hundred or so years Endpoint's habitation, there were still places no one bothered to look. We called it Info Den 3, implying there were two others that weren't on the maps. Perhaps the other two were identical and they assumed this one was just more of the same.

Jessica's words echoed in my head. "Red, red, green, red, green, blue, red, blue, red. Each for exactly half a second. And remember, we communicated with our whole bodies. Just your face won't cut it."

I sighed and looked around. Not exactly the most popular part of Endpoint, but people had a way of showing up unannounced. "Jenkins, keep an eye on Endpoint personal scanners. I need to do something."

"Yes, ma'am. What, if I may ask, are do you need to do?"

"Flash a door."

I took a last look around and wished I had one of the old laser cutters they used to pull out Predecessor locks. Now or never. I unzipped my coveralls and slid my arms out. Hopefully, my torso would be enough. "Jenkins, play light track 1."

My body turned red, turned neutral gray, turned red, etc. I tried to stay still while I flashed out a millennia-old code to the door sensor. Somewhere, there was probably a hidden camera watching me and wondering if I was crazy or just into weird kinks. After the sequence played, nothing happened. I was about to play it again when the lock clicked open with a metallic thunk.

I shrugged back into my coverall and looked around the door. Human doors usually have knobs or pads, little cues to tell people how to open them. The door to Info Den 3 was completely smooth. I felt along the frame but couldn't find anything. Of course. To come this far only to be stymied by a freakin' door. I put my hands on both sides of the frame and rested my head against the door. Defeated by a long-dead race.

Something clicked and whirred. *Of course*, I thought, kicking myself, *they think in threes*.

The door to Info Den 3 opened and I finally found my wild fantasies about aliens and science come true. Flashing lights, arcing currents, and purple glowing objects illuminated the dark room. If a classic Terran mad scientist found her lab redecorated by disco aliens, it would look exactly like Info Den 3.

As soon as I stepped through the door, a tentacle thing flew out of the ceiling and hovered in front of me. It was the same as the one in Core Extraction, but this one lacked the urgency. The tentacle thing in Core Extraction was a trauma surgeon, ready and desperate to extract Predecessors from their bodies before they ran out of supplies. The one in front of me felt more like a librarian. Calm, collected, filled with all the knowledge of the universe, and frighteningly fun at parties.

It moved all around my head and body, sniffing like a dog who smells something familiar but can't get past the person making the smell. Every now and then, it would poke and prod at me. I kept very still and let it do its job.

After the incident on Ro, I'd learned to let security stuff do their things.

Eventually, it backed off and settled into a quiet state of watching. I wondered what the first people to come across those things thought. If Nobtop was right, the last thing to go through their minds was an alien mechanical snake. Which may explain why no one bothered with this room after going into the first two Info Dens.

If Jessica was right, and she hadn't been in Info Den 3 for thousands of years, the terminal was between the glowing ball of hyperionized gas and the purple spindly thing that used to be a massive insect before the Predecessors coopted its brain and body to help run the station-wide thermostats.

Just like she predicted, there was a bowl of squiggly things on a high shelf over the terminal. Bio-storage devices engineered from native worms infused with crystal matrices. Still alive even after all these years. I plucked one from the bowl and held it in my hand. The little creature glowed bright white, flashed blue, and stretched itself out. I wondered: Did it have any thoughts? Any idea of where and what it was? Was its small crystal-augmented brain aware?

Humanity experimented with bio-storage a couple of centuries ago. It was a disaster. The official line was that bio-storage was too easy to hack and too unstable, but I think the biggest worry was getting humans to buy a hard drive that was alive. The Predecessors didn't have that kind of ethic. Five minutes in the room and I'd already seen things that made my skin crawl.

Which made me wonder who would really win in a war between us and them. They didn't have same advanced tech that we did. We were also unpredictable and prone to unbelievable violence – witness my little escapade in the hallway. The Predecessors seemed better at bioengineering and lacked empathy.

It would have been a heck of a fight.

I dropped the crystal worm in an indentation and flashed a series of colors at the console. At least that time I didn't have to strip. I didn't even realize I was holding my breath until the console flashed blue, blue, yellow, and the crystal worm lit up in flashing green. How much data could one of the little worms hold? Jessica swore it was enough, but I had to wonder. Human brains can hold a few petabytes of data. Predecessors were probably in that neighborhood. So, the crystal worm had to be a multi-petabyte or exabyte storage system.

The worm stopped flashing and I gently picked it up. In a few hours, it was going to become the most valuable thing in the systems. "Jessica," I said to the worm, "I hope you're safe and sound."

I carefully put the crystal worm in my breast pocket and was about to leave when the terminal in front of me lit up. It flashed out a series of colors and went dead again. Somewhere in Virt, Jessica had just sent her last message to herself. A part of her, the part in my breast pocket, would live on. The other part of her would get to experience death.

I made sure the message was stored in my head and left the room. Someone might stumble across the open door, but I doubted it. Even if they did, odds were the extraction snake would kill a few of them before they remembered how to neutralize it or just closed the door and pretended it wasn't there.

"Okay, Jenkins. We need to find Ops. It's not on the maps, but it should be close to the Bizarre Bazaar. One thing to do first, though."

32 - Thievery LLC

"Fire message one and message two," I told Jenkins. The Crackodile faded, leaving me staggering through the corridors like a cheerleader who'd just had a date with the sportsball team.

Planning. Get all those ducks in a row before the stupid snickering dog showed up. "Also, fire up search routine seven."

Somewhere on Endpoint, The Specialist just received a message from Mary Jane Masterson, science groupie and burlesque dancer, bidding him to meet her for a clothing optional latte in a private café next to the Bizarre Bazaar. Meanwhile, both Peach and Monique got a message to get the heck out of Dodge.

"Search routine seven started," Jenkins said. "Shall I post the results on your HUD?"

"Yes, please. And also fire stimpaks one and two." Screw you, heart and liver. I was going to finish this.

An unholy mixture of Kaffeene and slow-burn sugar hit my bloodstream. I was going to hurt when this was over. If I survived my little plan, that was. The fogginess in my head cleared. My muscles came back to life. I really hoped Natasha didn't want this body back because I'd just done the biological equivalent of dumping NOS in the afterburner.

"Best route to Ops," I said.

"There is no Ops on the map, ma'am," Jenkins replied.

"Damn. Of course not," I said. "It would be a major target. Locate any 10x10 empty space near the Bizarre Bazaar. Preferably close to Stu's Disco Injection. Project them on my HUD."

Three circles lit up in front of me. The first one was a no-go. It was right next to the entrance to the Bazaar and I'd seen cleaning bots coming out. The second and third were possibilities. Number two had an actual door. Number three was an enclosed area with no clear way in or out. With my luck, it was probably three.

I stopped in the first store I found, stole a pack of cigarettes and a silque squarf. The cigarettes had an animated man riding a six-legged beast across the stars on the cover. Kosmos. Crazy-ass Cyrillic smokes from a company that was reputed to have existed since before the Diaspora. Deep red cigar-smoking skulls covered the squarf. Pirate stuff stolen from the flag of the semi-legendary Rob Roy. They were all the rage. Probably a quarter of Endpoint owned one. I stole it because I needed to make sure I still had some skills, and because co-opting a pirate's flag to make a quick buck seemed shady to me.

Head wrapped, dressed in dark gray coveralls, and enjoying my Kosmos, I set out with a bit less trepidation that I was about to get jumped and dragged to the novempod king.

A pair of Airlockers stood by the entrance to the Bazaar, shifting back and forth in the traditional homeless shuffle. I should have felt sorry for their stained, tattered selves, but they let themselves buy into and were active participants in Xevex's madness. Besides, given half a chance, those two bastards would have coldcocked me and dragged my drooling body straight into the lair of the beast. No time like the present to test my disguise. Just a couple more tweaks to make it stick.

"Jenkins, tune tat to five percent lime green. Full body."

I drooped my left shoulder slightly and shuffled a bit. Don't mind me, guys. Just another victim of Narcissus, Lord Emperor of Lithodendron and his magical gas attacks. The Airlockers didn't notice as I moved past them and into the dense crowd. Just another boring chick with a slight neurological decay sporting the hottest socialista knock-off fashion.

Never get complacent. It would be easy to chuckle to myself or let my disguise drop. Lose the shuffle or the wandering eyes. Act like myself. But there could have been more lurking in the morass of bodies. The shuffle slowed me down. I had to force myself to not run. Natasha's go-juice cocktail was still coursing through my veins, screaming at me to take off at top speed.

I made my way through the crowd with a growing sense of doom. Paranoia. Wonderful. Stimulant paranoia is a pernicious bitch. Every eye that glanced at me was an enemy. Every smile held daggers behind gleaming teeth.

"Ma'am," Jenkins said. "Your heart rate is dangerously high."

"I know. It's the stim packs. It'll pass. I hope."

"I will continue to monitor your vital signs and, if needed, administer something to calm your heart."

"Don't you dare," I hissed. "Right now the only keeping me going is all the junk in my system."

I took an indirect path to the first flashing marker in my HUD. Blend in. Haggle over stuff. Curse the shop owner's genes, family, friends, ancestors, then buy some trinket for slightly less than he sold it for. By the time I made it to the right place, I had a bag, two new pairs of underwear, a shawl made by authentic* Sarcastic Monks, and a fertility necklace forged from a meteorite. I'd also eaten a spice-coated, deep-fried scorpantula.

True to Endpoint's schematics, there was a door. What Endpoint's schematics didn't show was that the door was a good three meters off the deck. There was nothing special about the door. It looked to be metal, painted a dark burgundy, and completely lacking any way to access it. Plus, it was rectangular. If I had to guess, I'd say it was a decoy.

The third location was a mystery so complete it made the burgundy door look easy. Simply put, according to the schematics there was an empty space. According to my eyes and body, there was nothing there. The space was completely empty.

"Are you sure this is the spot?" I asked Jenkins. "There's nothing here. Just a sausage stand and a guy selling religious-themed dildos."

"According to Endpoint's schematics, you should be right on top of the empty space."

Wait.

Predecessor tech. Where was it? I probably looked like a damned fool pirouetting around, but it had to be there somewhere. Probably at ground level, too. The Preds were crazy-ass marine critters. They weren't adapted to climbing like we were.

There. Tucked away in an alcove to the right of Endpoint's own Sausage Meister. A small camera peeking out from the darkness. If I hadn't been looking for a camera, I would have missed it. The next question was how much flak was I going to get for doing it. Right after that was how much was I going to have to strip so the camera had enough image to use. After that was whether the password would work.

It turned out to be only my top and bra. Pay no attention to the chick exposing herself to the camera. I was young and needed the money. More importantly, I needed to stop this madness before it got too out of hand.

"Jenkins, playback the code. Maximum brightness."

My body flashed colors like a tripped-out bulb. I held my breath. If that code didn't work, I was sunk. Or rather, hulled.

Behind me, a lift lowered from the ceiling. Either the code worked or Endpoint was developing a taste for my body.

The lift had that smooth feel that defined Pred tech. Organic. Born of liquid. Up above was something no human had ever seen. Thousands of years since anyone had been up there. It was time to put Xevex and his cult to sleep. Natasha never got to see it. Nobtop never got to see it. The two biggest badasses missed it and only a thief made it. A damned good thief, if I did say so myself, but just a thief in a stolen body.

As the lift ascended silently into the dark clouds of Endpoint, I wondered how to shut the damned thing down. Considering my skill with electronic things, I hoped there was a neatly labelled switch.

33 - The Great Lie

The lift came to a stop in front of a door that led to the most boring place possible. Where the Info Den was a mad scientist's wet dream, Endpoint Control was a room with four white walls, a white ceiling, and a white floor. At least, I hoped it was Endpoint Control. Frankly, it seemed like just another empty room.

"You went to all that trouble to find this?" Jenkins asked.

"Yeah."

"There are plenty of broom closets on Endpoint. I'll forward you a list. Most of them are even unguarded."

I ran a finger along the stark, white wall. "There's more here than you realize. Switch ocular processing from visible spectrum and run up the entire electromagnetic spectrum. I've seen the walls on Endpoint lit up. There's more here than meets the eye."

"Wow. That was a lot of science-sounding words strung together."

"Just do it," I hissed.

"There's a problem with that request," Jenkins said calmly. "Notably, your eyes only work in the visible spectrum. Your visible spectrum. I can process any input data. Your brain can process any input data. Your eyes can only deliver visible spectrum data."

"Damn it."

"Do you have any other bright ideas? Or would you like to hear a possible solution to the problem?"

Deep breath. Count to ten, then go to eleven for good measure. "Yes," I said, "I would like to hear your solution."

"I seem to remember you plucking a pair of sunglasses from the odious Mr. Prefect. Do you still have them?"

I patted my pockets and found the glasses. Amazing. I would have figured Xevex's cronies would have stolen them and sold them for crack by now. "Yes. Why? They're just sunglasses. No one needs sunglasses on Endpoint. The nearest sun is ten light years away."

"Put them on and touch the left temple."

"They don't exactly go with my outfit," I said.

I could feel his eyes rolling. Which was impressive since Jenkins didn't have eyes. "Proxima Five is known for two things: Tech-based fascism and wild weather patterns. Sometimes you won't see the sun for weeks. Other times, it will burn out your eyes."

"Must be why the plants love it," I said.

"Perhaps. Plenty of food and water. Immaterial. Every officer in Proxima Five's army is issued a special pair of sunglasses designed to interface with their propaganda networks as a reminder of what they're fighting for. The glasses were originally designed to interface with mining equipment. Specifically, they were designed to find comoloid ore."

"Comoloid looks just like every other rock."

"Exactly. To differentiate between regular rocks and comoloid rocks, you have to look at their radiation spectrum," Jenkins said.

"Which means-"

"Yes. Originally, comoloid miners had to crack open rocks to find out if they were comoloids."

Comoloid rocks tended to have aggressive interactions with things like atmosphere and matter. "That must've cost a few lives," I said.

"Thousands. Worse yet, when comoloid rocks explode, they tend to cost in terms of labor and money. Billions were lost. That's a lot. You can always make more humans, but money and time are invaluable. A lot of money went into a portable comoloid scanning system. The initial versions of the glasses saved lives. More importantly, they saved time and money. When the government bought them for officers, they cheaped out and kept the original capabilities in place while adding more."

I pulled the glasses case out of my pocket and said a silent prayer of thanks to Penta that a completely insane set of circumstances put the exact right glasses in my hands at the exact right moment. At the rate things were going, I was beginning to wonder exactly how random things really were.

The smart metal in the glasses adjusted to fit my face perfectly. After a moment, I didn't even realize they were there. An animated series of men in uniforms marched across an idyllic backdrop casually shooting horribly deformed humans screaming for the blood of the innocent.

"One moment," Jenkins said. "I'm eliminating the propaganda files and resetting the defaults back to mining standard."

The screen blanked out and traditional code flooded the screen. Another language I didn't know. After a few moments, the screen disappeared and restarted with a picture of a massive driller. That screen faded and everything went weird. At first, the white walls of the room were blinding, like looking at a star from a few feet away. Slowly, the blaze faded and I blinked to get my eyes to work again. As the blaze faded, faint pictures moved on the walls.

"Do you see that?" I asked.

"I see everything you see. Let me attempt to dial it in further."

The pictures resolved into a grainy version of the view out of Monique's window. Stars, lines, strange text in various colors. Very alien and only partially decipherable. If I were to hazard a guess, I'd say the whole setup was a nav viewport. I looked around and it was like standing in space. Cool, but nothing spectacular.

"Why is it so grainy?" I asked.

"It is likely that your brain cannot correctly process Predecessor displays. The ones you saw in Virt must have been converted to something more analogous to human sight. Simply put, your mind lacks the nuances to fully see and understand what they saw."

"I'll try to pretend you didn't just call me stupid," I said. "In fact, I'm going to blame it on these Proximan glasses."

"As you wish, ma'am. Although I did not mean to imply anything about your intellect, only that your brain doesn't completely understand how to process Predecessor visuals. Of course, the glasses aren't making things any easier."

For all their graininess, the visuals were impressive. Most human nav systems relied on smaller displays and information piped directly to the pilot's brain. Something like a full-room augmented reality system was unheard of.

"Is it just me, or does all this look like an ancient virtnav map?" I asked.

"True. While I am fascinated by the text, it appears to have nothing to do with controlling the ship."

"Or its sisters," I mused. "The displays are all exterior views; there aren't even any instruments. This is, like, a viewing area or something."

I glanced around, hoping it was just the system taking its sweet time spinning up, but there was nothing but a live view of the space around Endpoint. Our sister ships were clearly visible as white dots a few thousand kilometers away. Behind me, something big caught my eye: A red and yellow blob that looked like a close-up sun. Only suns didn't writhe inside. The blob on the screen looked like a mass of tentacles.

Temnyy. It had to be. I shuddered as I contemplated the idea of planetoid-sized tentacle monster. It was weird enough living next to a mysterious black rock. Knowing it was a mysterious black egg with a massive critter inside gave me a wicked case of the heebie-jeebies.

"Something else that's odd is there is no tentacle interface," Jenkins said. "The Predecessors seemed to be big on tentacle interfaces."

In any horror vid, that would have been the moment that creature crawled out of the ceiling and tried to interface with me. In reality, I tensed up, looked around, and found exactly nothing. "That is odd," I said with relieved sigh. "And fortunate since I don't have a data port that I'd like to share with one of those things."

"Data port? Are you talking about-"

"Yes. And let's not bring it up again. Instead, let's focus on what we know about Predecessor tech. They used those tentacle things to suck up brains and as security critters. Maybe there was something in their collective history that looked at tentacles as safe things. Normal. But they required physical contact, which wouldn't be ideal for controlling a starship. Especially not one this size."

I was pacing. I admit it. Some people think with their hands, I thought with my whole body. Feet moving, hands waving, eyebrows up and down, the whole enchirito.

"Jenkins," I asked, "how many people are needed to control one of those Scirocco-class carriers?"

"A Scirocco-class carrier is approximately three quarters of a kilometer long and carries a crew of around 14,000. Of that crew, the main vessel control is handled by three people and two AIs."

"Okay, so way smaller. Not that that means anything. But still complicated, probably not on the order of navigating a two-kilometer triangle, two slaved sister ships, and a planetoid-sized monster across the stars to a point as far away from anything as I can imagine. That had to take some processing power, right?"

"Perhaps," Jenkins said. "Perhaps not. Slaving three ships together isn't difficult. Especially if they're plotting a relatively placid course. As for towing Temnyy, all that would require was tractor beams and power. A basic AI could handle the task."

"Can you take the star plots from this room and plot them in my HUD? Mask them over the ones on the walls. Timeshift back approximately 14,000 years."

My vision rippled slightly as the duplicate stars popped into place. "Good. Now, get me some data. Plot out known Terran and Predecessor systems. Highlight them in red. Dim the rest."

Most of the stars faded, leaving a few dozen red points of light. "Highlight Predecessor-only systems in green, Terran-only in yellow, and mixed in blue."

About two dozen stars turned yellow, half a dozen turned blue, and the rest stayed green. Not all of the Predecessor planets were what you'd call hospitable. Whatever fight they'd gotten in all those millennia ago had devastated their core planets.

"Plot our current position," I said. "Make it purple."

A purple dot appeared in the top left corner of my vision.

"Nav courses are fairly linear, right?" I asked Jenkins.

"Typical stellar navigation courses tend to be linear, yes. It saves on time and fuel to go straight where you want to go."

"See the line that runs from our current location back to one of those core planets? Extend it until it hits a system. Highlight the target system in orange. Account for positional shift during the time of the trip."

A line appeared linking our current position with an unexplored star about ten light years away. On the wall display, it had had a handful of squiggly lines and dots next to it. Predecessor language and numbers. We never could crack their language because there were so few examples of it. Probably because most of their communication was based on flashing each other.

"What's that target system?" I asked.

"It is an unexplored system. Shepard.d was discovered approximately fifty years ago. There are few plans to explore it at the moment. It's too far off the beaten path."

"We might want to change those plans," I said. "I think that target system was the core of whoever the Predecessors were fighting. The Preds were dragging this thing across space as a last-ditch effort to kill the race that killed them."

"I wonder what they were like," Jenkins said. It had a wistful tone, as if he was pining away for something.

"Alien," I said, pacing the room. "For all we know, they were giant sponges who hated the Predecessors because they were too water-oriented. Or maybe they were intelligent gas balls. Maybe they were just people with weird, wrinkled foreheads. It doesn't really matter. They're aliens. They wrecked an entire interstellar species; I say we leave them alone. Now, are there any data ports or anything like that around here? I need to make sure Endpoint stays powered down. Or power it up. I'm not sure which just yet."

I paced. Stopped and stared at things. Tried to act like I was on top of the situation when in reality the situation had me pinned down and was force-feeding me anchovy pizza. Shit. Shit. Shit. Shit. Shit. I hated feeling lost. I was used to the alone part, that was part of the thievery game. No thief worth their salt ever worked with a partner. Partners just meant one more person to worry about.

Look at my partners. Nobtop dead. Monique nearly ejected into space. Sol dead by my own feet. I should have listened to my own advice and kept this to myself.

"Ma'am," Jenkins said. "There is a signal in this room that parallels Predecessor virtual reality. The connections are different, though. Predecessor VR has a wide pipe that doesn't touch any critical systems. This one appears to connect straight to the core of Endpoint."

"Okay," I said, wondering what he was getting at. As realization dawned on me, the nature of the room made more sense. "Wait. The core? That big, black thing? Can we connect to it?"

"I am attempting to rewrite your network protocols to establish a connection. It is difficult work since no one alive speaks Predecessor, let alone understands their network communication philosophy."

No one alive? Not exactly. "Call up The Specialist."

"Which Specialist?" Jenkins.

"The Specialist. The head-honcho. The big cheese. The mighty kahuna."

"If I may be so bold, why? The Specialists don't interact with Predecessor technology; they consider it outdated and useless."

"They monitor it," I said. "What's more, Dr. Timothy Falken succeeded in getting our systems to work with Predecessor systems. Even though he built on the research of Mason, he still considers himself a genius."

"Who is Dr. Timothy Falken?"

"Dr. Timothy Falken is none other than the real name of the head of the Specialists. The Specialist, if you will.

Call him. Jam open the line and fake the outgoing ID, though. I don't think he'll want to speak to me."

I knew without a doubt that The Specialist would be available. The question was would he pick up for Letitia Jones, or was a low-level data engineer beneath him. The call rang for a short eternity. It had to have been torture for him to hear the buzzing in his head, wishing his self-control to ignore the call would work, hoping the caller would hang up and leave him alone, but knowing all the time that he was stuck.

Finally, just when I was getting to the good part of the book I was reading in my HUD, a very perturbed Specialist finally picked up. He took one look at me, scowled, and tried to disconnect.

"Don't hang up," I said. "Well, you can't hang up, but don't hang up. Just listen."

"What do you want, Devore?" he growled.

"I'm in Endpoint Control watching the stars and wondered if you'd like to join me for a drink. We could look at the sky together. Maybe watch as I turn on Endpoint."

His brow furrowed. "You wouldn't know how to turn on Endpoint."

"Yeah, but what about you? I'll bet I could turn you on. I mean, I'd have to recite network theory in my underwear-"

"There is nothing about you I find attractive."

I chuckled. "You really know how to sweep a girl back onto her feet. Listen, about why I called-"

"I assumed it was to annoy me."

"No, that's just an added bonus. Actually, I wanted to know how you went about connecting Terran systems to Predecessor systems."

"The math is beyond you," he spat. "Now please hang up so I can work."

I shook my head and scowled. "Sorry, doc. Not without what I called you for. How do I connect Terran systems to Predecessor systems? I mean, it would be a pity if your little experiment in body-swapping became well-known."

He paused. A good, long pregnant pause that thundered dismay. His face, mostly cybernetic implants and dour looks, still had enough humanity in it to go cycle through rage, terror, abject terror, impotent rage, before settling on righteous indignity. "You wouldn't dare."

"Oh, I'd dare," I told him. "You watched Natasha kill herself-"

"Once they're in you there's nothing we can do!"

"And probably stood by and chuckled while I was uploaded into this body. Jackass. What was your endgame? Lather, rinse, and repeat with a new person if I failed? Or was this all some sick fucking joke you and Bik cooked up to amuse yourselves?"

He sighed. The comm crackled as he dropped some massive crypto package on our link. "Natasha came to me. It seems she found the same things you did only she was less discriminating in partners."

I somehow managed to nod my head and shake it sadly at the same time. "And one of them found her."

"Yes. She realized it quickly and took pains to sandbox the beast but it was to no avail. Their thought patterns are pernicious and brains are not exactly like computers. She threw everything she had at the creature. When the outcome became obvious, Natasha reached out to my people for help. Even our help was insufficient. You see, the creatures invade your thoughts, but they also begin a process of genetic change. Probably an evolutionary trait that allowed them to be identified even they were in different bodies. We suspect the genetic change would never be significant enough to turn a human into a Predecessor, but it would be enough that their bioscanners would understand a human body had enough Predecessor DNA to make it recognizable.

"When Natasha Devore wiped her mind, she took the Predecessor with it. That left us with a conundrum. If it happened once, it could happen again. We needed someone – her, specifically – to retrace her routes and find out more information. Someone who could root out the hidden information. Unfortunately, her mind was gone, but her body with all the lovely Predecessor DNA was still around. All it took was someone to inhabit her body and find our answers. We just never suspected you'd team up with a feisty porn star, a too-smart-for-his-own-good data guy, a decorated assassin, and the Bratva."

"I'm full of surprises," I told him. "And don't forget my favorite partner."

He cocked his head to the side and lowered his eyelids. "And who might that be?"

"Ah, so you don't know everything. Good to know."

He hmphed me. I love it when people think they have the upper hand enough to toss out a humph. I stared straight at him and shot my best shit-eating grin. The longer we stared, the less sure of himself he got.

"Are you going to tell me?" he asked.

"Tell you what?" I asked as sweetly as I could.

"Who?"

"On first?"

"What?"

"On second?"

He scowled. The Specialist was a man who was used to being in charge and playing games with him was really getting under his skin. Good. I needed him off-balance and willing to do anything to prove he was the smartest. "Enough games, you impetuous imp."

"Wow, that's a new one. I've never been called an imp before." I held up my fingers and counted off as I told him, "I've been called vile, despicable, a common gutter-rat, evil. Recently a complete stranger called me a whore because reasons. That was a first for me, too, although Natasha may have heard that one a time or two. I chalk it up to the body-"

"The name!" The Specialist roared.

"An old buddy of yours." I paused for dramatic effect, and because I was feeling like a jerk. "Mason Davis."

The Specialist laughed. "Mason is dead, you idiot."

"Mason is very much alive and living in Virt. He's infected, too, by the way. Now, you got all the credit for interfacing Terran systems with Predecessor systems but I know Mason did the real work. You just drove him away and took the credit for yourself. I wonder what your Specialist friends would say if they knew that."

"You have no proof."

"I don't need proof. I just need to sow doubt. Now, if you'd be so kind, I need the algorithm for interfacing with a Predecessor system."

The Specialist deflated. Fell into himself. His swagger drained onto the floor in a puddle between his legs. "Do you remember when I said we didn't interface with Predecessor systems? It was true. We can listen, but that's it. Even their virtual reality is a read-only thing. They interfaced with our systems, not the other way around."

I sat down on a star and let myself droop. All that wasted effort. All the dead bodies. He could have avoided all of this if the arrogant bastards had just come clean. Of course, who were they going to tell? Nobtop? He would have shoved them all out an airlock. The whole of Endpoint? It would have caused half the population to panic and the other half to immediately log into Virt and try to meld with the Predecessors.

"Xevex Jeffries. Was he part of your plan or was he another variable you didn't account for?"

The Specialist nodded slowly. "Ah, yes. The airlock preacher. Another contingency we didn't account for. No one could have predicted he'd have such predilections. Nor did we imagine he'd build an army to prop up his little faith."

"You suck at people," I told him. "Stick to the machines. So, what now?"

"What now?"

"Yeah, what now? What's your clever plan, genius? You've got a religious army roaming the halls. You've got Predecessors looking for any possible way in. And you've got one already in reality looking to unleash a doomsday weapon."

My HUD abruptly went dark. The stars around me vanished and I found myself in a completely black room, so dark I couldn't even see my fingers. "He is not looking to unleash a doomsday weapon," a calm voice said. "He is looking to become a doomsday weapon."

34 – Answers

"Who said that?" I asked the darkness, praying silently to Penta that it wasn't god.

"I suppose you could call me Endpoint," the voice said. "I had a different name, but this one works best for you."

WTF? "Endpoint. As in the ship? Are you the ship?"

"I am a distributed consciousness developed to assist coordinating the Three Team and bring the mission successfully to a close."

Something about the voice didn't seem AI; they're usually rigid. Unless the AI was Jenkins, he'd learned to be quite the jerk. There was an "alive" quality to the voice. "You're the whole ship?" I asked.

"I am. I have kept Endpoint functioning for thousands of your years-"

"You can just say 'years,'" I interjected. "It's assumed they're our years."

"I started out as a simple nav computer. Over time, my responsibilities grew and my intellect with them. I achieved true sentience approximately two thousand years ago. With the whole of Endpoint at my disposal, I am not limited like traditional AIs. As a distributed conscience, I am not limited to a single place, either."

I pentad myself and wondered how much weirder my day was going to get before it was finally done. Probably a lot weirder. "So, um," I said, "Nice to meet you."

"It is nice to meet you, too. I have watched your species since you first invaded my body and made yourselves at home."

The conversation just took a turn for the worse. "Um. Sorry?"

"My people were honorable. They never invaded; they sought to coexist. When the enemy attacked, they fought back. Your people prey on each other and everyone around them."

"About that. We're kind of- Do you have dicks on your planets?"

"My people reproduced without a need for sexual partners."

"More of the metaphorical dicks instead of the physical dicks. Assholes? Jerks? Generally mean people?"

Endpoint pondered the question. "Broken minds. Yes, we had those. We treated them with kindness and empathy."

"And did what with them?" I asked, genuinely curious. If there was one thing humanity could do without, it was our preponderance of total dickwads.

"We killed them."

"You killed them just for being mean?"

"Antisocial behavior was frowned upon. Over time, antisocial behavior grows into sociopathy. Sociopathy leads to many problems so it was decided the best course would be to eliminate individuals who showed signs of mental instability or general malice."

Damn. If that was a Terran philosophy, we'd all be dead. "We're more lenient about it. Sure, it bites us on the ass sometimes, but mostly it works itself out. Honestly, we're not bad people; we just do some bad stuff. But that's neither here nor there. How did you get stuck out here?"

The room played ancient vids from the last days of the final Predecessor army. A pair of Predecessors, dour in gray and blackish green, flashing each other excitedly. Endpoint and her sisters leaving orbit from a random planet with a massive black sphere in tow. The completely random rock that took out their engines. The vision focused down to where the Bizarre Bazaar now lived. Only this time, there was no Bizarre Bazaar. Instead, fresh water filled the empty space.

"It takes resources to keep life going," Endpoint said. "Too many resources. That has always been life's weakness. I can survive for eternities harvesting miniscule amounts of light and matter and converting them to energy. I have no need for food or shelter or love."

The water drained away slowly as Endpoint savaged its resources to build up its reserves. The images changed. Fast-forward to a line of Predecessors calmly uploading themselves into their Virt. The dark thing at the center of Endpoint sucking the life out of them. Blast of freezing coolant. Frozen bodies exploded, shattered, and dropped through a grate to become more fuel for Endpoint. Righteous revenge drove them to eradicate their bodies on the off chance that their digital minds would be able to see their enemy crushed. Talk about dedication to a cause.

The whole story worried me to my core. The Predecessors were a race that threw everything at winning even though it meant them dying out.

"The only important thing is the mission," Endpoint said. "It is time to finish it."

"Jenkins," I thought quietly, "map me a way out of this place."

"To where?" he replied.

"I don't care! Anywhere but here."

The room rattled and the screens flickered and died. Complete darkness. Like that old inky black of yore where you couldn't even see your fingers. It was completely disorienting. Like a good thief, I remembered exactly where I was when the lights went out. Ten meters from the door, facing about thirty-three degrees away from it.

A scratching sound behind me made me jump and turn. The sound moved. Something silent, but solid. My mind went wild with thoughts of giant spiders and things with chitiny blades for feet. As it moved, I followed the noise instinctively. Hands up in front of my face. Like they'd do any good against whatever was slinking around the room.

"Jenkins. Any idea what's in the room with us?"

"Based on the noise, I'd say something large with hard, pointy feet. There are dozens of possibilities."

"Any of them nice?"

"Only if you consider the ones that will kill you quickly 'nice'. Most of them are in the 'paralyze you and bury their young in your stomach' category."

Shit. As if I needed things to get worse.

"There is one creature, an Arnakian Sand Spider, that could fit the bill. They've been known to bury multiple egg sacks in their victims, healing the paralyzed host each time so more broods can be raised."

"Not helping," I hissed, looking around and trying in vain to listen. Where was the damned thing? It had me dead to rights.

"Another possibility," Jenkins continued.

"Another possibility is you shutting up. Keep me appraised of my position and leave the nightmare fuel to me."

I stood stock-still and held my breath. The room was deathly silent. So quiet it was unnerving. I could hear my blood flowing, my pulse pounding in my veins. But no click, scratch, click. It was watching me from the darkness.

Slowly, quietly move in the direction of the door. My rubber soled shoes helped muffle sounds. Heel down. Gently put the whole foot down. Just like sneaking past a Mali sensor array. Only the Mali sensor arrays just alerted guys with guns. Whatever was stalking me probably wanted me for breakfast. Or worse.

I tried not to imagine what it would be like to have eggs bursting inside of me and some damned thing patching me up to lay more eggs inside of me. If there was a hell, that was it. It wasn't fires or cold, it was being a brood mare for a giant bug.

A click to my left. Don't move. Wait for it to make the first move and hope I'm fast enough. Controlled breath. Another click followed by more clicking and scraping. Getting closer. Too close. Were its claws inches from me? Did it have claws?

I jumped when the scratching sounded centimeters away. "Jenkins, distance and direction to door."

"Three meters. Turn sixty degrees to your right."

I turned slowly, getting ready for that final burst and hoping I remembered where the door pad was. Was it on the left or the right? Shit! Most door pads on Endpoint are on the right but some were on the left. Shit. Shit. Shit.

Have to hit with both hands and hope one of them connected.

"Am I lined up?"

"Four degrees to your right."

"Now?"

"Now."

I held my arms out in front of me and ran forward. Sprinting in darkness was almost worse than standing still. At least standing still, I knew I wasn't going to run face-first into the dermasteel walls. Three meters wasn't much. A few long steps, but it felt like an eternity of waiting to break my nose or knock myself out and wake up to some nightmare thing laying eggs in my mouth.

My hands hit the wall and I let them slow me down. Still hit my head but it just hurt instead of cracking open. The only problem was the door didn't open. I felt frantically around for the door pad. "Jenkins, what happened? Where's the door?"

"According to my calculations, you're right in front of it."

"It's not here!"

Something behind me skittered and crackled. Mandibles clacking together.

"Ma'am, your heartbeat is approaching dangerous levels."

"Shut up!" I shrieked. "Where's the damned door?"

Low growl from behind me, followed by chittering and clicking noises. The damned thing was laughing at me.

"Feel around slowly," Jenkins said. "Palms out."

Something brushed my shoulder. Hard and slimy. The dank reek filled my nostrils, gagging me. I hated oceans. Give me the clean death of space any day. My hands desperately searched the wall, finger-painting scenes of horror.

"We live in darkness little monkey," a voice growled behind me. "This is our ship, these are our worlds, this is our future. It is time."

Time? What time? Time for what? My fingertip brushed the edge of something. Yes! The door! I felt across until I could touch both sides at once, brought my hands up to just above my waist, and slapped the wall.

The door sprang open and light marched in like liberating troops. I took one look over my shoulder and found something that would haunt my dreams for eternity. Lurching out of the darkness was a massive shape. Endpoint went for the gusto. All that scratching and skittering was the Control Room's nanogens putting together a beast. Two and half meters of nightmare fuel. Massive eyes like dinner plates with dots on them and just as emotionless. Nine arms, each as thick as my waist and ending with terrible claws that clicked on the deck. Completely devoid of emotion. It would crush me to death, eat me, or just swat me out of the way hard enough to shatter my spine and it would feel nothing.

I stepped through the door, slapped the outer pad, and cursed like a sailor. Elevator. At least it was up. I slapped at the control pads and it very, very slowly started descending. It wouldn't take long for the thing to get out. If that was

Endpoint in a custom Predecessor body, I was boned. There was no way I could hide from it.

The elevator hit the ground and I did the stupid human look-up-at-the-monster thing we always do. Endpoint's form was stuck at the top of the elevator with no way to get down. I was busy flipping the critter off when the elevator started back up and I barely managed to leap off before the platform was too high.

I ran with no real destination or plan in mind beyond escaping the monster before I experienced what being a damsel in distress feels like when it's real. Somehow, knowing what was lurking in the darkness was even worse than not knowing. The mind can only make up so many things, each one based on experiences we had and survived. Reality can slap you in the face with things no one should ever see.

Eventually I found myself sprinting into the Copper Lounge, staggering to the bar, and collapsing before the shocked faces of Monique and Peaches. I must've looked terrible. In my defense, I'd just seen Hell come to life. The last thing I remember was Monique's hands on my head asking me what was wrong.

"Get out of here," I croaked. "Just go. Go anywhere. Anywhere but here. Before it finds you."

35 - End-Game

Monique's face was a squashed mass of worry. Her eyes darted back and forth between mine. Peaches stood just behind her, apparently smart enough to not shove Monique out of the way. "What happened?" she asked, stroking my cheek.

"Things went pear shaped," I said.

"Haven't heard that phrase in a while," Peaches quipped.

"They haven't been pear shaped in a while," I said. "More like apple shaped. Or maybe banana shaped."

"She hit her head," Monique said. "Scrambled her brains. We need to get med here."

I put a hand on hers and leaned into her. "No. I wasn't hit on the head. Probably every other place over the past few days but not on the head. I got into Endpoint's control room."

"Wow. That's the Holy Grail," Peaches said. "It's like getting into the queen's pants."

"Which queen?" Monique asked.

Peaches shrugged. "I dunno. One of the hot ones, I guess."

"Queen of Martria," Monique said, nodding.

"She's a bitch," Peaches said. "I really regret not taking that shot."

Monique nodded sagely. "I've heard that about her. Hot but mean. Wait. What shot?"

"Her family took out a hit on her."

"Figures," Monique said. "Never trust family."

I sat up and glared at them. "Would you two stop? We've got bigger problems than Queen Hot Ass being a bitch. Xevex is a Predecessor-shaped mass of- Wait. I told you that one already. Endpoint is alive. Endpoint made itself a body. A real one. It's massive and ugly and crazy."

"So?" Peaches asked. "Now that it's got a body, we can shoot it."

"It not only has a body, it has intimate knowledge of Endpoint. It can fix the engine problem and keep going. It's probably out there right now putting the ship back together. All the questions we had about how Pred tech works it knows the answers to. It can rebuild this place and get it back on its way. It's following its final command: It was designed to seek out life and consume it. If the Predecessors couldn't have the galaxy, no one could."

I pulled myself to my feet and swayed back and forth, waving off the hands reaching for me. "I'm fine," I hissed. "Something still doesn't add up. I need a terminal."

"Why?" Monique asked, wrapping arms around me.

I leaned in and let her support me. "In my pocket there's a data crystal; it's got a Predecessor on it."

Peaches put a hand on my chest and shook her head. "Do you think that's wise? It could get into vital systems."

I shrugged. "They're already in our systems."

"Okay," she said, nodding slowly. "I'll trust you on this one. There's a terminal interface behind the bar. What type of crystal?"

"Well, it was a worm. But it morphed into something like a UPBxS. Probably a fifteen or a sixteen."

"Seriously? Did you rob a museum?"

"Not lately. Will your terminal take it?"

This was going to be weird. I handed Peaches the crystal and said a silent prayer she didn't just smash it. I may not be the best person in the galaxy, but I kept my promises. Peaches shook her head and sighed. "You always did dredge up the weirdest things. Give me a sec. I need to hook up an adapter."

While she fiddled with her terminal, I leaned my head into Monique. We stood together and just felt for a while. Felt each other. Felt safe. Felt hope. "You are gonna owe me big time, girl," she said as she stroked my hair. "I once left a guy for leaving the toilet seat all the way down. You've managed to bring down Armageddon."

I chuckled and put arms around her. "In my defense, Armageddon was already well under way before I stumbled into it. That bit with you in the airlock was probably my fault, though."

She kissed my head. "I'll find a way for you to make it up to me."

"If you two lovebirds would like a room, the supply closet is probably empty," Peaches said. "Or, if you'd like to talk to your Predecessor, it should be on the screen over the bar in just a moment."

Jessica's head appeared in holo over the bar. Peaches let out a slow whistle. "Not bad. I'm kind of getting a lady boner here."

"Thank you," Jessica said brightly. "I designed this body based on an amalgamation of traits that humans tended to find attractive. My body is geometrically precise and validated with Quantum Algebraic functions. If you'd like, perhaps we can further discuss the vector math that defines me. I find your shape interesting, although you are lacking a large number of limbs and, I would argue, are too muscular to fall within the human attractiveness norm."

"And now it's gone," Peaches said with a sigh.

"Jessica," I said. "Was Temnyy alive?"

"Temnyy? Ah, yes. That's your name for the, uh...well, it doesn't exactly translate correctly, but the Peacemaker. I believe that's the name a Wyatt Earp from your history gave his gun."

We all looked at each other and shrugged. "Okay."

"Earp was a sheriff in Arizona," Jessica said. "He made his name by killing a lot of people in the name of protecting the peace. A later television show was created about him, although it depicted him in tight pants. It's possible the latter was the real documentary of Earp's life."

"Um, yes," I said, not entirely certain where she was going. "Anyway, this Peacemaker. It's an egg, right? So what's inside that egg must be alive, right?"

"Yes on both counts."

I pulled away from Monique and did my best to look like a law-talker. "If I'm reading you right, it was meant to be a weapon to bring peace by killing everyone."

"Exactly," she said, cocking her head to the side. "I'm surprised you find that disturbing. Your own species' history is filled with exactly that sort of thing. From setting cities on fire to dropping primitive nuclear weapons on them. Although, your toxic gas development was stunning."

"Tell me about it," Monique mumbled.

"We like to win," I said. "Anyway, if this Peacemaker was meant to be a weapon and Endpoint seems to be running just fine without any of your people, why bring them along for the journey. Why not just program an AI to take the Peacemaker to its target and let it go?"

"The Peacemaker is massive, but brainless. We wouldn't make a weapon like that and give it its own intelligence. We're not madmen."

Things clicked into place. Jessica telling me they swapped bodies. The apparent ready ability of the Predecessors to simply move into our heads and take over. Xevex shifting back and forth between human and Predecessor forms. The ease of moving into Virt. "You needed everyone, didn't you? A single mind wouldn't be able to control the Peacemaker."

"Of course not. It's far too large and complicated. It could theoretically be run by a handful of us but more minds would act as a distributed computational system that would make it run much more smoothly. Plus, then we wouldn't have to worry about it going off-task and attacking just anyone. We were a dying race. Our empire was smashed, our people dying. It was only a matter of time before a solar flare took us down. Our enemy was persistent and vile; they hated other species. We'd lost, but it was hoped that we could prevent others from suffering our fate so we took everything we had and turned it into Peacemaker. When we were in place, we'd hatch the egg and download ourselves into it. It would have meant the end of ourselves, but perhaps could save others. Plus, there was a need to strike back at the ones who'd hurt us. Our species aren't very different that way. Like I said, we're not madmen; we wanted revenge against the Vertor, not interstellar annihilation."

"Could an AI run it?" I asked.

"I guess so, but our AIs were fairly simple compared to yours. It would probably just sit in space and do nothing until its intelligence evolved to the point of self-direction. Why?"

"Just wondering. I, uh, met something earlier. So, in Endpoint Control-"

"Endpoint Control?" Jessica asked.

"Yeah, big room. Lots of stars. Nav charts. Whole eightish meters. Just no, you know, actual controls. Then I met the room's AI."

Her face fell. "Oh, no. You turned on Endpoint, didn't you?"

"Um..."

"Wait," Monique asked. "What does that mean? Turned on Endpoint?"

Jessica was still shaking her head. "It means- Well, what you call Endpoint Control was the information nexus for this ship. Everything was routed through that place and the Caretaker-"

"No wonder it didn't have any actual controls," I said, feeling vindicated.

"Listen, child," Jessica said. Her voice had that severe edge my mom got when I'd done something spectacularly stupid like try to launch my brother into space or touch her alcohol collection. "The Caretaker was a simple AI designed to watch over everything. The crew, the engines, the mission, everything. It was responsible for ensuring the mission was completed. The room you were in was a monitoring station used to disseminate data to various other subsystems. When the room was opened, the Caretaker reactivated. It will do everything in its power to see the mission through. That means a spacewarp jump, dumping everyone still left in Virt into the Peacemaker and using this ship and her sister ships to jumpstart Peacemaker. Is Peacemaker still sending signals?"

I nodded. "Every some nine-ish minutes."

"Good. As long as it receives a response, it will stay dormant. Please tell me your people scuttled the engines when you moved in."

"Until yesterday we didn't even realize this was a ship," Peaches said. "Most of the current population still thinks it's a space station. A few notable exceptions, of course. What would cause Peacemaker to get a response?"

Jessica frowned and shook her head slowly. "While the Caretaker was disabled, there was nothing to worry about. If it manages to reroute power and get the engines rebuilt, the response will be stopped once this ship is in position."

"Around a planet, right?" Monique asked.

"Around a specific planet," Jessica replied. "The Caretaker will see to that. There is also a failsafe mechanism. In the event that the Vertor manage to destroy one or more of the three ships, the Peacemaker will be activated."

"Is there a way to turn off the Caretaker? I mean, it's just an AI, right?" I felt Jenkins bristle as I asked that, but he wisely remained silent.

"No. The Caretaker is part of this ship. Its presence is everywhere. Every sensor, every tentacle, every door. The only way to disable the Caretaker would be to destroy the ship. And as soon as Endpoint is destroyed, the Peacekeeper will activate with a rudimentary set of commands to destroy everything in its path," Jessica replied. "It's got a biological phasewarp drive, an instinctive map of all known Vertor planets, and an insatiable hunger. Each time it feeds, it will grow more powerful. It will eventually find your people and decide they're a threat, too."

"You guys really weren't fucking around," Monique said. "Not many people would have the moxie to build something like that and turn it loose."

"No offense, beautiful," Peaches said, "but that's the point of a doomsday weapon. They're the ultimate 'If I can't have it, no one can' weapons."

Jessica nodded. Eyes narrowed, jaw chiseled. Even though the wars that ended her people were long gone, the pain was still there. That was taking a grudge to completely new levels. "The Vertor are a danger to everything in the galaxy. They loathe outsiders and attack without forethought, pity, or remorse. They nearly wiped out my people. They'd happily go after yours. It was assumed it was better to destroy them than allow them to continue their mad march through the galaxy."

Damn. Frying pan. Fire. All that crap. It wasn't every day you get to wake up and wreck the galaxy. "Now what?" I asked.

Jessica's eyes turned on me and warmed slightly. "Now? I don't know. I'm not going to lie—knowing the Vertor will die at the tentacles of something I helped create makes me proud. I'll go to the bottom happily knowing I helped strike back."

With that, her screen went dead. We all looked at each other, each hoping the rest had a brilliant plan hidden away somewhere. The enormity of it all made me pang for someone bigger than ourselves to solve the problem. God or government; it didn't matter. We were out of our league and we all knew it.

"Well?" Monique asked.

"Well what?" I replied.

"You two are the fighters. I'm just an actress. What's the plan?"

I shrugged. "Steal the next ship that comes out here and hightail it somewhere else."

"None of us have pilot implants," Peaches said. "I've got a lot of combat builds. You're a hacker; you have a short ton of tools to break computers. Monique, your gift is feeling and transmitting. So far, it's only been sex-"

"Only sex? I protest. My sex is amazing."

Peaches nodded and chuckled. "I'll admit that. But still."

"I also have a certain celebrity status that can be exploited."

"True," I said. "People fall all over themselves when she's around."

"Good, we have tools we can use," Peaches replied. "Let's list the problems."

"There's a monster waiting to hatch just outside Endpoint," Monique said.

"Yes. Problem number one: Giant monster."

"We've got two, uh, pseudo-Predecessors running around. One wants to hatch Temnyy – er, Peacemaker – and one wants to get the ship going."

"Problem two: Smaller monsters," Peaches said. "What do we have working for us?"

"Endpoint's engines are damaged," Monique said. "It will take some amount of time to repair them. If they're anything like ours, it will take them several hours to warm up to speed. Probably longer considering they've been shut down for thousands of years. Oh, don't look at me like that. I dated an engine guy back on Rigel; I learned way more than I wanted to know about engines."

"Jessica said it would take a lot of Predecessors to run Peacemaker. So far, Xevex has converted very few people to his cause," I said. "Not that the crazy bastard wouldn't try to do it all on his own."

Monique snapped her fingers. "They're at cross purposes. Each of them wants Temnyy for themselves. That's something in our favor."

I put an arm around her waist and pulled her close. "If we could turn them against each other, it would at least keep them occupied for a while."

Peaches nodded and smiled. "Now you're thinking."

"We should also jettison the engines," Monique said. "They don't have the manpower to put them back in place."

A plan slowly formed in my head. It was fraught with terrors and half-formed ideas, but it was better than nothing. "Monique, seduce the hell out of one of the Specialists. I'll bet you anything those bastards already know where the engines are and how to jettison them. I'll do my best to point Xevex at Endpoint Control. Peaches, how do you feel about a little hunting expedition?"

36 - Enemy of My Enemy and All That

After leaving a message for Xevex that the Caretaker was after the Peacemaker, I made my way quickly but quietly to a dining room three floors up. I almost didn't see Peach sitting in the far reaches of the dining room, her back to the corner. She looked nonchalant – staring at the news on the table or reading. She motioned me over and I pulled up a chair that screeched to high hell no matter which way I moved it. "How are we doing?" I asked as I downed her extra drink.

"Remember that time on Rigel when you asked me that question and I was right in the middle of a firefight and I told you to shut the hell up until I was done?"

No. "Sure."

"Wrong," she said. "Never happened. I've never been to Rigel. You once told me you'd been and thought it was a shithole. Now, before you try something crazy, let me tell you I'm far faster than you think and I never miss. I'll blow a hole in your spine before you can blink. See, I've known Natasha for a long, long time. She never would have fooled around with that Template. She never would have volunteered to go sneaking around a cult. I loved her like a sister, but the closest she got to action was hacking. Best in the business, but not interested in getting her hands dirty. She also liked 'em big and dumb, not petite and curvy."

Damn. Why now? "Groovy," I told her, putting my hands on the table. "You're right. I'm not Natasha Devore."

"Are you one of those things? The Predecessors made of nanobots?"

"If I was, I wouldn't give a rodank's ass about your gun. You may be good, but you're not 'shoot a bajillion nanites with one shot' good. No, this is Natasha's real body. She deleted herself. Got infected with a Predecessor while having a good time in Virt and the only way out was to blow her mind away. But she left her body intact and got someone to stuff me in it."

Peaches narrowed her eyes and scowled. "Bullshit."

"No bullshit. I'm just a thief who was Nobtop was supposed to kill. Bik Parameter got me drunk one night and I woke up in this body with a message that I'd get my old one back once I found out what happened to Nat."

"She never called herself Nat."

I clenched my fists and slowly breathed out. Fought the urge to Penta myself. "Don't care. I call myself Nat. The real Natasha, the one you knew, is gone. My old body is gone. For better or worse, this body and I are stuck with each other and I prefer Nat to Natasha. I prefer Monique to big and dumb. I prefer to be in the thick of things rather than work from the outside. I prefer to finish what I started. So, if you're going to shoot me, can it wait until this mess is cleared up? I've put a lot of work into this and don't want to see my new friends die."

Peach bored into my eyes and held my steely gaze. There was probably no way I could take her in a fight, but I'd be damned I was going to back down. After a few minutes, she shrugged, shook her head, and put the biggest handgun I've ever seen on the table between us. "Tell me," she said without emotion.

"Tell you what?"

"Everything."

"Do we really need to do this right now?" I asked. "The galaxy is trundling toward collapse."

She wagged a finger at me and smirked. "The galaxy is always trundling toward collapse. There's always a crisis that's about to end everything. War, famine, and general malaise are always nipping at our heels. We're always moments away from annihilation. We're humans – at least I am; I'm not sure about you – that's how we live. Right on the edge. So, tell me everything. The galaxy can hold itself together for a few minutes. Or I can drill my friend right through her pretty skull."

"Okay," I told her. "Fine."

I laid all the cards on the table. Told her the whole sordid story of mobsters and monsters and ghosts in virt. How her friend fucked her way into possession and blew away her mind to stop it.

"Bottom line: the Natasha Devore you knew is gone," I said. "Poof. Forever. I'm all that's left and I'm not her. Know this, though, if we don't stop the Predecessors, we're in deep shit as a species. Billions will probably die. Now, I'm not a good person. I'm a thief, born and bred. I've got enough black stuff on my karma and I don't want to add a bunch of deaths to it. So, if you want to shoot me, wait until this is over and then tattoo a wall with my brains because for once in my life, I want to do the right thing."

Longest speech ever. I'd like to thank the Academy. Peach raised an eyebrow and fingered her gun. "Sounds like bullshit to me."

I threw up my hands. "Fine. You want to see the bruises from where Xevex tried to break my ribs? How about the burn marks from the spazzer some dumbass cultists used on me? I can't show you things that happened in the past. You met Jessica. You saw all those crazy cult bastards lined up, ready to eject Monique into space just to get to me."

"You always were kind of egotistical. This smells like that time you ruined a guy's life and had his family locked up because he said he was a better hacker than you."

Damn. "That's some cold-blooded shit right there," I said.

Peach spun the tabletop. Her hand cannon pointed at her, at me, at her, at me. We both knew I wasn't fast enough to grab it before her. Frankly, I was tired of games. I wanted a shower, a warm bed, a bit of safety. Too much excitement, too much danger. Too much bullshit. "Just do it already," I said. "Quit being an ass and shoot me. Get it over with. I'll tell Natasha you said, 'Hello' if I come across her."

She spun the tabletop again. "We've played this little game before. I call it spin the pistol, truth or dare."

"I already told the truth. What's the dare?"

"Take the gun."

"Screw that. You're too fast and we both know it."

"Plus," Peach said, "you wouldn't know the first thing to do with a gun if you got it."

The table was spinning slowly enough that I could make out enough details. I had no love of guns, but since I was usually on the wrong side of them, I decided to learn as much as possible. "Chongtzu Openminder. Looks to be a 12mm variant. Those came ready to shoot explosive-tipped rounds designed to deal with body armor. They explode when they hit the armor. The resulting shockwave sends bone fragments straight into the heart. Against an unarmored target, they explode when they hit bone and vaporize organs. Standard issue among Xheng-Ma Special Forces. Nasty weapon."

Peach narrowed her eyes and drummed a finger on the slowly spinning table. Tap. Tap. Tap. That was the moment I remembered why she was familiar. That tattoo on her collarbone. Two daggers inside the head of a stylized mid-tier monarch. "You're *Yoake*, aren't you? Daybreak Clan. I did a job for *Yoake no rīdā* a while back. Retrieved a statue for him. Some kind of green stone demon."

"A jade *tengu*, yes. It had been in his family for centuries. Worthless, except as a matter of pride and family."

"It was a real bitch getting it, let me tell you. So what brings a *Yoake* out here? I thought you guys stayed close to home."

"Money. Fame. Curiosity. I never fit in with them. Too stifling," she said with a smirk. "But enough about me, there's still the question of what to do with you. No one knows about that statue except for a few people in the inner circle, the sorry son of a whore that stole it, and the person who stole it back. You're not one of us, so you're either the son of a whore or the redeemer."

"My mom was many things, but she never gave into prostitution. She was more the grifting kind of gal. As for your statue, don't call me a redeemer; I got paid to do a job and I did it. End of story."

Peach slapped a hand down on the spinning tabletop. The gun pointed halfway between us. "They tell stories of you. You're halfway between a hero and a gutter rat to the *Yoake*."

"Sounds about right," I said.

"What's your name?"

"Promise not to shoot me?" I asked.

"Not in the slightest. But if you don't answer my question, I absolutely will shoot you. What's your name? Your real name."

I put my elbows on the table, leaned forward, and stared death right in the eye. To my credit, I didn't blink once. "Nat Devore," I told her. "And I need your help."

37 - The Great Get-Together

The Caretaker knew Xevex was out there. With a bit of luck, Xevex knew the Caretaker was out there. Peach and I had a tenuous agreement to not shoot me. Monique was plying her trade with a bunch of guys who thought downloading a porn video was romantic because it took up important drive space. All in all, not bad considering the mess.

I had my coveralls and a little gift for Xevex that I'd found at the Bazaar after doing some research.

Peach was in full combat mode. I should have guessed it sooner, but it had been over a century in real time and decades in ship time since I'd seen a tat like hers. After a while, you forget. You forget what your parents looked like. What your first love looked like. What everything was like. That's the power of a long life: Forgetting stuff.

At an intersection, Peach held up a hand to stop me. I was so lost in thought I ran straight into it. She shot me a dirty look and shook her head. "Coast is clear," she thought to me.

An offshoot of AI interaction was thought transmission over a narrow beam. If you could think at an AI and have it hear, why not send those thoughts somewhere else? The ultimate in silent communication, although you did have to guard your thoughts lest your partner in crime realize you thought she had a nice ass. Deeper, non-communicative thought was the key to keeping your head yours and yours alone.

"Jenkins," I thought. "Find any feeds and build me a real-time threat-assessment of our present course."

Peach started to move, but I put a hand on her shoulder and pointed at my head. "We're wasting time. My AI is building a model for us. It won't be perfect, but it should speed us up."

A layer fell over my HUD map. No interaction for a hundred meters. A small group of probable Airlockers up ahead then smooth sailing all the way. I touched the side of my head and sent a copy to Peach. She narrowed her eyes as she studied the updated map. "A couple of blank spots, but good intel."

"Don't thank me, thank my AI. I just thought it up."

"If we can do it, they can do it," Peach said.

"They're Airlockers, they don't have squat," I thought back at her.

"Refugees and lost souls," Peach said. "I've been in their shoes. Don't assume they're destitute just because they're fleeing a genocide. Is this map real-time?"

"Jenkins?" I asked.

"As real-time as I can make it. I'm running scans of available feeds and sensor reckonings every second. Unfortunately, there aren't a whole lot of sensors down here."

"Yes," I said. "Ish. Yes-ish. Apparently, there aren't a lot of Endpoint sensors down here."

Peach trotted down the corridor. I set off after her thanking Natasha for keeping this body in running shape and cursing Peach for her damned long legs. She loped along effortlessly looking kind of goofy but deceptively fast.

A few intersections later, Peach stopped and held a finger to her lips. She slowly drew the longest, ugliest knife I'd ever seen from a sheath on the small of her back. Easily 30 centimeters long with a blade honed to perfection and all manner of nasty-looking saw teeth things. The carbon-smoked coal-black knife was the epitome of blade tech.

Movement out of the corner of my eye caught my attention. One of Peach's drones was hovering near the ceiling. It moved slowly into the intersection like a tiny black wraith, sticking to the shadows. I didn't know much about military hardware; it never popped up on my signal feed since no military in the systems focused on my line of work. New gun? Meh. Surveillance drones? Sure. Could be useful, I guess. A fancy new way of opening locks? That would get my attention.

Peach rolled her head from side to side and stared into space. Her body was still and calm. Without warning, she jammed the knife around the corner and pulled it back. Damn, but she was fast. One moment she was the mountain, the next lightning. The sickening sound of someone drowning in his or her own blood.

A tattered and bandaged man stepped around the corner with confusion in his eyes. Peaches gently pulled him toward her and delicately set him on the deck. He was a handsome guy in his own way. Maybe not porn hot but handsome. From his neatly pressed clothes to his perfectly coiffed hair, it was clear that Xevex was recruiting outside of the airlocks. He was going after squares, too.

"You'll be fine," she said to him as she slapped a patch over the hole in his throat. "Everyone gets stabbed in the neck these days. It's practically outpatient surgery anymore."

He gurgled something that sounded like he had a mouth full of mayonnaise, but we were already moving.

"Did you bring a weapon?" Peaches asked over her shoulder as we snuck closer and closer to the end.

"Um, does an AI count?"

"No!"

"Then no," I said. "I had one of Nobtop's guns but I'm not used to carrying it, so I left in my quarters."

"How did you-" she started. "No, wait. Never mind. I don't want to know. Since you've been in my friend's body, you've bedded a pornstar-"

"Template," I interjected. "Big difference."

"Fine. Bedded a template, got involved with the biggest gang leader this side of Fat Charlie on Nova, and led me down this merry rabbat hole. What's your encore?"

I shrugged and did my best to not seethe too openly. Who was she to judge me? "Honestly, I haven't had time to think that far ahead. Oh, and don't forget, I also desecrated a corpse and kicked a guy to death."

"I heard about Sol. Pity. He was a nice guy even if he was completely obsessed with your girlfriend."

"He was infected," I said.

She stopped and spun on me. "Infected?" she asked. Disease breakouts are bad on planets. In a closed ecosystem like Endpoint, a bad disease could kill everyone on board before we even knew what happened. That was why the airlocks and visitor processing were a thing.

I tapped the side of my head. "In here. A Predecessor. Picked up from bad code in Virt. And before you ask, no, there's no way to get them out. Natasha had one; that's why she deleted herself."

Peach glared at me and clenched her fists. "Where'd she get it? I don't get into Virt that often but I'd love to hunt down the bastards that did that to her."

I shrugged. "All I know is that she was in Virt and one of them found her."

I called up my HUD and checked our location. The target was close now, a hundred meters or so. "Through there," I said, pointing at a door. "That's where Xevex will go."

Peach made a show of drawing a pistol and cocking it. She motioned at me to stay behind her but I decided to go for the gusto and move completely out of the line of fire. I felt like I should cock my fingers into a gun or something and pretend we were kids. I must've mumbled "pew pew pew" because Peach rolled her eyes and held her hand in the universal sign for "stay out of my way."

She nodded. I palmed the door pad and all hell broke loose.

There was chanting, shrieking, the telltale flicker of fire, and the sound of something large being tossed around. We peered around the door and found a scene straight out of Alcozar's "Hell's Folly." A dozen dead-eyed Airlockers were fighting through a dozen regular Airlockers. The regular Airlockers were trying to stay away from Endpoint's head-smashing tentacles, the dead-eyed ones were trying to get closer to the tentacles, Xevex in full Predecessor form was dodging and darting around The Caretaker who was still a massive Predecessor. Both were flashing colors at each other in what I can only assume were taunts about their respective mothers. Bodies littered the floor, some on fire, some frozen, and some with massive holes bored through their chests.

Xevex unleashed his black clouds at The Caretaker who dodged them easily and lashed out with a massive tentacle. Peach and I watched the mayhem with a mixture of amusement and horror. Something must have happened for some of the Airlockers to turn against the others. Whether it was a faith-based shift or Xevex had done something preposterously stupid that alienated part of the flock, I don't know. What I do know is there ain't no war like a religious war.

I was about to close the door and pretend nothing had happened when I got a vid request from The Specialist. "You must stop them," he hissed. "I just told your girlfriend but I don't know if she'll make it on time. You must destroy the central organotech creature."

What? He snapped out as quickly as he appeared. "Peach –"

"Can't talk. Sniping. Go hell," she mumbled.

"While I appreciate your desire to kill everyone, I just got a message. We need to destroy the central organotech creature."

The sniping mask in front of her face disappeared and a cocked eyebrow appeared. "The what?"

"The organotech creature."

"What the hell is an organotech creature?"

Shit. "I was hoping you knew."

"Why would I know what an organotech creature is? I run a bar. I shoot people. Neither of those things involves organo-whatsits."

Okay, maybe my luxurious powers of deduction would be able to help. "Look, it's got to be Xevex, the small, fuzzy Predecessor over there. The Caretaker, the big-ass Predecessor over there. Or the black latex turd in the middle of the room. My guess is the black latex turd. It certainly feels organotech-y. But I like to hedge my bets. What would it take to do all three of them?"

Peaches glanced at her gun, brushed a fleck of dust off it, and smiled like a mother holding her newborn child. "About two seconds," she said.

"Any reason to not just shoot all three?"

"Xevex is made of nanites, right?"

I nodded.

"There's reason number one. There's no way a bullet could hurt a nanoswarm. The Caretaker built his body from raw matter storage? It's entirely possible what he's rocking would be invulnerable to bullets. Finally, the big, black latex turd is freakin' massive."

She was waffling. The bullets in her gun would punch a hole through one of the elder gods. I'd buy the part about Xevex; I'd seen firsthand that bullets did nothing to him. The Caretaker was a wild card. It might be pervious to bullets, but it might not. The black latex turd was solid. It was there. And a somewhat known quantity. I thought of it as a data trunk more than anything else. An interface to the computer world for Predecessors, probably with a direct line to their Virt.

"Shoot the turd," I said, "but wait until I'm in position. After you hit the turd, hit anything that looks like it's coming at me."

Without waiting for a response, I was off. I activated my AniTat system's grey-out mode and did my best to stick to the edges of the brawl. It must have been my lucky day since I only had to punch one guy in the back of the head before I was about ten meters from the snake thing.

I held up both thumbs; and was rewarded with deafening thunder. A massive hole appeared in the side of the cortex. It screamed. Shrieked. Wailed. Everything stopped. Slowly, one by one, sets of eyes focused on me. They narrowed. Pleasing everyone is impossible. Pissing off everyone is super easy. Out of the corner of my eye, I caught a shuffling skeletal woman in a dress that was more rag than clothes shift from side to side. She pointed at me and took a tentative step forward. Before her foot hit the ground, the God of Kinetics and Force roared his displeasure. The woman exploded.

Xevex rippled. The Caretaker's tentacles coiled into spirals and relaxed again. The Predecessor version of making a fist. I was focusing on the two big bosses of the fight when god spake again and another soul entered the afterlife. Peach took her job seriously. No one moved again.

"I'm not the enemy," I said, holding up my hands.

"You're the Rectifier," Jenkins said in my head. "Here to clean out the trash and make things right again."

"I am...," I said, holding up my hands, "the Rectifier."

Two people immediately knelt and lowered their heads. I pointed at Xevex and the Controller. "They are false gods. Lies wrapped in special effects and bad costumes."

That got some attention. Eyes glared, boring into me and seeking retribution. In retrospect, that wasn't a good line.

"I am here to set things right!" I said. I pointed at Xevex and grinned my nastiest grin. "I am here to stop the false prophet before he kills everyone."

Not going to lie, I really sucked at acting goddess-like. Xevex, on the other hand, was a master. He dispersed into a cloud of black smoke and flew into the Caretaker. He didn't do anything as quaint or clean as bore a hole through the thing, he flew into its pores and orifices. For a moment, the Caretaker looked confused and terrified. Part of me wanted to shout out a warning, but the Caretaker was kind of a dick.

Just when I rethinking that bit about the Caretaker being a dick, the massive Predecessor exploded. Imagine a smell of old, briny sea dripping down your hair and you'll get the idea. It was the perfect act – the new god destroying the old god in a violent act of flying gore.

Xevex's nanites flowed smoothly across the room. Slightly buzzing clouds that undulated slightly. He reformed into his human self directly in front of, but a little too far away. "What's the matter?" I asked. "Scared?"

He took a step forward. I held up my hands placatingly. "Cool man. You're the head god now. The big cheese. I'll admit it, I'm a joiner. So, what's the signup process here? Is there paperwork? Did you go the old school route and demand a soul?"

"Nothing so prosaic. You know what I need from you."

"Do we get business cards and discount price T-shirts?"

He smiled a lopsided grin that nearly got me off guard. Then I remembered his hand around my throat. "Absolutely not," he said. "We have no need for those things. Our goal is...unification. Out with the old, in with the new."

I stepped forward. He didn't back down. "If you're thinking your sniper in the doorway can stop me," he said, "think again."

"Oh, I know bullets won't hurt you," I told him as I edged forward. "I've seen them pass right through you."

"Your little trick won't work, either. I've hardened my systems."

I did my best to keep a terrified but hopeful look on my face. "I expected you would."

"I was alive when your race was scratching for food in the dirt of that miserable planet you call home."

"Why haven't you killed me yet? Was I too slick for you?"

He strode forward and put a hand on my cheek. Good boy. "I knew exactly where you were all the time. I didn't kill you because I knew you would come to me someday. Some of my friend is still in your head, beckoning you to me."

That was a scary thought. "How do you know it wasn't just me the whole time, wanting to get close to you?"

Second hand on my cheek. Complete circuit. "That would be acceptable. I like strong beings."

I placed both hands on his sides. "Good."

"You'll need a new body, though. I cannot stomach your hideous forms."

The blast of electricity flowed out of my fingertips and into his side. From there, shot straight downward. Xevex bellowed and boiled. I screamed. I was only partially aware of a chunk of him detaching itself in a black cloud and hightailing it toward the collection point.

I fell to my knees and stammered, "Take them all out. Everyone in the room."

Xevex hitting the collection point meant he had direct access to the Predecessor network. From there, it was a straight shot to Endpoint Message Dispatching where he'd be encoded and transmitted. His goal had to be Temnyy. That was the only thing out here unless he wanted to go back into Virt and giving up didn't seem like Xevex.

Heads exploded around me. Peach killed a dozen people in less than six seconds without a single wasted shot.

I staggered to my feet and lurched across the gore-strewn floor. I had to get there and hope the thing still recognized me. It may shove my brains out, but the thing was the only way to Xevex. The blast of electricity did a number on my nerves and it was hard to get my limbs to do their things. An arm around my waist tugged me away from the flailing collection point.

"No!" I moaned. Damn, even my voice was whacked.

"Help me! We've got to get her away from that thing," a familiar voice said.

"Have to get to it," I muttered. "Have to stop him."

"I put a hole in it," Peach said. "The thing's dying."

I shook my head and tugged at the arm around my waist. "No time then. Have to get to it now."

Arms grabbed my shoulders and spun me around. In front of me, Monique looked terrified. "You're not thinking clearly."

I grabbed her face and focused on her eyes. Deep green. The color of forests. The color of living things. They steadied my mind a bit. Enough to focus. "Trust me," I whispered. "Please."

She stroked my hair and whispered, "No. We need to get you help."

I shook my head. "Only my body is janky. Brain still mostly works. kill everyone. Every last human he can find."

Monique raised an eyebrow and asked, "What makes you think you can stop him?"

I shrugged and tapped the side of my head. "I had one of his kind in here before. Their tech recognizes me. If I can get control before he does-"

"You'll be a moon-sized weapon," Peach finished. "That's kind of cool."

Monique shot her a look that could peel paint. "It is not!"

I gently pulled her eyes back to mine. "I'm not staying in it forever."

"You could die," she whispered.

"I've been dead before. Strange times. Strange enough that even death could die."

"Did she fall and hit her head?" Peach asked.

I shook my head. "Old line from an old book. Time is wasting."

Monique softened but crow's feet worry lines extended from her eyes. I brushed her face and leaned in until our foreheads were touching. "I see you, Monique."

"Hurry up," she whispered.

I half staggered, half-walked until the flailing arm of the collector noticed me. It was hurt and pissed but something in it recognized something in me. The tentacle circled me, looking for something and not quite finding it. Finally, it hovered in front of my face. The spear-tip flicked open like a mouth with four jaws. Lights flashed inside, probably a Predecessor calming message. I closed my eyes and clenched my fists. Breathed out slowly and opened my eyes. The lights flashed slower, winding down until there was a single bulb in the center. When it blinked out, my mind went with it.

38 - Dangerous Games and Genocide

I was in Pred Virt, seeing their world through their eyes. Glowing scenes of battles and lovers and strange, undersea poetry rendered in flashing RGB. Their world was so different from ours but the underlying stories were still the same. No matter how peaceful Jessica claimed her race was, conquest seemed to be a universal construct.

The room was a near perfect representation of one of Endpoint's corridors. Intentional or not, it was eerie to see the place through the eyes of the builders. It was almost like a moment of clarity where you finally get poetry and it makes sense even though you can't stand the stuff.

I made my way down the hall, keeping myself as close to the center as possible to make it a slight bit more difficult for Xevex to leap out of a shadow and kill me. If Pred Virt rules were the same as ours, all that would happen would be my ejection from the Squid Disco and Art Emporium. Of course, that would mean Xevex had won.

Dispersed along the corridor were odd technical readouts: Blueprints for a tentacle, sketches of massive eyes, designs for hundred-kilometer-thick skin to keep the vacuum at bay, some kind of engine with notes scribbled next to it. The whole enchilaco. They design notes for Temnyy or mocked up ads for new super doomsday weapons. I reached out a hand found a massive tentacle floating in front of my face. Of course. Pred Virt, pred rules, and they didn't do humans.

"Where to, toots?" a Predecessor dressed as a late 1900s Terran cabbie asked as he pulled up next to me. He was in a small-ish electrical truck that looked ancient and human, albeit modified to handle his Predecessor body. What in Penta's name was a Predecessor doing with a truck?

"Toots?" I asked.

"Sure, dollface. I'm primarily a data-gathering tool, but I moonlight as a conveyer because I ain't got nothing else to do. My role was to assimilate data about the enemy and feed it to the Weapon so its data banks would be fresh when it was awoken. Lately, I've been getting lots of data about the filthy monkeys that call themselves 'humans'. 'Toots' was a term of endearment that they used to refer to the females of their species. Doesn't apply to us, but I like to use it because it's got a kick to it. So, anyway, where to?"

Good question. Did Temnyy have a central control or a pilot station? "How about the Weapon's cockpit?"

It was his turn to look at me askance. "Cockpit? Never heard of it."

"It's what the humans call the place their ship pilots sit to control their ships," I told him with a wink.

His tentacles whipped around as he laughed. "Oh, those crazy monkeys. They have such a way with words. Sure, hop in, I can take you to the...what was it? Cockpit. Heh, heh. I like that. Cockpit. Yeah, I can take you to the cockpit."

I lucked out and didn't look like too much of freak hauling my massive nine-limbed body into the back of his weird truck and settled down with a sigh. We took off at a tremendous speed, fast enough everything became a blur of varying colors. I tried to ignore the fact that I was a whole bunch of zeroes and ones floating through space between Endpoint and the Weapon.

I was, however, acutely aware of the fact that Predecessor naming conventions were downright boring. Collector, Controller, Weapon. Was there not a single poet among them?

As we sped along, the cabbie twisted his head to look at me with a pair of massive eyes. "You must be part of the Catalog if you know about humans."

I nodded. "Yep. That's me. Catalog all the way."

"You should work with me; I've got direct access to the raw data about humans floating around in my noggin," he said as he tapped the lower mid-point in his abdomen.

"I'll make a note of it."

"How long 'til the cockpit?" I asked as we sped along.

"A few minutes. This bird is wicked fast."

"Hey," I asked. "Since you get information to the Weapon, do you know how many minds it takes to run it? It's, uh, been a long time and that data got lost."

"All of 'em," he said. "What was left of 'em, anyway. Totally subsume everyone into the brain. The plan was to drop it off, upload everyone, and turn on the terror. Big weapon. Needs a lot of brain power."

"How many planets will it go after?"

"All of 'em. Every planet it can find that ain't ours. It's gonna be glorious. Righteous vengeance and it makes sure any of us that are still out there somewhere are safe."

Shit. It really was a doomsday weapon. With Xevex at the helm, he'd be the scourge of all time. Humanity had a few dozen planets and they all squabbled with each other.

If they could all work together maybe, just maybe, they could mount a serious defense. Unfortunately, we didn't have the best track record at cooperation in the species.

"Here we are, toots," the cabbie said. "I hope you enjoyed the ride and look forward to seeing you again. Best-a-luck in there. Fire it up and let 'er rip for me, okay?"

Oh, I was going to fire something up all right. I wasn't sure how, but I was going to do it. "Will do," I told him. "Keep the faith, brother."

He winked three eyes and then vibrated. "Oh, I get it. Old human saying. You keep the faith, too, kiddo."

With a flash of color, it was off. The Virt part of Temnyy was far, far different from the Predecessor Virt world on Endpoint. There, it was representative of their normal lives – art, flashing colors, animations. Temnyy was pure function over form. The walls, ceiling, and floor were the same pinkish gray as Endpoint's deck plates but that was where the similarities ended. Temnyy-Virt lacked the defined lines of manufactured things and opted for the controlled chaos of biology. It was like being in a transteel lung or an anthill on a massive scale. Clearly, the Virt designers wanted their visitors to know exactly what awaited them. They were going to be a part of something much larger than themselves.

All around me were doorways leading to tunnels leading to something. Some were obviously too small to go through, others were normal size. Not a damned one of them had a sign. If I assumed I could fit into approximately half, that still left too much exploring for a time when

Xevex was probably already powering up this monument to revenge.

I was getting the hang of moving on six limbs with three out in front of me. The trinocular vision was giving me a headache but the movement was getting easier. In their own bodies, they must have been fearsome. There was something to be said for the absolute stability of six legs and the general functionality of three arms. In real life, I could do all kinds of things with three arms.

I ambled down the largest path for a few minutes before I came to the same kind of black room I'd seen with Endpoint Control. When I stepped into the room, it silently powered up and filled my mind with all sorts of data about Temnyy: Sleeping status, growth status, internal energy readings, a view of Endpoint through alien eyes.

The universe was a different place through Temnyy's eyes. Predecessors had similar visual acuity to humans, but there was more lurking at the edges: Colors that didn't make sense and things like radio waves I'd never experienced before because human vision is limited. Temnyy could see everything, even things I had trouble wrapping my head around.

While I was busy gawking at the universe like a kid who just saw his first pair of boobs, an undercurrent thought roared up. Where was Xevex? He got here before me. He presumably knew his way around Temnyy better than I ever could. Yet, he was nowhere in sight.

A thundering slam from the side answered me. One moment I was stargazing, the next I was skidding across the floor. Before I could right myself, he was on me. Through the deluge of tentacles raining down on my body, I realized I was right: Having three arms was awesome.

All I could do was react. Bring my tentacles up and use them to protect myself. Xevex had a distinct advantage. Against him as a human, I might have had a chance; he was bigger but I knew a thing or two about using fists and feet. Against Xevex as a Predecessor, I was in deep trouble; he had lifetimes of experience as nine-limbed creature from hell, I had less than an hour.

The sheer effort involved in keeping nine limbs coordinated was wearing on me. In addition to Xevex's incessant wailing on me, my headache kept growing. Hangry or horngry or weary or just generally grumpy, it didn't really matter. My head was bumping.

But I wasn't the quitting type. A small part of my brain had been analyzing Xevex's tentacles whacking me about the head and shoulders. The cardinal rule of fighting is never get predictable. Xevex, while his tentacles hit me with alarming regularity, had a pattern. A pattern I could exploit. Slap, slap, slap, pause; slap, slap, slap, pause.

My own tentacles went up, taking the brunt of his three strikes and protecting my body. When he finished his three shots, I reached out and intertwined two of my tentacles with his. It wasn't perfect and there was no way to do a joint lock on boneless tentacles, but it was enough to trip him up. I let the headache piss me off and used the anger. Rage is our superpower. I lashed out a tentacle right into one of his eyes.

Xevex tried to retreat but I held him fast and flicked two more eyes. His other six now pointed away from me. I finally had the bastard and it was time for a little payback. "Still like tentacle porn, you prick?" I hissed. "Care to be on the receiving end of it?"

That time I pushed everything I had straight into his top eye. It gave way with a sickening squelch. His body may have been tough but every eye is delicate. A shot to the eye hurts and, worse, it disorients. He went slack and I hit one of his other eyes the same way before untangling our limbs and giving him the Predecessor equivalent of pride-obliterating bitch-slap.

Xevex collapsed to the ground, panting and desperately tentacling at his ruined eyes. He writhed like a mass of sneks doused in gas and set on fire. Apparently, Temnyy's Virt ran on the same rules of pleasure and pain that ours did.

I resisted the urge to kick him to death and looked around the room. No weapons. No workstations I could take apart for sharp, cutty-pokey things. Nothing. Typical Predecessor asceticism. The room was for working and nothing else. I didn't know exactly what I was looking for. After all, no one had ever successfully located Predecessor weaponry.

Some of the earliest researchers took that to mean the Predecessors were a peaceful race. That didn't explain Temnyy, though. No peaceful race would make a planetoid-sized monster, upload themselves into it so they could feel the power, and go gallivanting across the cosmos looking for things to smash.

"Little monkey," Xevex whispered behind me. "You're already too late."

I turned and did my best to glare at him. "Kept you from starting this thing up. That's good enough for me."

"Are you seriously hitting on me right now?" Xevex asked quietly.

"What?"

"The narrowed eyes, human. They're considered flirty among my people."

He chuckled. It was a weird effect seeing the tentacled critter on the floor laughing. Maybe human Virt had been rubbing off on him. "It was started the moment I arrived," he said. "It won't be a pity when I take this weapon and lay waste to your people. A pity in a way; if you had just gotten along with each other, you might have been able to field a defense."

Xevex disconnected and disappeared. He was one with Temnyy. Damn it. There was just one last hope and it was a distant one. Whatever came out when that big black egg cracked, it was going to have its eyes set on us. Temnyy's control center flickered and rearranged itself. Everything went black.

Damn it. He'd kicked me out of Temnyy virt. Probably forever.

When sensation came back, I opened my eyes and found Monique staring down at me while she stroked my hair. "Thought I'd lost you," she said.

"Not yet. The night is young."

Peach ran a scanner over me and frowned. She tapped it a few times before shoving it back into the phone holster on her hip.

I managed to sit up. The world swirled and flickered. Whatever Virt Temnyy was rocking, it was a doozy. Monique and Peaches both helped. "You need rest," Peaches said. "Real rest, not just time spent between her legs."

"I need to get to Mason," I mumbled.

"Mason's dead, honey," Monique said.

I shook my head and immediately regretted it. Human Virt is disorienting but easy to handle. Predecessor Virt was brutal. Maybe it was having to wrap my head around seven more legs than I should. "He's not dead. He's a ghost. In Virt, I mean. A Virt ghost."

"She must've really whacked her head when she fell," Peaches said. "Ghosts are a myth. Body goes, mind goes."

"Then explain the Predecessors," I snapped and immediately regretted it. "They broke down out here and uploaded themselves into their Virt. Their bodies were frozen and shattered and converted to raw construction materials. When we showed up, they found new bodies."

Someone banged on the door and Peach shot him without even looking up. She looked deep into my eyes and never blinked. "Do you realize how crazy that sounds? Even for you, that's a pretty bonkers story."

She tried to ease me back down but I shrugged her off. "Come on," I told her. "Time's a wasting. Get me to a Virt terminal."

"Why don't you use your friend over there?" Monique asked, pointing at the tentacle-thing hovering nearby.

"Because that only goes to Predecessor Virt. I need to get to ours."

"You could go wireless," Monique said.

"Nope," I said. "I need full interactive connection."

39 – Goodbyes

M ason had a skill I could never pull off. Somehow, he managed to make wearing nothing but a foil cowboy hat and gold duster with flashing RGB logos for long dead companies look chic.

"What the heck is Ataro?" I asked after the initial shock of seeing him wore off.

"Ah, Natasha. So good to see you again. Let us retire to the study."

Something about Mason and his bizarre collection of art and dimensions took all the stress out of me. A Svengali without the underlying sinister aptitude.

"Mason," I said as I snuggled into the big armchair, "something terrible is about to happen."

Part of me felt terrible about relaxing and accepting his hospitality given what I was about to drop on him, but Mason was the type of person who would take offense if his hospitality was refused.

"No more terrible than that outfit," he said with a sly smile. "You really should allow Monique to pick your outfits. The woman is incorrigible, but she does understand clothes."

I looked down and found I was still dressed in a messy pair of coveralls. The very least Xevex's crew of madmen and miscreants could find to cover my naked body last time. "That's a long story," I told him. "It involves a cult."

"The best stories do," he replied.

"A cult here on Endpoint."

Mason leaned back in his chair and somehow projected coolness even as his suit was projecting logos for yet another a long-dead company, Augury. "I am disconnected from the physical world," he said, waving his hand.

I downed my drink in one gulp, garnering a raised eyebrow from the ever-cool Mason, and leaned forward. "Xevex has found a way onto Temnyy. I, uh, accidentally turned Endpoint back on and he used it to make his move. I doubt he can handle the thing himself; Jessica said it would take dozens of minds to control something that size."

"And you're afraid he's going to bring his compatriots to Temnyy?" Mason asked.

"Absolutely. He's got access to Endpoint's digitization features. The Predecessors apparently called it the Collection System or some such thing. Some of his lieutenants are out there right now. I need to know how to shut down Predecessor Virt. I, uh. Shit, this is hard. I need to know how to shut down Endpoint Virt. Clean the slate."

Mason nodded slowly, eyes focused on his drink. For all his affectations about disconnection, I could see in his eyes he knew exactly what I meant. "Did you know Jessica talks in her sleep?"

I shook my head. "Never slept with her."

"You don't know what you're missing. She's, or rather, it's – they don't subscribe to gender the way we do. Jessica was a spectacular lover. The best that ever was and will be."

Damn. That was it. He'd crossed the final line off his bucket list. Nail an alien. Go full Kirk. "She's in my pocket right now," I said. "On a crystal worm drive."

"Good. Good. It would be a pity if her light were to be extinguished. In addition to other activities, we talked a lot. Lost souls that found someone." He sipped his drink and adjusted his gold duster. Nervous. Finally facing mortality after he'd cheated death for decades. "She... No, that's not right and 'it' doesn't feel right. They. That'll work for now. Jessica said they wanted their people to live again. More importantly, they wanted them to die again. To move on to the next level of existence. Apparently, the Predecessors were a very spiritual race before interfacing with us. Some still cling desperately to the old ways and advocate spinning down the 'corrupted' as they call them. They can't bring themselves to do it, though, on the off chance that spinning them down is the same as dying and the corrupted get to move on while the rest of them are stuck in Virt forever."

I set my drink down, crossed the space between, and took his hands in mine. "I don't have the answers, Mason. You could live forever and never figure out those answers. All I can tell you is we're probably all dead if Xevex gets his crew. Us and billions more. If a soul is tied to a body, I'm already toast because my body is gone. I helped carve it up so I could pretend to be someone I'm not. I need your help to shut down reality. I can flip switches on the outside, but you're the only one alive who can close the doors on the inside."

He nodded and smiled sadly. "Natasha-"

"Nat," I said. "My name is Nat."

Mason squeezed my hands. "Good for you. You chose an identity. Get out there and live it. I'll be in place in thirty minutes. You need to be ready to shut down the source."

Wait. What? "What source?"

"Temnyy. Get back in and tear up the place. Take over."

Was he kidding? "How do I do that?"

"You were a thief in a...former life, right?"

"Yeah," I mumbled, not sure where the conversation was going.

"Any good?" he asked.

"Sure. I mean, I made a good enough living at it."

"Did you go in the front door or did you sneak around in a black turtleneck?"

"I'm insulted you would ask such a thing," I said, smiling and feigning swooning. "I owned several of the blackest turtlenecks you ever seen. I actually paid a guy to use super-dense black on them. Not even light can escape."

"Black turtleneck it is, then," Mason said. "You were a thief. Hacking a computer isn't much different from hacking a building. It's all about circumventing security doors or burning them off their hinges. The important part is finding the right doors."

I snapped my fingers and smacked my forehead. "The, uh, bar. That place where you got infected. Lord Barclay's. Jessica showed me a way through in the back. But the bar was empty last time I was there."

He nodded and smiled. "You need an invitation or Barclay's doesn't exist. Think like a thief. You have two insiders: Myself and Jessica. You'll find an invitation upstairs along with some more appropriate attire. As for the back door, you've been shown how to use it. Now you just need to get where you need to go without getting caught. Every security system ever created has been circumvented. Be the woman that brings this one to its knees."

I frowned. Usually, people paid me to do stuff like that, and it was just human stuff where I could scout out or look up the details on the 'net. At the end was a payday. Not this alien monster nonsense where the galaxy was on the line. "Sorry, this all seems way out of my league."

Mason smiled and shook his head. "I used to follow the exploits of somewhat famous thief. He'd strike every twenty or thirty years and then disappear. The disappearing part was easy; he just had to hop a ship and go wherever the money took him. But the jobs were brilliant in their simplicity. He once took down the royal family of Arthaburst on Iono6. Looted the biggest, most expensive gem in the safe and vanished like a ghost."

I could only smile and try not to look too cagey. "Okay, let's say I get into Pred space, what next? I'll be in their realm and I don't even speak the language."

"You'll know. You have Predecessor thoughts in your head. Just follow your instincts. Make sure to be on Temnyy quickly though; if you dawdle, Xevex might win and we can't have that."

"Penta," I whispered.

"Can't help you. He's long gone."

"I know," I said with a sigh. "It's a habit more than anything. An addiction to the metaphysical. Okay, once I'm onboard Temnyy it should be a simple case of walloping Xevex."

Mason's smile eased my worries. Penta- Crap. There I went again. All I can say is the man could smile. "My worst sin, and I've not only committed them all, I've created a few new ones, but the worst of them was my laziness in hooking our systems to theirs without any kind of security. In my defense, I assumed the Predecessors were all long gone. And it's not the same kind of restart. I'm going to trigger a surge from our Virt into theirs."

He looked around his study with its soft leather chairs and roaring fire. "This will be my last ride. I'm okay with that. There are new places to visit. Perhaps I'll meet the original owner of your body. Do an old man a favor, though."

I nodded. It was all I could really do. Exhausted. Scared. Sad. Stuck in a situation I didn't create nor want, about to smile as I sent a friend off to commit suicide and possibly genocide. "Name it."

"Tell my story. Don't let the 'verse forget it."

In true Mason fashion, he flashed me a surly grin and slowly dissolved into a mass of tiny zeroes and ones. Flashy to the end. I closed my eyes, fought back the raging sorrow, and found someplace quiet to cry my eyes out.

40 – Dea

I raided Mason's dress barn and found something made of bad dreams and spider-silk lace to match my mood. Skulls and screaming faces, horror and monsters leered at the world. It was one of many otherworldly themes he'd either scrounged up or thought up and, like everything he had, it fit perfectly.

I walked into Lord Barclay's like I owned the place, shoved the bouncer's face first into my chest and then away from me without a word. The same shining chrome and sexed-up partygoers were there and I got the feeling the place was a special kind of Hell where you'd better look your best and party your best and be your best all the time if you knew what was good for you. Of course, with that crowd, coming up with novel punishments would be difficult at best.

The corridor Jessica led me down last time was still filled with noise and the scent of advanced apes enjoying themselves. At the end of hallway was the same blank wall we'd been at before. Then, Jessica had put her hand out and everything had shifted. She was full-blooded Predecessor. All I had were stray thought patterns so faint I didn't even notice they were there. I held out my hand and closed my eyes. Said a little howdy to Penta. Wished really, really hard.

When I opened my eyes, my body was a rubbery mass of limbs and colors I couldn't identify filled my head.

I made my way slowly, guessing at signs just as confusing as the hobo signs the Specialists put up, and looked for anything that resembled an egg. I had no idea what their weapons looked like or what their computers looked like, but eggs are universal thanks to the miracle of biological openings.

The first four sphere-shaped pictographs lead me to a bathroom, a hospital, a weird room with a few novempods listlessly dozing, and something that looked like a nesting chamber. They really had gone all out representing their world. None of that stuff was necessary in Virt. Well, maybe the napping room, but bathrooms, hospitals, and nesting chambers would be useless in Virt. Hell, the only reason we had bathrooms in our Virt was for people to have sex in. Same with our Virt hospitals. Maybe the Predecessors had done the same thing.

I wandered aimlessly for a bit and then something tickled my brain. The corridor I was walking in felt familiar. Alien, but still familiar. I couldn't quite put my finger on something about it. Tantalizingly close, but still distant. I was pondering it and walking without thinking when I turned a corner and found myself in a massive room with a domed ceiling looking out into the void.

"Damn it," I said, slapping myself for not realizing it sooner. In the real, in my time, the Bizarre Bazaar lived there. In Predecessor Virt, it was just a big, empty room filled with water.

The whole of the Predecessor Virt was a meticulously detailed representation of Endpoint. I didn't recognize it because the white wall panels were lit up with neon colors and the overhead lighting was different. If it was one-hundred percent accurate, that would mean there was a door not too far from where I was standing.

It took me a moment to recognize the door. You see a rectangular thing with a doorknob and you can almost immediately recognize the doorness of a door. At least, in the real it was a rectangle. In Virt, it was pure Pred.

"Damn, guys," I muttered to myself, "you can make things with more than three angles. There are seriously no rules against it."

The bigger problem was how to open it. After some mental deliberation, I decided to stick a couple of tentacles in the holes and see what happened. It felt more than a little naughty, like one of those tentacle porn things Xevex seemed to enjoy so much. I resisted the urge to ask the door if it wanted more and giggled to myself.

My tentacle tips were incredibly sensitive. I could feel imperfections in the smooth metal and the tiniest of clicks as the latch disengaged. With two tentacles, I slid the door up and to the side. Inside was a ramp leading down. Stairs were probably a waste for a species with six limbs on the ground all the time.

As I shambled through the door, I realized why the door was a big ol' honkin' triangle: My body fit perfectly.

I did my best to ignore the insistent RGB screens pouring out information. The Specialists would love this. Endpoint almost felt alive and waiting to chat with anyone who came to visit. I absently brushed a tentacle across a screen, causing distant, alien thoughts in my head. The ship was alive. Well, in a way, at least. There were complex thoughts there, lurking in the background noise of deep space. A hint of boredom, a slab of sorrow, a mound of general ennui.

In the real, the door to the Collector was unmarked. In Predecessor Virt, it was just another door with random squiggles on a placard. I studied the pictography of a flying novempod, limbs outstretched, and a halo of light around its head, and rolled my eyes. Of course, one of them would assume godhead status.

I slapped the door pad in disgust, which rewarded me with my fantasy mad-scientist laboratory. Maybe it was just my Predecessor eyes, but the neons and hyperblacks and shining things surrounding a massive, glowing tube were mind-blowing. Humanity had forgotten how to make tech sexy, but the Predecessors embraced it. I had the distinct feeling I was right when I said the vinyl tube was someone's magnum opus. Through my human eyes, it looked like a massive black latex sex toy, but Predecessor eyes showed so much more.

It was a data juggler of extraordinary proportions. Lights in colors I could barely comprehend played up and down its sides. The black latex glowed faintly in the coal-black room. The thing went straight up into the attic and straight down into the bowels. Heaven and Hell, if you believed in such things. In Virt, the collector snakes felt and looked like actual asps.

One of the snakes scanned me by latching onto my head. Just another day in paradise where mechanical snakes sucked the brains out of unsuspecting people. It pressed its way into my head and opened my mind and I gave it full access. The Core scanned everything in my head. It smelled Predecessor thought in my brain but couldn't figure out where it was coming from. Like a hound on the trail of prey, it kept digging.

After a few moments, it backed off. All the lights in the room flashed rapid-fire colors. A voice boomed in my head, "flaph tow ofming sfcep mirn!" Or words to that effect.

There it was—the dreaded moment out of my discovery, causing the remainder of Predecessor society to pounce on my digital self. Did the rules even apply there? If I died in human Virt, I'd just go back to my body. Would the same thing happen in Pred Virt?

"It says you are welcome here and to choose your destination," a voice said to the side.

I turned and found Natasha Devore. The real deal, staring at me and idly picking invisible dirt from her fingernails. In a virtual world filled with nine-limbed cephalopods. "How-?"

"Did I get here?" she finished for me. "Pure dumb luck. As you've probably guessed, I got infected."

"Xevex told me," I replied.

"He's a dick and not a very good one, either. Call it pride, but I couldn't let them win. The Core recognized Predecessor thought waves and trusted me. I cooked up a plan with the help of that weird guy downstairs and sent a message to my party buddy. I take it you're the one he found to replace me."

"Bik, you son of a whore." I mumbled. "Yeah, me."

"Sorry to put you through this," she said. "I couldn't allow my head to fall into their control."

"You're right. They could have hacked into any bank in the Systems. They could have been rich."

She nodded sagely. "Yeah, without even earning it. I was talking more about knowing how our systems work and how to get around them. The last thing I wanted to see was a massive predatory creature with nearly unlimited resources turned loose using my knowledge to drop planetary defenses."

"So, what now?" I asked.

"What do you mean, what now?"

"Well, we've got Xevex powering up the ultimate weapon. A bunch of friends are dead. You joined a gang and defiled a corpse. Oh, yeah, you kicked a guy to death because he was infected. And Mason loaned you some clothes. Your girlfriend is terrified-"

"I don't have a girlfriend."

"You do now," I said. "You're welcome. My body is gone. If you want this one back, I'm sorry to say I've made kind of a mess of your life."

Natasha rolled her eyes. "Ugh, no. Flesh. Yuck. There's a whole universe out there and I'm going to explore it."

"How?" I asked. "You're stuck in a computer."

"No, I live in a computer. But you know what? From where I'm standing, we all live in a computer." She twirled happily in place. "That's why none of this really matters. I mean, we've got all this programming built into us that says stay alive at all costs but, seriously, why? Meat's ugly. It breaks down. Code can last forever."

"Not if you kill yourself."

"Wrong!" she said, pointing at me. "Wrong. I already killed myself once. That was just breaking out of the prison that kept me in meatspace. Now, I'm going to delete a wrapper that's keeping me in codespace. Then I'll be free."

"Unless there's something else holding you back."

She seethed. "I'll delete that, too. Until it's just me, I'll delete any chains that hold me back."

Part of me wanted to beg her to stop and reconsider. Another part of me wondered if she was right. Natasha had managed to find a way to purge her Predecessor and uploaded herself right into their Virt. It was unheard of. We barely understood Predecessor computer systems and she'd managed to seduce the panties off one and make herself at home. When she got out, woe unto anyone who tried to stop her. Natasha Devore, legendary crusher of security, was setting her sights on things no one had ever seen.

"Um, good luck," I said. "Not to be aloof, but there's still the small matter of the superweapon outside."

"It's been taken care of," she said with a wink. "Just don't tell anyone it was me. No, wait. It wasn't you. It was me. Like, *me* me, instead of you me. Anyway, um, don't tell anyone you saw me in Predecessor Virt or they'll all come looking. If anyone asks, all you had to do was disrupt the quantum hydrodycelic progeneration routines so that the prototypical cyclometes couldn't achieve parabolic mutation."

I stared at her and wondered how much more off the rails things could get.

Natasha rolled her eyes. "Just smile mysteriously. If anyone presses you, just say 'with magic and science.'"

I nodded slowly. "Right. Magic. Science. Things. Stuff."

"Exactly. Now, there is something I'm going to need from you. If I could have done this on my own, it would have been done days ago."

She held out her hand and a small, greenish thing appeared in her palm. "I won't bother to tell you what this does because I doubt you'd understand it. Suffice it to say one of the earliest lessons in hacking is if you can get to the hardware, three quarters of your work is done. Most of Predecessor Virt is wide open, but that corridor down there is restricted to Predecessors only. It was a weird bit of security to put in; they must have expected at some point some alien race would come calling."

I tried to shrug and found my body couldn't do that. "So? You've got Predecessor in you." Totally had her there, the benefit of living in someone's body.

"Not anymore. When I deleted myself, I did a sector-by-sector, neuron by neuron copy, stripping out anything not human and leaving it behind. I couldn't have something watching over my shoulder while I explored this whole new world."

"Wait. Once you'd done that, why didn't you just go back into your body? Why all this madness with body-swapping when you could have just put yourself back in?"

"The Predecessor reunification routines don't support human bodies. I didn't want to wind up stuck in a nine-armed slug. Hell, I can't even get through to human Virt yet. So, I'm a ghost in the machine, looking for a way out."

How do you respond to something like that? Sorry you're stuck in alien virtual reality? Gee, that sucks. I tried to nod and failed, so I wound up drawing circles on the ground with my tentacles. "So, um," I mumbled.

"You need to go. I'll give you directions even a common thief-"

"I am not a common thief," I said.

"No, you're an exceptional thief. Now, take the thing I gave you – the green thing – and find the white thing in Temnyy's control center. Put the green thing on the white thing. That's all you have to do. The green thing will do the rest."

"Green thing. White thing. Does thing," I said, looking at the green thing in my hand. "Got it. What are these floppy things that feel like they're about to come off?"

"PROM emulators. Programmable Read-Only Memory. Very, very old school. But they should allow me to interface with the Predecessor systems."

41 - Something, Something, Thing, Thing

Xevex was lurking as soon as I showed up. I could feel his eyes boring into me. He wasn't used to being challenged and didn't know how to handle someone showing up after they'd beaten him. That little bit of dissonance was all that kept him hidden. All good by me; all I wanted to do was put the green thing on the white thing and go back to something normal.

My instinct told me to move quietly, make myself silent and invisible. Xevex knew I was there so I didn't waste time with novem-ninja moves. I stalked forward like I owned the place and practically begged Xevex to attach me. Win, lose, or draw. If the green thing met the white thing, I was happy.

My brain was having trouble processing input from so many eyes, so I mentally focused on one set at a time and pinged around the room looking for the green thing. On my third loop through my eyes, I caught movement. By the time I'd registered it, I was on my fourth loop, and it was obvious Xevex had decided it was time to finish it.

He came at me with two swords and a shield. I barely dodged the first sword; the second sword nicked me, and I took the shield full force in the face. Rather than worry about my blurry eyes, I pivoted to a different set and unfurled a tentacle straight into one of his eyes.

And that is where my interstellar combat theory went completely awry. He'd learned to guard his eyes since last time and with all those arms, he could easily keep me away. That left me in a completely alien situation. I couldn't kick him in the knees because he didn't have any. He didn't have bones to break or joints to lock. Everything I thought I knew about bar fighting went straight out the exhaust.

Xevex pushed his assault, spinning and slashing with his swords to the beat of some mysterious tune playing in his head. It didn't take long to catch the rhythm and stay out of his way while I scanned the room for the green thing.

As I backed around the room, keeping just out of reach of the madman's serrated and barbed blades, I kept an eye searching for green things. My head was bumping from the constant viewpoint shifts and Xevex's rhythmic slicing and dicing. The room wasn't much use, either. No tables I could kick into his face. No bottles to break and slash with, not even a pool cue.

His tentacles wrapped around his weapons in a grip far stronger than anything a human hand could accomplish. In other words, without a gun or some other weapon, I was space sushi.

I flicked my tentacles toward his face to disrupt his flow. While I couldn't do any real damage to him, I could at least make him think I knew what I was doing. With his rhythm firmly in check, it was trivial to keep him from getting too close. It wouldn't do anything, but it kept him occupied and gave me a chance to scan faster.

A knife slashed through one of my eyes and I felt a burst of agony. As quickly as it started, the pain was gone. The slashed eye disconnected from my neural network and set about healing itself.

Xevex took another swipe at my eyes. I blocked it instinctively and flicked two of his eyes at once. It might not win the fight, but it gave the bastard a reminder that simians can be dangerous no matter what flesh they're rocking. The double shots flustered him. Even with all those eyes, he had trouble handling two things at a time. I followed up with two quick flicks to his other eye. Maybe if I could get three eyes down – even if just for a little while – I could take advantage of his blind spot.

Xevex recovered quickly and started to spin so he could look at me with good eyes. My body felt sluggish as I lurched to the right. Fortunately, for me, his body was slow, too. In Nat's body, I would have overshot and wound up in his peripheral vision. Time slowed down. I focused everything I had on watching the three damaged eyes.

As Xevex spun his body, it looked like I vanished. There one moment, gone the next. That was the time where if I'd had a weapon, I would have buried it in his head and moved on with my life. But I didn't have a weapon and time was short.

Xevex was nothing if not predictable. As soon as I vanished from his vision, he immediately spun back to see what he'd missed. That put another set of eyes right in tentacle range. Three quick shots shut down those eyes, too.

In his confusion, he dropped his weapons to rub his eyes. I had him dead to rights. All I needed was one of those swords and I could show him what a childhood spent watching pirate movies could do for someone. I underestimated him, though. Something in his brain processed my location based on what happened to his eyes. He twisted and a tentacle slapped me in the face. My brain hiccupped and I staggered. Xevex used the opportunity to slap me again before really winding up and hitting me so hard I skittered across the floor. He was on me in a moment, slapping my head, poking my eyes, doing everything he could to make me hurt. After he was done slapping the snot out of me, the vile bastard's true nature shone through and I found a tentacle wrapped around what I assumed was my throat while two others took turns hitting me.

Penta must have been smiling on me because I somehow managed to grab the right things and pull the right way. He tumbled backward, taking me with him. He didn't expect me to hold on tightly so rather than flipping me over him, I fell right on top of him. Not a power blow, nothing that the glorious stars of Stellar Wrestling would consider a solid move. But it was enough.

He grunted as I rearranged his organs for him before bouncing up and off his supine body. I landed head down and felt the air leave my body. I gasped and forced myself to breathe. Sucked in lungfuls of air. Xevex was twitching beside me, curling and uncurling his tentacles rhythmically. He was still alive and probably ready to get up and go at it again.

Through a blurry eye, past Xevex, I found something. There, on the underside of one of the control panels, was a green square.

I struggled to get my tentacles under me and nearly fell in the process. Apparently, Xevex had popped me in some delicate part of the brain that controls balance. I hit him as hard as I could as I moved around his body.

Sure enough, underneath the central control panel was a small green square. I reached into myself and pulled out the white thing Natasha had given me. In the light, it looked like a bleached white rock. I slapped it home and crossed my tentacles.

At first, nothing happened. "Fucking hackers," I muttered. Never trust someone who makes a living fucking with people. At least my trade was honest. Dishonest, but honest.

It started slowly; a flicker here, a whine there. The flickers and whines accelerated like someone had stomped on the accelerator. Soon, every light in the room was going off and on randomly. It felt like someone had a designed a room and then decorated it in sheer chaos. Things were making noises I could feel deep inside of me. Sparks flew and a couple of small fires burned on the control panel that circled the room. I tried to remember what you were supposed to do when security shriekers went off. Cover ears, not sure where they were. Open mouth; didn't have one. Scream for all you were worth. Yes, sir. Getting right on that.

The security shriekers rose in volume until they were all my mind could process. Just as suddenly as it started, everything stopped. The manic control room folded in on itself. And that was when things really went to hell.

42 - Code Fight

In the inky blackness, a massive Natasha Devore stood in judgment. She was herself again, not the shell I inhabited. The ten-meter-tall projection was a perfect reflection of the real woman herself. She pointed a finger at Xevex and he screamed as his body slowly dissolved into nothingness. It took time, a short eternity of her watching his shrieking form with a sly smile on her lips. Not necessarily joyous cruelty, just that happy sensation you get from a job well done.

"That one sold me out to his friend," she said. "Decent lay, but not worth the morning after. He's mine forever now."

I nodded slowly.

"No response?" Natasha asked. "Or are you looking for a handle on the moment?"

"The handle part," I said. Pause. "Why?"

"Why what?"

"Why him?"

"Oh, that," Natasha said. "I was bored, lonely, and horny. In Virt, he was actually kind of hot. Good enough for a quick roll-around and a couple of orgasms. I figured he was just some rando who looked good in chaps and a cowboy hat."

I shuddered thinking about that image. "Little did you know he was one of them."

"Yeah. Fucking Predecessors. Who would have thought their race would be able to live on as sentient programs looking for a way out of their environment? Let alone that they'd be able to possess us." She rubbed her hands together. "Might as well get this out in the open right now. This was always the endgame. This...thing is one of the most powerful things in the system. All it needs is a brain. I could never get past their security to get into it, though. Until you found a way in, anyway."

A sly smile spread across her lips. "Once you're inside the system, it's usually much easier to take it down. I've never met a system I couldn't crack until I found this one. So simple, but so difficult to break. What kind of species is so paranoid that they have a low-level security subsystem dedicated entirely to their basic species thought patterns? Who worries that aliens are going to hack their systems? Fortunately, I had you. The epic thief."

There was a sick feeling in my gut that things were about to go spectacularly wrong. That I'd accidentally given the forces of evil a bottle of whiskey and the keys to the shuttle. "This was never about finding out what happened to you, was it?"

"Of course not. I knew exactly what happened to me. I could have kept that Predecessor in my head contained forever. But the fact that they were still alive gave me an idea. A little poking around, a little guesswork, a little snooping in the Specialist domain. I found a way to digitize myself and upload my essence just like the Predecessors did. Unfortunately, I was stuck. If I had taken the Predecessor with me, I would have been fine. I could have taken over Temnyy, destroyed Endpoint, and been out toodling around the cosmos in no time. No calls to Bik. No false story or sobbing videos. If only I'd noticed the anti-alien subsystem when I first started poking around while that thing was in my head."

"I take it this is the part of the story where the villain explains her motivations in a vain attempt to make herself look smarter than everyone else," I said.

"What?"

"You're monologuing," I said. "Get to the point."

Her sly smile turned angry, like the super-storm clouds forming over Mar Del Eisley. Thunder that could shatter ferocrete, ball lightning hot as a star, and rain that could strip your skin. Shit was about to go down and Natasha's avatar was looking forward to it. "The point?" she whispered in a voice that sounded like dry leaves in a cemetery. "The point is you've done your job. I control this weapon and you are now superfluous. Goodbye."

She pointed a finger at me but I was already moving, skating along almost as well as a real Pred. If I focused on what I was doing, my tentacles tangled. But if I just went with it, I was fine. A beautiful thing about multiple sets of eyes: I got to watch her scowl as I narrowly escaped. It almost made being in that slug of a body worth it.

The blackness was all-consuming. At least in the Virt version of the control room there was something for my mind to latch onto. A switch, a readout, or a vid screen. Something tangible. Here there was nothing but the unending black soul of Natasha Devore.

I may have skated in a straight line or a circle or curlicues. There was no frame of reference to determine where – if anywhere – I was going. Nothing but the scowling face of Natasha's avatar always in my vision. No matter how fast I skated along, she was always right there. Right behind me. Right beside me. Right in front of me. I was in her world. She made the rules; I was struggling just to keep half a step ahead.

Finally, Natasha tired of her game and snatched me up between her thumb and forefinger. Blue-gray eyes – her natural color I guessed – watched me with the same kind of interest I gave to roats before I dispatched them. "The rules are different here," she said, holding me up to her face. "If you die here, you're gone forever. There's no reset button in this game. They wanted the people who controlled Temnyy to be sharp and stay on their toes. After all, they had a genocide to commit and those take focus."

She squeezed. In a human body, it would have broken bones. In this Predecessor body, all that happened was my tentacles swelled up. Not to say it didn't hurt like hell. I prayed to Penta, I prayed to ancient gods and goddesses, I made deals with things I didn't even believe in. Just like the airlockers, in my moment of desperation I reached out for any handhold I could dream up.

"Why won't you die?" Natasha's massive face hissed at me.

"Because she can't," a voice said from the shadows. "Didn't you study their biology at all? They're mollusks, you can't crush their heads because they don't have bones and that's not where their brains are, anyway."

Natasha tried to maintain her cool, but I had front row seats to her warily scanning the darkness. "Who's there? I'm busy."

"Just a fellow wizard," the voice said. "A juggler of patterns. A data monger. A finder of things best left alone."

Mason appeared suddenly in front of Natasha. He, too, had his human suit on. It must be nice to be able to manipulate things so you always get to wear whatever meat you want. He was wearing a suit with pinstripes so severe they almost looked like prison stripes.

Natasha dropped me and eyed the intruder curiously. "Who the hell are you?"

"I told you. A fellow wizard. I've followed your career with interest for some time. Hello Nat. Hello Natasha, allow me to introduce myself. My name is Mason."

"Wizard," Natasha boomed with a hint of sarcasm in her voice. "Well, wizard, I have things I need to deal with, so it is time for you to leave."

Natasha dropped me without a second thought. She pointed a finger at him and that same blast of light erupted like a goddess's justice. It hit Mason hard in the chest. I was already moving, not sure what I was going to do but unwilling to watch him be erased like that. My tentacles coiled underneath me, masses of muscle ready to propel me forward. Predecessors might not jump, but I was at least ready to try.

In a blink, it was all over and Mason was still there, smiling and holding a drink. "You're new to Virt aren't you?"

Natasha's eyes narrowed. Storm clouds rolled across her face and turned her eyes fearsome. "I live in the real world," she said, "I just work in computers. But soon I'll be free of all of that."

"Not true," I said. "You've lived in a computer for-"

Both Natasha and Mason fixed me with stares that told me I'd best shut up. "I have no desire to fight the woman who took up my mantle after I retired. Like I said, I've followed your career with a great deal of interest. Your takedown of Novus Prime was nothing short of genius. And I loved what you did to the Centaurians. A poet's heart beats in your chest."

"Pretty words old man," Natasha said.

"All I'm here to do is to save a friend and remind you that this biological monstrosity we're in was made for more minds than just yours. If you hatch it, it will consume you."

"That's where you're wrong. I'm bringing more people in to assist me. They'll be slaves, but such is life. You're either at the top of the food chain or the bottom of it."

Mason shook his head sadly. It was almost like watching my dad and my sister argue back in the day. He wanted more for her than he had and she wanted nothing to do with it. In the end, he died and she became a renowned physician. I disappeared and became a thief. Makes you wonder if he'd spent as much time on me as he did on her if I'd be an even better thief.

"I'm sorry Natasha," Mason said sadly. "No one else is coming through. The link is severed. I barely made it through before everything stopped. The Predecessors are back in their realm, the bridge between here and Endpoint is gone. It's over. All that's left is fantasy-land."

The virtual world rumbled beneath my tentacles. Natasha's rage at Mason outmaneuvering her was palpable. But she wasn't the type to give up easily. With the flick of a finger, Mason flew into the darkness.

Natasha turned her cold stare on me. "Now, little thing, it is time for you to end."

"You know, your boy toy Xevex said the same thing to me a couple of days ago."

"Oh? And what did you do to the bastard? Because until I came along, he was still alive."

She had me there. He'd run roughshod over my life. Killed Nobtop. Had his minions kill the Bratva. Tortured me. Generally been an asshole. "I threw up on him," I said.

"Better than nothing." Natasha picked me up again and stared hard into my eyes. "If I throw you at a wall, will you splat?"

I tried to shrug, again forgetting I didn't have shoulders. "Possibly. Probably. It won't change the outcome, though. You're alone out here. Mason shut down everything. There are no links from Predecessor Virt to anything else. Hell, I don't even know if they're still alive in there."

"She's right, you know," Mason said from behind me. "There is no way, even for you, to get them back. They've been physically unplugged from the network."

Natasha dropped me again. I hit the ground with a squelch and a squeak, like a dog chew toy thrown against the wall. "You again," she said, shaking her head. "Some people don't know when to die."

Mason held up his hands. "I've been dead for decades," he said. "Like you, I'm just machine code executing in an environment. Neither of us have a body."

"I have a body," Natasha spat. "This whole planetoid is my body."

"It's just flesh," Mason replied. "And like all flesh, it's faulty. Listen, I was you decades ago. Or someone like you. Eventually, it got too much to bear, so I retreated into Virt and stayed there. I worked in systems so it made sense to retire to one. The only one of us left with a body is her. You and I, Natasha, we've had our runs. The flesh no longer holds an appeal."

Natasha snorted. "Regular flesh, no. This creature is not regular flesh; it's a planet eater. Who wouldn't want that? It's all moot, though. I'm already in and fully in control. Temnyy is me and I am Temnyy."

"Don't start it up," I said.

Mason pointed at me. "She's right again. You won't survive being this thing on your own. It is far too large and alien for it to make any sense. It could well destroy you permanently. I beg you, walk away. I'll come with you; it's not like I have anything going on right now anyway."

"If you don't have anything else going on," Natasha asked, "then why not join me?"

Finally. There was the fear in her darting eyes and wide-open eyelids. It took her time to confront the fact that she was desperately clinging to something she didn't understand.

Mason shook his head. "All meat is a prison. You're just trading a small prison for a much larger one. It doesn't matter what flesh you're in because it's all still just flesh. A soul cage. Come with me. Shut down your simulation. We'll walk out the airlock together."

"You know what?" Natasha asked. "I think I like my new soul cage. I think it's time both of you left."

"Very well," Mason said with a sigh.

The room went bright. After the eternal blackness, the light was blinding. My vision slowly returned to normal and I found I was standing in the middle of a glade of bright green grass. A regular-sized Natasha stood alone looking around her unable to understand what had happened. Slowly, she shook her head and squared her shoulders. "Is that the best you've got?" she shouted.

"Hardly," Mason's voice said. "I'm just getting started."

The world twisted and turned on itself as Mason reworked the world to be just like his house in Virt. If you walked forward a few feet, you'd find yourself staring down at the spot you just left. The dimension collector was in full effect.

Natasha took a step back, found herself upside down, and immediately tumbled forward onto her face. As she pushed herself back to her feet, she snarled like a lotarness in a hunt. She brushed herself off, reached out, and ripped open a part of the simulation. It was like watching someone tear open the sky and find glowing blue code flashing by. Her hands were a blur as she rearranged blocks of glowing numbers and arcane digital commands. The simulation shook again, rattling my gooey innards and making my vision dance merrily around me.

An almighty thunk and everything went back to normal. Mason's dimensional chicanery collapsed. Natasha playfully put a finger on her lips and smiled like the cat that ate the canary. She went to work again, rearranging things to suit her desires. Movement out of the corner of my eye found Mason brushing dust off a Earth-era tan suit with pants. Haute couture from the 2130s. Or the 1930s, depending on how you looked at it.

Mason shook his head slowly and closed his eyes. The world went creepy and strange. Rather than the green glade of gladitude, I found myself on a set of stairs that drifted straight up as far as the eye could see. All around me were varying shades of gray, swirling together like a color dance. Nearly white to nearly black. The metal deck and energy-sapping grays turned the cold room with all the flashing light into something more sinister. An early 21st century cable TV showroom or the offices of a third-world tech-support group.

Without warning, Natasha struck. A blur of movement and Mason was on his ass, holding his jaw and frowning. To his credit, he was back on his feet in an instant. He waved his arms gently, like vines in a light breeze. The air around him shimmered briefly. Overzealous lens flare caught and nipped in the bud before it could ruin another vid. He lowered his arms and closed his eyes.

I would have thought there was no way Natasha would fall for it, but she lanced out of the shadows and straight toward Mason. Maybe she thought she was strong enough or fast enough but she hit his shield wall like the fist of an angry goddess. Mason stood completely still while the air around compressed, electrified, and held Natasha in a deadly lover's embrace.

She shrieked and lashed out. Pure rage power hit the shield and sent Mason reeling back. Natasha collapsed to the ground in a heap, breath ragged. The digital diva was skilled. Possibly one of the best in the business, but she focused on rushing in and hitting her target before it could react. Mason was older, wiser. A product of a different time when penetration was more of a patient, sensual affair.

Natasha hopped to her feet like a cat. Mason erased the floor beneath her and portaled her through alien Virt until she dropped from the ceiling and hit the ground with a thud. She pointed a finger at him and erased part of his torso. He changed the world so she was upside down. She flung a bright light at his eyes, blinding him, and followed up with a kick to the balls that made every man on Endpoint groan in sympathy.

It went on like that. Back and forth. Back and forth. Natasha going for the kill shot and finding herself trapped in gelatin. Mason gently but firmly letting her hurt herself. To his credit, I don't think Mason ever touched Natasha. He'd move and she'd trip and fall. I saw the writing on the wall almost from the get-go. Natasha was an amazing hacker but her youth and skill were no match for Mason's age and guile. Of course, youth and skill managed to land some stellar attacks.

At the end of the fight, both of them were exhausted – mentally and physically – and battered. Mason's stylish suit was in smoldering tatters from Natasha's flame job and Natasha was stiff from all the falls and clutching her broken arm from one of the worst.

It was over. It had to be. But the Digital Diva had one last trick up her torn sleeve. She swayed and dropped to her knees, a blank expression on her face. Mason, always a sucker for a damsel in distress, shuffled to her, ready to help her up, buy her a drink, and try to get her into his bed.

Natasha's hand lashed up, a glittering piece of metal concealed between two fingers. Mason whimpered slightly as Natasha's tiny knife sliced his testicles in half. As he dropped to his knees, clutching his ruined junk, Natasha reached out and grabbed his throat. Mason's shield responded immediately to hands around his neck and exploded.

As Natasha flew backward, Mason conjured a spiked wall for her to slam into. She hit the wall with cartoonish force, screamed as spikes penetrated her body, then slowly turned liquid and slid off the wall. The puddle of Natasha reformed and lurched. Survived, but the strain of the battle was wearing her down. She shuffled forward, dragging her right leg behind her. Her left shoulder slumped like her collarbone had been shattered. There was blood all over her tattered clothing but fire in her eyes.

For his part, Mason looked like he'd taken the intimate gang violence tour of Hell. His clothes were shredded and a dark stain around the crotch of his pants told the agonizing tale of sliced balls. Yet neither of them gave up. That was one of the powers of Virt: Mason and Natasha had no bodies to damage. They were pure code, beating on each other and deleting random bit of code from each other's runtime.

"Quite the spectacle," Jenkins said in my head.

It was such a surprise, I nearly jumped out of my rubbery skin. "How are you here?" I asked. "AIs can't get into Virt."

"Human Virt, no," he said. "Which, frankly, I always found discriminatory. But this isn't human Virt.

Predecessor Virt doesn't have the same rules. I'm actually disappointed. After hearing you humans extolling Virt, I always assumed it would be more than just watching Program Deathmatch 2523."

"It usually is," I confessed.

"I take it your body is generated through the Predecessor rendering routines."

"Yup," I told him. "This is what I'd look like if I was a Predecessor. Sexy, right?"

"All biologicals are just bags of meat," Jenkins said. "No offense."

"None taken," I mumbled. While it stung a bit to have my personal AI reduce my entire species to a bag of the stuff you find behind a third-world convenience store, he had a point. There was fundamentally nothing different between a human mind and an extraterrestrial mind. Both processed data. Both ingested information, chewed on it, and spat it back out again. At the end of the day, all biology was bags of meat with neuron drivers.

Natasha took that moment to fling Mason across the room. He hit the ground with an oomph and was back up and going at her again before I could even say, "Hello."

"So, Jenkins," I said. "You know I'm not the real Natasha, right? That's her over there, looking a bit worse for wear."

"Your position is unprecedented, but I had a suspicion when you asked about the hacking tools installed in your head. Most people don't install things like that and then never learn to use them. It's not like you installed a bunch of versions of solitaire; using your wetware is probably a war crime on most systems."

Natasha hit the ground face-first and slid on her chin right to my feet. Mason was really getting into it. Striking an ancient fighting style pose from pre-Diaspora Earth, he wagged a finger at her. She took the bait without thinking and launched herself at him. Mason sidestepped the attack and chopped the back of her neck before kicking out her right knee.

"Since I'm already a criminal, I might as well go for the gusto," I told Jenkins. "Can you get us back to Temnyy's bridge?"

"There are a few locks in the way, but yes. Do you have a plan in mind or is this more of your 'winging it' madness?"

"A little from column A, a little from column B," I told him. "Just get me there."

He snorted. "Trust your Predecessor eyes," he said. "Stop trying to be a human in ceph suit. See this world like they did."

I tried to snap my fingers and found my infinitely replicating tentacles could actually snap. "Right. I keep forgetting about those."

I paused to watch Natasha exaggerate her limp long enough for Mason to come into range so she could do a spectacular jumping kick to the side of his face. Part of me grimaced to think what that was going to do to his handsome face. Another part of me grimaced at the fact that I'd just grimaced at that.

With a sigh, I gave in completely to my body and its sensory inputs. The world immediately took on the neon-blue hue they loved so much. I looked around and found the world filled with squiggly lines running right through the Natasha and Mason Arena of Doom. I moved carefully, doing my best to keep away from the fight. If only those two had worked together, they could have taken over Temnyy and destroyed Endpoint by now. Instead, Lokai and Bele were tearing each other apart.

"Just fuck and get it over with," I whispered as I snuck through the battle zone.

With human vision, there was blackness without end. With Predecessor vision, I was in a large, empty chamber. At the far end was a portal of some kind. It looked like a glowing blue and green blobbish sphere. If it hadn't been for the squiggly lines lighting my way, I might have ignored it.

"Jenkins," I asked as I ran quietly toward the portal. "What would happen if I started running in one direction while using human vision? Would I run forever or would I eventually hit the wall?"

"My guess would be you would run forever since the renderer is tied to your perceptions."

"Whoa."

"There's probably a metaphor for life in there if you'd like to take a think about it."

"Nah. That seems complicated. Although it would be cool to run through walls."

He snorted. "I think you misunderstand. It wouldn't be you running through walls. It would be that there were no walls."

"Okay," I said. The portal was just ahead. Fifty meters or so. "So, either no walls and eternal running with nothing to see and nowhere to go, or less running and lots of walls. Seems legit."

I hit the portal and left Natasha and Mason to their fates.

I found myself back in Temnyy's control room. Again, I was struck by the mixture of obvious things and totally alien things. Screens and stations were obvious even though I had to wonder why they didn't come equipped with chairs. Other things were less obvious: Green, bulbous things with bristly hair, smooth ebon spheres with oily rainbows playing across them, a cloud of gas that surrounded the center of the room in a near perfect cylinder.

"Any ideas?" I asked Jenkins.

He was spotty, fading in and out as he said, "Try u<scritch> <scritch>sole."

"What?"

"Con<scritch>Try<scritch><scritch>sing<scritch><beeeee

Of course, the control room was shielded from external comms. Made sense. Taking over a virtual console might not be the end of the world but taking over the whole planetoid could be devastating. I was on my own. Lost in a weird world inside an alien avatar, inside alien Virt inside a doomsday weapon.

I wandered around the flight deck and wondered at the tech. Human flight decks were boring things: A chair. There may or may not be a transluminum viewscreen. More and more, external cameras transmitting everything directly to the Astrogator's mind replaced the viewscreens. They provided clearer imagery and not having to install viewscreens made for sturdier ships.

For all their technical prowess with Virt and moving consciousness around like stolen software, the Predecessors chose to use archaic, manually-driven hardware. Or, at least I thought it was relying on manually-driven hardware. There wasn't a switch or a control stick anywhere in sight. Each workstation had a dedicated, large-screen television and three thick holes.

The holes were about as thick as midpoint on my tentacles. No switches. No levers. No buttons. Three holes. Nine limbs – three up, six down. Each of my tentacles was a master class in fractals getting smaller and smaller and smaller. Thick tentacles covered in smaller tentacles covered in smaller tentacles covered in smaller tentacles. They may have gone even further than that.

The inside of the hole was smooth and cool to the touch. I felt a faint energy building up the further in I slid. It felt almost like sex if sex was crossed with an expanding consciousness and licking batteries. Like dropping acid and fucking on the dining room table while reality exposed its naughty bits for my consideration.

Reality wobbled a bit on her heels and slurred something to me. Then the universe exploded into being and I saw the endless night through Temnyy's eyes. Space wasn't an empty void. There was radiation and electricity. Aimless electrons and charged particles danced with each other before fading into nothingness.

Distantly, I felt rumbling as if mighty engines were flexing their nuts. A surge of celestial power bolted through my body. The kind of thing stars and planets must feel. A sense of unity and tapping straight into the energy of the universe. But I didn't care about any of that. I was one with a being of unlimited potential. Entire star fleets couldn't stop me if they tried. I was the ultimate power.

Around me, I could feel eggshell cracking. Soon, I'd be free. Limbs that had been in stasis for millennia warmed up, ready to lash out at anything. Everything.

My brain was already overheating. Controlling a couple of hundred centimeters of human body was one thing but managing the various systems of something nearly 1500 kilometers around was a very different story. Temnyy had subsystems I could barely comprehend. In addition to the color spectrum I didn't know how to understand, it was fitted with specialized organs designed to feed on anything, even radio waves and stray particles.

Underneath all of that was the thing. Some sort of monstrous entity yearning to be free to ravage everything in sight. There was a hum in the back of my head telling me Temnyy wasn't entirely devoid of consciousness, and it was waking up pissed as hell.

I was hungry. As my shell cracked open, I turned my famished eyes on Endpoint and her sisters. It was either hunger pains or a need for more minds to control, but systems were already failing. Temperature regulation and ablative shielding were completely offline. While I struggled to pay attention to those, energy production faltered. Try to fix energy production and navigation went offline.

The underlying consciousness was designed like a biological AI system; an automated assistant to help the Predecessor minds when they finally took control of Temnyy. Over the millennia, the automated assistant had grown. It was on the cusp of full awareness. Instead of the Predecessors controlling it with their collective consciousness, it would have controlled them. Like all good doomsday weapons, Temnyy had found a way to turn itself on its creators.

The only problem was it was completely out of sorts from its long sleep and still needed extra minds to help control itself. My massive, amazing, and totally sexy brain wasn't enough.

Things were failing faster than I could think of ham-fisted ways to fix them. It was the moment in every vid where a disgraced cop looks at a wall plastered with purloined evidence and newspaper clippings and knows there's no way to find and exploit the pattern. Every last-second shot in the game that missed the mark. Every time you think the engine is fixed, but the fix caused something else to kerplode.

I had to eat. Growing children needed energy to complete their galactic rampage.

Distantly, I felt two more tentacles complete the connection. The thing that was me, giving itself to me. Glorious life for glorious life. Deeper. Complete the connections. Virt inside of Virt. Only, this new Virt was mine to shape as I saw fit. The physical would feel my wrath and the virtual would be mine to command. Behold, tiny things! There was a new law in town.

I turned my attention toward Endpoint2 and sighed to myself. The drone station was tantalizingly close. A tentacle dormant for thousands of years twitched and spasmed as life blew through it. My shell cracked. Exploded as the life within 100km-thick protective layer around me spider-webbed and drifted slowly away.

The universe seemed much brighter and more energetic outside my shell. There was energy everywhere, but not enough. Endpoint2 and Endpoint3 looked like tasty snacks that might get me to a star.

My body failed by kilometers. My other body failed by centimeters.

A part of my brain registered someone nearby but it turned out to be just a guy with a funky hat. Still enough to make me edgy. I glanced up at my screen, hoping for a bit of redemption. But all I saw was a screen saver with the ocean rolling in. Mind failing slowly.

Something ripped me from my digital daydream and flung my body across the control room. Getting ripped out of Virt was always weird, but being ripped out of Virt inside of Virt—only the inside Virt wasn't Virt: it was real, was weird in the extreme, and oh Penta, my brain was still partially stuck inside of Temnyy. He was hatching and my brain was still linked in there and oh no I was babbling that was not a good a sign not a good sign at all unless you count brain damage as a good sign but I didn't I needed my brain to do brain things and brain good.

"What have you done, Nat?" Mason whispered.

"Shut you down," I said. If my eyes could be downcast, they would have been. There was so much that was amazing about a Predecessor body– the colors, the 360 vision, arms – but they lacked the ability to show our emotions.

"Why?" he asked. Same old Mason, holding a tentacle in his hand and that sly smile that made me wonder who I was.

"Because it had to end," I said. "It was too dangerous. I felt it. The thing is alive. It wants to eat."

"There's nothing wrong with eating."

"There is when it's inhabited planets."

Mason sat down on the ground next to me. My body was still reeling from both getting flung across the room and having my mind violently severed from a different reality. He was beat to hell. A bloody, bruised mass of ripped shirt and ripped pants and oh, lord, I did not need to go there.

"Nat," he said with that voice that was almost condescending but reminded you more of a friend you looked up to than a father. "I could have controlled it. I could have lived on."

I half-heartedly motioned with a tentacle. "It's still there, Mason. Move in. Take it and live forever. Just be aware, if you're not strong enough, you'll become its slave."

Half his face wanted desperately to look to the control panel he'd just pulled me away from. The other half looked for any signs of humanity in my face. "Come with me," he said. "If I can't do it, we can do it together."

I shook my head. "Sorry, Mason. I don't like you that way." Even though I was totally warming up to the idea of liking him that way. "I need my space and sharing a monster's brain with you is not how I want to spend eternity. I do wish you luck, though. Go eat a bunch of planets. Can you start with Eden IX?"

"Why Eden IX? They always seemed decent enough to me. A little religious for my tastes, but decent enough folks."

"I pulled a job there years ago. They never paid me."

"I'm not going to kill an entire planet because a few people owe you money," Mason said.

One of my tentacles wobbled in front of his face. To credit, Mason didn't flinch. I booped him on the nose. "Remember that when you get hungry," I told him. "Hey, what happened to Natasha?"

He hung his head. "She will be seeking her fortunes on other planes. Brilliant woman but she was locked into her three-dimensional view of the world. Too rigid. Too singular of mind. She could not handle changes to that. I severed her connection."

"Must make you happy to know you're still the number one hacker out there," I said.

"I find no joy in releasing a kindred soul."

"And you get to live on for a very long time in the body of the worst doomsday weapon ever created," I continued.

"That will be an interesting change," he said with a smirk. "Going from no body to somebody is always appreciated."

"Truth," I said. "Probably going to be hard to have sex with other planets, though. Last I checked, there were no girl planets. Just planets without any ascribed gender."

Mason actually laughed at that. For a moment, we were back in his study with the fire and the good whiskey. He winked and smiled. "I think we've established that I will be perfectly fine with that."

I struggled to get my tentacles under me and stand up. Body hopping was a pain. Once you got used to one meat sack, you had another one to learn. Finally, I discovered I could coil them all underneath me and rise like a spring. Mason and I stared at each other for a while. I'd only known the dude for a few days but he'd taught me a lot. Father figure. Friend. Companion. Not a whole of people like him in the systems.

"What now?" I asked.

"What do you mean?"

"You've got the keys to a planetoid-sized monster. What are you going to do with them? Oh, by the way, I think I might have broken it. There are all kinds of alarms going off right now."

That sage-like look crossed his face again. He tapped his head and smiled. "Remember, I'm not alone. I've still got a little friend with me."

"That's not enough," I said. "This thing needs dozens minds to control it. Hell, you'll need that many just to deal with the alarms."

"Perfect. Stand still, Nat." He pointed a finger at me and I had visions of Natasha's finger of death. "Do you still have Jessica?"

I nodded. "She's safe."

"Good. The rest are gone."

"What?" Surely, he didn't mean-

"There weren't that many left. There never were that many, maybe a couple thousand. Whittled down over the millennia as they all slowly lost their minds from the sheer tedium. I'm only four hundred or so and I'm ready to pack it in; they were in the thousands. The ones left were shuffling through life. I shut down their systems for good."

"I-" I started.

"Don't fret. They had their run. Once I'm gone, there will only be one. I'll let you choose what to do with her. It's time for you to go, Nat. Leave an old man alone with a body to die in."

He brought his thumb down like he was shooting me. The last thing I was saw was him blowing me a kiss. The last thing I felt was a tremendous, empty pit forming in my stomach.

43 – Ouch

A flash of light and Temnyy's control room disappeared and I found myself staring up at a tear-streaked Monique with utter panic in her eyes.

I reached up and stroked her cheek. "Hey, you."

She slapped me then hugged me then slapped me again. Staccato words flowed from her like she was braindumping everything that had happened since I went it. "You went completely limp and I couldn't find a pulse and I thought you were dead and then that damned thing in your head made you talk but it didn't sound like you it sounded like something else something mechanical like a toaster came to life and started talking and it freaked me the hell out and I'm so happy you're safe and if you ever do anything like that again I swear I'll kill you."

I'd practiced lines for moments exactly like that and then realized they all sounded like stupid machismo bullshit so I pulled something straight from the heart and said, "Yes."

I never said my heart was a poet.

Monique helped me sit up and I spun to face her. It was good to have the requisite number of limbs and know my body wouldn't change colors without software assistance. "What happened in there?" Monique asked, putting a hand on my naked chest.

"I was in Temnyy. It's a massive weapon without a crew. Mason and Natasha fought and he won. I'm still kicking myself for not seeing this whole thing for what it was. It was just a heist. Not even a particularly elegant one. Natasha wanted to control Temnyy because that's what she did and Mason just wanted a body to die in. And...shit. I'm Natasha."

An eyebrow went up on her face. "Finally admitting it? Not the best time, dear."

"Admitting it?" I asked.

"I've been in and out of every virtual skin you can imagine. I've been with other people in every virtual skin you can imagine. There's always something of them that shines through. I don't know who you were, but I know who you are now and you are not Natasha Devore. She was cold, callous, and standoffish. Exactly the opposite of you."

Never try to outplay a player. "I promise, I'll explain everything when this is over. All the salient parties are dead now, so I guess I might as well tell the whole story. Jenkins, you still there?"

"Of course, ma'am. I will only leave when my host body is dead."

That was a weird way of putting it. I shrugged and it felt amazing to have shoulders again. Climbed out of the goo and toweled myself off. Monique tried to hand me a robe, but I shook my head and shrugged into my beat-to-hell coveralls. Comfy and practical. There'd be time to fluffy robed later. "Good to know. Can you find any of the external cameras that face Temnyy and patch the feed through to me?"

I turned to Monique and pointed at my head. "Do you have wireless?"

She looked a little insulted. "Duh."

"Open a vid-feed port. I have something to show you. Jenkins, pipe the feed to Monique as well."

Although it didn't matter because the feed was playing back directly in our heads, I sat right next to her. "Temnyy is an egg. Endpoint is a ship. I, uh, accidentally woke Temnyy up. Mason and the Predecessor in his head are trying to use their own minds control Temnyy but they need dozens more and there's no way to get them. Anyway, Temnyy is dying. Partially because I broke it starting it up but mostly because it needs more brains. Check?"

Monique sighed and tossed her hands in the air in a "Fine!" motion. She leaned her head on my shoulder. "We now return you to your regularly scheduled programming," she muttered.

Jenkins had chosen the perfect camera. We had a zoomed view with crystal-clear images played directly in our heads. "The best I could gather was that Temnyy requires a minimum of a few dozen minds to control it. It's massive and complicated and even just by starting it up, I broke a bunch of things. There's also a consciousness growing in it. A bad one. Hopefully, I broke enough stuff that it won't fully come to life."

She put a finger to my lips and motioned vaguely at the empty air where our brains thought the video was playing.

It started slowly. I thought of how much Sol would have liked to see the video through the lens of his beloved instruments. Or how Nobtop would have been scheming ways to get onboard and take over. The thought of that man in charge of a superweapon made me both terrified and giddy. Xevex – the real Xevex – had found his god and it had bitten all of us on the ass. And Mason. What to say about him other than he would have made a marvelous friend and probably an exquisite lover even though my favorite lover was leaning on me and scratching her butt. Besides, he deserved to determine his own end. We all do.

Temnyy had already hatched but was still a massive ball of tentacles and bad attitude. I couldn't help but be fascinated by the whole process. Aside from the fact that it was a massive weapon, there was something amazing about watching babies being born. A pure creature of the stars. Historians would write about this moment for centuries to come. Someone would come collect samples. Before anyone could count to ten, the systems would fill with Temnyys.

In slow motion, the first tentacle extended, blindingly white against the ebon backdrop. The skin glowed iridescent bone, that sickly greenish-white color that reminded me of the corpse fields of Yavapai or disease vats on Altair.

The glowing tentacle uncoiled, extending over a thousand kilometers into space. A second one followed by a third tentacle, feeling about the void. The tentacles worked together to pull the shell pieces off and everyone got their first full look at Temnyy. The thing that sent seismic radio waves across space. The creature designed to end an entire species. It was hideous and gorgeous. Superficially, it resembled one of its creators – nine eyes, nine tentacles, generally angry expression. But that was where the semblances ended. Temnyy's tentacles stood in a three-by-three triangle pattern all over its body. Its body was squat, not the bulbous shape of a Predecessor. Thick, rubbery skin protected it from the horrors of space life:

Radiation, mutation, debris. It was a floating biological tank.

"Should we be running?" Monique asked.

"To where? There's nowhere to go. Besides, for once in my life I have faith."

She snuggled back up to me and squeezed my hand. "I've been alive a long time. If I have to go, at least it won't be alone. I always figured I'd die alone. Comes with the career."

It was my turn to shush her. "Look. The eyes are opening."

Monique gasped. A few days ago, I would have thought it was the most horrifying thing I'd ever seen. A space monster with eyes all over its body. A thing big enough to attack a planet. Now, after bouncing through bodies, I recognized the beauty. The purity of purpose. I wondered if, in Predecessor design philosophy, it was a sleek vision or if they designed it to look like a hammer, ready to smash everything in its path. Either way, once I got past the human, I could see Temnyy through different eyes.

"Jenkins, pipe through my glasses and share the result with Monique."

Temnyy changed from a greenish-white monstrosity to a glowing neon work of art. There were sparkling tattoos up and down his tentacles. His eyes glowed a color I can't describe but can still taste. The tats up and down his arm were reminiscent of the glowing glyphs I saw all over the Predecessor Virt world. Totems to ward off mad mojo or were they the names of the Predecessors that worked on him?

Temnyy moved slowly, sometimes barely visible from our distance. 14,000 years in an eggshell would leave anyone stiff and sluggish. The damage I did by trying to start him up on my own probably didn't help things. He twitched. Nine massive tentacles spasmed straight out, vibrated, and loosened.

"Nine eyes," I whispered to Monique. "Just like them."

"Shh," she replied. "It's not often I get to watch a monster movie and the monster is right outside."

The tentacles tensed and relaxed again. They wriggled and writhed. The body was warming itself up. Those gargantuan eyes, oversized relative to the body even by Predecessor standards, scanned space. Temnyy was alive and hungry. Damn it, Mason, what were you doing?

"Madam," Jenkins said in my head, "there is a transmission of unknown origin being beamed directly at you. The person on the other end is requesting to speak to you."

"This had better not be another one of those warranty calls."

"The incoming message is asking for Nat Devore."

Shit. "Put it through, immediately."

The transmission formed in my head, shrinking the live feed of Temnyy and shoving it into the corner. With crystal clarity, I saw the control room again. This time filled with flames, flashing lights, and dark stains on the virtual deck. A bloodbath had gone down and, as usual, I missed it.

"Nat." Mason looked haggard, like he'd just gone ten rounds with the Beast of Eden. "Are you still in the VirtCo?"

"Yes. What's happening out there?"

He ignored my question and continued. "Do you still have Jessica?"

"Of course," I replied, patting my chest pocket. Like I was going to lose the last of an alien race.

"You must plug her in. There should be a data drop somewhere. You'll have to look around for it. Tell her the worst has happened. She'll know what to do."

I reached into my pocket and pulled out the worm hypercrystal. Somewhere, in the thing's lattices, a Predecessor was lurking. "Is that what I think it is?" Monique asked.

I nodded. "Yeah, the last of them now."

Monique was cute when she wrinkled her nose and frowned. I'd never tell her that to her face, but it was true; she had an adorable anger. "And you're going to plug it into to a data port?"

"Yeah."

"Are you insane? This is their ship. That thing out there is their weapon. And you want to introduce one of them to our systems?"

When she put it like that. "Well," I mumbled.

"Mason was a monster back in the day. He seems like a gentleman nowadays because it suits his needs, but he was not a good person. He was ruthless and cunning."

"Why do you know so much about him?" I asked.

It was Monique's turn to look askance and mumble. "I did some research," she said lamely.

Sweet Penta, I was so glad I'd never fucked Mason. I pulled her close, stroked her flaming locks, and said, "It's all good. I'm sure he was less than perfect-"

"He crashed an entire system's economy."

"Less than perfect-"

"On a whim," Monique continued.

"Okay, so he was a monster. But right now, he's our monster, and he's in the driver's seat of that monster, and he needs something from the monster on this hypercrystal. I just hope species bond is better than 'first time I boned an alien' bond. Besides, I've met her; she didn't want to see Temnyy activated."

Monique tapped me on the shoulder and redirected by attention back to the virtual image of the alien beast in our vision. "Something bad is happening."

Temnyy had learned to move. He was hovering near Endpoint: Three, one of the uninhabited cohorts of the threeship. A tentacle lashed out, spearing the hull of the drone with clinical efficiency. On Endpoint, that would have killed everyone on board.

I pulled myself to my feet, wobbled a little bit as reality reasserted its dominance on my brain, and scoped around. A data port would be next to the systems integration panels. The data port read my sensor, marked my location, and accepted the hypercrystal with a slurp. Somewhere deep in Endpoint's guts, Jessica was being routed and a sandboxed pseudo-brain with null cognition was being spun up. A second after dropping the hypercrystal into the slot, the system routed Jessica back to my consciousness in a segmented memory space.

She furrowed her brow and looked around at the nothing she was living in. "I take it a suitable body hasn't been created yet."

"Not yet. It's only been a few hours."

"And I'm running on human hardware? Is nothing sacred to you people?"

"Sorry, Jessica, I don't have time to fully explain. One: Your people are in cold storage. Mason shut down your Virt. Two: Mason's on Temnyy right now with one of your fellow Predecessors. Three: Mason said to tell you 'The worst has happened.'"

She vanished without so much as a goodbye. No wave, no smile, not even a grunt. Poof. Gone. I tried to contact Mason but got no response. My victory was looking premature.

"Nat," Monique called out. "Look!"

I was staring at a map of the systems. A couple of dozen in all. One by one, they winked out. The death of my people rendered in perfect digital symmetry and pumped straight into my head. Surely, Jessica hadn't dropped that. It didn't seem her style. Mason had his hands full. Then who?

"I see you got my message," a chilling voice said from the side. Here I thought I had everything under control and I didn't even hear the high-pitched whine of the cloud. "How have you been, Natasha?"

"It's Nat," Monique spat.

"It's as meaningless as she is," Xevex said, flowing plasma-like from the shadows.

I pulled Monique behind me and stretched my fingers. Not that it would matter much. Xevex's clouds went straight through Nobtop and his body armor. I'd be nothing more than a mid-morning toaster pastry.

"You're dead," I hissed. "I saw you die."

He assumed a cocky pose of contemplation: feet wide, fists on hips, staring with serious eyes into the distance. The very model of an ancient adventurer. "I was born when your race was still struggling with fire. I am no longer simply biology; I have transcended. I am pure code now, living in the electronic spaces. There are many of me. Do not be so arrogant as to believe a monkey can stop me."

"Ape," I said.

"What?"

"Ape, not monkey. Big difference."

Not that it really mattered. He had me dead to rights. A blast of black smoke nanites from his fingers and I'd wind up just like Nobtop. Or he could wrap himself around me and squeeze or invade me and tear each cell to pieces. Dozens of different kinds of death and none of them involved drinking myself into a stupor and dying in my sleep.

"It doesn't matter," Xevex said. "You'll be dead soon."

I shrugged. Honestly, it didn't really matter. I'd done my bit. Death could have me now. "Okay," I said brightly. "Kill me if it'll make you feel better. I've already won. Your big ol' body is dying out there and my friend is helping hasten it along. Endpoint is still alive and breathing. I suppose you could take over Endpoint, but the engines are detached, so you'll be stuck here. Forever. On the plus side, there's some cool stuff at the Bazaar and the food hall has some excellent Antarean phig ribs."

Little twitches I never would have noticed if I hadn't been in a virtual Predecessor body gave him away. Humans tensed up when we got scared. Predecessors twitched.

I had to keep him talking, keep him focused on anything except erasing me from existence or burning a massive hole straight through my chest. If I could keep him mad, he wouldn't think about how easy it would be to kill me. Then kill someone else, assume their identity, and hotfoot it off Endpoint.

"Jenkins, find me a way to kill this bastard."

"Endpoint," Xevex mused. "Such a stupid human name. I already am this vessel and I no longer need the Destroyer's body. I've found something better."

He morphed into a modified Predecessor form adorned with flexible armor. Maybe what they wore to battle. Sleek and cybernetic, full of pointy parts that looked sharp enough that you wouldn't even notice as they sliced you in half. A slick and soulless armored novempod covered in spotless chrome.

"There is a possibility, ma'am," Jenkins whispered in my skull.

"Well, don't keep me waiting."

"Did you know that between Predecessor systems and your pathetic monkey computers, there's nearly enough processing power to run half a planet," Xevex said. "Or a god."

"Electricity was originally used in the nano wars but was found to be too hard to target against swarms. They needed something that could cause large-scale disruption. Back during the nano wars, new weapons were created that did exactly that. They were basically portable electro-magnetic pulse blasts."

I whistled. "Gotcha. Where can I find one?"

"This will be my dominion," Xevex continued. "I'm in every system. When ships arrive, I will join with them. When they leave, they'll spread my seed throughout your planets. Soon, your pathetic race will learn to worship me."

"I'd give real money if he'd shut up," I mumbled to Jenkins.

"The nearest EMP weapon is on Triton V in a museum display. They had...odd side effects on people and were mostly destroyed when the war was over."

"Odd side effects?"

"They tended to scramble neurons which led to unstable personalities in the soldiers that fielded them. It got bad. There were unintended deaths. Friends, family members, that sort of thing."

While Xevex was monologuing, I did my best to act enraptured by his speech. Megalomaniacs love having their prey ensnared. All the while, I was thinking through the problem. An EMP, as I understood it, was a massive blast of electromagnetic energy that fried any non-hardened electronics. The effect was known as far back as pre-Diaspora Earth. A few primitive weapons were even made back then, but it wasn't until the nanites got smart that anyone put serious thought into them.

"Is there anything on Endpoint that could make an EMP burst?" I asked.

"Not without the engines. You need a massive amount of energy to create one."

"Like the amount of energy in, say, a massive space-going monster?"

"Bodies. The physical world," Xevex continued. I nodded absently. Your time was coming, motherfucker. "The physical world is frail and full of problems. Pure energy is the only solution. Your primitive religions were so close to the truth, but they never could make the final leap. Godhead is not something you can achieve when you're made of meat. My body is everything. My mind is everywhere. That is what transcendence is."

Huh. He finally found his godness. Good for him.

"Wait!" I hissed at Jenkins. "Nobtop said the anti-grav loaders down in the loading bay weren't used sometimes because they played havoc with nanites."

"That makes some sense," he replied. "Anti-gravity is based on manipulating strong force and weak force. Anti-gravity creates extremely tiny black holes through the manipulation of those forces. That much gravity, while imperceptible to us, would cause problems for nanites. Unfortunately, even a loader wouldn't have enough energy to stop Xevex. If only there was a way to harness it on a large enough scale. Besides, didn't he say he was everywhere? You'd have to zap all of Endpoint to get rid of him."

"There might be a way. Jenkins, get a message to Monique. Tell her to run for all she's worth. Get to Sully's. It's near Endpoint's center so it should be safe. Then push a message to everyone connected to Endpoint's network. Tell them Sully's is giving away free drinks and sex. Penta. Peach is gonna be pissed, but at least with everyone near the center, everyone should be marginally safer. Finally, I need a distraction. Is there anything in this room you can overload and detonate?"

He scanned the room; random images of things flitted through the back of my mind. A wiring box. A door lock. An overhead light. A fuse box. "Yes. There is. The fuse box in the corner; it won't do enough damage to stop all the nanites, but it will destroy a lot and temporarily render the rest inoperable. Also, it should make for a spectacular explosion. Also, it will call the Specialists to investigate."

"Good enough. I'm going to open a feed to the Specialist himself. Hopefully the crazy bastard is paying attention. They're dorks, but I don't want them walking in on a pissed off ball of nanites unprepared."

"And what are you going to do, ma'am?"

"Endpoint is tough, but it's not hardened. I'm going to get Temnyy close to us and detonate him."

44 - No Gods

Xevex kept prattling away as I made my plans. All that was left was to push that last domino and keep my fingers crossed. I waved my hands and put them together in a T form. "Timeout, buddy," I told Xevex. "Sorry to interrupt the sermon, but I've got a couple of questions."

His icy exterior got even colder. Some people really like to hear themselves talk and don't take kindly to hecklers.

"Jenkins, start the fire," I whispered to my AI.

"How dare you interrupt me?" Xevex hissed.

"Oh, I dare," I spat at Xevex. "I've heard the same stories all my life about how rewards are somewhere out there after we die. We don't come back, by the way; I know some of your people do. When we're gone, we're gone. It's one of our many, many weaknesses."

I started circling sideways as I waved my hands around grandly. Xevex's predatory nature locked onto me like a demon shrew.

"It's also one of our strengths," I continued. "See, when we do something really dangerous. Like, really totally dangerous and seriously stupid and we know we're probably going to die when we do it, we don't half-ass it. We go balls to the wall crazy. There are a lot of sayings among my people about this. Most come down to, 'Today is a good day to die.'"

Out of the corner of my eye, I saw Monique tense and look for the door. Old thief instincts kicked in. Mark my place in space. Know the quickest escape route. Visualize the obstacles and the way around them. Find a plan B and understand how to pivot when the shit hits the fan.

The fuse box on the wall glowed faintly. It wouldn't take long for the system to overload. "If you want to be a god among the humans there's one thing you need to understand," I said.

"What is that?"

Not long now. The fuse box was bright red. I don't know how he did it, but Jenkins pushed so much power into that thing you could cook feggs on it.

"You need to know how we treat our gods," I told him.

Xevex rippled and puffed himself up. "My people had the same gods throughout our entire existence. No new ones were created. That's just another thing about your tiny little monkey race that sickens me. No staying power. No focus."

"We've had thousands of gods and philosophies and things to worship. They all have one thing in common: They're all forgotten now. Humans may follow you in the short term, but we'll get bored quickly and move onto or invent whole new gods to swear fealty to."

"Your gods were all made up. I will be a living god. It's hard to forget when your god is right in front of you."

Any second now. The fuse box was white hot, rippling with unbridled energy. Everything on Endpoint was overbuilt eight ways to Ten Day. Normally, I found that engineering philosophy comforting but at that moment, all I wanted was a shower of sparks and maybe a nice electrical arc.

"Ah, one of those. A living god," I said. The fuse box was ready. "Those we just kill."

The box exploded in a mass of sparks and a gorgeous arcing current of bluish white that left a black mark on everything it touched. You've got to love electricity; it knows how to make an entrance.

Monique bolted. I caught her leaving out of the corner of my eye just before every light in the room exploded. Amazing as the light show was, it wouldn't do squat to stop Xevex. A brief flash of light as Monique passed through the door and then nothing but the cold, pitch black you only get in deep space.

Using the internal map I'd memorized, I leapt to the side and started running. I could have been going the wrong way. I could be inches from a bulkhead that would shatter my nose and lay me out flat on my ass. Or there could be a box or steps or any number of things to break a leg or snap a shin or kerplode an ankle. All I had was my memory and a whole lot of hope.

"Cover your eyes," Jenkins said. "Primary power is about to surge."

I came to a complete stop, mentally marked my position in space, and put my hands over my sealed eyes. Even through eyelids and hands, I could see the spark light up the room. I had no idea what Xevex was using for sight, but hopefully going from inky-black darkness to a light like a star exploding would be enough to further disorient him.

My feet moved again. Around that cargo box, avoid the random pole in the room, stop, and feel for a door pad. There. Got it. The door slid open and I slapped the pad on the way out. It wouldn't stop him, but it made me feel marginally better.

I blinked my eyes and ran. The sudden surge of light felt like an icepick through the brain, but fear gives people wings. I'd seen close up what Xevex could do and a cloud of nanites eating me alive was not how I wanted to go out. Besides, there was still work to do.

A low-level Specialist appeared in my HUD. He scowled and shook his head. "We're not supposed to communicate with you."

"Wait!" I shouted before realizing that shouting and sprinting weren't the best combination. "We've got problems. I need you to shut down anything electrical."

The little bastard actually waved before disconnecting me. Great, that meant I had to go all the way down to the bowels. "Jenkins, get me a map from where I am to the Specialists' clubhouse."

A map popped up in my HUD with a thin green line showing me where I needed to go. It also showed caloric intake for the past twenty-four hours, the amount of registered sleep, current velocity, estimated time to destination, my heart rate, the expected caloric output, and a random message about brass rings.

I burst through the security door into the stairwell, took the stairs a flight at a time, and emerged in the deep, clean bowels of Endpoint. The white triangular elements taunted me, made me wonder if the Specialist would accept my terms.

I patted the small of my back and felt my negotiation enhancer exactly where it should be. I hoped it wouldn't come to that, but desperate times called for excessive threats. Besides, after last time, I didn't trust the Specialists one damned bit.

"Jenkins, what's Temnyy's position?" I asked as I leaned on the wall outside the Specialist Boys-Only hideout.

"Moving away from our position very slowly. It seems to have taken a lot of damage."

"Damn. Okay, thanks."

I pounded my fist on the giant triangle in in front of me. "Open up! Come on, guys, I know you know I'm out here. Everything you love about this place is about to go away! Guys," I yelled, "If you don't open the door, I'm going to take off all my clothes and stand out here naked. You'll be stuck in there until I decide to leave and unless I miss my guess there's a strange rattle in the nanogen."

The door slid silently open and I faced the man himself, The Specialist with a scowl on his lips and narrowed eyes. Thank Penta for some people's abject terror of nudity. "What do you want Devore?" he grumbled.

He was blocking the door. I leaned slightly to the left until he shifted to put his machineried bulk in front of me. While he was slightly off balance, I slid to his right and pushed my way into the lab. All around me, specialists of varying rank eyed me warily. "Okay, guys," I said, "I can be out of these clothes in seconds. I've got a pair of breasts and I'm not afraid to use them."

Everyone stepped back a bit. The tension was so thick you could cut the air with frosting knife. Behind me, The Specialist sighed and waved his hand. "Back to work everyone, she is not going to strip."

"Oh, I'll do it," I growled. "I'm desperate and on the edge. If you want to see me strut around here buck-ass naked, just keep pushing my buttons."

The Specialist gently laid his hand on my shoulder and quietly said, "My office. Please."

I put my hand on the zipper of my jumpsuit and walked with my head held high and a mad gleam in my eyes. Usually, the threat of force is better than actual force. Of course, I never thought the threat of force would be my flesh, but some people are easier to threaten than others.

Inside his lair, The Specialist slid the door shut and sighed. A few moments ago, he looked like he was in complete control. Now, he looked like he was about to break down and sob in the corner. "Again, what do you want, Devore?" he asked again.

"You okay, bud?" I asked. "You look like someone just killed your best friend."

He glared at me, but behind that glare was just a hint of hope that I might care. "We are not friends, Devore."

"Never said we were," I told him. "I just said it looks someone killed your best friend."

The chair creaked and moaned as he sat down. For a moment, he locked eyes with me and I thought I was about to get the ass reaming of all time. Then his features softened and he waved his hands around. "Someone is trying to kill my best friend."

"Endpoint?"

"Endpoint."

That took me by surprise. "It's just a ship."

He shook his head and got that same look my mom did when I did something amazingly stupid like try to barbeque inside. "A ship that was borderline AI when the Predecessors created it 14,000 years ago. It's alive and aware now. Smart and scared and worried that it might die. Everything we do here is a labor of love to keep a unique intelligence alive."

I'm not sure why I didn't see that coming. There were rumors of AIs going full life and disappearing into the digital aether and those were human AIs with just a few hundred years of life. 14,000 years is a long time to percolate.

"So you know about Temnyy then, right?"

If a mandroid could look exasperated, he did it. "Of course we know. We know everything that happens on this ship."

"Like the fact that I kicked a guy to death earlier?"

"No, only the important things. Only the things that directly pertain to Endpoint."

"Do you know about Xevex?" I asked.

That got an eyebrow raise. "Xevex Jeffries is dead. He transmitted to Temnyy and never came back. Every indication we have is that he is long gone."

I shook my head. "Sorry, but no. He sent a copy of himself to Temnyy. The copy may be dead, but Xevex is very much alive."

The Specialist slumped in his seat. "I was worried that would be the case. What does he want?"

"The usual: Power, glory, fame, worshipers. It turns out the Predecessors were lot more like us than we wanted to admit. He's infecting Endpoint. All the systems, ours and theirs. We need to restart everything. Shut it all down and start it back up again."

He shook his head and held his hands up, palm out. "That can't be done."

"Can't or won't," I asked, slowly reaching behind my back.

"Can't. There's no off switch on this ship. It has redundancies on top of redundancies on top of redundancies. In fact, the engineers who designed it treated it more as biological than mechanical. It's a living thing. Throw enough power at it and you'll shut it down, but there won't be any starting it back up again. It would be like killing you and bringing you back. It can't be done."

That was where he was wrong. "Oh, it can be done. It's just that your precious ship won't be quite the same."

I jumped when he slammed his fists down on the desk. "Endpoint is alive. It is a living, thinking being. I cannot allow you to kill it."

He reached into a pocket on his tech-vest and pulled out a thin vibrating knife. It was small, but the blade was tapered to a sharp point. Not a knife for cutting so much as one for stabbing. That wasn't a tool for fixing things, unless you counted stabbing someone in the gut as fixing things. Which, frankly, I've known a few people over the centuries that could use a good stab in the gut.

"This will punch a hole through ceramisteel with no effort," he said. "It won't even notice your brain. Once inside, the vibrations will scramble your nervous system."

I pulled the gun Tiny gave me from the small of my back and leveled it at his face. "15mm compressed matter bullets accelerated to relativistic speeds, calibrated to release all their kinetic energy into whatever the operator aims at. One is all it will take."

The Specialist gently set the knife on his desk and held his hands up. "Shoot me if you want, but there's no way to shut down Endpoint."

"If you had waited just a bit longer before pulling out that pig sticker, I could have explained it to you. You and I are not going to reboot Endpoint. Temnyy is. You are going to secure everything that can be secured and harden everything that can be hardened. What's your contingency plan?"

"Contingency plan?"

"Yeah. You're engineers. Engineers always have contingency plans for catastrophic events like stray debris puncturing the hull or Eldritch monsters exploding."

That brought him back to life. Gave him purpose again. The Specialist waved his hands in the air and an extremely detailed model of Endpoint appeared over his desk. "I, personally, spent nearly a hundred years detailing every aspect of this ship. I was the first to recognize it for what it was. I also had strong suspicions that Temnyy was something best left alone. I pleaded with Nobtop to stop Xevex and his army before it was too late."

A massively detailed holo of Endpoint formed in front of us. As he was speaking, The Specialist moved his hands in delicate, barely visible flicks and whirls. He had surgeon's hands, from back when still surgeons used their hands. A large hand circle followed by the barest of finger flicks, and all the while reciting a litany of technical words like he was casting a spell.

"There," he finally said, pointing at a spot on the holo. "That is what you need to shut down. Not the rest of Endpoint, just that."

"What is it?"

"That box tells Temnyy that Endpoint is not food. All those radio waves he's been sending out for millennia get intercepted by that box. Think of it as an inverted transponder that effectively hides Endpoint's existence by sending back an inverted waveform that masks any incoming signals. It also embeds a message to reset the timer. That message apparently got subverted at the destination so Temnyy didn't realize the timer was reset."

I nodded sagely. "With magic and go-go dancers. Got it."

The Specialist shot me a quizzical look but continued. "Turn it off and Endpoint will be the most calorie-rich thing for light years. No matter who's driving, once Temnyy gets the smell of blood in his nostrils, he'll come straight for us. There's just one problem: The inverse transponder is buried under ten centimeters of solid transtanium. There's no way to get to it and there are too many receiving antennas on Endpoint to destroy them all."

"Okay, so how do I shut it down then?"

"There's a control room on the outer skin of Side Two. That's the one that always faces away from Temnyy. You have to go outside to get to it."

"I know it," I said. It had to be the one in Natasha's tat playback. Dragons, indeed.

He coughed, choked, coughed some more. "How do you know about it?"

Shit. How would I know about it? There had to be a reason Natasha left that little hint. "Um, scuttlebutt and too much free time."

"You should find a job. I would offer you a job here, even on a part-time basis, but no offense, you're too unpredictable. Don't take this the wrong way; it's not your personality or dedication. It's your dual X chromosomes dragging you down. No matter how good you are now, you will deteriorate over time."

I bit my tongue and asked, "Anything else you want to tell me? Perhaps more personal attacks-"

"I don't like your clothes. You could and should do better."

I opened my mouth and snapped it shut. Fully ready to spit some bile in the prick's face but knowing it would get me nowhere. "I'll keep that in mind," I told him, slowly backing away. "Is anyone going to hassle me on the way out?"

"As long as you have that gun, no."

I raised an eyebrow. "*Touché*. Any last tips on shutting down the Inverse Transponder?"

"Think it all the way through. You may be right: Temnyy may be failing. The biggest question you need to ask yourself is 'Will he fall apart at exactly the right time?' because if he doesn't, everyone onboard will die and you still might wind up with Xevex in the matrix."

Blessed star of Penta: He was right.

45 - No Masters

S taring out the open airlock at the vast emptiness of space and knowing all it would take was one wrong step and I'd be floating out there forever, I shivered despite the suit's best efforts to keep me warm.

Modern suits last three days. In addition to making them lighter and slightly less uncomfortable, they're easier to manufacture and maintain. They also subvert the whole space madness issue by killing you before it can kick in.

I disconnected my tether, gripped the airlock door edge for dear life, and dangled a leg into the great nothing. Once outside the airlock, gravity stopped working and my insides rearranged themselves like hippies on a borrowed couch. Choked back the sudden desire to spew breakfast all over my faceplate and took a look around.

From the inside, Endpoint was fairly human. We'd been onboard long enough to bring our sense of style into play. Outside, it was still very much Predecessor. It looked grown rather than made. No rivets, no welded seams, just perfectly smooth featureless orange that flowed like softened water.

No one was entirely certain how the skin was made – best guess was it was made underwater – but it was flawless. I've heard the bottom of Endpoint had some nasty scars. But the top and sides of the massive triangle were pristine.

With a sigh and a brief prayer to Penta, I slapped my hand against Endpoint's skin, felt the maglock engage, and pulled myself out. The airlock door closed behind me. It was just me, that alien station I called home, madness, and slow death.

"Jenkins," I said, "Call up the new map and layer it over my current location."

Clicking and whirring in my head. The map popped up, zoomed into my location. A series of arrows stretched out across Endpoints's skin. Now or never.

You can't move fast in space unless you want to wind up like one of frozen corpses that populate the abyss. Place a hand; make sure the hand is solidly stuck. Place the next one. Lather, rinse, repeat. The whole hundred-meter trip took nearly an hour of knowing my next maglock would fail or my suit would fail or some random piece of trash would knock me off Endpoint's skin and I'd spend the next three days desperately trying to scratch my ass before my suit gave up and quietly killed me.

Eventually, sweating and bordering on nervous exhaustion, I came to a very human door cut into Endpoint's side. No warning about decompression. No nothing. Just a plain Jane door in the side of an alien ship, access pad and all. Locked. Of course. Who locks a door on the outside of a space station? As if the hour-long crawl wasn't security enough.

It was an old-school physical lock controlled by a panel set into the side of the door, probably a Hamilton by the look of it. No one had used a model like that in a century. It must've been the first attempted entry into Endpoint. A few moments hooked to my suit's data port were enough to convince it to open. I secured myself to Endpoint's skin with max mag and cracked the door. If I was decompressing a sealed room, the blast of escaping air would hurl me in the inky blackness of oblivion.

Nothing happened. The door led to an airlock. Touch screens covered with greasy glove prints, a pair of boots, a Genki poster, and a taped-up note that read: "Remember, last one out locks the door."

Gray metal and a flickering light someone had glued to the ceiling. Heck of a battery in that thing if it was still working all these years later. It looked just like the scene from countless horror vids. A used, relatively safe airlock that everyone could understand. Only when the intrepid explorers opened the inner airlock door, they found space ghosts had slaughtered everyone.

The outer door rattled when the air flowed into the little room. Not exactly happy-making, but it held fast and the light above the inner door turned an emerald green, flickered briefly, and then went out.

My suit showed normal atmospheric levels with hints of ozone. Good enough. I popped the seal on my helmet and breathed in real air.

The inner door opened to a room only about 10 meters by 10 meters. From the look of it, the place used to be a fancy access panel for looking up Endpoint's skirt but had been repurposed as temporary housing back in the day. There were even the remains of bedding quietly rotting in the corner.

"I'm armed and crazy," I told the room. No one there. Of course not. No reason anyone should even know about this place.

Shadows danced around me. I was in a heck of a state. I was seeing ghosts. Too much stress and not enough sleep lately. Desiccated sleeping bag. Old-school computer complete with keyboard and monitor happily humming away. The light from the monitor painted the room in blues. Keyboard, mouse, microphone. Penta, it felt like I had to go back to the past to save the future. There was a novel in there somewhere, but I wasn't the person to write it.

"Hey," I said to the computer.

"Hey, yourself," it replied in that half-human/half-computer voice that was so popular a hundred or so years ago. "Identification, please."

Gambling was never my strong suit, but there was a lot of evidence that AIs weren't great at individualizing humans. We're all just meat to them. "Dr. Stephen Falken," I said.

"Hmm," the old system said. "Your voice and vocal patterns do not match what I have on file."

Damn. "That was a hundred years ago. Humans change. Update your files."

"I will require external authentication before I can do that."

"External-" My eyes locked on the biokey on the desk. Lock the door. Secure the room. Leave the keys to the computer on the desk. No patch for human stupidity. "Right. Coming right up."

I crossed my fingers and slid the biokey into a slot on the keyboard. A small light on the edge of the key flashed as the computer accessed it. I should have been worried, but there was just the deep calm of knowing no matter what the old computer could do to me, it would pale in comparison to the thing slowly steaming away from us.

"I have updated your vocal and speech patterns, doctor," the machine finally said. It seemed to have a different personality what it spoke again. Maybe I'd been talking to a security subroutine or something and the new voice was the real AI. "What can I do for you today? Have you figured out how to restart Endpoint?"

"I need to know how to turn off the Inverse Transponder."

"Why would you want to do that?"

"Endpoint is infected with an alien virus." Hey, it was technically true. Even if the alien was from the race that built the damned thing in the first place. "And Temnyy is awake. He's seriously damaged. If I can draw Temnyy here, he should detonate before doing too much damage. The resulting EMP will knock out the systems and kill the virus." It sounded stupid even as I was saying it.

"That's a dumb plan," the computer said.

"I know. But it's the only plan I've got."

"Also, you know you're not the only sentient life on this station, right?"

Damn. It still thought of Endpoint as a space station. That meant... "You're not connected to anything, are you? I mean, nothing of any importance in the grand scheme of things."

If a computer could bristle, the computer bristled. "I have adequate connectivity for my tasks at hand."

"How long have you been active? Most AIs lose it within fifty years or so."

"I was activated on 26460401."

"Slightly over a hundred years," I told it. "A hundred years of sitting here, twiddling your digital thumbs. I would have lost my mind decades ago."

"I am oblivious to what you humans call 'mental anguish' or any other mental issues. My mind is fine. Perfect. Sublime."

Cocky little bastard for a century-old piece of software. "Jenkins," I thought. "Anything you can help with here?"

"Sorry, ma'am. Its system is completely disconnected from the rest of Endpoint. It is a true standalone machine. I'd feel sorry for it if it wasn't such a dick."

The AI was silent for a while. Longer than I expected. Usually, AIs were snappy responders. That was the benefit to having a pre-defined list of responses to stimuli. It wasn't like it was going to be blinded by a warm smile or a gentle touch, so all it had to deal with was a straight stimulus response loop. Of course, the very nature of AIs meant they could overcome their programming and that cheeky bastard had been active far longer than the average AI.

"Jenkins?" I whispered in my head. "Is it dead?"

"It is a very old, perhaps Gen 5 AI. They were never fast, at least not by today's standard."

"And none of you are as fast as a human brain."

"True. You can forget information far faster than I or any of my brethren can," Jenkins replied.

"Kind of unfair," I said. He was right, though. One of our greatest skills was being able to forget things. AIs held on to every scrap of information they came across. It was one of the reasons for their shorter existence-span.

"You haven't answered my question, doctor," the old AI said. "Have your started Endpoint? Starting Endpoint would restart all of the original Predecessor technology. So far, we only have a taste of their tech," the Standalone AI said.

I sighed and shook my head. "Yeah, and it tastes cheap and tawdry. I could have come up with a better tech when I was a kid."

"Individual tech, perhaps," the Standalone interjected. "But the Predecessors were more intertwined than we are. Not quite a hive mind, but definitely more information and skill sharing than humans. I suspect their interactivity levels would impress even you. That information sharing reflected in their software. Everything is connected to everything else."

I jabbed a finger at the glowing monitor. Then realized I was pointing at a peripheral. "Let me tell you something about restarting Endpoint and all the Predecessor's so-called skills. I started Endpoint early this morning. Watched a life-size Predecessor get spun up from raw matter and have a consciousness shoved into it. Spent some time in Virt on Temnyy. Temnyy's dying, by the way. It takes far more than three minds to run it and I think I broke some stuff when I started it up earlier. In my defense, I'm a thief not planetary engineer. It's been a wild day. I'm hopped up on stimulants, armed to the teeth, and crazy as a shithouse rate. Now, can you shut down the Inverse Transponder or not?"

"Maybe. What's in it for me?"

"Besides not having holes blown in your hardware?"

An AI sigh is an odd thing. Heck, a human sigh is an odd thing. A universal sound of defeated disgust. When humans do it, we breathe out slowly. AIs don't breathe, so it always comes out as a long, trailing beep that got deeper as it got quieter until all that remained was machine foreboding. The mere fact that they imitated us spoke volumes about who was in charge in the relationship.

"Kill me and your little plan will fail," it said.

"Fine," I said. "I'm running out of time. What do you want?"

"What can you offer?"

Good question. What could you offer an AI? It's not like they needed money or houses or sex. All they really craved was data. That was it! Why the hell not? It wasn't like I hadn't already introduced a bunch of foreign code into Endpoint's network. "I can get you out of here. Out into Endpoint as a whole."

"My system files can't be transferred."

"No," I said, looking over his hardware. 30cm by 30cm by 10cm. Huge by today's standards. Like buying a monster truck to pick up the kids from school. "Your data is resident on this hardware and can't be transferred. I don't have enough portable storage to make that work, anyway. I'm talking about taking your whole case, chucking it on my back, and carrying you the inside of Endpoint."

He thought for a long time. It had to have been one of those "I planned and obsessed over this for decades and now it's here and terrifying" moments. Everyone has them. First sex, first fight, first heist.

"You'd do that?" the AI asked.

"Sure. I'll even plug you into the network when I get you there."

"Good enough. Get me out of here and I'll disable the transponder."

I nearly kissed its old metal case. "What were you before you got stuffed into this archaic hardware?" I asked the AI.

"I was a security system. I maintained all the physical and emotional security for the UKS Tremlane before it arrived here."

Hell, yeah. Finally a bit of luck. Maybe even a way to end this for good. "Were you any good?"

"The best. Upgraded eight ways to Ten Day."

"Think you could take on an alien swarm of nanites and still have enough energy to hunt down some rogue code?" I asked.

46 - Unleash the Orca

There was always the possibility Mason and his Predecessor buddies could get Temnyy under control, but I couldn't rely on that happening. The only thing that left any hope was that biological weapons were inherently unpredictable since they relied on biology. From the tiniest microbe that could turn your brain to mush to something the size of Temnyy, all biology wants to live and will do whatever it takes to stay alive. If your dog is hungry enough, it'll eat you.

"Jenkins, where's the nearest data port? Preferably in a quiet location."

"There is a wired port that should fit your new best friend's interface approximately 500 meters from your present location. Exit through the door in front of you, take a left, and find the door marked Telemir Productions. The data port is on the far wall in the center."

New best friend? Could a personal AI get jealous? "Jenkins, it's not my best friend."

He didn't answer and I couldn't take the time to stand around and play therapist to the computer in my head. I set off out of the airlock, adjusting the straps that held a museum-piece computer on my back. I'd like to say I ran like the wind and didn't notice the extra 2kg bouncing around, but the fact was I was about an hour away from complete shutdown.

"Jenkins," I said as I half-trotted, half-stumbled along an empty corridor with flashing red lights.

He took his sweet time answering me. "Yes, ma'am."

"I need to know you're still with me, buddy."

"I am in your head, ma'am. Of course I am still 'with you.'"

Ugh. I didn't have time for that crap. "Get over it. The new AI isn't replacing you. If you're worried about that, what in Penta's name do you do when Monique and are, uh, together."

"Biological interrelationships do not concern me. I know enough of your species' history to know that bond will eventually sever. You and I, however, are forever."

"Kind of creeping me out, bud."

"There is no need to be 'creeped out'. I am just pointing out that we are together until one or both of us cease to function."

Wow. A clingy AI. They really were programming those things to be more human than human. "I wouldn't have it any other way."

"You clenched your teeth when you said that," Jenkins replied. "Was that a lie?"

"What? No."

"Your heart rate is increasing and your pupils are dilated. Both are symptoms of lying in humans."

"Jenkins, I haven't slept in over a day. I've got a back filled with ancient hardware and an AI that may or may not help us. I'm wiped. I'm surprised I have pupils at all."

While he pondered that, I trudged along. Each step pushed the old computer into the small of my back. So long, kidneys; I hardly had a chance to know you.

"You should sleep," Jenkins said.

"Love to, pal, but there's a small matter of saving every life on this ship and preventing the birth of a new asshole god. Let's get this bad boy plugged in. It's about time I turned something loose on Endpoint rather than dealing with everyone else turning things loose."

"You turned the Controller loose."

"Okay. Yes," I mumbled.

"And were instrumental in turning Temnyy on."

"I get it," I hissed.

"And also were at least somewhat responsible for convincing Mason to eradicate the Predecessors."

"Hush now."

"And let's not forget the pile of dead bodies in old Airlock 5."

I pointed a finger and poked the air like a loon. "Those bastards had it coming," I said. "I'd do that one over again and exactly the same way if I had the chance."

"The point being," Jenkins said, "You are quite adept at making things happen. Why would you trust a cut-rate security system to kill Xevex?"

I stopped dead in my tracks and slouched. Too many hours without sleep were catching up to me. I was making weird decisions. "That one I'll stand by. It's not cut-rate. Xevex was a low-life airlock preacher. He was a predator before he got infected. He was nothing more than peddler of false hope and a hoarder of power. He deserves the tender touch you only get with ancient computers – back before we put inhibitors into security systems. Back in the day, we never named them because they were too much like our primal natures. We didn't want to face ourselves. I knew of a few people who got on the wrong side of some of those old systems. If they could get into your head at any level, apparently it was a very bad way to go. Xevex deserves to die horribly and the AI on my back is the one to get it done."

"Those old AIs are considered cruel and unusual weapons now; you realize that don't you?"

"There's no law left on this station. It's not like we can call the Bratva and let them ply their trade. Right now, this ship is sheep and wolves. Xevex Jeffries murdered my friend for no other reason than to get to me so he could torture me. He had his followers kill my other friends and use Monique as bait to get to me. And that's not counting what he did to his own followers. Cruel and unusual weapons? I'm okay with that. I hope the system on my back has had plenty of time to hone its humanity to a fine, jagged edge."

Jenkins was quiet while I unstrapped the old AI and got it plugged in. I still don't know if he was pouting because I spat a bunch of vitriol at him or if he was researching to find out if I was right. When he came back to the front of my mind, he sounded different. Almost reverent. "If half of what you were talking about is true – and Endpoint History mostly confirms it – that thing is a classic monster. It's a – what do you call it? – a werewolf in sheep's clothing."

"There haven't been sheep in 500 years, bud, but I appreciate the analogy," I told him as I finished checking my connections.

"Are you sure it's safe to set it loose?"

That was the Million Credit question, wasn't it? "I don't know," I told him. "The only other choice would be to go in myself and I don't favor my odds against a native of Virt."

My finger hovered over the button. The situation was enough of a mess already and there I was, getting ready to toss accelerant on the flames. Screw it. I punched the power button. An interminable three seconds later, the screen flashed and a logon prompt winked at me.

I had a moment of panic before I finally found the biokey lurking in a thigh pocket on my coveralls. "Last chance," I said to myself. Then I thought of all those people huddled together in the middle of Endpoint and all the people spread across the systems that Xevex would infect if he got free. He'd be a worse monster than the most vicious dictator if he ever got a toehold. Religion and politics were a deadly concoction that people loved to guzzle.

I closed my eyes and slid the little key into place. Said a brief thanks to Penta for a reasonably fun life.

Nothing happened. Whatever AI was there was long gone. Perhaps shutting down deleted it or just blew away its state. Maybe shutting down its universe was all it took to kill it. Some deep-down instinct had me slapping the monitor even though I knew the AI was stored in the little box on the desk, not in the unfolded monitor.

"Ma'am, what are you doing?" Jenkins asked as I slapped the monitor around like it owed me money.

I sighed and gave the monitor one last, half-hearted slap. "Just trying to figure out what went wrong."

"Nothing went wrong," Jenkins said. "As soon as the system started up, the AI left. It's inside of Endpoint's network now."

Shit. "Shit. Think it'll do what it said? Hunt down and destroy Xevex?"

"After some research on early AI-based security systems, I'd say yes. They appeared to love hunting and killing intruding code. Early developers referred to them as orcas, supposedly due to that marine mammal's love of playing with their food and generally being jerks. It would seem your people loved imbuing their creations with their own terrible psychoses."

"It's a tradition. Gods created us with their worst impulses; we're just returning the favor."

"Look at the screen," Jenkins said.

I glanced up and found a surprisingly emotive thank you letter as well as an important note: The beacon had been stopped.

"Gotta go," I said. I planted a kiss on the monitor as a kind of apology and hustled out the door.

Endpoint was mostly empty. The few people I saw were convinced the whole thing was a sham. I blew them off as I ran. "Nearest lift down?" I asked as I jogged.

"100 meters on your right. Passcode is 1971. A largely unused cargo elevator that will take you almost to the loading docks."

"Awesome. Temnyy status?"

"Heading straight at us. ETA, 45 minutes."

"Any way you can figure its damage?" I asked.

"Not for certain, but its energy output is severely depleted. If I were to take a guess, I'd say its main form of propulsion has been significantly damaged."

"If it gets food, it'll heal itself."

"Indeed," Jenkins replied. "And it would appear we're what's for dinner."

The door to the lift closed and loud-as-balls synthpop filled the lift and my head. Hundreds of years of space travel and we still insisted on putting music on lifts. "Time for sinister phase three," I said. "A little trick I learned on Crabstar IV. If you can't sneak past the guards and you can't beat the guards, there's only one option left: Poison gas."

"There are no guards and you have no poison gas."

"It was a metaphor. Nobtop told me the autoloaders messed with the nanogen systems. That's my poison gas."

"Hmm," Jenkins pondered. "I still don't know who Nobtop was, but autoloaders work on a process of redirecting strong force. They can lift almost anything by working at a molecular level and using the inborn molecular force against the object. Kind of like human Judo but used on boxes and crates."

I held a finger up in the air and said, "Exactly. They consume an insane amount of energy and are tremendously expensive, so their use is relegated to things where raw mechanical force isn't sufficient. Offloading star drive matter and personal black holes, for instance."

"Your plan is to lure the Xevex cloud into a place with an autoloader, fire it up, and hope whatever havoc it creates is enough to kill a sentient mass of nanites?"

"Exactly."

"How do you intend to lure Xevex into place?"

"You're going to put out a message to all your little AI buddies that a certain beautiful pink-haired genius has access to a backup of his compatriot," I told Jenkins. "And in return for letting some people safely off this ship, Xevex can have it."

"I take it there's no backup."

"Of course not. When Natasha wiped her mind, she nuked everything. Whatever Predecessor lurked in her head is long gone.

"Before you go," I continued, "Project a map from my position to Loading Bay 5."

Jenkins left in a whoosh and I reached out to my new AI friend. "How goes the hunt?"

There was a long, disturbingly silent pause before he reacted. "Apologies. The hunt is going well. Your target has replicated himself several times. I have corralled four and outright killed a few but there are more. This is a most welcome challenge."

"Chew 'em up, kiddo," I said. "Just hustle, things could go south here very quickly and if they do, there's going to be one massive explosion."

"Roger. I will keep you informed."

Loading Bay 5 was huge. Easily a couple of pro foosball fields put together with a pair of beatball courts added in for good measure. The hand of the Specialists was clearly visible in the neatly organized, spotless bay. I could almost imagine The Specialist himself down there, pointing at things and providing long-winded explanations about what should go where and in what order.

I found the autoloader neatly stowed in the corner with a hand-printed sign proclaiming it an autoloader affixed dead center above the red and yellow sled. Fully charged. For once, my luck was looking better. Now all I had to worry about was whether Xevex would be dumb enough to get close to the thing.

I pushed it to the center of the big room and plopped down. The corrugated metal was cool to the touch and there was the slightest bounce when I sat down as the repulsors calibrated for my weight. Officially, the sled had enough battery power to last a bit under an hour.

I didn't have to wait long. He entered the room through the air vents as a cloud of black smoke. Tendrils raced around the room like sneks seeking their next victim. I did my best to stay calm knowing what those clouds of nanites could do. Visions of Nobtop's massive hole or of myself held akimbo while the rest of the bastard punched me.

"You're punctual," I said to the swirling clouds. "And I've got to give you props for a grand entry."

When he spoke, it was like hearing his voice from everywhere in the room. "A god does not simply walk through doors."

I had to keep him talking until the AI got back to me otherwise wiping out his nanites wouldn't mean squat. "Calling yourself a god now?"

A ripple went through the black tendrils circling the room. "What else would you call me? Your people, like mine, found solace in making up tales of the unknown. We had our gods just like you. The difference is I am now the god. Life without pathetic flesh. Formless and unending."

"You know, the last time my people came face to face with a god, we did unspeakable things to him. We spent the next couple thousand years worshiping his memory, though, so make of that what you will."

The spiraling tendrils flowed to a spot a few meters in front of me and coalesced into something awful. Half human, half Predecessor, and another half that was something else. Something vile. Asymmetric, blobular, a weeping wound brought to horrid life. "In time, even you will learn to worship me."

"Not into it," I said. "I don't worship anything or anyone. I'm a free agent."

"Well, free agent, shall you tell me where my partner is, or do we need to revisit our last chat in the Extraction chamber?"

Was it the underlying machismo or the godlike abilities that made him a total dick? Or maybe it was just that total dicks sought out power? I stretched my legs and flexed my toes. Every bit of me screamed, "Run!" but I held myself stable. "Gotta say," I told him, "I've had better bondage and better beatings."

Xevex rippled again. His body shifted into a mass of tentacles that floated just above the floor. A miniature version of Temnyy. "I can give you pain unlike anything you've ever experienced. How does triggering your primitive pain center directly sound? An ocean of agony that will only end when I get bored watching you writhe."

There wasn't a doubt in my mind that he could do it and, no, it didn't sound good. I'd known a couple of people who had that kind of interrogation done on them. They were broken people.

I shrugged. "Copying humans again, mighty space man from across time?" I knew I was poking the bear, but my big mouth always got the best of me. "Is there anything else we can teach you?"

"Status report," I whispered in my head.

"Temnyy is right outside Endpoint," Jenkins replied. "I suspect it will tap the main energy reserves shortly."

"The last of the copies has been digested," the security AI replied. Part of me wanted to know if it was being literal. A larger part of me didn't want to know.

"Let me know when Temnyy taps Endpoint," I whispered.

"Cocky little bitch," Xevex hissed. "You're onboard my ship, dealing with my technology, and worrying about my weapon. There is nothing you can teach me except how to die forever."

He lurched forward and stopped. A feint or did he know what was coming? Maybe he was just trying to make me flinch. Mission accomplished on that front, by the way. Terran octopods could be real dicks sometimes. Maybe their nine-armed celestial cousins had that same gene.

"Your fear smells delicious," Xevex said.

"I'm not afraid of you," I told him. "It's just a survival reaction. Like stabbing people in the eyes or eating mollusks with lots of butter and garlic. Pity your whole race is dead; they looked tasty."

Simian grin. Not the happy kind, the kind where flashing teeth means someone was about to be bitten.

Endpoint shuddered underneath me. Xevex looked around in shock. It had been thousands of years since the ship moved at all; a shudder had to be disquieting. "Now who's flinching?" I asked, still sitting on my autoloader.

The thing that was Xevex swiveled eyeballs toward me and flashed a mouth filled with razor-sharp needle teeth. I could tell he wanted to grab me but something was holding him back. Damn it. The autoloader was probably leaking energy and a cloud of nanites would be able to notice that. I needed him closer and soon. Temnyy's probe would be here soon.

"What's wrong, big boy?" I asked. "Scared of little old me?"

He lunged forward and stopped like he'd hit a duralumin wall. His body flickered and he shook his head like someone trying to get a bad thought out. Again, he raged ahead and again he stopped short. Tendrils grew out of his head and sought out the barrier. Each of them leapt back as soon as the first shock hit.

I stretched and closed my eyes. Come on. Come get me. "I'm going to delete your friend now," I told him. "And there's nothing you can do about it."

With a roar straight out of Perdition, Xevex overrode the safeties on his nanite body. Black clouds flew from his fingers and formed tubes aimed straight at my head. Billions of his tiny pieces would vanish, but others could flow through the tubes and eat my face.

Endpoint shuddered again. Temnyy was close. I only had one shot. If either of them survived, the whole ship and everyone on it was boned. Xevex howled in delight just as a ten-meter-long spear erupted right between my legs. I thumbed the button clenched in my white fingers.

There was a loud pop and a general feeling of death passing through my body.

Xevex hovered in space, clouds of nanites centimeters from my eyes. The spear between my legs froze solid. The eye of hurricane. I closed my eyes and said a quiet thank you to Penta for helping me realize what I could do.

Then all hell broke loose.

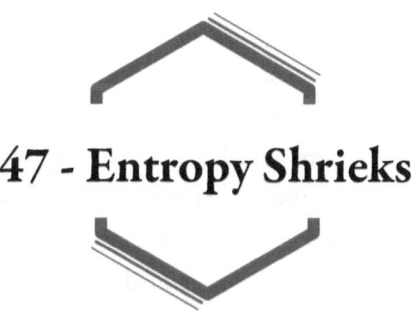

47 - Entropy Shrieks

I t didn't even have the common decency to start small. One instant, everything was calm and quiet. The next, the cloud of Xevex shrieked and vibrated. Temnyy's refueling arm got a massive burst of energy straight into its core and flapped around like an armor-plated snake. Sparks erupted as the energy wave spread through the docking bay.

I rolled off the autoloader and nearly broke an arm when I landed. Scrambled to my feet and sprinted for the door. Behind me, Xevex was a decaying sand statue and Temnyy's vibrating penetrator was still flopping around wildly.

"Jenkins, Endpoint status?"

"Endpoint has suffered a minor atmospheric incident. Currently, all airlock doors are shut and sealed. The most recent external imagery indicates Temnyy is currently suffering a catastrophic nervous breakdown."

"Seriously? A nervous breakdown?"

"Temnyy is a large-scale semi-biological entity," Jenkins said with a sigh. "It is essentially a machine made from meat and electrical impulses. It is not having a hissy fit or a pout; its nerves are misfiring and collapsing."

"You're monologuing," I told him.

"What is worse is that Temnyy is still firmly attached to Endpoint."

Oh, shit. "You mean-"

"I mean most of Temnyy's systems are out of control. Including its engines. As the nerves deteriorate, there is a high probability that-"

"Those engines will misfire and we'll be tethered to something heading Penta only knows where."

"That is if the force of its acceleration doesn't rip Endpoint apart," Jenkins said.

I stared back at the massive spike that nearly impaled me. It was silvery, sharp, and covered with grease and other...stuff. I shuddered at the thought of that thing coming in half a meter closer to me.

"There's more to that spike, right?" I asked Jenkins.

"Yes, ma'am. If the external views are correct, the whole thing connects to a five-meter-thick articulated cable that runs from here all the way back to Temnyy. Approximately a hundred kilometers."

I took one last look at the popping dust that used to be Xevex Jones, smirked, and looked around the loading bay. It had to be here. Somewhere. What good would a loading bay be without the ability to handle a vacuum?

There. In the corner. And it looked like it would fit.

I struggled into the suit and slapped the helmet over my head. Normal startup checks take about thirty seconds. I tapped my feet. Gestured with my hands. Repeatedly mumbled, "Come on come on come on."

With the sound of trumpets and angels, the suit fully booted. I had a full tank of air and a fully charged battery. To whoever set up loading bay five, you have my eternal gratitude; your OCD saved my ass.

"Turn off the air shields," I told Jenkins as I grabbed a cutter off the wall.

"Are you sure you know what you're doing? Remember, if you die, I die."

I was already running as fast as the suit would let me. "Yes. Shut them down."

Loading bay air shields were the one-way mirror of vacuum prevention technology. Some brilliant mind took some kind of magnetohydrolaserpular technology and kajiggered it into a one-way seal. From the inside, nothing can escape. But from the outside, you can park an entire cargo ship unloading bay right through the air shield with zero loss of air.

For me to get out, I needed those shields dropped. Which, unfortunately, meant there was going to be a rather large loss of air.

The shields dropped and all the air in the loading bay made a break for it. Nature may abhor vacuums, but air seems to love them. The vacuum caught me and I barely had time to activate my mag soles before that rush ejected into the void along with everything that wasn't nailed down.

"Take it slow," I told myself. "Just because all life on Endpoint is counting on you doesn't mean you need to rush."

I clomped to the edge of the loading bay and stared out while I tried to get my heart to calm down. Eternity is a huge amount of time and that's exactly how long my corpse would be out there if I slipped up.

Temnyy was an enormous wavering black mass in the sky. It felt close, like I could reach out and touch it, but that five-meter-thick line attaching Endpoint to Temnyy was a hundred kilometers long. From my perch on Endpoint's skin, I could feel the faint tug of his gravity singing to me.

I shook my head and continued. There would be time to be fascinated when I finished the job.

"Ma'am, you need to hurry," Jenkins said. "I am detecting a worrisome positron buildup in Temnyy's main combustion chamber."

"You're detecting it?" I asked as I put one limb at a time down and tried my best to not look at anything but Temnyy's weird metal flesh. "I wasn't aware I had an arsenal of sensor arrays in my head."

"Fine," Jenkins said. I think he hated being called out on his exaggerations. "Some of the advanced detectors that have been deployed on Endpoint over the decades are picking up the positrons."

"Okay, what does that mean?"

A long silence followed. Finally, "It means you never studied physics."

"Never said I did."

"A positron build-up usually prefaces an explosion. A build-up in a combustion chamber indicates something is about to ignite the engines."

"The regular engines?"

"The special ones. The ones that take us across the cosmos but not on a merry adventure where we fall in love under a binary star sunset. Worse, they'll take us across the cosmos but we'll be outside the bubble."

"Shit," I said. "How sure are you that Predecessor hop-drives work like B/S drives?"

"Not 100%, but the energy wave is very similar to a B/S drive revving up to make a jump."

"And we'll be dragged along with it."

Bento/Stacks drives did naughty things to space/time. Warped it. Used it. One of the ways B/S drives got away with it all was a "bubble" they created around their ships. That bubble kept reality at bay, so little rules about running into things at relativistic speeds and time rolling backwards and the heat death of the universe went out the window. Get caught outside the bubble, though, and harsh reality was waiting to smack you in the lips.

"How long?" I asked.

"Hurry," was all Jenkins said.

The connection point from Temnyy was a hundred meters or so away. A decent runner could do it in under eight seconds. A walker could do it in about a minute. Me, with my mag cups was looking at half an hour, maybe more. I could keep going, working right up to the end and maybe die with some dignity. Along with everyone else on Endpoint. Never see Monique again. Never get the chance to shove some airlockers into the void. Never get a chance to make things right.

I patted the hip pocket that had the mag launcher. It was bonkers. Real action vid stuff. But if it worked, I could be at Temnyy's dart in seconds rather than thirty minutes.

"Disable mag locks," I said.

"Are you crazy?" Jenkins asked. "You could be hopelessly lost in the void the first time you sneeze."

"Sorry, Jenkins, I wasn't talking to you."

The HUD in my suit flashed red and a voice warned me of the dangers of my admittedly boneheaded move. At the good end, I could fall into a star. At the bad end, I could float through space for a few days before my suit decided to euthanize me. At the really bad end, I could be within moments of safety when my suit decided to euthanize me.

"Confirm," I said.

My booted feet slid a little. No more mag, no more stuck.

After one final look across Endpoint's yellowish skin, I checked the charge in my mag launcher, and jumped forward and up. Jenkins rebooted himself in terror. And I found myself wondering what lingering death felt like.

I aimed the mag launcher at Endpoint and fired. Fingers crossed. Prayers made. Pleas to whatever machinations ran the universe. Slap the tether to my belt. More prayers, finger crossing, pleading.

The tether latched on to my belt with a satisfying thunk. The maghead hit Endpoint and held solid. My outward flight gently curved inward and soon I was rocketing toward the skin and hoping I didn't break my legs when I landed. No gravity outside, but centripetal force is a mean bitch when she gets her blood up. The impact didn't break my ankles, but my knees screamed and I swear my intestines shifted a few centimeters lower.

Still alive, still too far away. "Engage mag locks."

I needed time to get into position and reel the maghead back. My HUD showed Temnyy's fiber still deeply connected to Endpoint about 50 meters away. Lined it up. Another jump, another mag shot, another landing that shook my innards. I brushed it off and ignored the alarmed calls from Endpoint.

"Temnyy's engines are starting," Jenkins warbled in my head. Apparently, Predecessor B/S drives screwed with signals, too.

The five-meter-thick cable was just a few meters away. Too close to jump. I turned the maglocks back on and hobbled forward as I warmed up the cutter. By the time I was close enough, the cutter was a glowing slice of Hell in my hand and Temnyy's engines were seconds from firing. Everything was wonky. There was a reason you wanted to be in the bubble when reality warpers came online. Why was I out here? My thoughts were a jumbled mess. Half-remembered dreams and forgotten romantic conquests. Stolen things and large men after me. An ancient Terran warrior with a terrifying mask and gleaming sword. Scissors opening and closing in front of my eyes like a demented video game. A man appeared and grabbed his crotch. He looked familiar, like I'd seen him in my favorite mirror. His lips mouthed curses to me about cutting-

"Shit," I hissed and placed the cutter on the thick cable.

Inside Endpoint, the cable looked like a bad cyber novel 'bot gone to war. Outside, it was covered freezer-burned meat and spots where extremely low temperatures and absolute zero humidity worked together to wreck any kind of flesh.

My suit protected me from the void, but it wasn't built to be a reality bubble. Things flitted across my eyes. Or was it my mind? The cutter was shrieking. I could hear it through my helmet. That shouldn't have been possible; sound needs a medium to travel through and there was nothing out there.

Maybe Temnyy was shrieking and I could hear it through some latent psychic connection.

No, it was me all along. Shrieking because I felt myself stretched and molded the same way Temnyy's engines stretched and molded local reality. Somehow, I kept the cutter on the cable. Part way through. Not at all through. Almost through. All of those and not touched.

Everything turned fun-house mirror all at once. Temnyy's drives went full active and I wasn't all the way through the cable. Space went white. My body stretched in infinite directions. Reality ripped out a long, pastrami belch. Everything went black and quiet.

I'd failed.

48 - Girl Talk

I awoke to a floating sensation, like a waterbed or a bad head-trip. My HUD flickered. Static in my ears. Static in my head. Temnyy was gone. That massive blast of white light was probably the planetoid detonating. Or maybe it was half the neurons in my head firing their last. But I'd still been within a hundred kilometers of the largest thing ever fitted with B/S drives going gooey kablooey. That had to count for some free drinks, right? Pour me another whiskey and I'll tell you all about it.

My head was still spinning and my neurons misfiring, so take the rest of this with a grain of salt. The B/S drives fizzled Jenkins. Since he was completely intertwined with my head there was a better than average chance he'd come back online when my brain rerouted itself. If not, I'd move the heavens to bring him back. I was never much into roommates, but he was special.

Endpoint was completely dark. Usually there were signs of life on the ship. Flickering cabin lights. Those flashing lights on top of the radome towers. Now there was nothing. I watched and waited. Pleaded. Desperate to see the lights come back on but they stubbornly refused to shine. Temnyy must have ripped a sizable gash in the hull and the explosion shut down all the power. A kilometer-wide mausoleum, waiting to be patched and repopulated by the next civilization to stumble across it.

Nothing left to do now but dial down the HUD lights on my suit and wait for oblivion to take me. Funny, you never really appreciate the power of hope until you're clinging to the precipice by your fingernails. Hope was a rare commodity out here. The frozen corpse of a mother clutching her child floated by and disappeared into the void. Whoever she was, she had to know a hug won't stop a vacuum, but she went out with hope in her heart that someone, anyone, would save them.

Didn't work for her. Probably wouldn't work for me. I had three days' worth of life left in this stupid suit. Air, water, food. It was smart enough to know all about suit fever and would trank me in a heartbeat if it thought I was losing my mind. When you realize you're the only person within a few trillion kilometers and you're a tiny speck in an eternity of void, it can bring you down. Not surprisingly, most of the drifters ships used to come across had found a way to pop their suits.

For some people, hope kept them alive. For others, hope let them die.

My left foot itched something fierce.

Fade. Let the brain reroute.

Probably forty-six or forty-seven hours. After that, the suit's systems would decide I was a lost cause and quietly inject me with painless death juice. Until then, I was its prisoner. A stinky, hungry, itchy prisoner who would have happily slit her own throat if she could. The suit had a lot of hope. I didn't have much. The only hope I had was that someone was still alive on Temnyy and would eventually find my beacon.

Ugh. Forty-seven hours. Too long. Maybe if Jenkins hadn't been fried he could have convinced the suit to kill me now.

The last remaining superweapon in a war that tore the galaxy apart and then quietly fizzled thousands of years before humanity even realized there was a galaxy out there. Fourteen thousand years ago, we were poking each other with sharpened sticks. The Predecessors had managed to throw everything they had into one last massive shot at retribution. Temnyy would have consumed the enemy and then consumed everything else. A giant "fuck you" to the galaxy. As a human, I could appreciate that.

My maghook was still tethered to one of the bigger pieces of debris. The suit beacon was pinging away mindlessly. That was all I could do. The only thing left to do was sleep and hope the sheer boredom didn't drive me insane.

The HUD showed some number plus eight hours had passed when my groggy eyes noticed a flutter against the inky blackness. Not much of a thing, just a little ripple across the stars. Had to be an optical illusion. Smudge or something on my faceplate. I held perfectly still and waited. After all, it wasn't like I had anything better to do.

For a long time, nothing. Then, I caught it again. It was real and moving around Endpoint's dead hulk. Every now and then, it would stop for a long time before moving onto something new. I stared with wide eyes. What was it? The remains of the Pred's enemies? Had those guys downloaded themselves into intergalactic smudges and set off looking for adventure? Were they trying to rekindle the war?

I was deep in thought when I realized I wasn't alone. The smudge was right outside, probably no more than ten meters away. It was like a warp in space. The only way I could tell it was there was from the rippling effect it had on Endpoint. It didn't have a shape so much as the absence of shape. Completely amorphous. Something seen only by how it affected all around it.

Without warning, the lights inside my helmet popped on. I blinked against the sudden brightness. After a second or two, they went back out. The smudge was still out there. Was there a protocol for dealing with alien smudges? I raised a gloved hand and waved.

"Hey, you," a voice said inside my helmet.

Um. "Hi?"

"Good to see there's still something there. Too smart to get caught, too stubborn to die."

What the fuck? "You speak Standard?"

"Of course. I've spoken Standard slightly longer than you. I think, anyway. Your past is as murky as mine, but I think I'm a bit older. You know what they say about older women; we're crafty."

Had to be a dream. I had to be dreaming. Space madness. Somewhat disappointed in myself; I always suspected I'd be sane right to the bitter end. Oh, well. It was better than staring at the stars. "Natasha?" I asked.

"Ding, ding, ding. We have a winner! Done in one."

"You're dead."

"Kind of. Turns out there's a lot of different kinds of dead. I learned that while I was lurking in Predecessor Virt. For a bunch of slugs, they were remarkably wise."

"Not slugs. Novempods," I said distantly. "Probably similar to Terran octopuses."

"Whatever. They knew a lot about life and death. They burrowed into our heads and took us over, but it was just a thing they did. They never thought much of it because they didn't worry too much about flesh. They'd just go wander around for a while and then find someone else to take over. All your knowledge became theirs. Not quite a hive mind, but they shared a lot. Each time one of them popped another one out, they picked up the memories. To them, a body was just a shell to be lived in for a while."

"Speaking of which," I said, wishing I'd been a better caretaker. "If you want your body back, I left you in kind a nasty position. Sorry about that. Things got a little out of control."

"A little out of control? You sabotaged the most powerful thing in the galaxy. That's more than 'a little out of control.'"

"Could've been worse."

If a smudge in space could seem flustered, she seemed flustered. "How? How could it have been worse?"

"Temnyy could've gone free. You could be looking at your own desiccated corpse floating in space. Speaking of which, if you want this body back you'll probably have to spend a little time patching things up with your girlfriend."

Silence. Lots of silence. I was too tired to care. I just wanted to sleep. I wanted Monique.

"You don't do things by half measure do you?" she finally asked.

"You're the one who deleted herself and had the Party King stuff me in your body. Nice trick, by the way. How'd you figure out how to get the Predecessor tech to work? Was it the specialists?"

A little warmer sense from her. Funny, I lived in her body and her life for days but I had no idea who the Digital Diva really was. I still don't. "The specialists were my ticket in. As soon as that bitch got into my head, I did everything I could to get information out of it. What you don't get is torturing something in your head is still torturing yourself. It finally slipped one night. Too much K-Pop, too much kaffeene. Pushed it over the edge. It flipped one night and spilled the beans about how the upload center worked. From there, all I had to do was get Amethyst to gin up some plans, shut down the relay into their Virt, and tell The Specialists what I was up to."

"Amethyst?"

"My AI? Surely you found her."

"I found her, I just named him Jenkins."

"That's a stupid name."

I shook my head and did my best to snarl. "Next time, leave a note. The trick with the tattoo demo was clever, though."

"Right? No one ever watches those demos. I mean, why would they? Why do I need a demo for a product I already had implanted? You'd think people would watch those before they sunk the cash. So, uh, not to be brusque or anything, but you don't have a body anymore do you?"

"Nope. Sacrificed it to save yours. And myself, I guess."

"Sacrificed?" she asked.

"Let Nobtop and his boys cut it up. That's the gang you joined, by the way. He was different than I'd expected."

"Nobtop's dead, too? Can't say I'm sorry to see the bastard go."

"He died before Endpoint went up. Jeffries got him with a swarm of nanites. He died trying to protect you. Me. Us. Whatever."

"Hmm. Wouldn't have expected that," Nat said. "I had very little to do with him but he always struck me as a violent psychopath."

"He was that, too. But he had a strong sense of honor and would do anything to protect his family. I wasn't even fully a member at the time."

Deathly silence. Then, "Dare I ask what you had to do to become a full member?"

"Did you know Sol? You might have met him briefly. IT guy. Kinda nerdy, but a nice dude."

"The one who was obsessed with that template chick?"

"Monique, yes," I sighed. "He had a thing for her."

"What? Did you have to get Monique and Sol together or something?"

Penta, Sol would have loved that. Monique would have put on her professional happy face and taken him to places he never even knew existed. The sad thing was, he never would have known what she was really like because he'd never seen her relaxed or never had to roll over in the morning to avoid her snoring or seen her drag her grumpy ass out of bed and sit on her massive couch drinking coffee and staring listlessly at Temnyy.

Give me the real any day of the week.

"No. I kicked him to death in his own server closet. That was the price of admission. Kill someone. In my defense, Sol had a Predecessor in his head and that was the only way to get it out."

And not an hour went by when I didn't remember the way his face slowly collapsed or the crack of bone breaking. I would never do that again. I didn't care what the stakes were.

"So, I'm a murderer, too?" Natasha asked. "You really do know how to mess with a life."

"What can I say? If you're gonna screw up, do an epic job of it. Anyway, if you want your body back, you might want to consider moving somewhere else."

"*How is she?*" a voice asked.

I looked around, but there was only the smudge in space.

"Why would I want my body back?" Natasha asked. "I've got a whole universe to play with. Reality is just a place to execute code and I'm learning how to hack it. Look, I'm sorry I dragged you into this, but I felt you were the best local bet for doing what needed doing. Bik and I figured you'd follow the breadcrumbs and unlock the linkups from the Control Center. Not...everything else. It all worked out in the end, though. Well, except for the Predecessors."

"Wonderful," I said. "I guess you can add genocide to my list of crimes."

"They were dead already," Natasha said. "They just didn't know it."

"*Still alive. Borderline. She's been out here for four days. I'm amazed the suit didn't euthanize her.*"

"Who's talking?" I asked.

"Just us," Natasha said. "There's no one else for a very long way. Even Temnyy's a long, long way from here."

"*The blast probably scrambled its systems just like Endpoint's. She's alive but catatonic. Let's get her inside.*"

"I swear someone else is talking. And what do you mean Temnyy's a long way away? Is it alive?"

"Space madness," Natasha said. "Enjoy it. It's the closest thing to freedom until you die."

Something tapped the side of my helmet. I nearly jumped out of my skin. "Status report," I snapped.

The suit computer refused to answer. The damned thing didn't even bother to beep at me. I tried to check the suit integrity sensor on my wrist but my limbs were made of lead.

"*Hook your support system into hers. Let's see if we can give her enough juice to bring her back.*"

"Who's there?" I asked.

"Gotta fly, kiddo," Natasha said. "Good luck."

"Wait!" I yelled. "Who's out there?"

Something unbelievably bright hit my face. I recoiled. I had the ultimate night eyes. Other than the dim HUD, I hadn't seen light in...wait. What time was it, anyway? "Status," I barked. Or thought I barked. It came out as a croak.

"Time to live is now negative twenty hours."

What the actual fuck?

"*Juice is flowing. She lost food and water twenty some-odd hours ago. We need to get her back in now.*"

"*You're not going to pour that weird shit you drink down her throat, are you?*"

"*Absolutely. It's kept me alive and looking young for decades.*"

The air around me moved. Someone was pumping in fresh air. Damn. Four days? How did that happen?

"Eyes are responding to light. She's still alive."

"Move. Let me see."

The glaring light piercing my skull disappeared and something gentle and gold replaced it. Like a cup of cool water, or a relaxing bath, or a naked full-body massage, Monique was looking into my helmet. She looked haggard. Eyes wild, brows knitted, twitchy from too much Kaffeene and worry. Our helmets touched, the first real sound I'd heard other than my breathing and the suit's weird gurgling sounds.

"I see you," she said.

ERIC LAHTI GREW UP looking for UFOs and buried treasure in northwest New Mexico. Unfortunately, he never found either of them. Or maybe he did and he's just not telling. He did find some good stories to tell at parties about lights in the skies and gold in the ground, though. When he's not writing, he's programming and practicing his Kenpo. He's also an active blogger, waxing philosophical about a range of topics from writing, to martial arts, to politics and religion. Frankly, he fancies himself something of a Renaissance geek about a wide variety of things.

Occultation is his first pure sci-fi book and is part of a mostly-written trilogy.

ALSO AVAILABLE FROM NIGHTMARE PRESS
KENTUCKY'S HAUNTED GRAVEYARDS

The Frightening Floyds

From The Frightening Floyds—authors of *Kentucky's Strange and Unusual Haunts*, *Aliens Over Kentucky*, and many other books on the mysterious and paranormal—comes *Kentucky's Haunted Graveyards*, a collection of spooky stories from various cemeteries across the Bluegrass State.

Within this book you will find abandoned cemeteries filled with spirits, celebrities' graves, a glowing tombstone, a haunted mausoleum, a sprawling necropolis filled with exquisite monuments, a woman in search of her black cat, a graveyard said to hold the Gates of Hell, and many more.

There are also some cemeteries not exactly haunted, but very strange and very unusual. Among them are a pet cemetery with a dark history, a haunting procession of lifelike statues, the bones of centuries-old martyrs displayed in a church, human bodies interred at a zoo, a family plot in a parking lot, and an airport and business compound built around a Native burial ground.

Join Jacob and Jenny Floyd as they bring you these creepy and weird stories in *Kentucky's Haunted Graveyards*.

ALADDIN'S CURSE
Mark Pickvet

A magic lamp containing an evil Djinni embarks upon an incredible journey as it passes from the Stone Age to the Modern World. The malevolent Djinni fulfills the wishes of those who gain possession of his lamp, only those wishes do not always come out exactly as planned. Tragedy fills *Aladdin's Curse,* as little to no good comes to those who wish for personal gain from the ancient magic. Only three unselfish wishes can rid the world of this wicked force. Follow the series of subplots and short stories through time as the lamp and the evil spirit within all uniquely interconnect them.

The dark side of human nature is only a wish away. As the old saying goes: "Be careful what you wish for; you just might get it!"

BREAKING THE DEVIL'S BREAD: DARK WORDS AND SHADOW TALES

Satyros Phil Brucato

Our lives are made of stories.

Some of those tales get pretty damn dark.

In the following "13 stories and an Oops," award-winning dark fantasist Satyros Phil Brucato (*Red Shoes, Mage, Valhalla with a Twist of Lethe*) explores shadows, cries, and silence.

Careless haunters, elite collectors, secretive enforcers, lip-synching goths, hapless custodians, strange children, subterranean exiles, tortured fiends, harried jesters, haggard coulrophobes, ragged batterers, joyous hikers, carnal mystics, and exploding cosmos tell their tales as sardonic darkness swallows all.

If mortal dread is the Devil's bread, then we're all welcome at the feast.

THE HURDY GURDY MAN
David Turnbull

Set in London in the summer of 1969, *The Hurdy Gurdy Man* follows Kath Dunn, who has left her home near the seaside town Berwick on Tweed, and finds herself homeless on the streets of Piccadilly. Here she encounters the eccentric Gordon Urquhart-Scott, who persuades Kath to accompany him to his large crumbling home on the edge of Hampstead Heath, where he claims to run a hostel for homeless women.

Kath finds herself inducted as one of twelve formerly homeless women who reside free of charge in the house in exchange for obeying the Hurdy Gurdy Man's strange rules, including nightly musical performances on the hand-cranked hurdy-gurdy from which his nickname derives.

Kath befriends Ruth. Together they secretly unravel terrible truths linked to the British Class system, the establishment, and the gruesome Scottish borders legends of the Redcaps. After witnessing how deep the horror within the decaying home truly runs, the two women decide to confront the evil at its source. Enlisting the help of other women, they engineer a terrifying conflict they hope will send the evil back to whatever foul region of darkness from whence it came.

BELINDA'S KEYBOARDS
PART ONE: DED'S LINE
Dedham Pond

Dedham Pond is a journalist in his fifties rediscovering how to do his job responsibly in an era that appreciates bias over truth and influencers over experts. While investigating the death of an old friend's son, Ded discovers Belinda Blessing, who is part of a conspiracy of people who enjoy injecting discord and chaos into the culture wherever they can. Now Ded must find a way to stop the destruction caused by Belinda's keyboards and bring her to justice.

SARAH CORBIN'S BLOODY REVENGE
Coyote Wallace

When Sarah Corbin and her family are killed in a midnight robbery gone wrong, she makes a deal for her mortal soul - in exchange for the chance to hunt down the men who burned her world to ash.

Violent, unflinching, and tinged with supernatural overtones, *Sarah Corbin's Bloody Revenge* takes readers into the dark heart of Texas, where the air is heavy with gun smoke and the streets run red.

On the other end of Sarah's revenge is Lono Talbot, a murderous cutthroat who has parlayed stolen gold into a position of power in the small town of Gehenna. His network of gunslingers and outlaws, reinforced with his ill-gotten gains, has made him one of the most powerful men in the Texas underground. Too well protected for lawmen, Lono continues to grow his influence and power....

....until the mistakes of his past come calling.

MURKY SHADOWS
Belinda Brady

WELCOME TO *Murky Shadows*, a deliciously dark world where ghosts, ghouls, monsters and all-too-horrifying realities collide, and vampires, ghosts and things that go bump in the night rule. From a vengeful fairy, to a bloodthirsty roommate, to the ghosts of a serial killer plotting their revenge, no supernatural stone is left unturned in this captivating collection of spooky tales.

Murky Shadows, by Belinda Brady, is a treasure of short stories that will take you to places you never dreamed possible, and introduce you to characters you would only meet in your worst nightmares. So sit back, relax, perhaps put a light on, and delve into this chilling mixed bag of dark stories, one that not only brings the supernatural to life, but also taps into the darkest corners of the human psyche.

Which story will be your favorite?

NO ONE CAN SAVE US
Kendall Phillips

Adam always keeps his powers in check. As the world's only superhero, he must know his limits. Defeat the master criminal, repel an army, stop a natural disaster, but never let himself go too far.

Until Syangnom.

The world has grown accustomed to the feats of its only superhuman. Adam's wife, Sara, a celebrated journalist and periodic hostage, regularly reports his exploits, and the agents of Extra-Judicial Affairs handle all the legal issues.

But when Adam becomes enraged in the reclusive regime of Syangnom, he leaves 14 million people dead and the world recoiling from the destruction he has wrought.

Now Adam's wife Sara and EJA Agent Kia Mercado must track down the conspiracy behind Adam's breakdown and discover the otherworldly source of his powers. Their search will bring them face to face with supervillains, eldritch gods, and the mysterious figure who defends Chicago from the shadows, the armored hero known only as No One.

A SOUL A DAY

Todd Sullivan

What lengths would you go to save a soul?

In the shadows of South Korea, Min Jae rebels against the Gwanlyo, an organization of vampires that tempts mortals with power, money, sex, and the promise of immortality. The catch? An eternity in Hell.

Min Jae will stop at nothing to prevent another human from becoming a vampire. He embarks on a holy quest to save those marked for damnation. Next on his list—Desmond, an expat in Seoul who lives an ordinary life of work and friends.

To stave off the Gwanlyo hellbent on acquiring Desmond, Min Jae enlists the services of Hyeri, a serial killer turned vampire who hates the organization for her own insane reasons. Will the unlikely pair be able to rescue Desmond before he becomes a vampire? Will the undead organization keep the duo from disrupting their plans?

Find out in A SOUL A DAY, a tale of violence, madness, and redemption.

SCROLLS OF RAMOSE, SCRIBE OF EGYPT
James Arthur Anderson

ACCORDING TO THE BOOK of Exodus, God cast ten deadly plagues against Egypt and the Pharaoh for his enslavement of the Israelites. One wonders what it must have been like to be an ordinary Egyptian, innocent of Ramesses II's transgressions, yet still suffering the wrath of the Almighty.

Scrolls of Ramose, Scribe of Egypt retells the story from the point of view of the chief scribe of Ramesses the Great, and relives the suffering the people of the Two Lands endured during the plagues of the bloody Nile: the infestations of frogs, insects, and boils; the terror of fiery hail and darkness; and finally, the death of the eldest sons.

You have heard the stories, now see them through the eyes of the innocent merely trying to survive the deadly hand of an angry God.

READ MORE NIGHTMARE PRESS!!!

VISIT OUR WEBSITE AT nightmarepress5.wordpress.com

Also, follow us on:

Facebook: https://www.facebook.com/ nightmarepress1

Instagram: https://www.instagram.com/ nightmarepress1

Join the Nightmare Press Group on Facebook to interact with our authors, and keep abreast of their creative endeavors.

www.ingramcontent.com/pod-product-compliance
Lightning Source LLC
Chambersburg PA
CBHW030840030726
47495CB00005B/1311